O9-AIG-087

Y
FIN

THE CURSED QUEEN

ALSO BY SARAH FINE

Of Metal and Wishes

Of Dreams and Rust

Of Shadows and Obsession, an e-short story prequel to
Of Metal and Wishes

The Impostor Queen

THE CURSED QUEEN

Sarah Fine

Companion to
The Impostor Queen

MARGARET K. McELDERRY BOOKS
New York London Toronto Sydney New Delhi

MARGARET K. McELDERRY BOOKS

An imprint of Simon & Schuster Children's Publishing Division

1230 Avenue of the Americas, New York, New York 10020

This book is a work of fiction. Any references to historical events, real people, or real places are used fictitiously. Other names, characters, places, and events are products of the author's imagination, and any resemblance to actual events or places or persons, living or dead, is entirely coincidental.

Text copyright © 2017 by Sarah Fine

Jacket photograph of girl copyright © 2017 by Zlatina Zareva; photograph of fire copyright © 2017 by Olga Nikonova

Artwork and map copyright © 2017 by Leo Hartas

All rights reserved, including the right of reproduction in whole or in part in any form.

MARGARET K. MCELDERRY BOOKS is a trademark of Simon & Schuster, Inc.

For information about special discounts for bulk purchases, please contact Simon & Schuster Special Sales at 1-866-506-1949 or business@simonandschuster.com.

The Simon & Schuster Speakers Bureau can bring authors to your live event. For more information or to book an event, contact the Simon & Schuster Speakers Bureau at 1-866-248-3049 or visit our website at www.simonspeakers.com.

Book design by Debra Sfetsios-Conover

The text for this book was set in Goudy Oldstyle Std.

Manufactured in the United States of America

First Edition

10 9 8 7 6 5 4 3 2 1

Library of Congress Cataloging-in-Publication Data

Names: Fine, Sarah, author.

Title: The cursed queen / Sarah Fine.

Description: First Edition. | New York : Margaret K. McElderry Books, [2017]

Summary: "Ansa has always been a fighter. As a child, she fought the invaders who murdered her parents and snatched her as a raid prize. She fought for her status as a warrior in her tribe, but the day the Krigere cross the great lake and threaten the witch queen of the Kupari, everything changes"— Provided by publisher. | Companion to The Impostor Queen.

Identifiers: LCCN 2015045312

ISBN 978-1-4814-4193-3 (hardcover)

ISBN 978-1-4814-4195-7 (eBook)

Subjects: | CYAC: Fantasy. | Kings, queens, rulers, etc.—Fiction. | War—Fiction. | Magic—Fiction.

Classification: LCC PZ7.F495678 Cu 2017 | DDC [Fic]—dc23 LC record available at lccn.loc.gov/2015045312

FOR RUTA, GENTLE AND FIERCE WITH
BOTH HEART AND PEN.

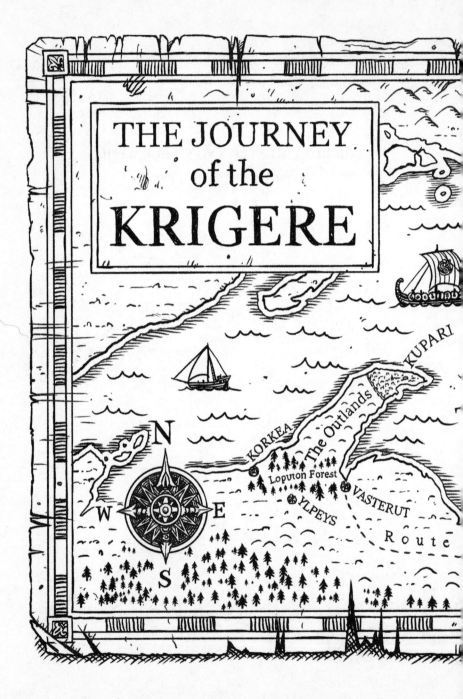

THE JOURNEY of the KRIGERE

KORKEA
KUPARI
The Outlands
Loputon Forest
YLPEYS
VASTERUT
Route

Jlvi Point

KRIGERE CAMP

Sikka
Harbor

Route of the Krigere

e Torden

The Marshlands

the Krigere

LEO-HARTAS

PROLOGUE

She'd never seen fire as an enemy, not until it crept like a snake along the grass to where she lay bleeding, not until it struck. And even then, Lotta didn't scream from the pain.

She screamed for Ansa, though. Screamed until the smoke choked off the sound. Her tears dried to a salty crust as she fought to keep her eyes open. Though she had no strength to rise, her fingers clawed in the blood-soaked dirt beneath her as she watched one of the monsters sling her daughter over his massive shoulder.

Only two days ago, she had resolved to hide Ansa forever and keep her safe, even if the priests from the city came calling with offers of copper piled to the thatched eaves. As soon as that red flame mark had appeared on Ansa's right calf, Lotta had known what it meant. When her brother's family had visited from the city yesterday and brought word of the Valtia's death, it had only confirmed her fear. She'd heard the fantastical tales of how the Saadella, the heir to the Valtia's magic, was chosen. She knew the Saadella lived in luxury at the Temple on the Rock. Many parents would give anything to see that kind of life for their child.

But once the Saadella became the Valtia, possessing the infinite fire and ice magic that sustained the Kupari people, the girl's life would not stretch far into the future. And she would never have children. Would never know love. Would never see her parents again, not once they handed her over to the elders. She would belong to the people and the priests until the day she died.

Lotta hadn't been able to bear the thought of giving Ansa up.

Now she was losing her all the same.

The raiders had come up from the water like demons, ax blades gleaming, the sweat on their grime-smeared faces glinting in the torchlight as they set fire to the outbuildings nearest the dunes. Grabbing his pitchfork, Anton had shouted for Lotta to take little Ansa and flee for the north woods, but they hadn't had a chance. Anton had been cut down not five steps from their cottage, and Lotta hadn't made it much farther.

Ansa, though . . . she had grabbed her father's knife and slashed at her enemies. Tears streaming down her face, shrieks bursting from her throat, she had dodged between legs, jabbed at soft spots, squirmed away from grasping hands, and sliced at thick-knuckled fingers. A tiny five-year-old exacting a blood toll from vicious barbarians. Even as Lotta's blood flowed fast and sure from her wounds, she'd felt triumphant at the sight of her daughter's speed, her ferocity. That was Ansa. She could never be stopped.

Until the one with the yellow beard caught her. She scratched at his laughing face and kicked at his chest as he hoisted her up. The monster called to one of his fellows in his throaty, garbled language, smiling until Ansa sank her teeth into the back of his hand.

He grunted and dropped her. Lotta's faltering heart leapt even as pain devoured her. But then Ansa threw her head back, and her ice-blue eyes took in the devastation around her, the cottage in flames, the screaming pigs being herded toward the shore, the demons plundering her world. . . . *Don't see me*, thought Lotta. *Keep running.*

But Ansa's gaze caught and held. And the sight of her mother, burning and dying, seemed to freeze the little girl where she was.

Yellow Beard scooped her up again. Ansa wailed, her skinny arms outstretched. "Mama!"

I love you, Lotta thought as the darkness closed in. *Never stop fighting.*

One day you will be powerful enough to kill all of them.

One day you will avenge us.

CHAPTER ONE

As the spray from the Torden kisses my face, I trace my fingertip along the four notched scars that decorate my upper arm, and then along the space below them, where soon there will be more. By the time the sun rises tomorrow, I plan to bleed all the way down to my elbow at least, and hopefully my wrist, though that might be too ambitious. I glance at Sander, to my left, dark hair, dark eyes, dark heart. He already bears kill marks down to his forearm, one at the bottom still new and scabbed over, earned from a reckless lone attack on wandering travelers a week ago.

He smirks when he sees me looking. "Down to my knuckle by morn," he says. "Catch up if you can."

I scowl at him, widening my stance to keep my footing

as the longship rolls into a trough. The black sails are full, lightening the load on the oarsmen and pulling us along at a ferocious speed. The collision of bow and wave jars my bones, but the last thing I want is to fall on my face in front of Chieftain Lars, who is squinting into the distance as if he can already see the Kupari peninsula. Both *his* arms carry over fifty parallel silver notches, from shoulders to the tip of his middle fingers. He has five on each cheek, too, beneath his eyes and above the edge of his beard. The marks of a true warrior.

Someday, I think. With those marks, no one would dare question whether I belong.

But today I will settle for holding my own. "If you can manage that many kills today without getting killed yourself, Sander, I'll be happy to cut you."

Sander leans down as if he wants to emphasize the difference in our heights, to remind me of the relative smallness of my body. My heart quickens, not with fear, but with triumph. He, like so many other men, doesn't realize how dangerous it is to give up the advantage of reach, to put himself within my strike range. It would be so easy to pull the knife from the sheath on my forearm and jam it into his exposed throat. He of all people should know better. Instead, he merely looks amused. "I'll do the same for you, Ansa, unless you're afraid I'll slice too deep. Your skin seems rather thin."

I laugh. "And yours is as succulent as lamb, if I recall correctly." Quick as a darting fish, I reach up and flick the base of his ear, where the smooth, soft drop of his lobe once hung.

Until I bit it off.

He grimaces, and his fingers close over the handle of the ax at his side. Thyra steps between us and elbows him. "What did you think you were going to get in return for goading her? Isn't the result always the same?"

He rolls his eyes. Thyra stands up straighter. "Either focus on what's coming or take another turn at the oars." She cuts her gaze to me as a gust off the lake blows her short light brown hair away from her forehead. "You too. Maybe take a breath before attacking." Her lips twitch. "For *once.*"

I force the corners of mine downward, though all I want to do is smile when she looks at me. "Oh, I'm focused—on getting as many kill marks as I can."

"Is that really all you think about?"

"No, of course not. I think about the copper and silver I'll plunder too." *I think about having so much that I will never want again.*

"Those people have no idea what's coming for them," she mutters. "But there are rumors of a—"

I hold up my hand. "No matter what's waiting for us, I'm ready."

"Let's hope so."

"You doubt me?" My gaze drops to the lean curve of her upper arm, where she bears three marks, one of which is rightfully mine. A forbidden gift to protect her; a secret that binds us.

She shifts so I can't see the marks on her skin, but her blue eyes are warm as she says, "I never doubt you, Ansa. Only fate and all mortal-made plans."

So like her. "Don't let *him* hear you say that," I murmur, nodding at Chieftain Lars's back. Thyra glances up at her father. Our chieftain is now in low conversation with Einar and Cyrill, his war counselors. Their cloaked shoulders are so broad that they block my view of the carved wolf head that juts from the prow of this mighty vessel. Ours is the lead, but the others, nearly one hundred fifty in all, sprawl behind us on either side like a massive flock of lethal birds. With a crew and a half on each, enough for all of us to have a break from the oars for part of the journey, we are a force of more than four thousand, tribes gathered from all parts of the north and united under Lars. Nowhere in this world is there a more dominant or deadly army, and we will cut through any Kupari resistance like wolves in a fat herd of sheep.

Not for the first time, I am confused as to why Thyra does not take more pride in all of this.

She will be chieftain one day. The only other rightful claimant to the chair—Lars's brother Nisse—was banished in shame this past winter. Thyra is our future.

She sees my frustration, I think. Something defiant and bold flares behind her eyes. "I wish us nothing but blood and victory," she says, her voice taking on a commanding edge that I envy and crave at the same time.

"Blood and victory," I repeat.

"They call us Soturi, I hear," she says. "Cyrill told me it means 'warrior' in their language."

I suppose Cyrill would know. He has a Kupari slave in his household. "That's nice. I'm happy to hear it doesn't mean 'dung eaters.'"

She gives me a half smile, and I stare at her face. She's a few inches taller than me, but on my tiptoes I can match our heights and bring us close. After she pushed me away the one time I tried, though, I won't do it again.

I so want to do it again.

"Skiff ahead!" shouts our lookout, his voice nearly lost in the wind as he calls down from his perch high on the mast.

"Probably a fishing vessel," calls Einar, the braids of his beard swinging as he turns to Lars. "It could warn them we're coming." He glances over and winks at me, and I grin—he's been like a father to me, and he's the only one I will claim. My real father was not strong enough to protect me, and on bad nights my dreams are haunted by his vacant eyes and bleeding body. He is always deaf to my screams.

"Do we know the size of their militia?" Cyrill asks, pulling me from unwelcome memory. "None of our raiders have encountered them."

"Whatever they have, they can't match us. A warning won't matter," Lars rumbles.

Thyra frowns, and I bump her with my shoulder. "It won't," I say. "Think of the stories from Vasterut."

She rolls her eyes. "And I'm sure tales of Nisse's easy conquest were not exaggerated in any way."

I bite my lip. Nisse now occupies the throne of Vasterut after his takeover of the southern city-state just before the spring. Though I meant only to offer confidence, mentioning him was probably a mistake. There are rumors he was plotting to assassinate Lars, since he could never best him in the fight circle. Thyra knows more, but she refuses to talk to me about it. One morning we simply woke up to find that Nisse had fled in the night, banished from the tribe. Lars allowed him to leave with those loyal to him, perhaps because he couldn't bring himself to slaughter his younger brother, perhaps to prevent us all from killing each other. With so many tribal groups gathered and sides to take, it would have been costly. Nearly one in five left with Nisse, including his only son, Jaspar. There's a pit in my stomach every time I think of him, though I haven't uttered his name in months. We all assumed he and all the rest of them were walking to their deaths in the dead of winter, so when news of Nisse's easily won victory and riches reached us, it was as good as a challenge for Lars.

Winter is coming once again, and Lars has told us we will spend it warm and fat and rich.

"Have you heard the stories of the witch queen of the Kupari?" Thyra asks quietly, moving close and raising goose bumps with the soft puff of her breath in my ear.

I shake off the tingles. "You doubt stories from Vasterut, but you're willing to believe *those* wild tales?"

Her tanned cheeks go ruddy. "I didn't say I believed them."

"Good." We've all heard stories about the source of the Kupari wealth and supposed strength. Not an arsenal, not an army—a witch. "But if she tries to use her stinking, evil craft on us, she'll end up with her head on the end of Lars's spear."

Thyra gives a curt nod. "She might anyway. The suspicion of witchcraft is enough."

"That little boat is definitely running," says Cyrill with a laugh. Standing at the front next to Lars and Einar, he leans on his spear, and its deadly-sharp tip gleams like a beacon. "I think it's going to be hard for us to sneak in unnoticed."

He gestures grandly at the warships in formation behind us, and the warriors all around me guffaw. So do I, louder than the rest. My blood sings as I feel their strength, the simple *aliveness* of us. I am so proud to be among these men and women. I wasn't born a Krigere, and I have spent the last several years trying to make people forget that. What should matter is my spirit, my willingness to fight. We all bleed red, as Lars always says, and I trust that he means it.

Thyra is smiling, but not laughing like the rest of us. And I can't help it—I grab her shoulders and shake her a little. "Come on!" I say, still chuckling. "Don't tell me you're not lusting to stick your blade into one of their fat merchants. Easiest kill marks you'll ever earn."

"Are those the only things that make a warrior?" she says under her breath.

Annoyance spikes through me, and I grab for the hilt of her dagger. Her fingers close over my wrist, hard. "Careful," she says in a rough voice. "Not here. Not now." There is something like a plea in her eyes.

It makes me want to push her. I want to replace that plea with *fire*. Thyra is not an eager fighter like I am, but when she commits, she is a thing of absolute, cutting beauty, and I hunger for the sight. I reach for her weapon with my other hand, and she catches that one too, right as I grasp the hilt. She presses my wrist to her side just as Sander leans over to watch.

"Well, you told Ansa to focus," he says with a sly glint in his eye. "And her focus is never better than when it's on you, Thyra."

With a near-frantic glance at her father, Thyra shoves me away so abruptly that I nearly stumble onto the front row of oars.

My cheeks burning, I right myself. "Say that again and I'll gut you, Sander."

He starts to step around Thyra to get to me. "Go ahead and try, you scrawny little—"

"Enough," roars Lars, turning on us like a bison ready to charge. "Dorte, Keld—take a break. Let these two cubs burn off some of their bloodlust on the oars."

Einar gives me an exasperated look. "Can you at least *try* not to kill someone until we make it ashore?" he asks, though he looks like he's about to laugh.

"I'll try," I grumble.

Dorte and Keld, who have been huffing away with their backs to us, lift their oars while the others keep at it.

I march over and take Dorte's oar, even though my break isn't supposed to be over until the sun sinks to quarter-sky. I don't want to hit the shore fatigued, but whining about it is unthinkable. Einar would probably throw me overboard himself for the sheer shame of it.

Dorte squeezes my arm with her scarred fingers. "By nightfall you'll show him what you've got," she says as she looks at Sander out of the corner of her eye.

"Assuming I let him live that long."

Letting out a harsh laugh that crinkles her weatherworn face, she lifts my elbow, examining the four kill marks. "I hope you'll give me the honor of making one of the new cuts after you've tallied your total."

"If you let me do the same."

She winks. "Maybe even two."

I plop onto the bench and place my callused palms over the skin-warmed wood of the oar. The simple, easy confidence Dorte has in me nearly makes me forget Sander's insult and Thyra's shove. Nearly, but not quite. I glance over my shoulder. Thyra's standing by her father now, her back to me, her posture stiff.

I face the rear again, telling myself not to look at her. Not to care what she thinks, not to worry about her. Frustration fuels each pull of the oar. Beads of sweat prick my forehead and glisten on the fine coppery-gold hairs of my arms. I hear the Kupari favor copper; I wonder what they'll think of me, the flame-haired warrior who will descend upon them like a starving wolf.

I'm not fooling myself. The sight of me does not inspire fear.

But it should. Anyone who has entered the fight circle with me knows it. Especially Sander, though he'll never admit it. I glance over to see him glaring at the vast array of ships following ours, the hard muscles of his arms taut. "Keep up, runt," he barks, reminding me of my task.

My back aches as I push the oar forward to match the pace of the lead oarsman and pull it to my stomach at the same time as everyone else. I treasure the cool breeze off the Torden and concentrate on becoming one with the others, as we all move in time like the flex of a horse's powerful loins. I've never rowed this distance before. Some of the warriors around me have; a few have made the journey at least a dozen times. Each time, they brought back livestock and tools the like we'd never seen. Each time, they gave us stories of a land so rich it practically bleeds copper. A few times, they've brought back slaves who wailed about how their witch queen, who they call the Valima or the Voltana or some such ridiculous name, will save them. Avenge them.

Surprise, surprise, she never did.

I hope I can be there when Lars marches into her throne room, when she begs for his mercy. He won't offer it. If you want to live, you must earn the privilege. I learned that lesson at a very young age.

I peek over my shoulder at Thyra again, and I blow out a long breath as I take another stroke of the oar. I want her to turn around and look at me, to punish me for provoking her. I want her to charge at me, take me down right here on the deck. Pin me. Dig her hip bones into mine. I want to feel her strength and know she's willing to do whatever she needs to. I want to bring the violence out of her, even if it means bleeding at her hands. I'd paint it on her skin, swirls of red to harden her spine and awaken her thirst for violence. It has to be in her. Lars is the greatest warrior the Krigere have ever produced, and Thyra's mother might have been an andener, a nonfighter, but she was a skilled iron smith who could fix any blade and would slice anyone who wasn't willing to barter fairly for her services.

Thyra carries this ferocity somewhere inside her; I know she must. She'll be a magnificent chieftain one day if she can summon it. My heart squeezes as she runs her hand along the hair at the back of her head. I cut it myself, just a few days ago, and she returned the favor. We'd let it grow a bit in the summer months, when the air grew too hot to ride out to raid, when we snuck away mornings and found a pretty spot among the dunes to tussle and eat the salted meat and biscuits we'd stolen from camp. In those moments, alone, no eyes on us, Thyra would touch me, just a hand on my back, or a brush of her fingertips to move my hair out of my eyes. Unnecessary, unbidden, but so, so wanted. She gave me hope. She made me wish.

Until I tried to make that wish reality.

I'm still trying to figure out if she pushed me away because she doesn't feel the way I do, or if she simply wishes she didn't. I think about it way too much, in fact. Especially because it's pointless.

We can't be together. We're both warriors now, but we are not the same status. I was a raid prize three times over, passed from one victor to another. I have no idea where I came from, only the memory of flames and blood. My history is so violent that some say it explains the red mark on my right calf, shaped like a burst of flame. I don't deny it. I usually add that it also explains how I survived—I am made of fire and blood myself, and it is why I fight so well. I have scrapped and killed for my place in this tribe, because without one, I have nothing. I *am* nothing.

Thyra, on the other hand . . . she is the daughter of a great chieftain, bred for war. She needs an andener as a mate, one who will keep her blades sharp, her fire stoked, her stomach full, her wounds bound, her bed warm.

One of us would have to lay down her weapons so the other could fight. It is forbidden and foolish to do otherwise—no warrior can survive without an andener to support him or her, and both of us must choose one soon to establish our own households now that we've reached our seventeenth year. Sander already did—a raid prize like me, taken from deep in the north. He was still able to win the heart of Thyra's sister, Hilma. He hasn't been the same since she died near the end of the winter season, taking their unborn son with her.

As for me, I've fought too hard for my status to give it up, but the thought of Thyra's skin against mine, of taking care of her and having her take care of me, makes it tempting. My heart skips as I glance over my shoulder yet again to find her looking at me, as if she felt the stroke of my thoughts.

"Three more skiffs ahead!" shouts the lookout. "Coming this way!"

"Are you certain?" Chieftain Lars calls. "Coming *toward* us?"

"Moving quickly!"

Still rowing, I turn as far around as the motion of the oar will allow. The water is piercing blue beneath the clear sky and bright autumn sun, and it's possible to make out a few specks on the horizon. I even think I can see the distant shadow of land several miles behind it.

"Closer now," calls the lookout. "Definitely approaching fast."

"Odd," says Einar. "They're coming against the wind."

"Maybe it's their navy," Dorte suggests, drawing a laugh from the rest of us. I check to see if Thyra's joining in, if for once she'll shed her seriousness and just enjoy herself.

She flinches and wipes her face, then looks up at the sky.

"Did a bird get you?" I grin at her, hoping to ease the tension between us.

Her brow is furrowed as she turns toward me. "Raindrop."

The oarsman in front of me tilts his head to the cloudless expanse above us. "Not sure how you came to that."

I tense as I feel a drop on my cheek, and another on my arm. A shadow passes over the boat, like a hand closing around the sun.

"What is *that?*" the lookout says, his voice cracking with alarm.

"All oars rest!" shouts Lars. I turn around and face forward as he peers at the sky.

We halt our rowing, our ship still cutting through the waves, blown by a sudden, fierce gust of wind that fills our sail nearly to bursting. Behind and around us, I hear captains in other boats calling for their oarsmen to lift their oars from the water and wait. In the space of a few minutes, the sky has changed color, from blue to purple to a faint green, and now clouds are bursting from nothing, swirling with the wind around a dark center. "What's happening?" I whisper.

"Freak storm," mutters a warrior behind me. "Bad luck."

"Skiffs still approaching fast," our lookout shouts.

I squint ahead to see the three silhouettes much closer than they were before—impossibly, they seem to have covered at least a mile in the last few minutes. The prow of the lead boat is grandly decorated, a column of copper that shimmers as lightning flashes within the clouds above. I don't understand—*is* this their navy? Just three tiny skiffs? And—

A deafening crash makes me yelp as rain lashes at my face. Thyra grabs her father's arm to stay upright. Our boat roils with a sudden wave, followed by another.

I blink rain out of my eyes—the foreign skiffs are even closer now, and I gape at the one in front. The copper column isn't a prow decoration, I realize. It's a woman, skin white as winter, hair as red as my own. Her dress billows in shimmery folds behind her as she raises her arms.

It's the last thing I see before the lightning stabs down from the sky like a Krigere blade, slicing the world apart.

CHAPTER TWO

I am thrown from my bench as our lookout's scream is silenced. The sail explodes into flame, a flare of orange heat above me. Warriors shout in fear while our ship is tossed by violent waves. I claw my way back to my position, knowing by the grunts around me that others are doing the same. My head is pounding and my ears are ringing.

As the white glare clears from my vision, I stare. Not at the chaos all around me, but at the woman in the skiff. She stands serenely at the prow, a coppery crown on her equally coppery hair. Her vessel and the other two accompanying it are floating on a patch of completely calm water, in a clear ray of sunlight in the distance. I swipe rain and bits of ice from my face, unable to comprehend the sight.

When my hands fall to my lap, she's still there. Arms

upraised, looking up at the sky as if it were a dear comrade. On one of her wrists is a thick copper cuff that glints red in the sunbeam.

"It's *her!*" shouts Einar, his voice strained as he clings to a rigging. Bits of fire from the burning sail rain down around him, mingling with icy rain. "The witch queen!"

"Starboard oars row!" howls Lars. "We'll give her a Krigere welcome, storm or no."

I spin in my seat and plunge my oar into the water, along with all the oarsmen on my side of the boat. We're not completely together, but our efforts are enough to bring the ship around, so that its bow meets the waves head on. We're perhaps a hundred yards from the witch and her peaceful patch of the Torden, but the waves are pushing us back.

"She's doing this," Cyrill shouts. "She's calling down the storm! Look at her!"

I crane my neck, as does nearly everyone else on the ship. How could a *person* cause a storm? And yet there she stands in her circle of sunlight, untouched by the gale, the arm graced by that copper-crimson cuff aimed at the sky. She's slowly twirling her fingertip—while the clouds above match the motion.

"All oars, row!" Lars bellows.

"You're going to ram her?" Thyra asks, shrill and shaken.

I close my eyes at the sound of her voice. She's right behind me. I could reach back and touch her, but I keep rowing, letting out a war cry that is answered by all my fellow oarsmen. Love for our chieftain beats fierce and proud inside me. No matter what happens, he fights. We will follow him into eternity. Nothing can stop us.

"We'll crush her," Lars shouts. "Row! R—"

His powerful voice is silenced by a sickening crack, a wave of heat, and a shuddering convulsion that throws me onto the oarsman in front of me. Thunder crashes around us as lightning brightens the sky, and I turn to the piercing sound of Thyra shrieking for her father.

The entire bow of our ship is on fire, the carved wolf engulfed, a blackened mass slumped over in the inferno.

It's Lars.

Thyra's back is pressed to my bench. Her blue eyes are wide, reflecting the flames devouring her father. Einar and Cyrill are sprawled in front of her, dazed and singed.

For a moment, there is a kind of hush, warrior cries smothered by a stunned realization that our chieftain is gone. My hands move on their own, reaching. My fingers skim along the soft, chilled skin at Thyra's throat, my fingertips slipping beneath the edge of her collar, offering strength. Comfort. Her palms cover the backs of my hands, pressing my flesh to hers for a moment. But only a moment.

I feel the instant she transforms. Her muscles tense, and heat flashes across her skin. She squeezes my hands and pushes them away as she shoves herself to her feet and turns to all of us. "You heard him," she shouts as the flames of our ship rise high behind her, the smoke billowing into the sky. "Row!"

My adoration for her is like a blade through my heart. I

whirl around and gouge the churning Torden with my oar. But a massive wave hits my back a moment later, water to my chest that nearly pulls me from the bench. Dorte screams as she's washed over the side and into the seething lake. Steam hisses as the fire behind me is extinguished. Thyra stumbles forward and clings to me as the lake tries to take her, too, so I wrap my arm over hers and try to row with one hand. I'm not strong enough, though, and the handle hits my chest. It knocks us both backward as the wave recedes, and I end up on the deck next to Thyra.

There's no one up here but us. Einar and Cyrill have also been washed away. A roar to my left draws my gaze to a massive waterspout shooting up from the deep, swamping two warships as it rises to lick the sky. The Torden is raging now, waves the size of large hills tossing our mighty ships as if they were toys. The hoarse cries of horror and fear drive the terrible truth home—this is an enemy we were not prepared to face.

"Row!" shrieks Thyra, still clinging to me. "If the witch controls the storm, we have to destroy her before she destroys us!"

"All in," roars Sander. "Blood and victory!"

"Blood and victory," echo the others, though I hear the cracks and strain of their cries. As I push myself up, I see several of our oarsmen and warriors are gone, carried overboard by the wave that put out the fire. Our burned bow rises as we're rolled by yet another. Thyra's fingers curl into my tunic for balance as she sits up on her knees and yells for everyone to give it all they've got. We'll be swamped if we don't. I need to get back to my bench, but I don't want to leave her alone up here. If the black water rising above us is our death, I want to go down with her in my arms.

We manage to make it over the crest of the wave and slide heavy and chaotic down into the next trough. Before we do, though, I catch a glimpse of the witch. "We aren't far," I call out to Thyra as needles of ice begin to rain down, slicing at our skin. I shield my face as our oarsmen battle the Torden, each back hunched as ice pricks at their flesh. Our beleaguered crew carries us up and over two more behemoth waves, the frigid water pushing at us from all sides.

And then we crest another wave, and she's right there. The witch queen watches us calmly, waiting in her little boat, on her tiny patch of smooth water. She's only twenty yards away, if that.

Thyra twists away from me and draws her dagger. She stumbles forward and cocks her arm back just as the witch queen's pale eyes meet mine. The witch's head tilts suddenly, as if in cold curiosity. Her eyes narrow. I feel her gaze inside me, a hand grasping for my heart, fingers slipping on smooth, pulsing muscle. The water around us suddenly calms, though the storm still rages behind us, all our ships caught in the jaws of the mighty lake.

Thyra gets her feet under her, preparing to hurl her dagger. She is devastatingly accurate at this distance, but I feel a flutter of uncertainty, like the wind has whispered a warning in my ear.

The witch's eyes slip from mine to hers. And in that moment, I know what will happen. As Thyra's body tenses for the throw, I hook my arm around her waist and fling us into the narrow space between rowing benches, just as a bolt of lightning slams into the deck where she'd been standing. A strange metallic scent fills the air and the prow begins to burn anew.

"Stay down," I snap, grabbing the dagger from her hand.

Thyra is struggling beneath me. "How dare you!" she screams. "This kill is mine."

I shove her against the planks beneath us. "She took your father only minutes ago, along with his war counselors. If she strikes you down too, we'll have no chieftain at all. Stay alive and lead!"

I bend over her as the waves begin to toss us again. My lips graze her cheek. "Besides," I say, "I'm a much better swimmer."

"What?" yelps Thyra.

Before she can stop me, I wrench myself up and stagger back toward the burning bow. Through the smoke, the witch's face shines white and fearless. Her eyes are like chips of ice. Raw hatred for her burns inside me, hotter than the flames eating our ship. Witchcraft is an abomination—unnatural and evil—and she is clearly steeped in it. If I can't kill her, she'll kill all of us. If my death is the price of victory, I'll happily pay it.

Just as we slide into a trough, I rip my cloak from my neck, clench Thyra's dagger in my hand, and dive off the side of the ship, praying I clear its hull. I hear my name called just before the water closes in around me, shocking me with the cold. My lungs beg for air as my body tumbles in the dark, swirling deep. Panic washes over me. I can't find the sky. My fingers clutch the dagger, and I flail, desperate to fight my way back to air. A flash of lightning below my feet tells me I'm upside-down, and I buck and kick for the green, flickering vortex above me. My face bursts to the surface and I gasp, frantically kicking to stay afloat. My weapons— knives in my boots and strapped to my arms—aren't heavy, but the collective weight of them and my clothes is pulling at me. But I'm close enough to the witch that the waves aren't massive, not like they are deeper inside the storm.

As I try to get my bearings, a wave hits our ship from the portside, causing it to falter. From here, I can see the damage, the broken mast and burned, shredded sail, the charred bow, the prow gone, half the oars either washed away or dangling useless next to empty rowing benches, all the shields stripped from the sides by the hungry Torden. Thyra's clinging to my bench and screaming orders, still trying to get our crew to ram the witch, but they can't control it. They're at the mercy of the gale and the waves. Right there, so close to me and yet out of reach. Fury warms my chilled bones, and I stroke hard to bring myself around again, to get the enemy in sight.

There she is. Watching our defeat with a tiny smile on her face. She's enjoying this.

I grit my teeth and swim as hard as I ever have. I can see

the wall of light that separates the witch and her boats from our peril. Only a few yards away. Before she even knows I'm there, I will lunge up from the water and slice her legs. As she falls, I will plunge Thyra's blade into her gut. Let's see her make it rain when she's drowning in her own blood.

These happy, savage thoughts drive me through the water, every muscle alight with determination. I am barely aware of the cold until a burst of warmth encloses me. The darkness peels back, and I am in her column of light. The water here is smooth, no waves to slow me down as I am coming at her flank. Her skiff is three strokes away, and she doesn't see me.

A bald, black-clad man in one of the other skiffs shouts, "Valtia!"

I jerk around to see him raising his arm, his chubby finger pointing straight at me. My eyes water as the air around me warps with heat and the lake turns scalding. Hissing with pain and twisted up with confusion, I kick away, desperate again for the icy feel of the storm. This water is cooking me. I face the sky, my legs pumping.

The witch turns and looks down at me as I wriggle like a speared fish. Her brow furrows. Her face is oddly cracked, the whiteness chipped away in places to reveal rosy skin beneath. The sight reminds me of my purpose, and I lunge for the hull of her skiff even as my flesh begins to blister. It doesn't matter, as long as I take her down before I die.

My raw, red hand clutches at the bow of the skiff. With her copper-decorated arm still raised to the sky, the witch stares into my eyes. She doesn't look scared. One corner of her mouth is still quirked up in a tiny, victorious smile, but I swear, there is a completely different kind of war within her pale blue gaze.

Another bald, black-robed man sitting at the stern lazily swishes his hand at me and speaks to the witch in the odd, trilling language I recognize as Kupari. He sounds undisturbed. Like I'm no threat, merely an inconvenience.

Hate is my fuel. My right hand raises the blade above the surface of the lake as I strain to escape the searing water, to heave myself into the boat and draw blood.

But the witch merely considers me as I struggle, looking pensive. "You're wrong. She's *not* a boy," she says softly, almost to herself.

I am caught by the sound of her voice—*and the fact that I understand what she said.* Like her gaze before, her voice reaches inside me, and this time, I feel when it takes hold, when it squeezes. My chest is filled with a feeling I cannot name, so powerful that it robs me of my will. I cannot possibly kill her. I cannot harm a hair on her head. My mouth drops open and the dagger falls from my upraised fist.

The black-robed man barks at her, trilling words gone harsh and hateful, lips pulled back from his teeth. I think he's telling her to kill me.

The witch looks over her shoulder at her dark companion. "I . . . can't." She sounds as puzzled as I feel.

He spits a few more words from between his bared teeth, and a ball of flame bursts from his palm.

I don't have time to be surprised. The witch whirls around again, and before I can blink, she pushes her palm toward me. A cold wave rises beneath me, ripping me from the side of the skiff and bearing me upward, away from the boat. I catch one more glimpse of her pale face and the glimmer of her crimson-copper cuff before I am plunged back into the jaws of the storm. A bitter wave crashes over me, sending me tumbling head over feet, helpless and lost and sure of only one cruel thing.

I have failed.

CHAPTER THREE

I am tossed up, sucking in a gasping breath, to see ships aflame and sinking, bodies all around me, emptied of the noble spirits who once resided there. The lake pulls them down, aided by the weight of their axes, their helmets, their cloaks. When I am forced deep by another swell, the lightning above reveals a lake full of thrashing arms and legs.

And me, clawing for air, battling the storm and my own despair. Surrender is weakness. I swim for one of the few longships still floating, only to watch a thick bolt of white lightning cleave it in two, sending warriors flying into the air with flames to cushion their fall. Another wave hits me, this one square in the back, pushing my face into the water and drawing my legs up, sending me into the depths yet again. Something hard slams into my head, a splintered mast or a rowing bench, maybe, lacing the water with my blood. My mouth opens in a gasp, and I inhale the Torden, which burns my lungs as my entire body revolts. Blackness rims my vision and then closes in.

The thought flashes in my head—*Give up. It's done.*

But I remind myself: A Krigere is granted passage into heaven only after a victory, or if she dies fighting. Though my only enemy right now is the lake, I will battle it until the end.

I stroke and kick and convulse. My fellow warriors do the same. The water invades and conquers, and as I struggle, I see so many of my brothers and sisters lose the fight. I know my time is coming too, but I don't—

The wind calms so quickly that it's like a heavy blanket smothering a campfire. The waves sink into the depths. The heavy, violent clouds swirl into nothing. The tempest folds in on itself like a melting ice crystal, and then it's gone. I blink up at the sun. Its beauty makes my eyes burn, and I let out a bemused croak of a laugh. I float on my back as the elation that comes with life after the certainty of death gives way to a completely different kind of understanding. Somehow I know to keep my eyes on the sky. If I gaze on the world as it is now, it will be the fatal, crushing blow. The silence alone is evidence of the totality of our destruction.

I should let the water take me. Sometimes wounds bleed too much. A warrior can die in victory on the battlefield if she fought to the end, if she gave all she had. And I did.

I gave everything, including the chance to die in Thyra's arms, to look at her face one more time. Surely I can simply let go now . . . ?

"Ansa!"

One word, one cry, one voice pulls me back from the brink.

"Ansa! Answer me or I swear I'll cut your throat."

I turn my head. Thyra paddles toward me on a large scrap of hull, her face smudged and dripping, her eyes bright with horror. Sander is behind her. He is bleeding from a gash on his temple, the blood staining his jaw and dripping into the collar of his tunic, but he still looks strong as he steers the makeshift vessel with a broken oar. Cyrill is draped across the middle, half his blond beard singed away, his formerly handsome face a mess of black and blisters.

I reach for Thyra's outstretched hand, so grateful that she's alive that I can't find my words. She clutches my shaking, scalded fingers and drags me up, and Sander lays down his oar and helps her pull me onto the raft. I clamp my teeth together to keep from crying out. It feels like I'm about to shed my skin, and right now, I wish I could.

While Thyra leans over me, Sander says, "We can't take on more weight. We'll sink."

She nods, then touches her forehead to mine, her palms on my cheeks. "Don't you ever try to steal my rightful kill again," she whispers harshly, but then she plants a hard kiss on the top of my head.

"I'm sorry," I say, my voice as broken as the rest of me. "I failed you."

She lets out a strained chuckle as she sits up and looks around. "We all failed."

Wincing, I push myself up on one elbow. We're floating in a sea of bodies and debris, beneath a rich blue sky and the sinking early autumn sun. A cool breeze ruffles my hair, but that's not what sends the cruel chill down my back. Not a single ship survived. In the distance, I can see a few warriors on another section of splintered hull, pulling a limp body onto their platform. But even as they succeed, a section of it dips, and all of them slide into the lake. They let out feeble cries as they struggle to climb back to safety. "We have to try to make it over there," Thyra says.

"Are you addled?" snaps Sander. "We'll be lucky if we don't meet the same fate."

She glares at him. "There were thousands of us on these waters. And we have andeners at home waiting for word—and protection."

Sander laughs. "Protection? Thyra, look around. We're dead."

"Not yet," she says, and begins to paddle toward the other survivors, her eyes scanning the waters for others.

Next to me, Cyrill moans. I put a hand on his back. "Keep breathing. Keep fighting."

"Blood and victory," he says weakly.

My throat tightens. "Blood and victory." But I know Sander's right. We're corpses with heartbeats. I peer at the horizon. Three tiny specks are receding into the deep blue. "There they are. The witch and her dark minions."

Thyra pauses in her paddling, drawing her soaked arms up from the lake. The fading sunlight glints off her silvery kill marks. If her gaze were an arrow, it would strike true and lethal. "For a moment, I thought I had the target," she murmurs.

It's as good as an accusation. "And if you'd stood your ground long enough to throw the dagger, you would have ended up just like your father," I say, coughing at the strain of so many words.

"And here I thought your dearest wish was to see me kill," she whispers.

"How did you know the danger?" Sander asks. "You pulled her away just in time."

"Instinct, I suppose. The witch had just struck Lars down the same way. I could see her looking at Thyra."

"You could see her that clearly?"

I turn to Sander, annoyance burning at the back of my tongue. "So could Thyra. We were close."

"If we'd had enough oarsmen, we might have been able to ram her," he says bitterly.

Another accusation. "We never would have reached her. She wouldn't have allowed it."

He arches an eyebrow, pure suspicion. "If you really thought that, why did you swim for it? Or were you just jumping overboard to save yourself?"

My brow furrows, and I look to Thyra. "The ship came

apart only a minute after you went over the side," she says quietly.

Sander's gripping the oar as if he'd like to hit me with it. "Did you know that by instinct too? We needed you on board!"

I rip one of my knives from the sheath at my wrist, but Thyra grabs my arm, which makes me hiss with pain. "Stop it now, both of you," she barks. "If you knock us into the water, I'll kill you before you have a chance to drown."

"So many dire threats, Thyra," drawls Sander. "You actually expect us to believe them?"

Thyra's eyes go wide at his insolence. He's never dared speak like this to her. No one has. But her father is dead now.

She strips my knife from my grip and has it pointed at Sander in an instant. "I said to stop it." She stabs the blade into the wood of the hull, leaving its hilt bobbing only inches from Sander's knee. "Though I choose not to shed blood often, it doesn't mean I won't."

"I'm just wondering what Ansa was really doing while our entire crew was battling the storm."

Thyra opens her mouth, probably to threaten him again, but it snaps shut as I murmur, "I made it all the way to her skiff."

Cyrill stops his moaning and turns his head to look at me. My cheeks burn as I gaze after the three black specks on the horizon. "I nearly had her, but the water . . . somehow, they turned it hot." I show them my raw, red arms and hands. "And one of her attendants had fire in his palm."

Sander rolls his eyes. "You're *both* addled."

"Our world was just destroyed by a witch-brewed storm," Thyra says in a flat voice. "What's more addled than that?"

Sander leans forward. A drop of blood from his chin lands on Cyrill's sodden tunic. "The fact that Ansa's still breathing. If she got that close to the witch, how is she still alive?"

All of them stare at me again, and I fight a strange fluttering inside me at the memory of the witch queen's face, the way she was looking at me before the end. "I don't know," I mutter. "I tried to strike, but then . . ." I swallow my next words, and they taste like shame. I dropped my weapon for no good reason. I had the chance and the strength. I might have been injured, but not severely. If I had lunged, I could have sunk that blade into her thigh. I was that close. But my heart went soft all of a sudden. And if I admit that, I might lose the thing that is most important to me in this world, more important than my own life.

Other warriors' respect.

"A wave caught me and pulled me away," I say quickly, realizing I have been silent for too many seconds.

"Why didn't she bring a bolt from on high to cook you in the water?" Sander asks. "Since that seemed to be her strategy for eliminating threats."

"Again, I don't know." Except . . . I don't think she wanted to kill me. Her attendants seemed to want her to do exactly that. The one in her boat, with the fiery hands, was going to do it himself. Instead of striking, though, she summoned the wave that bore me away.

She *saved* me.

The thought turns my stomach, and I lean over and retch into the lake, giving it back some of the water I gulped down as I drowned. I press my forehead to the soggy hull and listen to Cyrill's wheezing breaths, not wanting to raise my head and see how my three fellow warriors are looking at me. My skin is hot and cold at the same time, and hard shivers are making me tremble. A spot on my leg throbs, then sends icy bursts of sensation up my thigh. Startled, I shove the edge of my boot down my calf.

"Are you injured?" Thyra asks.

I stare down at my red birthmark, which is now pulsing hot, and shake my head as I pull my boot back up to cover it. "It's nothing."

Thyra curses. "They've disappeared."

I slowly raise my head and look out on the watery battlefield. The only sound is of gulls crying above us. Some of them have descended on our dead. The warriors we saw slide off their own improvised raft are nowhere to be found. Sudden fury rushes through me, and I yank my knife from the hull. I reel back to throw it at one of those hateful birds and nearly pitch into the water, but Sander brings up his oar and slaps me hard between the shoulders, sending me down with a huff on top of Cyrill. "Cursed to survive with only three baby warriors as my allies," he says with a moan.

"Quiet, Cyrill," Thyra says, command in her voice. "Your

eyes would be in a gull's stomach if not for us." But she squeezes his shoulder, and he offers a weary smile.

"What now?" asks Sander. "If there are others who made it through, they've drifted too far for us to find them."

Thyra stares out at the gently rolling waves, which are indeed carrying our dead and the remnants of our invading force further out into the Torden. "We go home," she says.

Sander laughs. "It took us nearly half-daylight to get here, and that was with the wind at our backs and twelve pairs of oars!"

He brandishes his broken oar, but Thyra rises on her knees with threat in her eyes. "And what would you prefer to do, Sander? Lie down like a weakling and let the Torden sing you to sleep?" She snatches the oar from his grip before he can think to stop her. "Take your spot next to Cyrill, then. Lie down and rest."

"Hey, don't cut me from the same cloth as this cub," Cyrill rumbles. He tries to push himself from the planks, but then groans and sinks back down. "If I wasn't so broken, I would help you row."

She grimaces. "Stay where you are." I hate the look in her eye, the worry and despair she's trying to hide. The twist of her lips and the bright sheen on her eyes—this is how she looked as she stood over the fallen, weeping old man in that coastal village during the summer's eve raid. When her hand shook, when she said in a broken whisper, *I will risk my father's wrath. This man has done nothing to warrant such a death*, and when the sight of her hesitation and shame made me draw my own blade and plunge it into his side. Though it is forbidden, I gave her the kill mark—her father had told her not to come home without a new one.

Like then, I cannot help but save her. I grab a floating plank from the water and hold it like a paddle. As Thyra plunges her broken oar into the Torden, I do the same, and together we move the raft, the shattered hull of what used to be a great warship, a few feet closer to home. The wind pushes my hair off my forehead as I glance over to find her looking at me in a way that warms me from the inside.

Red-cheeked, Sander snags himself the blade of another broken oar and joins us. He's at the "prow" of our unsteady little vessel, and so he sits on his knees and reaches forward, drawing the flat blade straight back toward the jagged edge before pulling it up again. The three of us paddle in silence as the sun dips at our backs and the sky turns dark once more, this time with night. Stars wink from the safety of the outerworld, mockingly cheerful as we slowly pull ourselves closer to our home shore in the northeast. The moon lights our way, showing us nothing but black waters all around.

Thyra is the first to notice that Cyrill's spirit has departed for eternity. She stops midpaddle and presses her fingers to his neck, then bows her head. "Stop for a moment."

Sander sits up and tosses his oar blade down next to him, rolling his shoulders and wincing. "What is it?"

"Cyrill's gone," I say unsteadily. I let out a shuddering breath and brace my palm on the planks. The birthmark on my leg is throbbing steadily now, to the point of pain. I can't tell if it's hot or cold, only that it burns. Thyra gives me a concerned look, and I wave her off. "I'm fine." I think I am, at least. The shivers haven't stopped, even though I'm sweating. Perhaps it's the scalding I took in the water. I've had fevers before, but it hasn't felt like this. Something inside me has gone unsteady and brittle, one collision away from shattering.

"We have to get rid of him," says Sander. "We'll be lighter if he's gone." He reaches over and plucks Cyrill's dagger from the sheath at his side, and I feel a pang of memory. Just last night, his beard dripping mead, his mouth split into a drunken grin, Cyrill drew that very blade and joked about how he'd ram it into the guts of any Kupari who stood between him and the twenty fine horses he planned to own before the invasion was done. His andener, Gry, laughed and kissed him, her fingers twisting in his beard, her joy and pride and love so big that all of us could feel it.

"Put that back," I say quietly, wishing I could stop shaking. My mouth suddenly feels too dry, like I could drink the entire Torden and still be parched.

"Why?" says Sander. "It's an excellent blade, and it'll do me a lot more good than it will him."

"It's *his*," I snap. "And a warrior is buried with his weapons." If he's not, he goes to the heavenly battlefield unarmed and shamed.

"We're not burying him, Ansa—you see any dirt around here?" shouts Sander, his voice breaking, his fingers white-knuckled on the hilt of Cyrill's dagger.

"He died with honor!"

"Stop it, both of—" Thyra begins.

"Death is pathetic, no matter how it strikes, and Cyrill died helpless and wounded and weak," roars Sander.

"Like Hilma did?" I ask quietly.

Sander hurls his broken oar blade at me, but I duck and snatch my dagger from the planks. Its edge reflects the moon. My palm is so sweaty that I almost drop it, though. "Stop letting your grief twist you up, Sander. Cyrill earned your respect in life, and I won't let you take it from him now!"

"How will you stop me, runt? You look like you're about to join him."

"You first."

Thyra yelps as Sander strikes with Cyrill's dagger, but I draw a second blade from the sheath along my calf. I block his strike with the back of my forearm, the impact rattling my teeth but forcing Sander to catch himself with his other hand to keep from falling into the lake. Taking advantage of his stumble, I straddle Cyrill's back to slide my blade up against Sander's throat. "Drop it," I growl, my teeth chattering. It feels as if someone's sunk a red-hot brand into my calf, and it's all I can do not to groan.

"Do it." Sander smiles as the blade bites his skin, and he leans forward to show he isn't scared. His dark eyes are full of rage and challenge. "Do it before I rip this knife from your grip and cut you open."

I am shaking so violently now that I can't hold the blade steady. Sander is grinning. "We're all going to die," he

41

whispers, even as his smile crumples into a grimace. "Do you think she'll be waiting for me?"

Thyra reaches for Cyrill's dagger, still locked in Sander's grip. "Sander—"

"Shut it, *Chieftain*," Sander snaps, his eyes glittering.

Our eyes are locked. He is past caring, past respect, past hope. Suddenly, the urge to kill him is almost as powerful as the massive, tremulous *thing* inside me that has been growing by the minute, taking me over. Sander used to be full of light and life, and now he courts death like he wants it for his new mate. I brace to make the cut before I fall apart, but Sander rears back, perhaps because his body wants to survive even though he has lost his will to live. But his weight and the sudden movement sends the other end of the hull rising into the air. As Cyrill's body starts to slide, I dive for the higher edge while Thyra tumbles off the other side. With a splash and a cry, Sander goes into the lake too, and Cyrill's body promptly lands on top of him. The hull splashes back flat onto the water, soaking me. I hear Thyra begin to shout at Sander, but a roaring fills my ears, deafening me.

I gasp as something monstrous in me stretches and spreads its wings, drawing its talons along my ribs. My red mark throbs once more, wrenching a cry from my mouth.

"Thyra," I say. Or, I think I say it. I'm not sure the sound ever leaves my mouth. An unseen force flips me onto my back and slams me down against the hull. My eyes open wide, but I'm blind, everything white. It feels like a giant's hand has descended from the sky and is holding me down. My heart is beating so fast that it's one long, painful squeeze. Panic and terror flash so hot inside me that I'm burned. Has the witch queen returned for us? For me? Is this her final victory?

My backbone bows, my chest and hips rising while my shoulders and legs stay pinned. I can't control my body at all. Fire bursts inside my mind, followed just as quickly by knives of ice that slice away my thoughts. I'm in a cage of flame and swirling snow, extremes that rip me apart and knit me together again, over and over. The feeling of being torn down my center is unbearable, but the force inside me is so huge that it cannot be denied or contained. It grows and grows and makes its home in my chest, crowding out everything I thought I was. Tears turn to ice crystals on my cheeks, then sizzle on my skin. The pain goes on and on. Now *I'm* the one who craves death as a mate.

The feeling goes as quickly as it came, dropping me limp onto the planks with a sudden *thunk*. My head cracks against the wood. My eyes blink open.

I'm alone on the raft. I bolt upright, looking around, my vision blurred.

Perhaps six feet from the makeshift boat, two heads bob in the dark water. Thyra and Sander. Both of them are staring at me with round, terrified eyes. "What happened?" I ask, still rocked by the aftershocks of whatever it was.

"Y-you—you . . ." Thyra swallows hard.

"You were struck by lightning," Sander says weakly.

I look down at myself, sinking backward because I'm too weak to stay upright. My clothes are intact. Nothing is singed. The only thing that burns is the mark on my calf. "No, I wasn't."

"You were," Thyra says, her voice high and tremulous. She swims toward the raft. "Hold still. I'm coming aboard."

"Me too," says Sander.

She gives him a hard look. "We're done fighting tonight. If you truly wish to join my sister so soon, stay in the water."

Sander lets out an annoyed breath, and the two of them heave themselves up on either side of me, landing at the same time and somehow managing not to tip our raft. Their clothes soak me, leaving me shivering between them as we all look up at the cruel stars, panting.

"We lost our oars," Thyra murmurs. "They floated away when we fell in."

"And both your daggers. And Cyrill's. I'm sorry," Sander mumbles.

"Fine by me, since all the two of you were doing was threatening to kill each other," Thyra retorts. She turns her head. "I can't believe you're alive. When I saw that bolt come from the sky, I thought—" She closes her eyes, and I know she's envisioning her father, charred and ruined within the fire.

Our faces are only a few inches apart. On any other occasion, this would make me unbearably happy. But right now, it's too sad. We're floating on an endless expanse of blackness, with no way home.

I would give everything I have to make it back. I would kiss the stony beach, dig my fingers in until grit burrowed beneath my fingernails. I would twist my hands in the long blades of grass that mark the edge of the dunes. I would lie by a warm fire and sneak glances of Thyra's face when she's asleep.

"I confess that this is not the way I wanted to die," Sander says quietly. The desperation is stripped from his voice, and he sounds like a little boy again, the one who I was friends with before he lost his love and turned cruel and careless. "I didn't want to have this much time to think about it."

"I know what you mean." I let out an unsteady breath. I have never been eager for death, but I always imagined it would be quick, a sudden, merciless slice instead of a slow unraveling.

"I still have a knife in my boot," Thyra whispers.

I squeeze my eyes shut. "No. It won't come to that." I find her hand and clutch it tightly. Her fingers are stiff as icicles, and the feel of them makes my eyes burn. What I wouldn't give for a good wind, a warm, blessed breeze to carry us to shore.

My hair flutters as a gust rushes over us, like a breath of summer.

"Oh, that felt good," Thyra says, scooting slightly closer to me so that our bare arms touch. "I'm so cold."

If Sander wasn't here, I would offer my embrace and take the risk she'd rebuff it. But since he is, and with all that's happened today, I don't think I can take another failure without breaking. I settle for imagining the wind is an ally that will dry her clothes and warm her skin as it moves us along the smooth surface of the placid lake. I close my eyes and hold her hand, focusing on that wish so completely that it's almost as if I can feel it stroking over me. I lose myself in the dream of it, even though I'm not sleeping. I'm too absorbed by the feel of Thyra's skin, the way she's caressing the back of my hand with her thumb, the way she's looking at me like she never wants to look away. If I move, if I sleep, I'll lose this final gift.

"I don't believe it," Sander mutters from beside me. "Is this really happening?"

I lift my head, but my vision blurs with dizziness, so I let it fall to the planks again. Waves of chill are cramping my muscles, but as soon as the pain makes me want to cry out, the cold is replaced by flashes of heat that make me sweat. I shudder. "Sorry. I'm still recovering from whatever happened earlier. Everything is moving. Spinning."

"We *are* moving," says Thyra, whose hand slips from mine.

My eyes meet hers. "What?"

Her hair is standing on end, blown by the warm wind that is gusting steadily now. Her pale eyes are wide, but no longer filled with fear and horror. Instead, they're filled with awe—and hope. "This wind," she says softly. "This wind . . . it's blowing us to the northeast."

I sit up, clutching my aching head and looking around.

Sure enough, our makeshift raft is leaving a small wake behind it as we're carried along the surface of the water. I let out a surprised chuckle, shivering as I feel the air caress my face. *More*, I think. I want to be home.

I sit there all night, fighting a squirmy, gut-churning feeling akin to snakes writhing beneath my skin, scared the miracle will end at any moment. But it doesn't.

By the time the sun rises, the shore is in sight. The very harbor from which we launched our massive force just a day ago. I can already see people gathering on the docks, the small group of warriors who made up the secondary force, and the andeners who sacrificed so much to prepare us to go into battle. Sander looks over at Thyra. "What are you going to do?" he asks her, sounding uneasy.

She clenches her jaw and lifts her chin. "I'm going to lead."

Sander gives her a skeptical look, and anxiety turns my stomach.

We promised them a victory. We promised them riches.

Instead we bring them ruin. We've survived one deadly storm—but we're about to face another.

CHAPTER FOUR

By afternoon, the sky is the color of slate and spitting icy drops onto our sprawling settlement, contempt from the heavens. I sit wrapped in a coarse blanket by the fire in the large shelter for unpaired warriors, shaking with weakness, knowing I deserve every wet reminder of defeat that reaches me through the leaky thatch. I'm alone in here—most of the young warriors who shared this shelter with me traveled in the first wave. We were eager to prove ourselves, and we fought for our spots in the boats. Now most of the people I came up with, the ones I was tussling and laughing with only two days ago, are sleeping forever at the bottom of the Torden.

Thyra has been in the council shelter for hours, explaining our catastrophic defeat to our remaining warriors, the few hundred mostly older or weaker ones who stayed behind to guard the andeners, led by a gray-bearded but thick-bodied warrior named Edvin. I begged to be by Thyra's side as she took her place on the chieftain's chair, stumbling after her on faltering legs as soon as our makeshift raft reached shore. Instead she put her arm around me and led me here.

She left me stunned and ashamed that I did not have the strength to follow.

Outside, the andeners are wailing, their quiet toughness shattered. Their warriors are not coming home. Their widows cannot cut themselves and bleed one last time over their lost loves. They cannot bury their mates with their swords on their chests, ready to meet eternity. This is worse than death, worse than loss—it is nothingness. Utter defeat. And there is more than grief in their cries—I can hear their fear. With thousands camped on these shores, stretched from Ulvi Point to Sikka Harbor, the southernmost tip of our territory and the launching point for our ships, we have been unassailable, a marauding people who sleep safe, unafraid of the nomad tribes that make their shelters as near to the lakeshore as they dare.

Now, though . . . as winter descends, and as news of our devastation spreads, we will become the hunted.

I raise my head as Sander and Aksel, Edvin's only son and another of the second-wave warriors, trudge into the shelter. Sander has a wineskin in his hands, and he holds it out when he sees me huddled by the fire.

I shake my head, and he frowns. "Have you eaten?"

"Not hungry. And we should save what we can." I stare at the fire to avoid their gazes, and the flames dance for me, twining together like the fingers of lovers.

"There's plenty," says Aksel, shaking raindrops from his mane of tangled brown hair. He doesn't remind us that the surplus is because half our number are dead, but I have no doubt they're thinking it, same as I am.

"We'll need it when the snow comes."

"Doesn't mean you should starve yourself today. If you expect to help keep watch, you can't be faint and weak." Sander's voice is sharp as his ax blade. "Unless weakness is your new preferred state."

Icy anger flashes across my skin, so cold I imagine I can see my own breath as I exhale. I almost say *Wasn't it* yours, *just a few hours ago?* But I don't have the energy or strength to fight him right now, so instead I mutter, "When have I ever shirked my duty?"

Aksel plops down next to me and nudges my blanket-covered arm with his bare, wiry shoulder. One kill mark decorates his upper arm, and bruises bloom like nightflowers around his left eye. He fought like a crazed animal to gain a spot in the first wave, but now I wonder if he's glad he and his father both lost. He gives me a sideways smile and offers a hunk of bread. "Put that in your stomach. We need you out there."

I take it, meeting Sander's dark eyes before looking away again. He sits down on the other side of the fire. "Thyra's still in the council shelter," he says, running a hand through his shorn black hair. "She won't be able to keep us whole."

I sit up straight, the hard bread clenched in my fist. "Don't underestimate her."

Aksel shifts uncomfortably next to me. "My father says she'll face a challenge soon."

I give him a peeved look. "Your father should hold his tongue. That kind of talk spits on the memory of Lars—and it could tear us apart."

"Or unite us." Sander leans forward suddenly, staring at me through the dancing flames.

The flames between us rise with a burst of cold wind from outside. "Behind her, I hope you mean. You've seen her fight, Sander. You know how clever she is."

"Oh, we all know that," he mutters. "Have you ever wondered if she's too clever?"

Jaspar, Nisse's son, used to say that all the time. "Stop it. She is a force to respect. Her father certainly did, and that should be good enough for you."

Sander looks into the fire. "What if she doesn't lead us down the path he would have chosen?"

I glance at Aksel, who is studying his boots. "Thyra is our new chieftain," I say. "It's her path to choose now."

Aksel sighs. "Our tribe is broken."

Panic punches through me. This tribe is all I have. "You sound like a weakling," I say savagely.

Aksel's fists clench, but he relaxes again as he takes in my sweat-sheened face. "I don't like it any better than you do, but some are already talking about taking their andeners and striking out on their own. Such a big settlement, with so few warriors to guard it . . . They think it might be safer if they head to the northwest. Or the south."

"Toward Vasterut?"

"Chieftain Nisse might take us in."

"Or he might skin us alive and turn our hides into saddles." I scoff. "He's a snake, and a poisonous one at that! We may have suffered losses, but we are not defeated. Why should we crawl to him as if we were?"

Sander clenches his jaw and tosses a stone into the fire, sending sparks into the air. "Because we might not survive the winter if we don't!" He gestures angrily outside, where a group of andeners, nearly all women, are beating their breasts and howling at the sky, while their rag-footed children watch with solemn eyes from inside the shelters. "We have herds of horses but no riders! We have thousands of mouths to feed but no raiders to plunder!"

Aksel stares out the shelter door. "Thyra thinks we should stay put, use our cached supplies for the winter, and plant in the spring. Like a bunch of farmers! She sounded like an andener. Several warriors walked out of the meeting."

"Including the two of you." Now I understand why they're here, why Thyra isn't.

Sander nods. "We couldn't stomach it."

"You must have misunderstood what she was suggesting," I say. "We're Krigere, and she knows that." We don't root ourselves in the earth—we rule it, taking what we want when we want.

Aksel shakes his head, pushing tangled locks off his brow. "She wants to be a sheep, not a wolf."

Sander's eyes narrow. "You know this, Ansa. You just don't want to see it."

He's pulling on the tiny voice of doubt inside me, and I hate him for it. "Are you just lashing out because we witnessed *your* despair and pathetic weakness after the battle?"

Sander gives Aksel an uneasy sidelong glance. "My weakness was momentary. Thyra's is part of who she is. She has no thirst for blood. The others see it. You would have walked out too, if you'd heard what she was suggesting. Whatever you are, Ansa, you're not a sheep."

I bare my teeth. "The first intelligent thing you've said since coming in here. But Thyra has my loyalty and my blades." My cheeks heat. "As soon as I earn myself some new ones," I mutter.

"You won't have to earn them," Aksel says, his broad face sagging with sadness. "We've lost nineteen out of twenty warriors, and many of them will have left weapons behind."

The thought of all those blades, made for vital, ferocious men and women who died scared and helpless, feels like a ball of ice in my gut. I hunch over it, my eyes stinging.

Aksel curses. "My teeth are going to chatter right out of my skull. I'm going to get more wood for the fire." I listen to the shuffle of his feet as he heads out.

"It would be warmer if we were in here with all our brothers and sisters," Sander says to nobody in particular.

"The least we can do is honor their memories instead of pissing on them."

"*Now* honoring the dead is important to you?" The crackling roar of the fire matches the rush of irritation through my veins. I jerk my head up. "One more nasty little insinuation about Thyra and I'll tear your throat out." The fire is burning so high that it's blackening the thatch above our heads, but it wanes as I slump, as if it somehow knows my mood. "I won't believe a thing you've said until I speak with Thyra myself," I say, suddenly tired.

"Fair enough." Sander eyes the fire, then glances at me. "You don't look well, Ansa."

I lay my blanket along the edge of the fire and sink onto it. "I'm fine. Just tired. Aren't you?"

"I am. But . . ." Our eyes meet. "I wasn't struck by lightning."

"Obviously I survived. So obviously it wasn't lightning."

"Your eyes glowed like lanterns. Your body arched up like it was about to snap in half. The light was so bright I was nearly blinded." He makes an impatient noise as he lies down on the other side of the fire. "If it wasn't lightning, what was it?"

I am so sleepy that I barely hear him. "Doesn't matter now," I mumble. I had wanted to stay awake until Thyra returned, but I can't. Exhaustion is pulling me under its waves. I sink into blackness, happy for the temporary respite from the memories of shattered ships and thrashing limbs and Lars's burning body lost in the fire.

Fire.

A spark, really. In the dark pit of my rest, it flares to life, orange and bright. I stare, fascinated, as it burns without fuel, growing slowly, licking the air around me with its serpent tongue. I have never seen the sun burn in the night, but I imagine this is what it looks like. The heat slides over my face. It's such a relief after all my cold despair, but as sweat beads my brow, I wish I could scoot away from it. It's growing by the second, expanding into my space. I cringe back, whimpering, as it nips at my toes, the tip of my nose, my eyelashes and hair.

I cry out as it licks my stomach and chest, as it presses against me, setting me aflame, boiling my blood, cooking my eyeballs. The shrill sound of my own scream pierces the roar and crackle, but the flames jump down my throat, and then they're inside me, filling me up.

"Ansa!"

My eyes fly open to find my dream made real. The air is filled with sparks and smoke and screaming. Sander's silhouette fills the doorway of the shelter, and he's beckoning me toward him while he holds a cloth over his mouth. Between us is a wall of flame. I'm surrounded by it. If I stand here, I'll burn alive, but my only alternative is to run through the fire. There is nothing between my skin and those flames, and the thought sends an icy chill over my body. Even in the inferno, I shiver; it feels as if frost is covering my skin.

I don't spend more time thinking about it. As the roof begins to rain chunks of burning thatch and splinters of wood, I leap through the wall of fire. Sander grabs my shoulders and tosses me through the doorway of the shelter. I hit the mud and roll.

The night is lit with the orange flames shooting from the top of the shelter. Andeners are running and shouting all around me, evacuating their own shelters for fear the blaze will spread. Some of them are tossing pails of water onto the fire, and the weather is helping—the rain intensifies, drenching all of us. I slide my hand over my short hair and sit up.

Sander squats by my side, the strangest look on his face. It's not fear, exactly, but it looks like a near cousin. "Why are you staring at me like that?" I ask impatiently, as he helps me to my feet.

"You were completely enclosed by that fire," he says as I wrench myself away from him.

"So?"

He gestures at my tunic and breeches, at my cloak that hangs muddy and wet from my shoulders. "You're not even singed."

I stumble backward as the air suddenly becomes too thick to breathe. "I don't even know what happened."

"You were thrashing in your sleep, and then your blanket was on fire." He takes a step away from me as the wind blows thick smoke between us. "You are the luckiest Krigere in the world, escaping death so many times in the space of a day."

Suddenly, I need to get away from his prying eyes. Every

glance feels like an accusation, and I'm going to kill him if he looks at me one more time. I whirl around and march toward the shore, needing fresh air and silence. As I walk, the rain thins to a mist. Andeners run past me every few seconds, carrying full pails up from the lake. On the other side of the docks lies a quiet hollow, and I make for it, desperate to outrun the shouts of fright echoing behind me. The scent of burning wood is sharp and rich, and like Sander's stare, it feels like a finger pointed straight at my chest. Reeling with rising panic and confusion, I reach the edge of the rocks and slide down the pebbled trail toward the hidden cove. Halfway down, I lose my footing and collide with someone climbing up the path. I end up on my back, staring up into Thyra's face, which is lit by the faint glow of the inferno in the settlement.

"What are you doing here? Is there trouble?" she asks, her voice high with alarm. "I heard screaming."

"My shelter caught fire," I reply. "It's good to see you, by the way. How are you?" I sound much calmer than I feel.

"You don't want to know." She lets out a strangled laugh. "I came down here to think." She grasps my shoulders and pulls me to my feet. "Are you all right?" Her gaze travels down my body. "You aren't burned?"

I shake my head, fighting the urge to press myself against her, to wrap my arms around her waist and cling. "I'm fine. And the rain is helping." As if it hears me, the drops grow colder, making my breath fog.

"I should go help," she says wearily.

My hands grasp her elbows, fingers digging into the lean muscles of her arms. "Don't go."

"Why not?"

"I—" My mouth hangs half open, words shriveling. "Sander and a few others came into the shelter a little while ago. . . ."

The edge of her jaw could cut flesh. "They want to go running to Nisse. And they accuse *me* of being a coward."

"Did they actually say that to you?" *And why didn't you cut their hearts out?*

She gives me a look that says she hears my unspoken thought. "No one's saying anything out loud." She lets go of me and runs both hands through her wet hair. "I wouldn't have spoken as I did, especially so soon, but the suggestion that we take a knee before my uncle, after what he tried to do . . ."

"I know." I swallow hard. "I'm with you. Whatever you want to do."

Her hands fall to her sides. "You might not say that if you knew what I've done—"

"Sander told me what you proposed."

"Oh . . . yes." She closes her eyes. "Ansa, I don't know if I can do this."

"Of course you can. You are Lars's daughter, and you were born to be a great warrior!"

"Sometimes I feel like it's just a skin I wear."

I squint at her. "How can you say that? It's in your blood and bones. All you have to do is embrace it."

She gives me an uneasy look. "And what, exactly, is in my blood and bones? War? Killing?"

I hate the distaste with which she says those words. "The thrill of conquest. Territory and triumph. Blood *and* victory." I laugh, but it carries an edge of frustration.

"How can that be enough for you, Ansa? It certainly isn't enough for me."

"Tribe, then," I shout. "You were born to lead this tribe. Born to keep us strong. And if you don't—" I clamp my lips shut and turn away. "Give us our pride back. Build us up. Remind us who we are. Plan our revenge on Kupari. But *don't* let us become prey." *Please.* I wrap my arms around myself as the memory of blood and fire and my parents' empty eyes makes me feel so small, so small, like anything could snatch me up and take me away from everything I love.

"Ansa." Thyra touches my arm. "*Ansa.*"

"Do whatever you have to do," I say in a choked voice.

"I always have." Her blue eyes are wide and unfocused as she stares at the lake. "But . . ." She blinks and tosses me a quick, sad smile. "Never mind."

"You will triumph. I know it," I whisper, reaching up to touch her hollow cheek. Perhaps, if she feels my faith in her, she'll find the strength she needs to fight, to keep us whole.

A tired smile pulls at her lips. "Your hands are so warm. As if you brought the fire with you."

That's what you do to me, I want to say. But I don't want her to push me away. "If I did, I'm glad. At least I can say I did *something* for you tonight."

59

She bows her head, but presses her palm over my hand, holding it to her cheek. "In the last day I have watched nearly everyone I love die," she says quietly. "And I suspected that what I had to say tonight might make the rest walk away from me, yet it was a risk I had to take. But I couldn't bear . . ." She looks at me through eyelashes sparkling with mist and firelight. "If *you* looked at me with disappointment, if *you* walked away . . ." Her voice is so soft that I have to move close to capture her words, my gaze focused on her mouth.

I'm your wolf. Your fire. Your knife, your blanket. If only you ask. "All I see when I look at you is my chieftain."

"Is that really all you see?"

"You want all my honesty?"

"Yes," she murmurs, and then slowly, so slowly, she turns her head and kisses my palm. A tiny but potent pang of ecstasy streaks along my arm and straight to the center of me like a ray of sunlight focused through a crystal drop of dew—one that awakens a wildfire inside.

My heart pounds, sending heat pulsing along my limbs. Caught in a storm of hope and searing need, I rise onto my tiptoes.

Thyra gasps and steps away from me, her hand clamped over her cheek, leaving mine suspended between us, reaching. She lets out a surprised laugh. "Are you feverish?"

I tuck my hand into the folds of my cloak. "What? No. Why would you think that?"

"I think you burned me." She pokes at her cheek, wearing a bemused smile. There's a reddish outline on that side of her face, her pale skin blotchy with heat. I blink at it, telling myself it's just a shadow as she begins to walk up the narrow path to the settlement. "I'm going to help get things calmed down. You coming?"

I nod, but as she turns her back, I stare down at my hand. At my fingers.

And at the tendrils of flame swirling merrily in the center of my palm.

CHAPTER FIVE

Now I understand why the witch let me live. It is the only thing that makes sense. And as the truth sinks in, it drives my hate for her deep into my bones.

She cursed me. Instead of giving me an honorable death, she filled me with her poison and sent me back to our people. She killed all our warriors, but it wasn't enough for her. I had thought the warm wind, which rose from nowhere to blow our scrap of hull back to our home shore, was a gift from heaven.

It was just a part of her plan to kill us all. She means to use me as a sword against my own, but I won't let her.

I crouch against the dune and stare across the water. The knife slips in my sweaty palm. My head is buzzing with lack of sleep—I haven't allowed myself to do more than doze since the second fire.

One burned shelter is an accident. But two makes people wonder. A third will make them sure. *Witchcraft*, they will whisper. *Witch*, they will think when they look at me. In the five days since we were crushed, superstition has sprouted like mushrooms from the soil of an empty burial ground—haunted by warriors who will never be properly laid to rest. Thyra has been working with the widows of our most senior warriors to plan a ceremony of farewell to soothe our uneasiness and grief. We will not get to share our blood with our lost brothers and sisters one last time, nor can we arm them for eternal battle, but Thyra says our spirits and memories will be the wind that carries them to their final victory.

She cannot silence the whispers, though, nor can she quell the fear. The wolves of heaven no longer guard us. We are prey now. We have been cursed.

And we are all looking for a place to lay blame.

A low sob bursts from my mouth. I could not bear it if they knew that I am the cursed one, but I am; I know it. Fire drips from my fingers if I do not focus on suppressing it. Just as bad, frost creeps along my arms and bitter cold whirls around me at the worst moments. So far, they all draw their cloaks around their shoulders and blame it on the coming winter, but soon they'll realize it comes from me. I feel the ice *inside*. It's a blade on a stone, growing sharper by the day, destroying me.

I pull the collar of my tunic wide and hold the knife

angled downward, the point touching the soft skin at the base of my throat. One solid thrust, and it will pierce my heart. I know how hard to push. I've felt flesh give way, the strike vibrating through a hilt to my palm, up my arm. I've felt the shield of bone, the resistance of gristle, the slide of viscera. I know to twist, to leave nothing untouched in my wake, to shred and tear and leave no possibility of recovery. I'm going to earn one more kill mark today, though I won't be alive to ask for it.

I squeeze my eyes shut and turn my face to the heavens. Why me? There were thousands of warriors on the Torden that day. Why was I the one she sent to hurt my people? Did she know how hard I'd fought to be one of them? Did she know my tribe means more to me than anything else?

I wrap my other hand around the one clutching the hilt. It will be over soon.

"I thought I saw you sneaking away."

I pivot on the balls of my feet, whipping the knife behind me. "I didn't sneak," I say breathlessly as Sander steps into view.

His brow furrows as he examines my face. "Are you crying?"

I grimace and swipe my hand across my cheeks. "Are you addled?"

"We were scheduled to take watch this afternoon, but—"

But I had planned to be dead by then. "Yes, this afternoon. So leave me alone."

"What are you hiding from? Why weren't you at noonmeal?"

I stand up, annoyance blazing through me. But fear is hard on its heels as I feel the heat sprout from my fingertips. I clench my fists, and sweat beads across my forehead as I wrestle the curse back. "Just because I wanted to get away from the gloom of camp, I'm hiding?"

He rubs his palm over the back of his head. "You haven't been the same since we returned."

"I can't imagine why. I only watched everything I love burn and splinter, and there was nothing I could do to stop it." My lip curls. "I think the better question is why you're suddenly the perfect warrior, Sander. Did you realize Hilma would have thought you a coward, for the way you acted on the Torden?"

With a strangled growl, he lunges at me. I sidestep, but he catches a handful of my tunic and sends me stumbling over his legs, into the sand. I roll away as he tries to dive on top of me, then land a kick to the side of his head as he comes for me again. He grunts and rises to a crouch, ready to pounce. But as he does, I hurl a handful of sand into his face.

"You conniving little runt!"

"Maybe I haven't changed as much as you thought."

Sander chuckles as he blinks sand from his eyes. "Oh, you have. Setting fire to your own blanket two nights in a row, and somehow you're untouched by the flames? Slinking around for the last few days with a cloud of bitter cold around you? Don't think I haven't noticed."

This time I'm the one who attacks, out of pure terror at

his words. I plow into him, wrapping my fingers around his throat for an instant before he yowls with pain and grabs my wrists. I slam my forehead into his face. Cursing, he wrenches my hands behind my back, barely avoiding my snapping teeth. "Cut it out, Ansa!"

"Why should I?" I'm still struggling, trying to get my legs beneath me so I can thrust my knee into his crotch. "Are you reliving our last turn in the fight circle? This time I could bring you death if you like. Fight hard enough and Hilma might even welcome you to heaven."

He shoves me away, and I land on my back in the sand, knowing I've poked an unhealed wound but too shattered to care. I need him to come at me, to give me a reason. I'm hoping he's remembering that bright spring day, when he thought I was easy game, when he beat me until I could barely stand . . . when he turned his back on me and gave me the moment I needed. As I scramble to my feet, blood drips from his upper lip while he gingerly prods several red streaks along his throat. I glance down at my hands and ball them in my tunic. Did I just burn him?

"Your fingers . . . ," he says slowly as his hands fall to his sides.

My heart thumps in time with my panicked thoughts. "I've had a fever lately."

He squints at me. "They were so cold that I thought my blood would turn to ice."

Saliva fills my mouth and I nearly retch. "I had just washed them in the lake."

"Liar," he says quietly, then puts his hands up as I start forward again. His steps are quick, like he's nervous. And he should be. If he accuses me of witchcraft, I'm going to kill him.

"Ansa, I didn't come here to fight you," he shouts as I start forward.

"Now who's a liar?"

"It's Thyra! I was coming to tell you—just listen!" He has his hands out in front of him as I move closer, alarm ringing like a bell in my ears. "She told me to come find you. She was challenged."

"What? By who?"

He glances over his shoulder, toward the camp. "Edvin laid his claim to the chieftain's chair at noonmeal."

"The second-wave commander thinks he can do better than she can?"

"He said he wouldn't let Thyra turn us into land drudges. They were going straight to the circle. And I knew that you—"

I'm running now, my only thought of getting to Thyra. Sander catches up with me as I hit the trail. My mind is a whirl of questions, but I'm too panicked to ask him. My feet pound the rocky path as I sprint into camp. I can already hear the shouts coming from the big open area in front of the council shelter—where the fight circle lies.

I should have been at her side. She said she needed me! Instead, I crept away like a coward, too focused on my own problems to watch her back. When I reach the crowd, I use my small size to my advantage, weaving between hips and shoulders and legs to get to the edge of the circle. Sander gets shut out behind me. I hear him grunting as he tries to get through. But I don't stop to wait. I can't bear the thought of Thyra facing this alone.

But she already is. When I get to the roped off circle, she's standing in the center, in her boots and breeches, wearing only her chest wrap and undershirt. Her kill marks are silver pink on her tanned skin, and the lean muscles of her arms are tense as she faces off against Edvin, a barrel-chested old warrior with arms the size of young oaks. He holds his battle ax and paces in a slow circle around her. He's easily twice her weight, but she's nearly as tall as he is. Her chest rises and falls slowly as she waits for him to attack, and she holds a dagger in her right hand, her grip light.

All around us, warriors and andeners shout and cheer. Some for Thyra, some for Edvin, most for the sheer normalcy and reassurance of blood, I suspect. Edvin's andener stands proud near the entrance to the circle, looking sure of her mate's victory. Aksel stands next to his mother, his brown eyes fierce with pride as he stares at his father. There is no one there for Thyra—her parents are dead. She has no brothers, no sisters. Not anymore. The open space in that place of prestige is gaping. Our chieftain is all alone. I am desperate to make my way over there, but I don't want to distract her now that the challenge has begun.

Most fights in this circle are for sport. Or to gain status. This is where I faced off with Sander the day I became a warrior, the moment I spit a part of his ear in the dirt and smiled at him with bloody teeth while Lars roared with laughter.

Warriors usually clasp arms at the end. We all bleed red.

But in a challenge fight for the chieftain's chair, only one will leave the ring. It's a fight to the death.

"I'll make it quick, Thyra," Edvin says in his scratchy sand and lakewater voice. "I respected your father."

Thyra's eyes flicker with pain. "You should have had faith in me, Edvin. You haven't even given me a season to prove myself."

"Too much at stake for that." He whirls his ax, and the blade catches the sunlight.

Cold emanates from the ball of ice inside me, wrenching a shiver up my back. A frigid gust of wind blows over us, making the people around me draw their shoulders up and wrap their arms around themselves. I glance over to see Sander giving me a queer look as he tugs his collar over the red, blistery streaks I left on his throat. I swallow hard and focus on the fight circle again.

Sander leans down. "Edvin's going to rely on brute strength. Always has. Thyra should be all right if she—"

"Shh." I can't listen to his detached, pompous observations right now. This is no ordinary fight.

Thyra looks so thin and fragile as Edvin lumbers toward her, but as she adopts her fighting stance, the cold inside me dissipates. Her face is solemn and smooth as he lets out a war cry and swings his ax in a sideways strike, like one might chop at a tree. Thyra throws herself to the dirt and rolls before jumping up again, her movements lithe and graceful. She never takes her eyes from his face. Edvin breathes hard, and his bushy gray-brown beard swishes with a burst of warm breeze. He strikes at her again, clearly aiming for her side—a height impossible to jump over and hard to duck under, too quick to run from. But instead of doing any of those things, Thyra spins *inside* his guard in an instant and leaves a slash across his ribs before dodging away. Like she's dancing, graceful and controlled. Edvin staggers, his mouth half open as he touches his fingers to his side. He laughs when they come away bloody. "Lars would be so proud! He used to boast about you when he was nose-deep in his goblet."

"He wouldn't have wanted to see this," she says, still in her stance, ready for his next attack.

"End it, Edvin," shouts a grizzled old warrior, wrinkled lips curling over missing teeth. "Stop playing with the child."

Edvin charges again, this time holding the ax closer and guarding his body as he swings. I grit my teeth. Thyra could throw the dagger, but if the strike isn't true, she'll be weaponless. Instead, she ducks under one swipe and blocks another, but the power of it sends her stumbling. Edvin presses, slamming his ax down in a blow that will cleave her spine, but she leaps to the side and the blade *thunks* hard into the muddy ground, buried deep.

Thyra's moving before Edvin can pull his weapon from the earth. Aksel screams a warning to his father, but it is no good. Her dagger slices into Edvin's throat just above his collar, and red drops fly as she pulls it loose and ducks behind him, transferring her dagger to her other hand. She strikes him again from the other side, a quick, mercilessly deep stab. And then she stands with her back to him, a sign of pure confidence—or contempt—and stares steadily at the shriveled old warrior who called for her quick death, while Edvin's blood slides along her blade, dripping onto the toe of her boot.

Edvin sinks to his knees, his eyes wide and stunned. Thyra turns around and stands behind him as his hands fall from his ax handle, leaving it sticking up from the ground. He's making the most terrible noises, animal grunts and cries, as he claws at his wounds, perhaps trying to find the air as he drowns. Thyra meets the eyes of Edvin's andener, a woman the age Thyra's mother would have been, had she lived.

"I offer mercy," she says to the woman, who bows her head as Aksel stands frozen beside her, white with shock. Finally, as Edvin lets out another pained cough, his mate nods, an abrupt jerk of her head.

Thyra grabs a fistful of Edvin's hair, wrenches his head back, and cuts his throat. He falls onto his stomach as his partner shrieks her grief, falling into her son's arms. Thyra kneels next to the fallen warrior and murmurs something in his ear, then rises and addresses the crowd. "I'll be in the council shelter if anyone else would like to challenge me."

A strange silence has fallen over us. Usually, at the end of a fight, there's celebration and drink. Blood and victory.

But this . . . there's a tang of fear in the air. I've never seen a battle for the chieftain chair—Lars was already chieftain when I was brought to this camp, and no one ever dared challenge him, including his ambitious younger brother. But still, I'd imagine someone would be cheering, wouldn't they?

I shove my way along the edge of the fight circle, but no one puts up any resistance. Everyone seems subdued as Preben and Bertel, Edvin's dearest comrades, trudge into the circle to carry Edvin's body away. As I pass, Aksel stares at me with a new, frigid blankness in his eyes. I manage to catch up with Thyra just before she enters the council shelter. Her head is bowed as she absently wipes her blade on her breeches and sheathes the weapon at her hip.

"Thyra!"

She turns as I run up to her. "Where have you been?"

"Who cares? Are you all right?"

For a moment, her cheek twitches and her eyes grow shiny, but then she sucks in a deep breath and lets it out. "Edvin had fought at my father's side since before I was born."

"But he challenged you. You had no choice."

"We only have two hundred warriors left. We need every sword arm we have. Even the old ones."

"Not if those arms are raised in defiance against you."

She lets out a sharp laugh and shakes her head. "You always make killing sound so easy."

"And you make it unnecessarily difficult."

"Maybe it should be, sometimes." She turns to walk away, but I grab her arm.

"I'll make your kill mark for you."

She rips her arm from my grasp. "I don't want it," she snaps. Her blue eyes meet mine. "I have to go meet with the senior warriors about distribution and storage of our supplies for the winter, and then I must meet with the andeners to make the final plan for the farewell ceremony. They need any measure of peace I can offer."

"I'll come with you."

"It would bore you. We need you on watch anyway."

She's pushing me away again, and it makes me desperate. "You were brilliant, Thyra," I offer. "Lars really would have been proud. Everyone will think twice before challenging you again. You proved that you will kill without hesitation."

She grimaces, and I know I've said the wrong thing, though I don't know *why* it's wrong. "That was the point," she says quietly.

"What did you say to him, as he died?"

She looks down at the spatter of Edvin's blood on her boot. "I told him I'd take care of his family."

Carefully, I reach out and touch her arm, focusing on keeping my skin cool. Normal. "You are a noble chieftain. You just united the tribe by earning their respect."

"I might have united them, but I'm not sure I won them. Those are two different things, and I need both to keep us whole."

"You deserve the chair."

"I must earn the chair every day. And I plan to. It's the only way to grow their faith in me—and in themselves."

She sniffles and wipes her nose on her collar. "But I need you at my side next time," she says, her voice breaking. "I had to send Sander to find you. Don't disappear again."

I grin, eager to raise her spirits. "Because I cheer louder than the rest?"

Her small, reluctant smile is the best reward. "Because of the way you look at me."

"I think perhaps I understand that." Because the way she's looking at *me* right now makes me feel like I could fly. "I'll come find you after I finish my watch."

"Good. We'll have supper together." She sounds so weary, and I vow to guard her sleep tonight, if she'll let me. I won't be slumbering anyway. I have to stay alert to hold down the curse. Now all my thoughts of killing myself are evaporating. Thyra needs me. I have to find a way to control this, and to keep it secret, so I can support her while she establishes her leadership. The last thing I want to do is shame or distract her, especially as her smile gains a delicious warmth that I feel in my bones.

"Chieftain Thyra," cries a guard as he sprints up the path. "Armed riders approaching!"

Thyra pivots quickly, her movements sharp. "How many?" she barks as other warriors jog over and gather around, looking to her for instructions.

"Dozens."

"Hostile?"

The guard puts his hands on his knees, breathing hard. "They're flying a yellow and white flag."

"That's Vasterut," she says in a flat voice as the men and women around us begin to murmur among themselves, even as the clatter of hooves reaches us from the edge of camp.

"To me!" Thyra yells, and draws her blade again.

I pull a knife from my boot, the one I was planning to use on myself not long ago. We stand shoulder to shoulder as the riders draw near, and a cold wind blows as Sander pushes into position next to me. "Chilly, isn't it?" he asks, giving me a pointed look.

I press my lips together and stomp that evil cold down as the first rider comes into view, cantering up the road with his followers just behind him. His golden hair shines with flecks of red in the sunlight, and though he's still yards away, I know his eyes are green, green, green.

"Jaspar," whispers Thyra.

Unease churns in my gut as he reins in his horse and halts perhaps ten yards from our assembled warriors. "Greetings, Cousin Thyra," he calls.

"It's Chieftain Thyra," I yell.

Jaspar's eyes flash as his gaze shifts to me. The corner of his mouth curls, and my cheeks burn with memories. "Ah. So Lars's daughter has claimed the chair." He inclines his head, a gesture of respect that somehow seems to drip with defiance. "Like she always wanted, and like we always knew she would."

Thyra's gripping her dagger so tightly that her hand is shaking. "Why are you here?"

"We heard of your misfortune at the hands of the witch queen of the Kupari."

"And did you come to finish the job?"

"Quite the contrary. I've come under orders from my father. We will escort you and your tribe to Vasterut immediately, *Chieftain* Thyra." He looks out over our force, a few hundred lesser warriors and the three of us who survived the storm, and then glances behind him as at least forty mounted warriors crowd in formation at his back. All of them have thick broadswords belted to their waists and shields strapped to their backs, and I recognize many as strong fighters, young and thick with muscle. Though we outnumber them five to one, if it came to a battle against those mounted warriors, we would be slaughtered, and the thousands of andeners and children we protect would be at their mercy.

"Vasterut is not an option," Thyra shouts. "We have just lost four *thousand* warriors, and we are in final preparation to bid their souls farewell. But not only that—we are settled along this shore all the way up to Ulvi Point, if you recall, and with this many widows and orphans, the priority is to—"

"Chieftain Nisse is prepared to provide for all of you in Vasterut." Jaspar's smile is warm, but there's no mistaking the danger. "He is eager to see our tribes united once more." He leans forward, his gaze hard on Thyra. "And he will be particularly delighted to welcome *you* within his walls."

CHAPTER SIX

There will be no ceremony of farewell. Jaspar insists we leave at new daylight, taking no chance that the snow will catch us out on our journey. We have no choice but to obey, and Thyra realizes it quickly as she sizes up the force Jaspar has brought. None of us argue, because most of us realize the same thing, and the others wanted this outcome from the moment our shattered hull washed ashore.

Thyra looks pale and troubled, but she keeps her chin up as she orders the warriors to ready their own households for the journey, and then to assist the widowed andeners in their preparations. It's an unbelievable amount of work, but Jaspar orders his warriors to help.

One look into Thyra's eyes tells me she's caught in another

storm, the kind that's tearing her apart inside. "What can I do?" I ask.

"Find out their true intentions," she murmurs as her gaze follows Jaspar, who is already speaking with Preben and Bertel, who have not yet had the opportunity to wash Edvin's blood from their hands. His smile flashes as he shows them his sword, a gorgeous blade that is probably of Vasterutian make, with a set of long blood grooves down its center.

"Why me? Wouldn't Sander be a better choice?" He's already headed over to admire the weapon, and Jaspar's clapping him on the back. I remember the first time they faced each other in the fight circle, two lanky eleven-year-olds determined to prove themselves. An hour later they staggered out, bloodied best friends.

"Sander would probably have gone with Nisse's rebels if he hadn't already paired with my sister, and if she hadn't been with child." Hilma died from the fever only a month later, and I can tell Thyra wonders if he regrets his decision to stay.

She touches my arm. "But I know I can trust you." Her blue gaze loses its warmth. "And you hold charms for Jaspar that Sander does not."

My mouth goes dry as Jaspar glances toward us and looks away just as quickly, as if he was checking to see if we'd been watching. "Please, Thyra. Let me stay with you."

"Nonsense." She gives me a humorless smile. "It will be just like old times."

Humiliation freezes my tongue to the roof of my mouth.

Thyra's fingers squeeze my upper arm. "Draw Jaspar away now. I must have a chance to speak to Preben and Bertel before he wins them over. Their support will be important as we begin this journey. If they are with me, the others will feel more confident."

I hear the pleading in Thyra's voice, the note of desperation beneath the authoritative steadiness she's trying to project. If we do not make this journey united, by the time we arrive in Vasterut, Nisse will be the chieftain of us all. A traitor and would-be assassin will be our new master. Honor will not protect us, nor will rules. And Thyra, as the chieftain of the defeated tribe, will be in the most danger. It's so clear to me that the only reason she's agreeing to this journey is to save our lives.

I throw back my shoulders, even as misgiving burns inside me. "As you wish."

"Make him remember." She leans close. "Because I will never forget."

How foolish I was to believe that when Jaspar fled on the heels of his father and the other traitor warriors, he would take our past with him. "As you wish," I whisper again.

"Don't make it too easy. He'll sense it if you aren't yourself."

I'm not myself, though. I've been cursed by a witch. I glance down at my hands, which are stiff with cold. My veins run blue beneath my pale skin.

"Have you lost something, Ansa?"

The sound of Jaspar's good-natured voice brings my

head up. *Don't make it too easy.* I scowl. "Nothing that can't be taken back with blood."

His laugh echoes through camp. "You haven't changed."

"You know nothing." I give Thyra one last look and then walk past Jaspar and the others, heading for the shelter where I've been sitting awake at night while others sleep. The crunch of his footsteps on the trail behind me brings me both triumph and dread.

"I know your temper is sweet as ever," he says as he falls into step with me.

"Am I supposed to greet you with open arms?"

"That might have been nice."

I give him a sidelong glance. "Why are you following me? I thought you were busy showing your big blade to the other boys."

That laugh. I close my eyes and push memories away as he says, "I'd show it to you, too, if I didn't believe you'd strip it from me and chop my head off."

I enter the shelter and glance around, realizing I don't have any great reason for being here. After a few faltering steps, I head for my little pile of scavenged belongings in the far corner, intending to pack them for the journey. "How long is the march to Vasterut?"

"Only four long days of hard riding, but on foot, with the andeners and children in tow, it will take at least two weeks. With luck, we could make it before the snow closes in."

"Nisse moved quickly then, to send you here."

"Chieftain Nisse, Ansa," he says quietly. "He is ruler of

Vasterut now and deserves respect. And as his heir, so do I."

I turn to him, wishing I was taller so I could look him in the eye. "At whose expense?"

"Thyra will be treated according to her status. I promise. Is that what you're worried about?" He reaches to brush my hair from my forehead, but I step backward out of his reach. His hand falls to his side, and he sighs. "I suppose we're not allies anymore. But I want us to be. And I only want what's best for the Krigere. Our warriors are too precious to abandon to the winter."

"We'd be fine here."

"I've been in this camp less than a quarter-day, and the stink of despair is everywhere. Don't tell me you're fine— and don't pretend a pathetic little ceremony will do anything but ease the guilt of your chieftain."

I stare out the doorway of the shelter, at the bustle of camp, all moving in the same direction once more, just as we were on the morning of our great invasion. "So the solution is to march to Vasterut and bow to a—" I clamp my lips shut over the word *traitor*.

"Ansa, Vasterut is only a four-day quick-march from Kupari. Two days riding. Five hours on the oars, up from the south."

The awful-beautiful face of the witch queen rises in my memory. When Jaspar sees the look on my face, he nods, his jaw hard. "Think of the possibilities."

"Tell me," I say in a low voice.

He waggles his eyebrows and takes a few steps back. "In

good time. But I think perhaps this is conversation best reserved for our chieftains, eh?" He gives me a mischievous grin. "As I recall, Thyra doesn't like to be surprised."

The fire at the center of the shelter flares so high that it frames Jaspar with light. He turns when he feels the heat at his back and puts a bit of distance between himself and the reaching flames.

It gives me a moment to think cold thoughts. "Then go talk to her," I say.

His look of surprise relaxes into a familiar, teasing smile. "When she's ready. I should go pay my respects to your surviving senior warriors." His fingers close over the hilt of his sword. "I hope we'll have more time to talk as we travel."

Thyra's plea to discern his true purpose is still in my head. "We might."

"We will." He looks me over, his eyes as bold as stroking fingers. "I missed you, Ansa. More than I expected to."

He turns and walks away, leaving me with a memory—a fall afternoon, my blood singing with victory after my first raid kill. The curve of Jaspar's mouth as he asked if he could make the cut, my very first. The slice of pain, the red trickle of warmth down my bare arm, the way his fingers closed over my elbow. And then we were kissing and I barely knew how it had happened, only that it *was*. That's *all* it was too. I had just wanted that moment, high from the fight and needing something vital to match the battle-lust still beating at my temples. Jaspar tasted of sweat and heat as he pushed me against that tree, as his knife fell to the ground with my blood still on the blade.

It was a moment. Nothing more than that. But when I heard the crunch of boots on fallen leaves, I shoved Jaspar away from me and saw Thyra standing, frozen, on the other side of the clearing.

I will never forget the look on her face. Her blank expression, her big, solemn blue eyes . . . the sinking feeling in my stomach, the pit that lasted for days.

But she pretended like it didn't matter. Like she didn't care. Like it never happened, even.

Until today.

I sit only a few feet from where Thyra lies, watching the flickering embers of flame chase shadows along her brow. She deserves this rest. Needs it. And I will guard her so she knows she's safe.

I'm her wolf.

I need sleep too. I'm woozy and addled after so many nights of startling awake for fear of sinking too deep. Sleep is dangerous right now, for so many reasons.

I spent the rest of the day helping the andeners in the shelters near mine ready themselves for the journey, bundling supplies into blankets, sneaking a few abandoned blades into my boots and arm sheaths. I always feel better when I'm armed. I watched Thyra during supper, when we took down the rope around the fight circle and gathered as a tribe, as she positioned herself right over the bloodied dirt that marked the place where Edvin fell, as if to remind the other warriors she had earned her status. She spoke to Jaspar and a few of the others with a smooth, assured voice. But when she retired to the shelter, I saw the wariness in her gaze. The weariness, too.

She feels hunted. When I told her that Jaspar had vowed she would be treated according to her status, she scoffed. "That's a deliberately vague thing to say, if you think about it."

"You are his fallen brother's daughter," I said. "Surely that means something."

Her laugh was dry as summer sand. "Oh, it most certainly does." Then she scrubbed her hands over her face. "I am only worth reckoning with if I have my warriors behind me," she said. "This journey will determine whether I arrive in Vasterut a master or a slave."

I scoot a few inches closer to her. We're in the council shelter—the chieftain's carved chair sits on the other side of the space. There are guards at the perimeters, and Jaspar and his warriors have set their camps at the hunting trails leading north and west, claiming to offer protection. I think they are trying to make sure we do not escape.

It's begun already. That's what Thyra said to me, just before she fell asleep. And now she breathes slow and even, and I hope that means she's shed the barbed pain of defeat, that her dreams are full of victory. An ache spreads through my chest as I think of how beautiful she was today, the lithe spread of her arms, the elegant strike of her blade, the way she made it look like a dance. I suspect I look like an animal when I fight, all bared teeth and frenzied motion, but not Thyra. She is long and lean and made of lethal grace. And now she is being forced to lead us into the unknown, because there is no other choice.

I reach out and take her limp hand. "I'm with you," I whisper. "I've always been with you."

If she'd ever asked me about Jaspar, I would have explained. But she never acted like she wanted or needed that, and so I would have felt foolish saying it aloud. She is so guarded, even with me, no matter how I crash against her walls. Until the witch queen plunged us into a new upside-down world, Thyra created no space for these sentiments, and so all of them remained stuffed inside me, hot as burning pitch. *If it had been you, I wouldn't have let go.* I have wanted to tell her this for so long. *If you had made the cut, I would have been on my knees. I would have pulled you down with me. I would have bruised you by holding too tight.*

Thyra winces and swipes her hand across her brow, which is drenched with sweat. I yank my hand from hers as heat warps the air between us. My breath bursts from my throat as I realize I'm doing it again. Fire kisses my fingertips as I rise to my feet, my eyes stinging, horror crushing me like a storm wave.

Why do I think I can protect her? She's facing the fight of her life. She needs all her wits—the survival of our tribe depends on it. What she does not need: the taint of witchcraft to make people doubt and question.

And I'm about to burn her alive with a witch's curse.

Pulling my cloak around me, I jog for the doorway, desperate for the open air.

A hand closes over my shoulder, and I whirl around, the fear like ice in my veins. Thyra yelps and stumbles back as our fire gutters out with a frigid blast of wind, then flares to life again when my gaze flicks toward the pit. When light fills the shelter once more, the flames are reflected in Thyra's round eyes.

"The fire," she says, her voice breaking.

It's massive, licking the thatch, and I give it a pleading look. The flames shrink like I've just reprimanded them, and Thyra gasps. Her fingers are clawed in her cloak. "Ansa. Did you do that?" Her voice trembles. "The two shelters that burned . . ."

My back hits the door frame of the shelter. "I'm sorry."

"But this is like—" She shudders as the air becomes so cold that it makes my bones ache. "Are you doing this on purpose?"

"The witch queen cursed me." I clench my fists because I can feel the ice and fire trying to seep through my skin. It's taken me over. Tears overflow and streak down my face. "Thyra, I'm sorry."

And then I run, my feet pounding the dirt, my heart a gash in my chest.

CHAPTER SEVEN

I sprint for the water, unsheathing a blade as I flee, the cursed red mark on my leg pulsing with icy fire. Each step reminds me what the witch has done, how she has taken the one thing I've always fought for—my family, my tribe. As I run, the fiery memory rises as if the witch herself summoned it—my mother's outstretched hand, the monsters all around her, their blades glinting in the flames. I am helpless as I watch her die.

I never wanted to be helpless again. I *refuse* to be helpless. I won't let the witch win.

Thyra hits me so hard that the dagger flies from my fist, and then we're on the ground, skidding through the loose stone near the shore. I claw my way toward the weapon, but Thyra grabs my wrists, pressing me to cool earth. "Have you lost your mind?" she says in my ear.

The sound of her voice only sharpens the pain. I slam my forehead into the stone. "Get off me before I hurt you."

She lets out a tight burst of laughter. "Try."

I buck, sudden and brutal, and my shoulder hits her chest. She slides off, and I lunge forward, spinning around to face her. I crouch, feral and panting, as she gets to her feet, rubbing a spot above her breast. The wary look on her face makes bile rise in my throat. "Walk away from me, Thyra."

"Not until you tell me what's happening to you."

"I have no idea!"

"You said she cursed you. How do you know?"

I sink forward onto my hands and knees, my exhaustion catching up and making my limbs heavy. "There's no other explanation. Fire bursts from my hands no matter how I try to hold it back, and I saw one of her black-robed minions do the same thing on the Torden. The cold rolls off me like a winter gale, and I can't control any of it! But I swear, Thyra, I'm not doing witchcraft on purpose. It just . . . happens."

"So that's what it was," she whispers. My head jerks up, and she raises her hands as if to calm me. "I saw it happen, Ansa. That bolt of light arced over the lake from the south, not straight down from the sky so much as something hurled from across the water. I've never seen anything like it."

My breath fogs from my mouth, chilled with confusion

and betrayal. Thyra's eyes widen as she stares. "Why didn't you tell me?" I ask. "You said it was lightning!"

"Sander said that, and I had no idea what else it could be. I was just glad you were still alive." She takes a cautious step toward me.

"Sander knows there's something wrong with me."

"I know. He came to me this evening. He told me about your escape from the shelter fires—I hadn't realized you were so close to the flames. And I saw his throat. He said he felt his blood turning cold when you attacked him. I didn't want to believe him." She rolls her eyes. "His instability after the battle made it easy for me to dismiss him, no matter how solid he has been since."

I draw my hand through my hair. "What was his theory?"

"He was at a loss. But he thought it might have been the arcing light that hit you as well. He didn't seem to think you were doing it intentionally."

"If he tells anyone, I'm dead anyway, Thyra. You've heard the talk around camp. They'll happily stone me just to make themselves feel a little safer." Our eyes meet. "Maybe I should let them."

"Stop that. Sander hasn't told anyone. I ordered him to stay silent, or I would kill him for telling lies."

"He wouldn't be lying." I inch backward, glancing around for my dagger. It was my sharpest.

"Looking for this?" She slides it out of the folds of her cloak.

"Sometimes I hate you."

The corner of her mouth lifts. "No, you don't."

My gaze drops to her lips and then away, because the sight weakens my resolve. "I can't stay, Thyra. I'm dangerous."

"You've always been dangerous." Her voice is heavy and makes me shiver.

"I can't control this." I wave in the direction of camp, toward the burned shells of the two shelters I razed with fiery dreaming. "It's a wonder I haven't killed someone yet. I think that's what she wanted." I get to my feet, drawing a dull dagger from my boot as I do. "It's why she let me live. She sent me back here to hurt our people. But I won't let her use me."

Thyra sheathes the dagger I dropped, tucking it under the rope belt that holds her breeches up. She watches me cautiously, a look I recognize from the fight circle. She's waiting for me to move. "Is there a chance it will go away? Wear off?"

I think of the way my red birthmark throbs as the cursed ice and fire rush through me. "It's inside me, Thyra. Like a fever."

"It's possible to overcome a fever."

I let out a bitter chuckle. "Like the one that killed your mother and Hilma?"

"But left me and my father alive. Many others as well. Those who were strong enough."

I take a step back. "There are some things that can't be borne or survived, no matter how strong the warrior. Some wounds are fatal."

She frowns. "Is it making you sick? You do look dead on your feet."

"This will be my fourth night without sleep," I say quietly.

"You can't expect to be strong and well if you don't rest."

"When I rest, things catch fire. When I'm scared, things freeze. When I wish for wind, it rises from nowhere and gusts hard over the camp." I swirl my dagger in the air, hot frustration coursing through me. "That happens even when I *don't* wish for it!"

As if to mock me, a burst of warm wind whirls around Thyra, blowing her short hair. She blinks as it makes her cloak flap. "I don't know what to make of this," she says unsteadily. "Did you really do that?"

"Not on purpose."

"Can you control it at all?"

I bite my lip and turn away. "As you have pointed out many times, control is not my strong suit."

"But maybe if you . . . try? You made the flames settle down in the shelter just now."

"I didn't make them do anything! I just looked at them!"

"Have you *truly* made an effort?" She takes a few slow steps closer to me, and I can't bring myself to retreat. "You're so strong, Ansa. Maybe you can keep it imprisoned inside?"

Tears burn my eyes. "I'm trying."

Her eyes crinkle with what looks like pity, and she closes the distance between us. She catches my wrist, her fingers sliding down to mine where I clutch my dagger tight. "Don't make me take another weapon from you tonight."

"You have to let me go," I whisper, even as I ache to lay my head on her shoulder.

Her fingertips smooth the hair off my brow, and as I did not do with Jaspar, I let her. "Your skin is so warm," she murmurs. "It always has been."

"Only when you touch it," I breathe, barely giving sound to the thought.

"I won't let you go this easily, Ansa. I can't."

I look up at her face, lit by moonlight. "Your leadership is being tested at every turn. How can you—"

"That's why I can't." Her forehead touches mine, and my fingers go slack, dropping the dull blade. "You're the only person I trust in this entire camp."

I can't breathe. I'm too shaky inside, working hard to keep the ice and fire in a cage.

"If you abandon me, I don't think I'll make it," she whispers.

My eyes fall shut, and my throat tightens as she swipes hot tears from my cheeks. I grab her hands and pull them from my face. Warriors do not behave like snotty-nosed babes, and I am embarrassing myself. In front of my *chieftain*. "I'm sorry," I say hoarsely.

"We survived the witch queen's storm. We survived the journey back." She takes me by the shoulders, refusing to let me turn away. "We will survive this. We'll show the witch queen that her curse is not strong enough to destroy the Krigere."

"You make it sound so easy." I choke on a sob and wrench myself away, feeling the ice creeping along my bones, pushing through my skin and crystallizing like frost on marsh grass.

Her eyes flash with anger. "You make it sound like she's already beaten you. Have you surrendered before fighting to your last breath?"

I rub the cold sweat from my arms. "This is not an enemy with a blade."

"What does it matter? It's an enemy nonetheless. And you're a warrior."

I look down at the dagger at my feet.

"Do you remember the day you earned that title?" she asks.

"Of course I do."

"Truly, it seems as if you've forgotten."

I snatch the dull blade from the ground.

"Sander left you in a heap, bleeding in the dirt. They all thought you'd lost."

I remember the cheers as he walked away from me, and then Thyra shouting my name, cutting through the haze of defeat. "He turned his back because he thought I wouldn't get up."

She smiles. "The sight of you leaping onto his back, the sound that came out of his mouth when you bit him . . ." Her laugh melts the rest of the frost on my skin. "I may have been the only one who wasn't surprised."

"That was different."

"It's not different at all. This curse has bloodied you, Ansa, but you're not dead yet." She ducks her head until I'm looking at her again. "And until you are, you have no right to surrender if you wish to call yourself a warrior."

My shoulders slump. "If I were to hurt our people . . ."

"I won't let you." She pries the dagger from my grip and sheathes it at my wrist before slipping her hand into mine. "We'll find a way to suppress it. If there's a way to lift this curse, we'll puzzle it out."

"We have no idea what we're dealing with." Even as I say it, I remember—Cyrill had a Kupari slave. If I can find her and question her, perhaps she can tell me more about the witch queen's magic. Cyrill's shelter is a bit of a hike, but maybe—

"Come back to my shelter," Thyra says. "We need to rest before we leave tomorrow."

When I hesitate, she tugs my hand. "We'll sleep in shifts. I'll watch over you, then you watch over me." Her smile is uncertain but so sweet that I want to taste it. "I'll wake you if anything starts to smoke."

"I'll come, but you must promise you'll let me go if . . ."

She squeezes my hand. "If it comes to that, you'll talk to your chieftain." She raises her eyebrows, and the laugh bursts from me unbidden. Then she leads me back to her shelter. I can practically feel the glares of Jaspar's guards as we trudge past their post, but I don't look up. The weight of relief and gratitude is so heavy on me that I can barely lift my feet. Thyra guides me onto her own blanket and wraps it over me. "You'll be better able to rid yourself of this curse if you aren't half dead from exhaustion. Rest, Ansa. I'm depending on you."

If I trusted myself, I would touch her face. But I am afraid I would burn her. "I'm sorry for asking this," I say quietly. "What is your plan?"

I hold my breath as she cups my cheek in her palm. "It's a worthy question, and you don't need to be sorry." She sighs. "My father would never have wanted us to be led by a traitor. But not only that—I don't trust Nisse to do right by our widows. He put forth some very backward ideas when he was still a member of our tribe, and I don't want that to infect us now, especially when they are so vulnerable. We have a commitment to honor with our andeners—and to the memory of our fallen brothers and sisters—and I am responsible for seeing it through."

Now I understand why she was discussing sowing crops in the spring. How else could we keep thousands of bellies full, with so few warriors to journey out to raid and hunt? "I don't suppose we could send a contingent of warriors while the rest of us remain here."

She shakes her head. "Jaspar was very clear. Our andeners are valuable, and Nisse requires their presence in Vasterut."

"Is it possible his intentions are good?"

"I don't know. I just . . . hope he will be willing to move on from the past."

She shakes her head, as if she were casting off something heavy, and not for the first time, I wonder what really happened last winter, and why she won't talk about it. "Go to sleep," she says, turning her face away. "I mean it."

I should be guarding her while she rests, but I can't fight my own exhaustion anymore. Tomorrow, yes. I will search for a way to lift this curse, and the Kupari slave will be the first step. Tomorrow, I'll rise and fight again.

But for now . . . the ice-fire throb of my red mark subsides to a faint pulse. I fall asleep feeling the sweet slide of Thyra's palm over my hair, and my dreams are black as the deep waters of the Torden.

We rise with the sun, and our fire bursts to life the moment I shiver with the morning chill. Thyra glances with alarm at the pit—there's no fuel there to burn. With a shudder, I walk away, and I feel the moment the heat fades to nothing, leaving only the stain of humiliation on my cheeks. She's counting on me to control this, to get rid of it, and to keep it secret in the meantime. It will all fall on her if I am revealed as some sort of witch. I'll be dead, my brains bashed out and my bones shattered—and she might be next.

For a moment, I think of that kind of death. The most awful thing about it wouldn't be the pain. It would be the looks on their faces as they hurled their stones. It would be the bite of their hatred, the despair of knowing my tribe was no longer mine.

If I'm honest, I'm not just fighting to keep Thyra safe. I cannot think of a worse agony than that of being abandoned. And with that realization, another memory creeps up like a snake—me clawing at the monster as he carried me to the boat. I stare at the glow at the top of the hill, knowing my parents can't reach me. That they won't save me. That I am truly alone.

I stomp at the ground, savagely crushing the past beneath the heel of my boot.

The mood in and around the sprawling camp is hard to read. People load horses and their own backs with all the things they own, all the things we've plundered and captured in our raids over the years. Some of the andeners have fled with their families—several shelters are empty, the fires cold. They must have snuck along the shore, avoiding the well-worn paths Jaspar and his warriors were guarding. They were willing to risk the bite of the north to avoid what awaits us in Vasterut, and I have a feeling Jaspar will be furious. Thyra will feel the loss too—those who left might have supported her over Nisse. Though our andeners may not be fighters, all of them have valuable skills—weapon forging and repair, food preparation and storage, breeding and child rearing, weaving and mending, wound stitching and healing. They know what warriors need, and how to keep us battle ready. We protect them and provide for them, and in return they keep us whole.

Now we are shattered. A broken people facing many choices with no good options. Our only chance lies with Thyra.

I thread my way past some of the older warriors who were meant to lead our second wave, those who called Edvin their commander. My stomach drops as I pass Aksel in hushed conversation with Preben, whose long beard is the color of wet iron, and Bertel, whose hair has gone white over the last few years, in contrast with his dark brown skin. Neither of the older men notices me, but Aksel tosses me a look as cold as the Torden in new spring, and I look away. I have no time for conversation or confrontation—once we leave, we'll be stretched over at least a mile along the perimeter of the lake, hiking leagues to get to the southern shore. I might not have another chance to get the information I want.

When I reach Cyrill's shelter, I find his andener, Gry, bundling her children into as many layers as they can possibly wear—she means them to carry all their clothing on their backs. Her thin blond hair hangs in a lank braid as she kneels in front of her youngest, a rosy-cheeked boy named Ebbe who Cyrill used to carry around camp on his broad shoulders. She glances over as I lean against the door frame. "No, you can't have any of Cyrill's blades," she says sharply. "Heard you were taking them from the shelters of the dead yesterday."

"I have all I need."

"Good. Because we don't." Her face crumples and she turns away.

There's a heavy cold in my chest that isn't caused by my curse. "Cyrill was a great warrior, Gry. I'm sorry he was lost."

She sniffles and shoos Ebbe off to play with his older sister, who is killing time with a game of jackstraws using sharpened twigs. "Not as sorry as I am," she says in a choked voice.

"We will make sure your family is provided for."

"I know. And I believe in Chieftain Thyra, no matter what the others say. But"—she gives me a pained look—"I miss Cyrill's laugh. I miss how he made *me* laugh."

I rub my chest. "He made me laugh even as he lay wounded. He was in good spirits until the end, Gry."

"You were with him?" She swipes the sleeve of her gown across her face.

"He cursed the fact that he was stuck with a bunch of baby warriors."

Her chuckle is raspy with grief. "Thank you for that."

I glance around. "Where is your slave?"

"Hulda? I sent her to gather kindling. Why?"

I shrug. "Just hoping she hadn't run away. Many have." I take a step backward, already knowing where I'm headed next. "If you or your children need anything on this journey, find me. All right?"

She gives me a flickering smile. "Thank you, Ansa." She looks away. "Cyrill always spoke highly of you. Said you were among the fiercest he'd trained."

My throat hurts as I say, "I will live up to that; I promise."

I jog to the other side of camp, the edge of the great forest. It used to lean right over the shore, but over the years as we built our longships, it shrank back and back and back, leaving only a muddy field of stumps. A few andeners, slaves, and children pick their way along, hunting twigs and leaves to stoke morning fires for the meal before we depart. I spot Hulda by herself at the far edge of the field, right at the forest's new edge, dropping handfuls of short twigs and splintered wood into a cloth bag. Her weathered brow furrows as she sees me approaching, and she backtracks into the woods as I draw near. "Cyrill's!" she says in a shrill voice.

She's afraid I'm going to claim her as plunder.

I put my hands up. "No. I don't want you."

Her eyes narrow. She's healthy and stout, with hair the same color as mine. The same as the witch queen's. "I need to ask you something. About the witch." I wish I could take back the word as she scowls. "I mean, the . . . Valtera?"

She gives me a quizzical look.

I try again. "The Valia?"

"Valtia?" she asks, leaning forward to look into my eyes.

I nod. "I need to know about her power."

From the scrunched-up look on her face, I can tell she's trying to translate my words. "Ice," she says. "Fire. She has the two, the same." Her accent is . . . round. And trilling. Even the Kupari language is soft and weak. I push down a swell of contempt even as I recall the witch's black-robed minion grinding out those trilling words—just before he prepared to hurl fire at me.

"Ice and fire," I say. "She controls both?"

"Both. Together and"—she spreads her hands—"apart. Many ways she has magic."

"And she curses people."

Hulda tilts her head. "Curse?"

"Yes," I say through gritted teeth. "She sticks this ice and fire inside people." I mimic the arc of the witch-made lightning that struck me six nights ago. "How might one break such a curse?"

Hulda blinks at me. "Curse?" she asks again. "Valtia has ice and fire, together and apart—"

"Yes, I *know*." My frustration is already making me sweat,

and I remind myself to stay calm. "But how do people get rid of it?"

She looks utterly baffled. "Get rid . . . of magic?"

"Sure, if that's what you all call it. How do they do that, once she curses them with it?" An idea occurs to me. "If she were to be killed—"

Hulda tilts her head. "Some born with ice and fire, some not. But Valtia . . . her power comes from other Valtia."

"You mean there's two of them?" Thyra will need to know immediately.

"No, not two."

My hands rise in irritation. "Then what in heaven are you talking about?"

The woman looks me over with curiosity, then touches her own coppery hair and points to mine. "First, Valtia is a Saadella," she says, though I've never heard that word in my life. "Her hair is this color. Kupari."

"My hair is *not* Kupari."

"Copper," she says slowly. Then she points to my eyes. "And her eyes is that color." She lets out an amused grunt. "You could be Saadella."

"*What* did you just call me?"

Hulda steps back in alarm as a frigid gust of wind swirls around us. Her gray eyes go round as the breeze whips her coppery hair from its braid, and her teeth chatter as she says, "Nothing! I said nothing!" She stumbles and falls backward, landing hard on her backside. Her eyes are bright with tears. "Please! Please!"

Her cries will draw attention to us, the last thing I want. Cold hatred for this stupid, cowardly slave rushes through me, especially when she screams again. She's staring at the ground and inching back, pure horror etched into the lines of her face. I look down to see what on earth could be frightening her.

Thick, silver-white frost is creeping along the ground around me, edging closer to the hem of Hulda's skirt, advancing like an army of ants. I gasp and clench my fists, trying to push the curse down, but when the ice keeps advancing, I rush forward, frantically shushing her. If she doesn't shut up, the entire camp will come running, and then they'll see the frost. They'll know I'm cursed, and I'll be stoned in the fight circle.

Hulda's fingers are gray with cold, and she's shivering violently as she points at me. She shrieks one word in her awful language over and over again, one that sounds like the hiss of a snake. The sound slithers into my ears, relentless and maddening, filling my head with memories of lullabies and fire and blood.

I drop to my knees and clamp my hand over her mouth.

CHAPTER EIGHT

I am so desperate to silence Hulda that at first I don't notice that I have. My fingers, rigid with cold, freeze to the damp flesh of her face. Her hands scrabble along my arms. But I don't feel it. I stare at her face, her coppery hair, and I hear her unfamiliar-yet-familiar language in my head, and suddenly her eyes are no longer gray. They're blue and pleading and the light in them is fading, and there's nothing I can do.

The distant whinny of a horse wrenches me back to the present, shivering and trembling, something hard tickling my palm. I look down, and with a cry, I throw myself backward, landing in a sprawl on damp, rotted leaves. Hulda does not move. Her gray eyes are clouded with frost, and her mouth is open. Her stiff fingers claw at empty air, as if she is begging heaven for mercy.

My breath fogging, I crawl forward and poke her arm. She is frozen solid.

I let out a wretched whimper as I wipe my palms on my breeches. "I didn't mean it," I whisper to her. And then I rise to my feet and kick her rigid body as my rage at the witch queen rises high enough to choke me. "I didn't want to hurt you!"

"Hulda!" Gry is shouting for her slave from across the field, and the sound of her voice nearly makes my heart burst.

If I'm caught here, that's it. My feet slip on the matted leaves as I sprint up the hill and deeper into the trees. I can almost hear the eerie laugh of the queen from across the Torden. Perhaps she senses what she's done. Perhaps she knows her trap has sprung.

But I didn't kill a Krigere. I killed one of her own. A slave. A Kupari. I have not killed one of my tribe. I double over and retch behind the fractured trunk of a lightning-felled tree. I should not feel this bad. Killing is as natural as eating or sleeping. It is the right of the victor over the conquered.

I grit my teeth over a sob and pull the collar of my tunic up against my throat with shaking hands. With my eyes closed and my head bowed, I imagine cramming the witch's curse back inside, burying it deep under layers of dirt, covering it with stones. Despite my frantic efforts, it still managed to slip free, and I can't let it happen again, for my sake and for Thyra's. I have to be her wolf. I cannot be the witch's sword.

I stay hidden in the forest until my breathing has

slowed, until it is once again warm and steady, until I feel like myself again. Faint cries from several hundred yards behind me make me wonder if Hulda has been found, and thinking about it nearly makes me retch again. So does my fear of anyone finding out what I've done. I weave my way further into the woods, to a stream that leads down to the beach, and then I trek back up to camp that way, so no one will suspect where I came from. I return to my shelter like a wary, kicked animal, ready to dart away from the slightest hint of threat, and for the first time, I am glad that we are starting our journey today.

As far as I'm concerned, we cannot possibly leave soon enough.

I shiver, even as sweat trickles across my shoulders and into the collar of my tunic. We are a fog of scent and noise and grief stretched along the shore of the thunder-gray lake, slowly drifting to the southeast. I stare out at the rough waters as a cool breeze sends another hard chill down my spine.

I can't stop thinking about Hulda's eyes.

My stomach clenches and I forget to watch my steps. I hiss with pain as my knee strikes a rock. A hand slides around my upper arm and yanks me up like I'm a sack of grain. It belongs to Preben, his eyes like lumps of charcoal. "It's only the first day," he says. On his other side, Aksel lets out a grunt of laughter at the implication that I'm already struggling to keep up.

I yank my arm from Preben's grasp. "And no matter what day it is, I can regain my footing on my own." I quicken my steps and get in front of the two of them, my cheeks burning. Up ahead, I hear a whistle. Smoke stains the darkening sky. I shift my bundle of scavenged belongings—blanket, spare tunic, sharpening stone—on my back. It's not heavy, but the weight of my secret bends my spine toward the ground. Hoping to relieve my burden, I slide the bundle—secured by one stretch of rope and a strip of leather I plan to make into a belt—down my arm and jog ahead to find Thyra. She's been hiking near Jaspar all day, surrounded by his warriors and some of ours. I think she's afraid that they'll scheme if she doesn't hover like a fly over a corpse.

She's probably been wondering where I am. She expected me to hike at her back. But for the first many hours of our journey, I did not trust myself to be around other people.

Maybe I still shouldn't, but I can't simply disappear either. I am needed.

"Ansa!" Thyra waves from next to a circle of stones that will mark the gathering place tonight for this camp. We'll have several, seeing as a few thousand of us are making this trek. Jaspar has assigned small squads of his own warriors to each cluster of people, in charge of making sure all of them keep moving in the same direction. We're being herded like sheep, and we don't yet know if our destination is lush new pasture or the butchering block.

"Where have you been all day?" She glances meaningfully at Jaspar. "He's being obstinately cagey," she whispers.

"I thought you said he wanted to be open with me, but he's full of smiles and smoke just like his father."

She wants me to ferret information from him, I can tell. She has no idea the extent to which I've already failed her. I shiver and rub my arms, scowling at the memory of frost creeping across rotting leaves, and then across skin. "It's been a long day," I murmur.

She gives me a concerned look. "You still look so tired."

"More than I want to admit." I swallow hard as I watch Dorte's widow, a woman whose skinny limbs belie her wiry toughness, striking flint against an old blade to light the dry leaves that have been stuffed amidst the gathered wood in the fire circle. Clinging to the back of her gown is a brown-eyed little girl, an adopted raid prize who Dorte brought as a gift two summers ago. If anyone has a right to be tired, it's this widow. If anyone deserves warmth and rest, it's her. If anyone deserves a reward for her determined strikes of stone and iron, *she* does. I stare at the flickering sparks, and they flare sudden and strong. The widow smiles as the flames take hold, and I blink in shock. Was that the curse? How could such an evil thing do something so merciful? I tear my eyes away from the woman. It was either a coincidence—or a trick, meant to lull me until it strikes again.

We pass around rations and tend to our weapons as the andeners gather enough wood to last through the night. Bertel, Preben, Aksel, and Sander share raid stories with a few of Jaspar's warriors just yards from where Thyra and I have settled in with our waterskins and hard biscuits. I am relieved that Jaspar himself seems to have disappeared for a while, and when he plops down between me and Thyra, I flinch.

"Any blisters?" he asks.

Quite a few. But our horses are loaded with supplies because we don't have enough wagons. "None at all."

The corner of Thyra's mouth twitches at my breezy tone. "It was a lovely stroll along the lake."

He chuckles and stretches his legs out in front of him. "Well, my feet hurt, anyway."

"You could ask an andener to rub them," Thyra suggests, "though the smell might prove lethal." She leans forward to grab another biscuit and knocks over the uncorked waterskin, which sends clean streamwater splashing over the stony ground, soaking the back of my breeches.

I grab it and lift the opening, but it's too late. The water is nearly gone. Thyra snatches the container from me. "I'll go fill it up again." She gives me a hard look before turning and walking toward the stream we passed several hundred yards back.

Jaspar watches her departure. "That was . . . unusually clumsy of her. One would think a chieftain would have better things to do than fetch water." He turns to me. "Does she hate me that much? I never actually did her any harm."

I'm not sure that's completely true—I remember the look on Thyra's face when she saw us together. But I shake my head and scoot closer to the fire, wanting to dry my breeches before I lie on my blanket for the night.

Jaspar moves with me, staying near. "So it's mistrust that drives her away," he says.

"What reason does she have to trust you? You're ingratiating yourself with her warriors and bringing us all to a foreign land, ruled by a man who tried to assassinate our chieftain."

"Is that what you were told?" he asks.

"You make it sound like Lars was spinning a tale, but he refused to speak of it at all."

"Oh, I don't think it was Lars who did the spinning." Jaspar laughs.

"Thyra won't talk about it either." No matter how many times I asked.

"Yet somehow all of you have the same belief, that my father is some sort of traitor."

"If he wasn't, then why didn't he openly challenge Lars?" My lip curls. I remember Nisse. Always in the council shelter, always drawing maps in the dirt, always full of plans and strategy, always thirsty for conquest—and rarely riding out to do his share of fighting.

"What makes you think he wanted to challenge Lars?" I give Jaspar a skeptical look, and he leans forward, his mouth tight. "Hundreds were loyal to my father, Ansa. Have you considered that he wanted to protect them from the consequences of that loyalty if he perished, even if it was based on an unfounded and unjust accusation?" He moves close enough that I can feel the skim of his breath across my cheek. "What would Thyra do?" He chuckles. "I'll bet she never imagined she'd have to face such a choice."

I wince and get to my feet. "Don't compare them," I say, my voice turning rough as my thoughts tumble with everything I've heard about what happened during the winter. A vial of poison was discovered in Nisse's shelter, along with the celebration goblet Lars always drank from when he returned in victory. It was found by a slave . . . or a child? Whoever it was took the evidence straight to Lars and his senior warriors, if the rumors are true. I cast a wary look at Jaspar, who is watching me with one eyebrow arched. I'd rather stab myself in the throat than ask him what he knows.

"Any chieftain would be privileged to have such a loyal wolf as you at her side," Jaspar says. "Or his side." My eyes narrow, and he smiles. "I simply meant that you were just as loyal to Lars."

I swallow the lump in my throat at the sudden, unbidden memory of Lars roaring with laughter after I spit Sander's earlobe at his feet. I had never in my entire life felt as mighty or fierce as when Lars looked at me with respect. "Of course I was. And you should have been too. He was your uncle."

"I would have been loyal to the end, if I hadn't been forced to choose."

"That's what loyalty is, you dunce. A choice." The flames flare, and I turn away quickly, my heart pounding with terror as I see them start to reach for Jaspar.

He jumps in front of me. "Don't walk away. Ansa, you can't fault me for following my conscience. I believe my father when he says he never intended to assassinate his brother. I would stake my life on it."

I blow a long, cool breath from between my lips, trying to slow my heart. "That is comforting," I whisper. *And confusing.* "But you can't fault me for not trusting you."

"I trust *you.*"

When I open my eyes, he's only a foot away. "You shouldn't."

His smile is sad. "I can't help it. I always have. You're not a schemer. You wear your emotions like a cloak. You laugh when you're happy and attack when you're angry. I always know where I stand."

"Don't pretend like you know me. A lot has happened since you left."

"Clearly." He glances over at Thyra, who is trudging toward us slowly, carrying a full waterskin and pretending she's not watching our every move. "Has she earned the loyalty you give her?"

I draw a dagger. "Are you suggesting she's not worthy?"

"I'm suggesting *you* are." He takes my wrist and guides my blade to the side of his neck. "Your loyalty should be rewarded with trust, Ansa. Pure, unwavering trust in return for your pure, unwavering devotion."

"Thyra does trust me."

"Does she?"

I do my best to hide the twinge of uncertainty that pricks in my mind. Jaspar's hand slides up to mine, and he squeezes my fingers as I watch my blade dent his skin. If I pressed, he would bleed. "*Such* devotion," he whispers. "I can see it in your eyes. A chieftain dreams of such a wolf, and here you are." He releases my hand, and I carefully pull the dagger away from his flesh, painfully conscious of my own unsteadiness.

"Ansa," Thyra calls out lightly as she returns to our side. "As much as I would sympathize, try not to kill my cousin before we reach our destination."

Jaspar bows his head, hiding a grin. "Ah, but who could blame her," he says good-naturedly, looking around at the other warriors who have gathered to share the warmth of the fire. "My own father threatens to murder me on a daily basis."

"Aye, but you earn that with your mischief!" says one of his warriors with a laugh. The woman has her long hair pulled back tightly and coiled at the back of her head. Her right middle finger bears numerous kill marks, which means she's already started on her left arm.

Jaspar dodges as she tosses a burning wood chip at him. "Yes, Carina, but—"

"There you are!" comes a broken voice, harsh with rage. We all turn to see Gry stalking up the trail toward our fire. Her finger is raised, a spear of accusation.

She's jabbing it at my chest, and I feel each thrust.

"Gry, what's wrong?" asks Thyra, rushing forward.

"I demand compensation," Gry shrieks. Her face is red, and her blond hair has pulled loose from its braid and hangs in pathetic strings around her face.

Thyra takes her by the shoulders and gives her a gentle shake. "What are you talking about?"

Gry leans around Thyra, and her eyes bore into mine. "I know what you did."

My hard biscuit has turned to stone in my stomach. "Then maybe you could share, because I have no idea what you're talking about."

Thyra looks troubled as she releases Gry, and stays next to her as she approaches me and Jaspar. "I was depending on Hulda to help me now that I've lost Cyrill," Gry says in a choked voice.

"Gry," Thyra says. "Tell us what's happened."

Gry turns to her. "Hulda didn't return from gathering kindling. I went to look for her." She glowers at me. "And I found her in the woods."

"Dead, I assume?" Jaspar asks. The other warriors around the fire are staring at us with rapt attention.

I wish I could melt into the ground like frost under the sun, but instead I'm frozen where I stand. I push the memory of Hulda's eyes out of my head as Gry nods.

"And you think I had something to do with it?" I ask, hating the shake in my voice.

"You asked where she was this morning!"

I force a laugh, sharp and high. "I merely wondered why she wasn't in the shelter, helping you prepare for the journey!"

"My oldest saw you follow her into the woods," Gry says, hatred soaking her voice.

Thyra gives me a questioning look, and I shake my head, terrified by the cold twist of ice inside me. I want to run, to get away from Thyra and everyone else I care about, but if I do, my innocence will be questioned. "I went to offer my assistance," I say. "I told you I would help take care of your family."

"And that included leaving my slave dead in the forest?"

"I never saw her!" I shout. I hate the way Thyra is looking at me, the questions in her eyes. Her doubt is a knife. "I went looking for her, but she was nowhere to be found."

Lies and lies and lies. What I wouldn't give to fly across the Torden and cut that witch queen's throat.

"How was she killed?" Jaspar asks, yanking me from my bloody thoughts. He glances over my arms and calves, where my weapons are sheathed.

Gry's mask of righteous rage slips. "I don't know. I just know she was."

A line forms between Jaspar's brows. "If Ansa killed her, wouldn't there have been a wound?" He gestures at me. "When she kills you, you tend to know it."

Sander lets out a begrudging grunt, but everyone else is silent. I look to the other side of the fire and see him staring back. He runs his hand over his scabbed throat and I look away.

Gry folds her arms over her chest. "No wound. She was cold when I found her."

I grit my teeth, and Thyra frowns. "And when was that?" Thyra asks.

"Midmorn. Just as we were leaving."

"So she had been dead for a while," Jaspar says, moving to stand right next to me. A vote of confidence that sits like honey on my tongue.

One I do not deserve.

"She was only steps inside the tree line," Gry snaps, her keen eyes on me. "How could you have gone into the woods and not have seen her?"

"How am I supposed to know?" I say, my stomach a pit of snakes. "Forgive me for the fact that I had a thousand other things to do this morning. When I didn't see her, I turned around and left. I don't have time to search for careless slaves in the woods."

"Could she have died of natural causes, Gry?" Thyra asks with a much more appropriate tone to take with a widow. "Hulda was reaching the end of her middle years."

"And was stout as an ox," says Gry. She closes her eyes and lets out a breath. "The look on her face, Chieftain." Her voice breaks, and her eyes fill with tears as she looks up at Thyra. "There was such terror there."

"That kind of look doesn't require an external source," I say. I am earning every second I will spend in hell someday. "Her heart could have seized."

Jaspar nods in agreement, but Thyra is still staring down at Gry, whose cheeks are sunken, whose nose is red. Gry, who used to wear a smile like the sunrise, whose laugh was a gift, and whose love for Cyrill was like a blazing torch. "So she died afraid," Thyra says, stroking Gry's hair. "Is there anything else to suggest she was killed, instead of a more natural, though deeply unfortunate, death?"

A tear slides down Gry's face as her eyes meet mine. "Nothing I can prove," she says, her voice trembling. "But when I say she was cold . . . there was melting frost on her skin. Her body was stiff with it." She shudders. "It wasn't natural, Chieftain."

A hissing, anxious whisper comes from somewhere behind me, but I hear it like it's been shouted in my ear: *witchcraft*.

"All right, I think we've let this go on long enough," Jaspar says loudly, and Thyra steps back suddenly, a look of shock on her face. "Carelessly hurled accusations are sparks on dry tinder after everything this tribe has been through. Gry, we'll compensate your household for the slave. And—"

Thyra gives him an imperious look. "Gry is of *my* tribe."

Jaspar pauses, his mouth still half open, and then he smiles. "My mistake, Chieftain Thyra. By all means. *Lead*." He gestures at Gry.

Thyra's cheeks are red as she puts her arm around Gry and guides her away from the fire, away from dozens of warriors' stares, back toward her camp up the trail. She murmurs quietly to the widow as they walk. Jaspar chuckles. "I suppose the same words are sweeter if delivered with a soft touch and a gentle voice." His warriors lift their waterskins to him in salute, and he grins before reaching over to squeeze my shoulder. "Are you all right? It's not every day one is accused of murdering a slave by"—his brow furrows—"freezing?"

I shiver, letting out a bitter laugh. "Yes. See? A lot *has* changed since you left. Now I don't need these." I hold up my arms, showing off the sheathed daggers strapped between my wrists and elbows. "All I need is to think cold thoughts."

He guffaws. "Then I'll redouble my efforts to inspire only warmth in you." He glances at Thyra's retreating figure before looking at me again. "Remember what I said, Ansa, hmm? Think about what you deserve in return for that iron loyalty of yours." He leaves my side and joins his warriors.

I turn and stalk toward the woods on the far side of camp, my thoughts a mess of ice and fire and panic. I've just reached the trees when I hear footsteps behind me. Thyra stalks through the dark toward me. She wears the moonlight like a crown, and her eyes are like chips of quartz. "Did you do it?" she asks in a harsh whisper.

"What?" I take a step back.

"You said the witch cursed you to hurt our people. Did you? Are you her weapon now?" Her doubt slices into my side, seeking my vitals. I should admit what happened. I should tell her. But she's looking at me like I am a stranger, and I recognize the suspicion in her eyes—it's the way she looked at me when I was first brought to camp all those years ago, a filthy raid prize passed from one tribe to another. She was the daughter of the chieftain, and I was no better than one of the wild dogs who prowl around camp looking for scraps. I fought and I fought and I fought to become one of the Krigere, to have a place and a home. I thought she accepted me as one of them, fully and completely. Now her doubt cuts through that hard-won safety, slicing me away from my tribe, from my love.

"Thyra, I swear I didn't do it!" The lie bursts from me before I can muzzle it.

"So Gry is a liar?"

"She wasn't even there!"

Thyra rubs her face and lets her arms swing at her sides. "I'm sorry, Ansa. What she described . . ."

I know what she must have described. I left Hulda frozen, her last breath a shred of gray vapor rising toward the trees. Gry must have found her not long thereafter. My handiwork. My curse. "I understand why Gry needs someone to blame." It's amazing how one lie builds on another, how once you start, the truth dies a quick death.

Thyra sighs. "I got her calmed down, but Jaspar succeeded in undermining me anyway. He looked like the strong one tonight. And perhaps I deserved that." She gives me a look full of regret. "I shouldn't have been so quick to doubt you, Ansa. You're the one person in this entire world who I know will protect my back. It was ungrateful of me to question."

"I understand why," I say. "But I *will* keep this curse under control."

"And you will be victorious," she whispers. "I am so fortunate to have such a warrior at my side."

I tilt my head up and kiss her forehead, even as my throat constricts with shame. "And the rest of us are fortunate to have a chieftain who respects every Krigere life, warrior or andener."

"Half of them still think I'm too weak to deserve any respect in return."

"You're going to prove them wrong." I smile. "Come on. Both of us need to rest." I pause. "I'm still not sure of my sleep," I admit. "Will you stay next to me?"

She slips her hand into mine. "No one could pry me away."

There, Jaspar, I think. *This is my reward.*

Together, Thyra and I walk back down to the fire.

CHAPTER NINE

We wake to a bitter, wet cold that has seeped into our blankets and breeches and clings to our hair in icy droplets. As we pack up just before sunrise and resume our slow progress to the southeast, following the shore of the Torden toward the unknown, I stay near Thyra and work every minute to keep the magic inside.

She was right; with a few hours of sleep, I am calmer, more able to push my thoughts and feelings into neat rows, keeping their jagged edges from thrusting the ice or fire to the fore. I focus on my adoration of her, and how she needs her strength to win allies and make strong decisions. I carry her bundle of possessions on my back, along with my own. She objected when I slid it off her shoulders this morning, but I wanted her to walk unencumbered as she speaks to our warriors, assuring them that we will be respected once we get to Vasterut—or else we will leave to plunder the south. We are not prisoners.

They cast nervous glances Jaspar's way when she says this. I'm not sure they believe her.

"Jaspar said Nisse is planning his own invasion of Kupari," Preben says, bowing his head and speaking quietly to Thyra as they trudge up a scramble of rocks, the gulls that follow us circling and diving overhead. "Apparently he's been repurposing some of the Vasterutian water vessels."

Thyra laughs. "Water vessels? How much would you wager he's dealing with half-rotten fishing skiffs? If Vasterut had a force on the Torden, we'd know about it."

Preben scratches his beard. "Aye, but Nisse's been in Vasterut for nearly three full seasons, so he could have built at least a dozen longboats, maybe. Depends on whether he's got Vasterutians working on them too. Jaspar would know."

Thyra looks out over the Torden as she and Preben reach the top of the rocks. "A dozen boats would be nothing to the witch. Nor would fifty."

"Sounds like our chieftain is spooked," Aksel mutters as he falls into step next to me. He's corralled his bird's nest of curls with a leather thong, and though the sun and wind have chapped his cheeks, his face is drawn with grief and taut with bitterness. "I for one am eager to slit some Kupari throats."

"Probably because you were safe at home while the rest of us were fighting for our lives on the Torden," I hiss.

Aksel's dark eyes become slits. "I never believed you of all warriors would shy away from a fight. I guess I should, given who you serve." He glares at Thyra's back.

Heat runs in rivulets down my arms, all the way to my fingertips, and I suck in a breath of cool air off the lake, fighting my rising irritation and the danger it brings. "It's not cowardice to reassess your strategy when your enemy turns out to be vastly more powerful than you first believed." I lean forward, clutching hard on the straps of my bundles. "Not doing so, however, seems like idiocy to me."

"I'd rather die fighting than wringing my hands and *reassessing*."

"Stop arguing like a pair of children," snaps Thyra.

I look up to find her peering back at the two of us as we descend the rocks. "Apologies, Chieftain."

Aksel mutters something insolent before echoing my words. Thyra stops right on the trail, forcing the rest of us to do the same. "Aksel, go see if the andeners at the rear of our line need help carrying anything. We're nearly to noonmeal, and they're bound to be getting tired. A strong arm will be a relief to them."

Aksel stiffens at the dismissal, but she's framed it in a way he cannot refuse without looking like a weak and selfish ass. "Yes, Chieftain," he mutters.

With concern Thyra watches him go, but Preben merely gives him an amused look before returning to his conversation with her. "Will you be able to offer Nisse some information that might speed a victory over Kupari?" he asks. "This might enhance our status within his tribe."

"I have not yet decided if we will unite our tribe with

his. Remember that he's a traitor who stooped to assassination," she says in a voice that promises any defiance will be met with iron.

"Still, it's our best chance of victory," says Preben.

"And of killing the witch," I say. My hope that her death will break the curse has been filling my head as I hike, along with the traitorous thought that perhaps uniting with Nisse will give us the strength and strategy we need to defeat the queen.

"I will consult with Nisse," Thyra says, turning around to glance at me. "I can't say I'd advise another invasion over the Torden, though. Over land seems wiser, but I don't know the terrain." She nods at Jaspar, who is several yards ahead with Sander, swapping raid stories in loud, jovial tones. "And I believe I'll trust my own eyes over blind promises of easy victory."

Preben grunts. "Lars would have said the same."

I'm not sure he's right. My heart sinks as I think of how blindly confident Lars was of easy victory . . . just before he was struck by lightning. His drive for plunder became insatiable after Nisse took Vasterut. But Preben's compliment must feel like a win to Thyra, because she presses her advantage. "I think this is a chance to consider all the alternatives before rushing to war. We have so many to provide for—stability and safety is my priority."

Preben frowns. "That is *not* something Lars would have said."

Thyra freezes midstep, but only for a splinter of time.

"He had many thoughts about our future that he did not share openly. We'll never know what he would have said, had he made it through that battle."

"The only way he would have made it through the battle is in victory. He wouldn't have had it any other way."

Thyra looks up at Preben, her chin raised in defiance at the implication—perhaps she should not have returned either. "If it had meant safeguarding the future of the Krigere, you had best believe my father would have done anything, including not carelessly squandering his own life. Think of the mercy he showed Nisse and all the warriors who followed him."

Preben chews on the inside of his cheek. "I suppose you're right, Chieftain," he mutters.

"He would have hated to see us like this," she says. "But he would have been proud to see warriors like you still loyal to the tribe, not letting greed or fear of enemies and the unknown tear us apart." She grasps Preben's arm. "I'm sorry about Edvin. It would not have been my choice to lose such a strong and valuable warrior like that."

Preben gives her a long look, then bows his head. "I know, Chieftain. You did it because you had to." He shrugs off her arm and keeps walking.

Thyra's hand hovers in the air before she clenches her fist and brings it to her side.

The days pass full of moments like that, her losing a foot of ground for every two she wins, her wooing while the others warily watch for signs of how she will lead. All along the trail, there is constant talk of what awaits us, and the hum of speculation about Kupari and Vasterut and Nisse and being caught within his newly acquired kingdom for the winter. Thyra does not waste a single opportunity to speak to our warriors while Jaspar is laughing and joking with his. She assures them she is with them, that she will not lead us into certain defeat over the water again. She speaks of our responsibility to the widows and orphans, and how we must be creative and determined as we consider our way forward. It all seems to add up to one thing—she is not at all eager to attack Kupari.

I try to understand it. With the exception of me and Sander, none of our warriors saw what happened on the Torden that terrible day. None of them saw the floating bodies of their comrades. None of them watched the seagulls descend to make a meal out of their corpses. None of them tasted the keen tang of despair that came with watching those waves bow over us, that feeling of being so small that there is no escape from the jaws of the beast. They imagine, yes, but they don't *know*. They are thirsty now, not just for Kupari wealth, but for Kupari blood.

I wait and hope for Thyra to promise them satisfaction and revenge, but she doesn't. Instead, she urges caution. She urges patience.

Part of me knows this is wise. But only part of me.

The rest of me longs for the day when I bring vengeance to the witch queen's door—and possibly win my freedom back. I can feel her curse inside me, carving on my bones, snaking through my veins, twisting along my spine, trying to escape and kill once again. At night it coils inside my mind, with scales like iron filings, scraping away my soft parts with every flex and shift of ice and fire. I hate the way it feels, the way it seems to think it's entitled to burrow in my body and make itself at home.

I work very hard to stay calm at all times. I won't allow the curse to control me, to hurt my people, to condemn me, to reveal itself to Thyra and make her doubt me again. But as days pass and we near the marshlands that mark the turn to the southwest—the long miles of trail that will lead us to Vasterut—I have to wonder how much harder my task will become.

The morning we're to traverse the marshlands, Jaspar's warriors rouse us when the moon is still in the sky. Thyra pokes at my shoulder, her teeth chattering. "They want to cross while the ice over the marsh is still firm," she says. "When the sun gets high, the ground goes soft again. We have to get everyone over before that happens."

"Especially because the rear of the caravan is mostly old ones and andeners with children," I mutter as I stand up and strap my sheaths to my arms.

Thyra frowns as she tries to light a torch in the fading embers of last night's fire. When the pitch bursts with flame a moment later, she looks over her shoulder at me. "Was that you?" she whispers.

I flinch. I think it might have been. "No! I told you. Everything is under control." I look around to make sure no one is listening. "The witch hasn't beaten me yet."

"Is it getting any easier?"

The opposite. But I flash a confident smile. "I haven't heard a single whisper of witchcraft in days. Have you?"

"No, actually."

"There you have it."

She ruffles my hair and then laughs as she takes in my appearance, probably because she's made my fiery hair stand on end. "That's my Ansa." She turns away and walks toward Jaspar.

"I *am* your Ansa," I whisper, and then I follow, feeling lighter and happier than I have in days.

By the time we reach the edge of the marshlands, an expanse of swamp a few hundred yards across that extends at least two miles inland by Jaspar's report, the eastern horizon is as pink as a newborn. Jaspar summons us all to gather around as those at the rear begin to catch up.

"The ground should be firm enough to cross until the sun is midsky," he says loudly. "We made it across at this time of day on our way to your camp."

Thyra puts her hands on her hips. "But that was with forty warriors. We number in the thousands. Perhaps we should go around it."

Jaspar sighs. "Going around this marsh will add at least a day to our journey, and probably two, and I've been told we're running low on rations." He gestures at the sky. "And the first snow could come anytime. Seems to me that getting to Vasterut as quickly as possible is best for everyone."

Thyra glares at him. "Getting there *alive* is best for everyone. If we must do this, we should all rope up."

Jaspar and several of his warriors groan. "Crossing like that will take hours longer."

"And it would ensure that *no one* is lost to the marsh."

"Ah, Thyra, so careful and calculating, as always." Jaspar chuckles. "Risk is part of life."

"But foolishness doesn't have to be. If your warriors are so greatly affected by the *risk* of snow and hunger, then perhaps you should take them and ride ahead. I'll stay and get my people across."

"Or she'll turn around and run back to the north," says a hulking dark-haired warrior next to Jaspar. Several others echo his suspicion.

Thyra draws a dagger. "Say that louder, Sten," she invites. "Let's discuss it, by all means."

The warrior's lip curls, but he remains silent, and Jaspar claps him on the back. "Nonsense, Sten. Until *proven* otherwise, I will choose to believe Thyra is as full of honor as she is of caution."

Thyra's eyes blaze with sudden hate and, to my surprise, a flicker of fear. "An insult wrapped in a compliment. How uncharacteristically clever of you."

Jaspar chuckles drily as his hand moves to the hilt of his dagger, and the sight jolts me into action.

"We don't have time to argue." I stride over to one of our horses and yank a coil of rope from its back. "Let's get to work."

I catch Thyra's eye as I loop the rope around my waist, and she smiles. The people behind me each use belts or shorter stretches of rope to attach themselves to the longer rope as Jaspar leads his warriors across unroped. The horses' flanks twitch as they pick their way past clumps of grass and stretches of black ice, as if they sense the danger. I follow, leading a long line of our own warriors over the treacherous ground. I know about marshes—I've watched one swallow an ox whole. First it sank to its knees, then to its neck, and then it disappeared all of a sudden, its bellowing cut silent in a fountain of bubbles and froth. There are layers to these places, thick vegetation that grows a few feet below the surface and is firm enough to hold weight—until it doesn't. If we go through the ice, there's not much time before the rest gives way.

By the time our first wave is across, the sun sits fat and yellow on the treetops in the east, watching our slow progress. Jaspar and his warriors camp themselves on a hill just beyond the marsh, clearly impatient with how long it takes to secure ropes to each individual crossing the divide. Thyra ignores the eye rolls and muttered comments . . . along with the grumbled complaints that come from a few of our own people. She's sweating from traveling back and forth across the marsh with our rope and keeps glaring at the rising sun as if she'd like to sink a blade into its cheerful golden face. But the ice holds, making our toil over the rope seem fussy and overcautious.

The crowd on the opposite side grows as the sky brightens, and the trailing caravan shrinks as those at the rear catch up and prepare to cross. I fight my growing anxiety that Thyra's caution is playing as weakness and fear.

But then Gry and her family emerge from the woods and reach the edge of the marsh, and my heart speeds for an entirely different reason. She's glaring at me as if I'm a snake and clutching her daughter's hand hard enough to make the girl wince. I cross the distance between us, hefting the loop of rope around my shoulder with Thyra carrying the rest.

"Just be kind to her," Thyra says softly as we reach the midpoint of the marsh. "She's grieving, and she just needed a face to pin her anger on."

She's scarily accurate about who she's chosen. "As long as she doesn't go spouting stupid and baseless accusations again, I'll be as kind as a lamb."

Thyra snorts. "You, a lamb?"

"Baaaa—ah!" My bleating is cut off as my foot sinks through the ice. I yank it back up and spread my arms, looking at the dark ice all around. It shines wetly in the sun. "This isn't good."

"Come on, Chieftain!" Sten shouts from the other side. "We've been here half the day, and we have ground to cover!"

Thyra mutters something about putting him *in* the ground before saying, "Come on. We're almost finished."

"Are you sure you want to risk a crossing?" I wiggle my mud-coated boot.

Thyra pauses and looks over her shoulder at the crowd on the other side. "If I call a halt to this for the day with only fifty people left to cross, I'll never hear the end of it.

They'll blame *me* for letting the sun get too high."

She's right. Which means we have to risk the most vulnerable of our group. Grimly, we rope up and begin a careful plod back across the ice, single file. With each step, I feel the tug of resistance, fifty bodies behind mine all attached to my rope.

I'm within three yards of solid ground when a scream rends the air and I'm yanked backward. I land on Thyra's squirming body as a terrible crackling sound echoes across the marsh.

"Mama!" shrieks a little boy. I turn to see him splashing, submerged to his chest. I roll off Thyra just as she lunges backward toward the shore and tries to brace her feet on a clump of grass, her slender fingers wrapped around the rope as she attempts to hold the line while the others move to pull the child out. But four more andeners fall through the ice, their faces white with fear. Several others are on their stomachs, arms spread wide as the ice cracks and shatters. Still tied to the rope, I'm pulled several feet away from the shore, icy water soaking my breeches. I can hear the crunch of boot steps and frantic shouting behind me as warriors rush forward to help, suddenly pulled from their boredom by the catastrophe playing out on the marsh. But they stay at the edge of the bog, afraid to be sucked down. Someone shouts for more rope to bridge the gap.

It won't be soon enough for the andeners and their babies, though. Shrill wails and sobs drown out everything else.

"Find your footing and pull!" yells Thyra, even as her

boots sink through the ice. She's leaning back with all her might, her teeth clenched and mud-speckled water dripping from her hair. But her voice is lost in the noise. Half the line is at least up to their thighs in icy marsh water, and most of them look terrified to move for fear of sinking further, even though not moving means freezing to death. We're not close enough to shore to get the help we need from the other warriors, and we're not strong enough to pull all our andeners and their children to safety. My throat tightens as I watch Gry clutching tightly to her little boy, even as she sinks to her waist.

Deep inside me, something stirs, monstrous and unpredictable. I tense all my muscles, holding tight to the rope as I fight to keep the curse from breaking loose at the exact wrong moment. The memory of Hulda's frozen eyes rises, a grisly specter inside my skull. My breath huffs from my mouth in a glitter of frost, and I whimper. My feet have broken through the ice, and frigid liquid permeates my boots. The rope vibrates beneath my palms with the struggle.

Thyra gasps as the marsh begins to take her. She's still pulling on her rope, which is streaked with blood from her torn palms. She'll hold on until the marsh devours her, just to give her people a chance to get to the other side. She glances over at me, her eyes shining with unbidden tears.

The wave of cold bursts from me, sudden and awful, and I grit my teeth to try to press it back inside, my every thought focused on keeping the curse from killing the innocents of my tribe.

"Oh, heaven," murmurs Thyra as a muted crackling sound reaches me.

I open my eyes to see the frost creeping across the previously wet surface of the marsh. "No," I whisper. But I can't stop it, and I'm quickly growing tired of fighting it. The only thing that keeps me from letting go is the memory of Hulda's clawed fingers, the way her mouth froze open in a silent scream. Any moment now, Gry will look that way. Thyra, too. I'm going to kill them all.

"All of you, come to me!" Thyra shouts, jarring me from my horror. "Come on," she says, clutching at my shoulder. "If we get to shore, the others can help us pull them out."

I blink my eyes open again, shivering and stunned. A thick layer of ice has formed along the top of the marsh, and those who fell in are climbing out onto the newly stable ground. The frozen crust of it beneath me trembles as our people crawl to safety, pulling themselves up from the marsh's black mouth and across its deadly skin toward the rocky shore. Sobs of relief fill the air, but it's not until someone tugs me onto solid ground that I realize I'm still lying on my back, clutching at the rope as if my life depends on it.

Thyra's pale eyes meet mine. "Are you all right?"

I look down at my muddy hands, my soaked boots and breeches. My arms tingle with the sting of frost, but the pain is manageable. "I think so."

She grins. "So are they." She gestures toward a wet and shivering group of children and andeners. Others have gathered around to wrap them in blankets and dry their dripping hair. I look back out over the marsh. The holes made by the splash of bodies are iced over, and the rest of the marsh is laced with white frost. Cold wind blows in my hair, making me shiver. Thyra slides her hand into mine and laughs, a strained, broken sound. "Usually your skin is so warm."

We're at the rear of the crowd, many of whom are fussing over the ones we nearly lost while the rest are already hiking forward. Either Jaspar and his warriors didn't want to acknowledge that Thyra was right in using the ropes or they're so focused on covering the miles that they don't care. But I see Sander standing at the crest of the hill, staring down at me before he disappears over the other side.

I start to fall into step at the rear of the group, but Thyra pulls me to a stop. "They all would have been lost." She turns me to face her. "But you called to the ice, didn't you?"

My heart skips as she moves closer. "No. I didn't—"

"It's all right, Ansa." She touches my cheek. "I know what you're doing."

I gape at her, my world crumbling. "I swear, Thyra—"

"You somehow managed to turn the enemy's sword against her," she murmurs, the corner of her mouth lifting. "I'm in awe of you."

I should tell her the truth. Or at least admit that we're lucky I didn't just kill everyone out on the marsh, that the curse broke free and it took everything I had to hold it back. But the way she's looking at me keeps me silent. The spark of desire in her eyes turns my blood hot.

Her fingers slide over my cheek. "Oh, there's that warmth I was missing."

When her lips touch mine, shock explodes inside me, but also happiness, pure and fierce. Thyra pulls back quickly, looking stunned, possibly a mirror of my own expression. "I've been telling myself not to do that," she says.

She shouldn't have. I'm not worthy of it. But . . . "Just give me this moment." Any compromise. Any bargain. I need her lips on mine again.

As soon as she nods, I wrap my arm around her waist and pull her body to me, and she takes my face in her hands, lifting my chin. I rise on my tiptoes, my tongue sliding hungrily along her bottom lip, our chests touching, my whole body tingling. *This,* I think. *This I would happily kill for, every day of my life.* I press her closer, craving more even though I know very well that if she knew about my lies, she wouldn't want to touch me at all. It's a stolen treasure, and I am the greediest of thieves.

Thyra lets out a whimper and pulls back, tugging my wrists away from her body. "Too hot," she gasps. My throat tightens as I see the black scorch marks on her tunic. Horror rushes in like the black water of the marsh, quenching the flames of my joy. I give her a pained look, still burning at the loss of her kiss.

She gives me an unsteady smile. "I know you're still trying to figure it out, and I know you'll succeed, just like you figured out how to save Gry's family. You'll make this curse your dog. It will cringe at your feet."

I stare at the black, singed fabric just above her belt. Her smooth skin lies just beneath it, so fragile. So precious. I was seconds away from setting her aflame.

This curse is far from tamed.

I force a smile. "Of course I will."

She kisses my cheek, a flutter of sweetness. Her body is shaking. "Maybe all you need is practice," she says breathlessly, her cheeks pink and lovely. She looks into my eyes for a moment, then lets out a sudden, surprised, unbearably bright laugh. "I never thought I would be happy again after all that's happened."

Then she turns and marches up the trail.

I follow her, hope and dread waging a war inside me.

CHAPTER TEN

Over the next few days I am very careful, but Sander stares at me whenever we're near each other. Still, he hasn't said anything, and the farther we go, the more days we have without mention of witchcraft, the more I begin to feel almost normal again. Finally, we reach a vast stretch of dunes, and the sun sets on our left instead of our right, and I realize I'm facing north. We've hiked halfway around the great lake.

"Tomorrow!" Jaspar announces as the warriors in our camp crouch in front of the main fire for the evening meal. "After one final push we'll be at the gates of Vasterut by sundown. I've sent riders ahead to let them know of our approach."

"So there's no escape," mutters Bertel as he warms his

gnarled hands, looking at Thyra with concern. In the last few days, she seems to have won over many. I think many of the warriors who were left behind during the invasion were the ones with milder spirits anyway, but Thyra's endless efforts to connect with them, to listen, to speak with wisdom, appear to have solidified the support of our tribe—as did our rescue of the andeners and children on the marsh. I was afraid it would be seen as overcautious, but in the end, many warriors were shamed by their failure to protect our widows, as was their duty to their fallen brothers and sisters. Thyra's unfailing dedication to that purpose, her willingness to sacrifice herself to save them, and her steady refusal to apologize for it have all reached them, and I am so proud of her that it makes my heart hurt.

She hasn't kissed me again. We haven't had a moment. But she sits closer to me at meals, and lies near at night. Every time her skin touches mine, I shiver and tell myself to focus. I am working to get over my terror at nearly burning her so that I can earn the pleasure of touching her again. It is impossible not to resent the curse for stealing that joy from me.

Her shoulder nudges mine as she turns to slap Bertel on the back. "We have each other, brother, and we'll face our future together. United."

Jaspar's green eyes meet mine over the fire, and then he looks at Thyra. His handsome face twists into a grimace as he wings a pebble into the fire, throwing up sparks. I wonder if he senses something has changed between us. He hasn't approached me in days.

"I still want you to be his friend," Thyra says. "He knows more than he's sharing. I need to know Nisse's intentions."

"How do you know he hasn't shared everything with Sander? Our earless brother is standing right next to the new prince of Vasterut." He's speaking to Jaspar in low tones while he casts suspicious glances my way, no less. On Sander's other side, Aksel isn't bothering to glance. He's glaring at me and Thyra with his jaw set as he waits for his share of hard biscuit and dried meat. We're down to our last rations, and tomorrow we'll be hungry until we reach our destination.

"I've never been to a city," I say to Thyra. "Have you?"

She shakes her head. "Father said they were like camps, but that the buildings are set on stone blocks, and sometimes they are tall."

"How tall?"

"As the trees in the forest."

My eyes go wide. "How is that possible?"

"We always used wood to build boats, to explore. Other tribes use wood to root themselves in one place."

"Which is exactly what we would do if you'd had your way, right?" Aksel says to her as he plops down on my left.

Her smile disappears. "Can you truly not tell the difference between a plan to provide for a populace and the complete abandonment of who we are as a people?"

He gives her a quizzical look. "I suppose not. You were going to strap us to plows like oxen."

"How else did you propose we eat, after nineteen out of

twenty of our hunters and raiders were killed?" Thyra leans around me to look Aksel in the eye. "Be at peace with it, Aksel. Your father challenged me. If he had trusted in my leadership, he would still be at your side."

Aksel grimaces and shoots to his feet, so violently that he stumbles. "Someone had to do it," he mutters.

"What?" I snap.

He takes a few unsteady steps back from the fire. He's drawn most of the eyes around the fire, and he looks into each as he raises a waterskin in Jaspar's direction. "I am grateful to be in this company," he says in a loud voice. "Grateful to be entering the embrace of a true leader." His red-rimmed eyes are shining with grief and he looks unhinged. "As a Krigere I want to hold my head high and my sword higher!"

It's the kind of statement that would usually draw shouts of agreement, so it's a testament to how much work Thyra's done on this journey that he's greeted only with strained grumbles of appreciation over the sentiment, if not the insult to Thyra's leadership.

I slowly curl my fingers around the hilt of my dagger as Aksel draws his and thrusts it at the sky. "Does no one hear me?" he roars, a tear slipping down his cheek, shining on his almost-faded black eye.

"I hear you," Thyra says.

I jerk my head around to look at her. She's risen and is facing him. Her face is smooth, not red-cheeked and petulant with offense. "You grieve," she says. "And I grant you one final night to howl and rage." She slides a blade from the hilt strapped to her rope belt, and I feel the tension around the fire heighten just like the flames, which respond to my own rising emotions.

Thyra steps around me, putting herself within striking distance of Aksel and showing she is not intimidated by his wild-eyed posturing. "But make no mistake, Aksel. If you cannot put this aside by the time we reach the walls of Vasterut, if you cannot show me the respect I am owed as your chieftain, I will leave you drowning in your own blood at the gates." She drops one leg back and spreads her arms just slightly, the graceful arc that indicates she's ready to fight, ready to strike. "Or I could do it now, if it will relieve your pain."

Aksel's face is crimson, though whether it's from humiliation or the roaring flames, I know not. His muscles are knotted, and his hair is a tangled mess around his grimy face. His knuckles are white as he grips his dagger, and his hand is shaking.

I take in the expressions of the warriors around the fire, and I know they see what I do—if Aksel strikes at Thyra, she will destroy him. Yes, he is taller, with better reach, though not by much. He outweighs her by at least a stone. But he has always been a step slower than most of us, and no one is faster than Thyra is—or better able to read her opponent's moves before he makes them.

"Put it down, lad," Bertel says, his deep voice obliterating the taut silence. "It's the last thing we need tonight. Let our chieftain eat her biscuit in peace."

Aksel looks over at Jaspar and Sander, who are standing still as boulders on the other side of the fire. Sten, the dark-haired warrior who criticized Thyra's decision about the ropes, looks like he agrees with Aksel, but Jaspar shakes his head and lets out a weary chuckle. "I don't know about you, Aksel, but I'm disinclined to fight on an empty stomach. Use that waterskin to wash this down." He tosses his own biscuit over the fire, and it hits Aksel in the chest.

Aksel blinks and steps back abruptly, sheathing his dagger as he does. He smiles like his lips are being wrenched up with metal hooks. "I suppose I could use a good meal. It's been days," he says, his voice unsteady. He picks up the biscuit and dusts sand off it. "Many thanks, Jaspar."

Shoving the hard lump of flour and salt and lard in his pocket, he marches toward the shore, his strides jerky and stiff.

"That boy needs an andener. *Immediately*," says the warrior named Carina, twirling her thick braid and rolling her hips, and everyone bursts into guffaws, probably not as much because of the joke as with gratitude that the tension has been shattered.

Thyra is smiling as she sinks back down onto the sand, but her muscles are still drawn tight with readiness. She accepts the toasts of our warriors and the begrudging nods of a few of Jaspar's—it seems her quiet confidence has impressed them as well. "Follow Aksel," she says in my ear as everyone returns their attention to their food. "Make sure he's keeping wise."

I meet her eyes. "You're afraid he'll do something rash?"

"He's lost his grip on reason. I wouldn't put it past him to poison my water or sabotage the horses. Give him space, but watch him."

"I'm your wolf," I whisper, and stuff the rest of my biscuit into my mouth. It tastes as good as I imagine the sand beneath my feet would. I pull a strip of dried meat from my pocket and chew on it while I follow Aksel's trail through camp, where people are settled around small fires among the gently sloping dunes. His footsteps turn abruptly at the edge of camp, cutting toward the shore, and I peer around me, noticing his mother—Edvin's widow—gathered with a few others near a small fire of their own. She gives me a hard look as I disappear around the edge of a massive sand hill and follow a rocky slope toward the pebbled beach. Stony outcroppings jut toward the water every several yards, and waves reach for them and fall short with each grasping effort. Aksel is nowhere to be found.

I eye the ground and see a smashed sprig of greenery, freshly downtrodden. Thyra didn't want me to get too close, but I need to make sure Aksel's not looping back to ambush her at the western edge of camp. Surprise is his only hope of beating her. My steps quicken, but I plant my feet on larger rocks to avoid the crunching sounds that would announce my approach.

I pick my way along slowly, peering around each outcropping and expecting to see Aksel, but he's gone. Finally, as the sun kisses the water, I lean against a boulder and sigh. I must have missed his trail. I've never been the best tracker—I'm better at charging in and killing head on. And I'd better get back. I turn to retrace my steps.

The blow comes from above, a hard punch to the side of my face that sends me sprawling in the sand. Panting, I roll onto my back and draw a dagger, blinking up at the dark form descending on me.

"You're not Thyra, but you'll do."

I roll sharply to the side as I hear the malevolent whisper of a blade being drawn. "Aksel, cut it out."

The kick lands right in my ribs, and my breath explodes from my mouth. "What's a warrior without her wolf?" he asks in a low, shaky voice.

"Still strong enough to kill a conniving weasel," I say, launching myself to my feet even as my lungs scream for air. Fury courses through my veins, hotter by the second. I leap back as Aksel slashes at me, a clumsy swipe of his blade, but I misjudge his distance in the shadowed twilight. Pain slices across the top of my forearm, forcing me to stifle a cry. "For heaven's sake, Aksel, this isn't a fight circle!"

"Right, this is the real world, Ansa. And you're serving the wrong master." He stabs at me, but I throw myself to the side and parry the blow. His dark eyes glitter wetly in the gathering dark. "She'll betray you, too, you know. As soon as you cease to be useful."

"Thyra's never betrayed anyone."

"That's what she'd like people to believe."

I take a step back. "Aksel, I know you're grieving. But

Thyra would give her life for this tribe." My throat tightens. "She wouldn't have traveled to Vasterut if the threat to us hadn't been grave."

"From what I hear, she created that threat!"

"Who have you been talking to?" But even as I ask, I know. It can only have been Jaspar and his warriors.

Aksel's lip curls. "She's blinded you, Ansa. Ask yourself who had the most to gain from Nisse's banishment."

The accusation sparks in my chest like flint on iron. "Stop blaming her for everything and accept that she's chieftain now!"

He lets out a strangled roar and dives at me, and I catch his blade arm as we go tumbling to the ground, rolling over each other in the loose sand. It flies into my eyes and ears and mouth, but I ignore the scrape of it as I jam my knee up to throw him off me. He grunts and jerks upward with the impact, but then flattens himself on top of me, the edge of his dagger pressed to my shoulder as I fight to hold it back. His teeth are bared as he stares down at me.

My skin flashes hot, and I try to quell the fire in my veins, thinking of ice and snow and cold marsh water even as I hold his wrist, keeping the dagger a few inches from my jugular. "Stop this. You'll regret it if you don't."

He chuckles, the vibrations spreading from his body to mine. "I can be a wolf too, Ansa."

My grip tightens as he tries to push his dagger closer to my throat.

"Thyra doesn't want what's best for us," he says. "She

only wants the power, but she doesn't want to fight."

I let out a startled laugh. "She's ready enough to fight *you*."

"But not the Kupari."

"Who cares about that right now? She's more focused on keeping us whole in Vasterut! Who are you fighting for, Aksel? Yourself? Your family? Or someone else?" Jaspar's green eyes flash in my mind.

His only response is to force the blade toward my skin. Panic strikes hard inside me—he's intent on a killing blow. Aksel, with whom I've joked and tussled since childhood, who was one of the first to congratulate me after I became a warrior, who I sat next to in quiet support after he lost the fight to be part of the first wave, both of us staring out at the water and craving what lay across it. And it turns out it's us, fighting for our lives.

"Stop." I gasp as the iron bites at my throat. The pain hits me like a bolt, traveling straight down my spine, awakening heat like I've never known before. I stare up at Aksel, my vision going red, lighting his face with an orange glow, enough to see his eyes going wide and his mouth dropping open in a grimace.

"Your eyes!" he cries.

Taking advantage of his surprise, I roll onto him as he tries to escape me. "Tell me why you're so intent on killing," I say as my breath rushes searing from my mouth. "Whose lies have you chosen to believe?"

Aksel screams, and I keep one hand wrapped over his wrist while I clamp my fingers around his throat. He thrashes beneath me and makes a strangled sound, and I abruptly realize his skin is blistering, sizzling, splitting, and steaming. I throw myself backward, frantically trying to calm my panicked heartbeat, but the pain in my neck, the hot trickle of blood over my throat, the sight of Aksel writhing in the sand, clawing at his chest and stomach . . . The curse will not go quiet, no—it rages and roars. My own flesh burns and stings, and then ice rushes up, making me shudder and ache. This curse works its will, though I try in vain to muscle it down.

Aksel's eyes go so wide that I half expect them to pop out of their sockets as his body arches up and begins to smoke. Then, slowly, it sinks back to earth, curling in on itself. He's still moving, but I realize it's not because he's alive, not anymore.

It's because I've cooked him from the inside, drawing his muscles taut with blazing heat.

I sag onto the sand, pressing my palm over the wound in my throat. The air is filled with the scent of cooked meat, and I stare up the bluff toward the camp. I've just done it again. Lost control. Killed one of my own. Aksel sealed his own fate when he drew my blood, but if anyone sees this, they'll know I'm cursed. Shaking, I lick my finger and hold it up, nearly crying with relief as I realize the wind is blowing toward the lake.

Aksel lies, still smoking, in a pathetic ball. His messy hair is gone, and his scalp is a charred dome.

"Aksel?" a voice shouts from up the beach, jolting me from my dazed pondering.

It's Sander.

I leap to my feet and hook my fingers beneath Aksel's rigid, greasy shoulders, and I haul him backward, further behind the outcropping that hid him from me in the first place. I can hear Sander's footsteps on the pebbles—he's not trying to be stealthy. He shouts Aksel's name again.

My heart is thumping like the wings of a dragonfly. Sander is close to Jaspar. He already suspects me of witchcraft. If he sees that I've killed Aksel—and how—the entire tribe could turn against me . . . and Thyra, too. My fear rises hot inside me, and a glow at my sides draw my gaze down.

My fingertips are dripping fire.

"Aksel! Where in heaven are you?" Sander shouts. He's just on the other side of the outcropping. I have to decide how to handle this. I have to get control of this evil force inside me before I kill again.

Unless Sander is also Jaspar's wolf. That would change things.

I clench my fists in an effort to contain the curse-fire. Then I step from the shadows.

CHAPTER ELEVEN

Sander freezes when he sees me emerge from behind the outcropping. I inhale the thick night air, wishing for a cold wind to blow the stink of cooked flesh out over the water.

Sander's short, dark hair flutters as the breeze gusts over him. He squints at me in the darkness. "Are you bleeding?"

I glance down at my tunic, the collar of which is stiff with my blood, dried under the heat of my curse. "Just a little." I whip out one of my own daggers. "I lost my footing while I had it unsheathed."

His eyebrows shoot up. "And nearly cut your own throat?"

"The trail is treacherous in the shadows."

"Such truth," he says, his voice thick with suspicion. "Have you seen Aksel?"

"Not since he went away to pout like a child." The heavier my conscience, the easier the lies flow, it seems.

Sander chews on the inside of his cheek for a moment. "Any chance he slipped and fell onto your dagger too?"

My laugh is ugly and loud. "He always was a little clumsy." My stomach turns as I catch a whiff of him. "But I'm sure he's around here somewhere."

Sander steps toward me like he means to go around the outcropping, and I move to block him. "He's definitely not back there. I've just walked along that stretch. I was the only living soul for miles." I smile and tuck my arm—the one Aksel sliced as he attacked me—behind my back. "Why are you looking for Aksel? Thyra sent *me* to find him."

"I was concerned for him. He acted very rashly by the fire."

I squint at his face, trying to read it in the dim light of the winking stars. "I think Thyra would rather have such things said to her face than whispered behind her back. Though it seems there's quite a lot of that going on."

He doesn't take my bait. "Of course she prefers open challenge, especially from someone like Aksel. It allows her to prove her mettle in front of everyone, at his expense."

I scoff. "What would you have done?"

"Avoid the need to prove myself in the first place."

"Are you still doubting Thyra? Has Jaspar drawn you into his nest of intrigue?"

"Jaspar just wants what we all want. Victory." Sander's chin juts out. "If our tribes are united, we'll be able to attack Kupari in the spring."

"And no doubt he sees Thyra as a barrier, especially now that she's gained the loyalty of Edvin's closest comrades."

"You said that. I didn't."

My fists are tight balls, holding the flames inside, but just barely. "But you're thinking it."

He sighs. "I don't know what I'm thinking, Ansa. Everything has fallen apart. I just want to be part of something powerful again. And I'm not one for intrigue. I like things simple. Don't you?"

"Of course. But that doesn't mean I'll cozy up in the arms of a traitor."

"Jaspar told me there's more to that story than we were told." He carves a divot in the sand with the heel of his boot. "He hinted that Thyra was involved."

I groan. "You sound just like Aksel. Maybe Jaspar's simply trying to sow doubt among us, to undo the work Thyra has done."

"Or maybe we were lied to!" He shakes his head and turns to look out on the water. "Don't you ever wonder if Thyra's hiding something from us? Nisse is a strong leader, Ansa. One of the best strategists we've ever had. Lars listened to him."

"Lars listened to Thyra, too!"

"Thyra was always trying to poke holes in their plans, though. Nisse and Lars weren't at odds."

"But Nisse wanted the chair for himself."

He turns to me, regarding me quietly for a moment before saying, "Or someone wanted Lars to believe he did."

"This is dangerous talk, Sander. You'd better be sure before you repeat it."

"I'm only sure of one thing, Ansa. I want to be strong again. I want Kupari blood on my weapons. I want them to suffer for what their witch queen did. I want to see her head on the end of a spear."

"So do I," I say, remembering her terrible white face. It's her fault that Hulda and Aksel are dead. Killing her may be the only thing that can set me free.

"And I'll serve the chieftain who can deliver me to her threshold."

"We already do." I hope.

"What if Thyra doesn't have the stomach for it?" he asks, speaking my fear aloud. "Every time it comes up, she's the one reminding us of what happened, instead of planning to change the outcome next time."

"She's never said she didn't want to defeat them. She's only urged caution so we don't get decimated again. Jaspar and Nisse should be grateful." I stare at his sharp profile in the moonlight. "And so should you. It's only by the grace of heaven that we survived the first invasion."

"Maybe for me. But I think you might have survived for a different reason."

Everything in me goes still. "I have no idea what you're talking about."

"Yes, you do." He looks at me out of the corner of his eye. "The witch left her mark on you."

"You've gone soft in the head."

He scratches at the dark, short beard that has grown during our journey. "I don't want to fight you. But I will if you've become our enemy."

I close my eyes as the fire inside me rages, hungry and hot. I hold it tightly, but my control is slipping again. "If you spread lies, I will kill you."

Sander's footsteps crunch on pebbles as he backs away from me. "So you can add me to the list?"

My eyelids pop open, my eyeballs hot and aching. "Is that an accusation?"

"I don't have proof yet, apart from the fact that you've just threatened to murder me."

"I threaten to murder people all the time. How is that proof?"

"If my concerns are baseless, why would you want to silence me?"

"Do you have any idea what we're walking into in Vasterut? Any rumor you spread will weaken us, no matter how unfounded. And you're already doing exactly that— echoing stupid stories to frame Thyra and absolve Nisse, just to make it easier for him to take us over!"

"So I should stay quiet and let the witch's poisoned dagger inch closer to the throne of Vasterut, and the home of all the remaining Krigere warriors? Does Thyra suspect that the witch has tainted you? Would she want you at her side if she did?"

"I would never hurt our people!" I shriek, cold tears brimming in my eyes as I realize I already have. First ice and now fire. The storm on the Torden was nothing compared to the gale raging inside my body. "Sander, you need to get away from me."

"Why, Ansa? What will you do if I don't?"

I sink into a squat and wrap my arms around my knees. "Nothing," I whisper. The weight of death threatens to pull me straight into the ground. "Nothing. I just need to be by myself right now."

Sander looks over his shoulder. "Too bad. Greetings, Chieftain," he calls out, stepping toward the shore to reveal Thyra striding toward us, a torch upraised.

Thyra catches sight of me and begins to jog. "Ansa, are you hurt?"

Sander snorts. "She claims to have had a little mishap with her own dagger."

Thyra's eyes go wide. "By accident—or on purpose?"

Sander looks both surprised and troubled as he gazes down at me, and I bury my head in my knees to hide my burning cheeks. "I didn't realize—" he begins.

"Sander, go back to camp," Thyra says in a flat voice. "I'll deal with Ansa."

I raise my head to see her catch his arm as he walks by. "Think about your loyalties, Sander," she says quietly. "Whatever happens now, please know that I love our tribe, and I will die before I allow harm to come to them. You and Ansa are my only first-wave warriors, and I will not succeed without your strength—and your discretion. My sister is waiting for you in the eternal fields. In her name and memory, if not in my father's, stay with *me*."

Sander swallows hard as Thyra raises the specter of his lost, beloved mate. "I hear you, Chieftain," he says hoarsely, then sets off through the dark. Something tells me he needs some time by himself now too.

Thyra squats beside me as soon as his footsteps fade away. Her fingers slide into my hair, and my eyes fall shut as I treasure her touch. "What happened?"

I press my forehead to my knees again. "Nothing. I'm just tired."

She puts her arm around me, gathering me to her. I feel her lips graze my temple. "I know you've had to work harder than all of us, and that your burden is great. But I also know you're more than strong enough."

My throat is so tight that I can't breathe. "I'm trying." It comes out of me broken and rasping.

She touches my elbow, near the shallow gash across my forearm, and I flinch. "Did you really slip on the rocks?"

"You doubt me?"

Her arms drop away. "I didn't say that. But before we left the northern camp, you seemed intent on—"

Killing myself. "It was an accident, Thyra, I swear."

She gives me a long, questioning look. "As you say. And Aksel?"

I shoot to my feet. "I lost track of him—he must have kept to the rocks. No footprints. Let's go back to the camp."

But Thyra doesn't follow as I start to walk back the way she came. Instead, she looks up and down the beach . . . just as the wind shifts. The stink of burned flesh makes her grimace. "Ugh. What *is* that?"

My heart seizes. "Oh, probably from the camp—"

"No, it's close by," she says, taking a step toward the place where Aksel's corpse lies.

I grab her arm. "But nothing we need to—"

She pulls herself from my grip. "Aksel might have been stupid enough to make a fire nearby," she whispers, drawing her dagger and creeping toward the rocks.

I lunge between her and the evidence of my crime. "He's not back there! I already looked."

Her eyes narrow, and then she tucks her face against her upper arm as the smell surrounds us, heavy and bitter. "What's causing that stench, then?"

"It's . . . um . . ." I pause a moment too long, and her expression hardens. She pushes past me, her torch held high, and I'm too paralyzed to stop her.

My stomach turns as I hear her gagging with disgust. She returns to me, spitting onto the sand and looking like she's about to lose her dinner. "You did this," she says slowly.

"No, I swear!"

"No?" Her voice rises high, matching the blaze of her eyes. "You don't even look surprised, Ansa! You know exactly what lies behind that rock."

My lips tingle cold with the realization that she's caught me out, that my mountain of lies has crumbled to dust in the space of a moment.

"Why would you do something like that?" she says in

a choked voice. "I can understand meeting him blade to blade, but why did you have to—"

"He attacked me!" I gather enough courage to look up at her, and immediately wish I hadn't. "I didn't mean to."

"But you said you could control the curse." She's staring at me with that wary look in her eyes again, as if I'm a stranger. "You killed Hulda, too, didn't you?"

The sob wrenches itself out of me as Hulda's frozen eyes rise in memory. "Please, Thyra—"

"No." The sound lashes from her like the bite of a whip. She backs away from me. "You lied to me, didn't you? You've been lying this whole time."

"I didn't want you to think—"

"That you murdered an innocent slave in cold blood? Or—and I find this hard to believe—did she threaten you somehow?"

"N-no," I stammer.

"Hulda was Kupari. Did you do it as revenge, to get back at the witch for what she did to you?"

"What?" I hold my arms out, but it only causes Thyra to move further away. She looks disgusted, the back of her hand pressed over her mouth. "I had no intention of harming Hulda!"

"But you did, didn't you? Only with ice that time." Her voice is dead. Emotionless. "And now you've killed Aksel with fire. Did he really draw first blood?"

"Yes," I shout, my voice cracking. "How can you question that?"

"Because you *lied* to me," she roars. "Right to my face! Knowing what was at stake, knowing where we were going, knowing that I was *depending* on you, you lied to me. Your *chieftain*." She rolls her eyes. "Not just once, either. Over and over again, it seems. And I ate your lies like honey cake." Her voice shakes as she adds, "I was so eager to believe."

"I *can* control it, Thyra. I'm getting better every day," I say.

"How can you say that, when Aksel's roasted corpse lies only feet away from us? His death had to have taken minutes, Ansa, not seconds. He was cooked, not devoured by sudden flames. Either you *were* controlling it in the most evil way, or you were out of control for longer than you want to believe. Which is it?"

Evil. My stomach clenches and I nearly heave as I recall the way Aksel clawed at his belly as his innards boiled. I had no idea how to stop it—the enemy inside me was in control. "It won't happen again. I swear on my life. I'll kill myself before I let it happen again. Please."

I take a step toward her, but stiffen when she leaps out of my reach. And when the flames of her torch flare, she yelps and hurls the stick into the lake, as if she thinks I would use it against her. Hot tears burn their way down my cheeks.

"It's been you all along," she says raggedly. "When the fires flare. It wasn't just the ice on the marsh."

"I helped you," I say with a sob. "I saved all those children, all those andeners. They would have perished in the marsh if not for me. You couldn't have saved them."

"I thought you were controlling it, but now I see what a

fool I was." She stares at me with a cold kind of fear. "We all could have ended up like Hulda, though. We're lucky you didn't kill every single one of us."

"I did everything I could to keep that from happening!"

Thyra nods slowly, never taking her eyes off me. "And I'm grateful for that. But it doesn't erase your lies."

"So I make one mistake"—I grit my teeth as her eyebrow arches—"*two* mistakes, one of which was to kill a warrior who had ambushed me with the full intention of cutting my throat, and now you abandon me?"

"I'm doing no such thing!"

"Really?" I walk toward her, and she backtracks.

"Nothing I do is because you killed Aksel! Or even Hulda." Her face is solemn and exquisite in the starlight reflected off the water, so beautiful that it's splintering me. "But you lied to me, Ansa. The reason why doesn't matter. We were alone that night in the forest after Gry accused you. No one else would have heard the truth. It was just *you* and *me*, as it is now. You could have trusted me. Confided in me. And instead you put a wall between us, to protect *yourself*."

I swipe my nose on my sleeve. "Please," I say, my voice thick with tears. "I'll never do it again. Don't push me away."

Her smile is unfocused. Like a fog off the lake. "When you've done it once, the way becomes easier. The paths unblocked, the hesitance rubbed away with repetition."

Cyrill said that to us, as he prepared us for our first raid. He was talking about killing.

I never thought one simple lie could be just as deadly. Except it wasn't just one lie.

"But I had never deceived you before that moment," I say in a low voice. "It's just that with everything that was happening—"

"When it is difficult, your decisions mean the most. Then we discover what we're made of."

I want to howl with rage as she quotes her own father, standing on the deck of our longship just before we pushed out onto the Torden. The night swirls with a rush of hot and cold air. Thyra staggers backward under the force of it, a look of betrayal and shock on her face.

I sink to my knees, my fists pressed to my thighs, shaking as I try to hold my curse captive. "Kill me, then, if you hate me so much. Just don't banish me from the tribe."

Her expression crumples. "I *wish* I could hate you," she says in a strained voice.

Hope glows warm in my belly, like a flame on a windy night, precious and fragile. "You know I'm yours. You know I would never do anything to hurt you."

She winces, her eyes bright with pain. "You already have, Ansa." She holds up her hands as my arms rise, trying once again to reach her across the chasm. "Enough. I'm not banishing you. We will tell the others that Aksel ran away after being rebuffed by both me and Jaspar. You will tell everyone that you found his tracks along the shore, headed back to the north. I will say the same."

"They'll ride after him."

"No, they won't. He was one of our weakest warriors, and he had proven himself unstable. Jaspar will let him go. He's too eager to reach Vasterut to pursue a broken warrior."

"What about Aksel's body?"

She takes a step forward, her expression smooth. Cold. "We bury him in the stones. It won't be visible from the bluff if anyone looks down. And then we will go back to camp, tell our story, go to sleep, and get up tomorrow as if nothing has happened. You will not tell anyone of your curse, and you will use every ounce of power and will you possess to suppress it. This is for your safety and that of *every* member of our tribe. Do you understand?"

I understand so many things, each piece of knowledge a blade of sorrow inside me. "Yes."

She stares at me for a long moment, letting me feel the twist of her weapon, the way my heart gives way beneath her will. "Good. Let's get to work."

CHAPTER TWELVE

I do not sleep at all. Thyra walked away from me the moment we reached the camp again. She stared at me coolly while she slowly and deliberately poured water over her hands, rubbed them together, and dried them on her cloak. Perhaps it was just to clean the stink of burned meat from her skin, but I could not help but think she was washing me away too, the way she's touched me, the bond we shared, my place at her side. When she was finished, she crossed to the other side of the dying fire and laid her blanket next to Bertel.

I am curiously numb as I rise from my blanket and roll it around my spare weapons and bloodstained tunic. My muscles ache with fatigue, and my steps are heavy as I fall into line behind Thyra and a group of warriors who are loyal to her—today Sander is among that group, and Jaspar hikes at the front with the warriors he brought from Vasterut. However, they seem more like one tribe, the distance worn away by the shared journey, talking and teasing as we slowly make our way up a sandy trail that winds along between grass and forests and dunes. The sand is marbled with black, and the Torden is smooth and blue as the sun arcs over us. The wind bites at our ears and the tips of our noses; the snow will come any day. In a fog, I find myself wondering if the weather is the same here as it is in our northern camp. I hadn't lived there all my life, but it is the only place I truly remember thinking of as home.

The realization that I will never see it again brings on another numbing wave that fills my head from ear to ear. This is how it felt under the waves during the witch's storm. Knowing I was going to die, and only wondering how and when. It crosses my mind to simply decide and do it myself, but there is something in me now, hard and unmovable, that crushes that thought as soon as it forms. Maybe that's the curse being willful. Or maybe it's the tiniest spark of hope—Thyra didn't banish me, and it was well within her power to do so. Perhaps, if I'm strong enough, I can find my way back to her.

That's the thought that lifts one foot and places it in front of the other, that draws air into my lungs, lifts my chin, and points my gaze to the west. Somewhere out there is the Kupari peninsula, the home of the one who tried to strike us down. My heart roars at the thought of delivering her filthy witchcraft right back to her threshold.

Someone pokes my shoulder. "Obviously you're very busy daydreaming at the moment, but I was wondering if you wanted to ride out and see if we can't hunt up something for noonmeal. Several flocks of wild turkeys call the woods home."

I blink at Jaspar, who has dropped back into step with me. "Me? Why?"

He glances up at Thyra, who does not turn around and acknowledge us. "Well," he says quietly, "I get a bit bored when I hunt alone, and I do remember you are a keen shot with a bow."

"I haven't hunted in a while." I was focused on gaining my prizes and food through the plunder of two-legged prey.

Jaspar holds out a fine bow of black ash with a string of hemp. It's not very big—clearly made for small-game hunting and not for battle, which is good because that's the only kind I'm strong enough to shoot. "Will this do?"

I touch the taut string. "Maybe."

Jaspar gestures up to his horse, which has been freed of the load of rations it had carried at the beginning of our journey. He leans down to whisper in my ear. "Let's get out of here, just for a little while. It's our last chance before we reach the city, and I'm feeling lucky today."

I soak up the friendliness in his tone like a sunflower thirsty for water and follow him to his mount. I get on behind him, wrapping my arms around his lean waist. He might not be a bulky, muscular warrior, but he is solid and sure, and I hold on tight. He chuckles. "Either you don't trust my horse, or you've missed me."

I need it too much to let go. "I'll let you figure out which."

Thyra's request to get closer to him echoes in my memory, and I glance over my shoulder at her. As she so often does, she looks up as if she feels my gaze. But her eyes are solemn as she turns away to say something to Sander.

I fight the ache in my chest with hope—perhaps following her order to become Jaspar's confidante will help me regain her trust. "Are you eager to be back within city walls?" I ask as Jaspar gently kicks his horse's flanks and turns its nose toward a wood about a mile to the south.

"Yes and no. I had missed sleeping under stars, but it's hard to beat a stone hearth and fresh bread. You'll see when we get there."

"Will there be enough shelters for all of us?"

He shakes his head. "For tonight, the andeners and many of the warriors will camp outside the city. My father has been preparing for their arrival, so there will be food and blankets aplenty. I've already discussed it with Thyra. She and her most senior warriors will be welcomed into the castle. I hope you'll find it to your liking."

I'm not sure she'll count me among that group, but I don't admit that to Jaspar. Instead, I close my eyes as his wood-smoke-scented blond hair brushes at my face, blown by the chilly breeze. I don't know if I'm causing it or not.

Jaspar steers his mount to the edge of the trees. He loops its reins around a branch, and then we're striding into the damp and cool of the forest, spongy needles beneath our boot soles and the sharp smell of pine sap in the air. We've just reached a clearing split down the middle by a burbling stream when Jaspar says, "You wear your unhappiness like a veil today, Ansa. I can barely see anything else when I look at you."

"Nonsense. I'm just thinking about what lies ahead."

"You're a terrible liar. You always have been."

I scrub my hand over my face. "What do you want, Jaspar?"

"How has she rewarded your loyalty, Ansa? I want to know. A few days ago I could have guessed, but this morning . . ."

"Since when is this your concern?"

He turns around, his green eyes reflecting the colors of the pines. Muted and deep. "Whether you wanted me or not, you've always been my concern, ever since you were brought to our camp by one of my father's warriors. His andener didn't want you as a slave because you were too fierce, almost feral. But Lars and my father recognized that you had a warrior's spirit. That was when they gave you to Einar and Jes to raise. That was when you became Krigere."

I touch my short hair as I remember Jes drawing his knife and cutting my matted, filthy locks from my head. "The first time they put a weapon in my hand, I couldn't wait to use it."

His grin says he remembers the moment. "I wouldn't be alive if that cursed dagger hadn't been completely dull. But I think that was the instant that linked us forever."

"I tried to kill you!"

"You *chose* me. Of all the warriors in training under that roof, you came for me. Not Sander. Not Aksel or Tue. And not Thyra."

"I don't even remember who else was there." Just blurred faces with bright eyes, surrounding me, closing me in. A test of my courage, but I didn't feel brave. I felt desperate. I had been alone and scared for so long that I didn't realize things had changed at first.

He touches the sheath strapped to my forearm. "Dismiss it if you want. I never will. I may have been a mere boy with barely eleven years under my belt, but I knew it was important even then. And we have had other moments since—you can't deny it."

My skin flashes hot when I see the passion in his eyes, the same heat I felt the moment before he drew his blade across my skin and marked me forever. "We don't know each other, Jaspar. Not anymore."

"I know you love Thyra. That, at least, hasn't changed." He gives me a sad smile. "It doesn't stop me from craving your happiness and your victory."

"I'll be happy when I know our tribe is not in danger of extermination."

He chuckles and shakes his head. "Why would we have gone to the trouble of bringing all of you on this journey if we intended to slaughter everyone? Please. I had enough warriors with me to raid the camp. But we are tribe, Ansa, whether you sense it or not."

"Tribe," I whisper. His words are a balm, soothing my fear.

"My father needs you. All of you." He leans forward, placing his palm on the tree behind me, bowing his head over mine. "And perhaps especially *you*."

My blood slides cold through my veins as the fear returns. "What?"

He points to the bandaged wound on my neck, and the other on my forearm. "Something tells me Aksel didn't walk away from our camp." I open my mouth to speak, but he holds up a finger. "As far as I'm concerned, you have done your tribe a service. Thyra would do well to be grateful instead of treating you as she has."

I don't know whether she would want me to admit to the killing or to keep up the pretense. We've walked far enough so that it's likely no one would volunteer to retrieve Aksel's charred body, but I can't be sure. "Whether I killed Aksel or didn't, he's gone, and his mother grieves. I wouldn't say that's a service to our tribe."

Jaspar grabs my arm, pressing his thumb over my kill marks. "Shall I give you another scar, Ansa?" he asks, his voice low and rough. "Since it seems Thyra didn't offer. It certainly appears that you've earned it."

My breath rasps from me, harsh and frigid. "No need." I pull myself out of his grip.

Jaspar gives me a shrewd look. "Sander has come to me with a very interesting theory about Aksel's *departure*. Would you like to hear it?"

I duck under Jaspar's arm as frost creeps down my neck

and blooms across my back. Behind me, Jaspar shudders. But if I run from him now, it's as good as admitting guilt. "Sander's been jealous of me ever since I took his ear for a trophy," I say as breezily as I can manage. I peer up at the sun through a break in the trees, welcoming its warmth, and feel it stroke my cheek only a second later.

I turn to see Jaspar watching me. "Sander is a good warrior, Ansa. He hates the idea of defeat, and you gave him one of his most memorable. But I think, in a way—and though he would never tell you this—he's grateful for it. You taught him an important lesson that day. Never turn your back on an enemy who isn't well and surely dead."

I scoff. "So he's telling you lies about me out of gratitude? Of course. Why didn't I guess?"

"Ah. You're denying even though you don't yet know what he said. Interesting."

I start to walk back toward our horse. "If this is why you brought me here, we'd best get back. I'm not clever enough to play your game."

He catches my arm as I pass. "He said the witch queen did something to you, and that you're trying to hide it," he says, holding tight as I try to jerk my arm away. When I reach for my knife with my other hand, he grabs my wrist. "Hear me out! Please!" he says as I take a step back to slam my knee into his groin.

"I'm not hiding anything," I say, my voice barely more than a growl.

"Remember what I said about your prowess at deception?"

I stop struggling as the ice creeps up over my shoulders, as it starts to reach for Jaspar. My nostrils flare as I draw a deep breath. Concealing Aksel's death was one thing, but if I kill Jaspar, our entire tribe will be slaughtered to pay for the affront. "Fine," I tell him. "Let me go, and I'll talk about it."

He releases my arms but stays close. "That's all I wanted."

"When we made it back to shore after the witch-made storm, I began to have dreams. Terrible dreams."

Jaspar stares down at me. "And?"

"And—that's it."

"Sander said you were struck by lightning on the Torden and survived."

"It's a miracle any of us survived that journey home."

"He said you caused two shelters to burn."

"Yes. At night. When my tortured flailing must have knocked a burning ember or log from the fire."

"Sander thinks you *created* the fire."

With everything inside me, I focus on the sincerity of my words. "I did. By sleeping too close to it, apparently, and scattering cinders over sleeping blankets."

"He told me that you attacked him, and your touch was so cold it burned his skin."

I shake my head. "Like all of us, Sander is trying to make sense of what happened, and of what the witch has done to our tribe. Do you really believe I can create fire and ice at a whim? What kind of witchcraft would *that* be?"

"The useful kind," Jaspar says simply.

My mouth drops open. "Is that how they think in Vasterut? Because among our people, witchcraft is only useful for getting oneself stoned and speared in the fight circle. And maybe that's Sander's goal, to see me defeated that way."

"It's not, Ansa. He only wants to understand what he's seen, to keep his tribe safe—and to take his revenge on the witch queen."

I throw my hands up. "I want the same thing! No one so evil should be allowed to live."

"But is it possible to use witchcraft like hers for good? I've heard stories of her power from the Vasterutians. She keeps the entire Kupari kingdom warm in winter. The gardens of Kupari flourish even when the lake is frozen solid. And she keeps the brush fires away from their gates. She wields ice and fire to take care of her people. She meets their every need."

"No wonder they're all so soft and happy. Do they do anything for themselves?"

"Apart from hoarding their riches, you mean? Really, it's an excellent question. From what I hear, there is no Kupari *army*," he says. "We are almost certain of it."

"A few minutes before she struck that day on the Torden, we were joking about her lack of a navy. It turned out she didn't need one."

"But if we could understand her magic, perhaps we'd have a chance to defeat her." His eyes are bright now. Eager. "That knowledge would be valuable."

"I wish I could help you."

"Are you saying Sander is telling me stories?"

"I'm saying Sander has lost everything. His chieftain, his war, his home, his pride. Like me, he has no family—and his dream of creating one died with his mate last winter, just weeks after you, his closest friend, were banished along with your father. Sander has nothing left except his weapons and his wits. Perhaps he's using them to gain your trust and enhance his status with Nisse by feeding you lies. Interesting ones, but lies all the same."

"So you're saying you do not control the wind, or the chill in the air? You didn't make fire?"

I laugh, so relieved as the ice in my veins melts. "Do you hear yourself speaking right now?"

He gives me a keen, searching look. Then he grins, though I swear it doesn't reach his eyes. "Sadly, yes. It does sound rather unhinged."

"Please don't make Sander face consequences for this," I say, praying he will let this go. "He's suffered enough. But if you can, encourage him to turn his mind toward serving his chieftain instead of telling unfounded tales. If you care for him as your friend, help him keep wise."

Jaspar takes a step back from me, his gaze drifting from my boots up to my face. "You could challenge him to the fight circle for this." He chuckles. "Maybe you can claim his other ear!"

I can't have his blood on my hands. Not now. "As Thyra says, we need every sword arm." I smile. "And ear."

"My father still speaks highly of Sander." He pushes his long hair away from his brow. "I'll tell him to hold his tongue if he comes to me again." He gives me a rueful look. "And here I was sure I understood why you were looking so pale and miserable. Now I'm back to wondering what has happened between you and Thyra."

"Nothing," I mumble.

Slowly, as if he's afraid I'll flinch away, Jaspar reaches up to slide his fingertip along my hairline, smoothing my coppery short hair against my skin. "I stand by what I said. You deserve so much in return for your loyalty. You would be welcomed into any tribe."

"Thyra is a good chieftain." My voice falters as I think of the coldness in her eyes this morning. "I'm her wolf."

The corner of his mouth lifts. "You're only illustrating my point, Ansa." He gazes down at me, his green eyes full of so many feelings that I can't read a single one. He leans in, slowly, until his mouth is only a few inches from mine. My heart beats frantically as I inhale the scent of sweat and leather and pine. "And now . . . ," he whispers.

Part of me wants to beg him to kiss me, just to make me forget the taste of Thyra. And part of me knows that nothing could ever erase it. "Now?"

"It's time to hunt." He pulls his bow from his back, then grins at me. "What did you think I was going to propose?"

I let out a relieved chuckle and shake my head before happily following him across the clearing. As much as I'm grateful for Jaspar's light heart and teasing manner, though, I refuse to let my guard down.

Something tells me that hunting is what he's been doing all along.

CHAPTER THIRTEEN

My very first raid was on a settlement along the northwestern shore of the Torden. A large tribe of people who called themselves the Svalerne, recently migrated from the west, not realizing they'd entered our hunting territory and that they were our chosen prey. They had shelters like ours, mud and thatch. Apart from our own camp, which grew by the year as distant tribes united under Lars, it was the largest gathering of bodies I'd ever seen.

Until today.

The sun is setting as we reach the city wall of Vasterut. Made of stone and wood and mud, it is higher than three men standing on each other's shoulders, and I cannot see the end of it once it comes into view. It blocks the sight of the shore and the lake. We stare in awe until Jaspar says, "There is no wall between the city and the lake." He laughs as if he can't believe it—they had no defenses against attack over water. "Kupari is the same, I hear. Only fishing vessels guard their harbor."

"And a witch who controls the clouds," Thyra reminds him.

Jaspar's warriors grumble, but he simply smiles. "All challenges can be overcome with the right strategy."

We reach a place where the trail meets another, this one wide enough so that several of us can walk shoulder to shoulder. "This is a road," Jaspar says. "They are made for carts and horses, and the south has many—they connect their kingdoms this way, for trade."

We all look up and down the wide path, which is rutted with the tracks of wooden wheels. "They provide us trails we can use for raiding?" Preben says, his voice full of amused skepticism. "I like this place already." Our laughter reaches the sky.

I watch Thyra, who is wearing a small smile, but her brow is furrowed. "How different this place is," she says softly to no one in particular.

Jaspar points up ahead to the gate, where a massive door hangs open like a giant mouth. "And here we are—welcome to Vasterut, warriors. The city lies at our feet."

We march toward it, and my heart kicks in my chest like it wants to run. As we reach the gate, the smells overwhelm. Human and animal waste. Rotting vegetables and fish. Next to me, Sander curses in a thick voice, pressing his hand over his nose. "What is this hell?" he mutters.

"This is twelve thousand people living in close quarters like animals in a pen," says Jaspar. "We don't exactly trust the locals, so the door stays closed. No one but Krigere allowed in or out."

We clear the gate, and my stomach lurches. It seems like all twelve thousand Vasterutians have gathered to watch our arrival. An eerie silence hangs heavy in the air, along with greasy smoke from the torches that line the city wall and the road. Shelters taller than any I've ever seen jut up from the ground on either side of us, and faces peer from windows, from the muddy spaces between buildings, from doorways. Many Vasterutians have darker skin like Bertel does, brown like turned earth instead of sandy pale, but among the crowd there are so many shades. Perhaps they are like the Krigere, then, accepting in their midst anyone who earns their way instead of relying on blood relation and sameness. Most of them have dark hair and dark eyes that stare with sharp wariness at our daggers and axes and spears and swords.

Jaspar has invited Thyra and her senior warriors to the front of the line, and I walk a step behind. She did not invite me close, but she did not tell me to stay with the andeners and the rear guard outside the city either. That would have required her speaking to me, though, something she hasn't done since last night, when she told me to keep my mouth shut and hide my curse at any cost. Now I am like smoke, drifting along, not sure whether she sees me or not. Jaspar, though—he sees me. He catches my eye as he gestures at the

Vasterutians. "Once their militia was destroyed and their king and his family executed in the square, they put up no resistance. You see they don't mind us so much. We protect them from other raiders."

Thyra's gaze slides from face to face. "Were they threatened by other raiders?"

Jaspar gives her a sly smile. "They certainly won't be now."

His warriors guffaw, and I fight a tangle of uneasiness. As Krigere, we raid. We take what we want. Weapons. Tools. As many horses as we can corral. Sheep and pigs and sometimes an ox. Sacks of grain, stores of wheat and barley. People, if they strike us as useful. But until now, I have never witnessed a tribe occupying another tribe like this. I suddenly realize that is exactly what Lars had in mind for Kupari. Would they have looked at us like this? Silent and stony-eyed? I'd never really thought about it—I hadn't thought past the fight, the victory, the knowledge that I was the conqueror. Is this what comes after? There is something in their faces that sends a chill down my spine. "Twelve thousand?" I say quietly. If they stood up and fought, their sheer numbers would be like a giant wave on the Torden.

Sander grunts. "None of them warriors. And Nisse had several hundred."

"Over a thousand, now that you're here," Jaspar calls out. "And we need every arm if we're to fulfill my father's vision."

"I am eager to hear about that vision," Thyra says drily, tossing me a questioning look.

"And so you shall!" Jaspar gestures up the road, which winds through the stinking, silent city to where the biggest human-made pile of rocks I've ever seen blocks out the setting sun. The shelters of the people seem to fall away as we hike a gently sloping hill that levels out at the top. The city surrounds the rock shelter on three sides like mushrooms around a tree stump.

"This is the tower castle," Jaspar tells us. "This inner stake-wall around it provides some protection, as does the ditch around the perimeter."

"How did Chieftain Nisse overcome these defenses?" Preben asks as he stares up at the tower, which juts like a massive stone oak, the height of five shelters piled atop one another. "A siege?"

Jaspar shakes his head. "They thought the bluffs on the lakeside would protect them, but a few warriors simply scaled the rocks, crept inside, and executed their guards—they were soft and ill trained—before capturing the king and his family. It was like goats defending sheep."

I smile at the thought. "And then you opened the gates for the others. You took it by stealth."

Thyra gives Jaspar a cold, accusing look. "Something your father is particularly skilled at, as I recall."

"He's not the only one, is he, Cousin?"

Thyra glares at him, but Jaspar doesn't look the slightest bit apologetic. In fact, he squares his shoulders, his pride obvious. "My father saved countless warrior lives with his decision to attack with stealth. Lives that would have been wasted in an out and out frontal attack. We lost fewer than ten in the taking of this entire kingdom. Could Lars have done the same? Could you?"

Thyra's eyes flare with the insult. "Well, my father did prefer a bloody fair fight to a—"

"And here we *are*," Jaspar shouts, cutting her off. His smile is knifelike and the sweep of his arm sharp as he points to an opening in the stake-wall, presenting us with entrance to this castle. "Welcome to Chieftain Nisse's domain, *Chieftain* Thyra."

His words are pure warning, and I pray she heeds it. She looks so small between Preben and Bertel, both stout and broad-shouldered, standing in the shadow of this ugly stone monster that's about to swallow us. She does not cower, though, or show any indication that she is afraid of what will happen now. Instead, she gives him a breathtaking smile. "Many thanks. I look forward to meeting my uncle again, face-to-face."

Jaspar merely gestures for us to pass. We have entered a broad clearing lined on one side with shelters that are clearly meant for keeping animals, and on the other by a huge area marked off by square pegs of green wood hammered into the ground, strung with thick rope, with plenty of room around its perimeter for spectators, including a set of raised wooden benches.

It's a fight circle, but the ground within is smooth and untrodden.

"Niece!"

From the entrance to the stone tower strides a man I

haven't seen in a year, one that I never thought I'd see again when he rode from our northern camp, disgraced.

His long, graying blond hair is pulled back in a queue, away from his face, which is handsome in a weatherworn way, a fading echo of Jaspar's. But it's his eyes that overpower the rest, and they sweep over us like they see all, measure all. Like I always did when he noticed me during trainings or tournaments, my body seems to shrink back, as if to escape his assessment. I hold my breath, waiting to see how he will greet Thyra.

He raises his scarred hands, spreading his muscular arms in welcome, his wide smile radiating triumph and joy. "Thyra, I spent days believing that my brother *and* his heir had been wiped from the face of this earth by the witch of Kupari. I cannot tell you my relief at hearing you had survived."

Thyra remains still and stiff as he rushes forward and pulls her into an embrace, clutching her head to his broad chest, which is covered in a rich brown leather vest. When he releases her, she looks up at him with a surprised gaze. "How I want to believe that, Uncle."

He grasps her arms. "All grievances are washed away with time. I told Jaspar to do everything in his power to see your tribe made this journey whole. We must be united again."

She doesn't try to pull away from him, but I can tell by the tension in her posture that she wants to. "*If* that is what is best for my warriors. I have not yet decided."

"Nor should you." He puts his arm over her shoulders

and guides her toward the tower entrance. "Come inside and let your warriors settle their bones. Tonight we will feast. You will tell me what has happened, and I will tell you everything I have planned." He turns back to all of us. "Are you ready to stuff your bellies full of fresh meat and warm bread?" he shouts.

"Aye!" Jaspar and his warriors roar, along with several of ours. My stomach growls at the thought of bread, in spite of the wariness in Thyra's gaze as she looks us over. But then she jerks her head toward the tower, telling us to get inside.

I obey, along with all the others. Our trek to the south is over. All the Krigere warriors are within these walls or just outside the city, but as I see Nisse enclose Thyra in another embrace she cannot possibly want, I know our journey has only just begun.

We lay our blankets down in a dank collection of little chambers set along a stone walkway that Jaspar calls a corridor. My shoulders are hunched up around my ears the whole time—it feels like this whole place could cave in and crush us at any moment. All our own warriors look equally nervous, eyeing windows and arched doorways and staircases as if pondering escape. I share a chamber with four other warriors, one of them Tue, Aksel's best friend, who slinks around like a whipped dog, eyeing me with resentment. Thyra has taken Sander, Preben, and Bertel into her own chamber, and she seemed to be deliberately avoiding my gaze as she made the assignments.

Once again I wonder if I should be here at all. My curse has been quiet today, and I have done nothing to call attention to myself, just as she asked. Despite his questions this morning, Jaspar seems to have believed my lies, though he sought out my eyes numerous times this afternoon. Sander hasn't said a word or thrown me a single suspicious look all day. Things are as she wants them to be—I am just another warrior. I am nothing out of the ordinary. But she gives me no window or doorway back to her side.

Jaspar's words return to me over and over again—she has had my loyalty, and what has she done with it? She's treating me as one of her secondary warriors instead of her wolf, the one who has guarded her sleep and stayed by her side. The one she *kissed*. The one she was cruel enough to give hope to. She's discarded me like a bone. She's stripped away what was useful and tossed the rest. The hurt burns in me like a smith's fire, low and hot and utterly unquenchable. It doesn't help that the others look at me warily, no doubt wondering what has changed.

We wash the dirt from our faces and hands—not in a stream and not in the lake, but with water that comes from a metal tube stuck in the ground, which only flows when you crank up and down on a pump attached to its head. The others shiver, telling me that it feels like the water came from the heart of winter herself, but somehow, it simply feels cool to me. Thyra's skin is bright red as she splashes it over her cheeks and hair.

The others change into spare tunics if they have them,

but I remain in mine, as my other is stained with blood and smells like burned flesh and I'd prefer to keep my wounds from my fight with Aksel well covered. They itch and ache and are barely closed, and I clench my teeth as I tighten the sheaths on my forearms. We all keep our weapons strapped to our hips and calves and arms and backs by Thyra's order. Until she is sure of Nisse's intentions, she wants us to remain ready. We all know that fighting would result in death—they outnumber us three to one—and fewer than fifty of us are actually within the castle walls. But we would take a staggering number of Nisse's warriors down with us, and Thyra is obviously hoping the threat is enough to stave off a possible ambush.

Jaspar appears long after the sun sets and our bellies have begun to growl. "Chieftain Nisse waits in the grand hall!" The bright look in his green eyes softens when he looks at me, and he frowns and glances at Thyra, who is deep in conversation with Bertel. I close my eyes and look away. I don't want to see the confirmation in his expression that she has abandoned me.

We follow him down the corridor to another and another. This place reminds me of the ant mounds we used to dig up as children, searching for their queen so we could watch them scramble and scatter without her. Now I am part of such a mound, and I feel for those little ants, lost within their mazes.

The way is lit by torches, but it feels gloomy and close all the same. That is, until we reach a high arched doorway and enter a massive cavern of a chamber. Ten long wooden tables that seat at least fifty each are arrayed within, and at the front of the room, on a raised platform, is yet another long table. I look for where we will sit and realize that Nisse has already filled many of the places with his own warriors, but they have left spaces hither and thither to accommodate the few of us that Thyra brought inside the castle.

"How clever," Thyra murmurs as she realizes what he's done. United with former friends and kin they haven't seen in a year, her senior warriors' loyalties are about to be tested.

Jaspar starts to walk up to the head table, where Nisse stands, waiting for us to join him. Half the seats at his table are empty, allowing Thyra to have an equal number. She begins to call out names, the warriors she has drawn close. Sander, Preben, and Bertel are among them. I am not. As that group marches up to the table, Jaspar strides back to our group with a hard look on his face. "Ansa, please join us."

Thyra whirls around, and Jaspar smiles at her. "Ansa and I were only just renewing our friendship on the road," he says. "I assume you don't mind if we continue to do so over our meal?"

I can see the conflict in Thyra's eyes. She doesn't trust me. She doesn't want me near. Perhaps she's afraid I'll accidentally set fire to someone's hair or freeze the wine. Perhaps she's afraid of *me*. But if she refuses Jaspar, it is not only rude to him as the host—it's an open rejection of me, which makes her look weak and petty at a time she needs to be strong, with a united tribe. Everyone is watching us, including Nisse and his most senior warriors, who used to be high-ranking warriors in her dead father's tribe.

I believe that she regrets allowing me inside the castle, and another pang of resentment turns my stomach sour.

"By all means," Thyra says in a light voice. "I was about to call her name."

Liar, I want to scream. But Jaspar only grins. "Of course you were."

I force my shoulders back as I join the group headed for the table on the platform, and the maelstrom of emotion, ice, and fire inside me is temporarily quelled by the most amazing scent. In the center of the table is a whole hog, beautifully roasted and lying on a thick bed of greens, with a rosy apple in its gaping mouth. Surrounding it are wooden bowls piled with steaming carrots, sweet potatoes, and many other things I can't identify but that smell like I imagine heaven must. Fat skins of wine, piles of crisped turkey legs and brown loaves, so much of it that I can barely see the surface of the table. Around the table are a few Vasterutian attendants, who remain hunched against the wall watching Nisse with rapt attention, responding to the slightest wave of his hand. All except for one—a woman with cheeks round as plums and a wild spray of black hair who is eyeing all of us newcomers with a curious, bold stare.

I edge in next to Jaspar as we surround the table. Nisse is at one end and Thyra is at the other. Jaspar has guided us to the middle, right next to Sander, which is good because as angry as I am at Thyra, I cannot openly abandon her now by sitting on Nisse's side.

Nisse sweeps his arm over the feast, and then looks out over the assembled warriors with a rapturous smile on his craggy, blond-bearded face. "Blood and victory!"

"Blood and victory," we all echo, loud and sharp as we've done since childhood.

Nisse takes his dagger from his waist and plunges it into the pig in front of him. "Eat your fill, warriors!"

With a shout of appreciation, we dig our own daggers into the food, spearing loaves and chunks of meat before plopping them down in front of us. I could be mistaken, but the Vasterutians look vaguely disgusted, though I don't know why. We're sitting at a table, aren't we? I've never eaten at a table, but I've seen them in other camps and I know the council used to sit at one. I decide the Vasterutians are ignorant, and lucky to still be alive if they commonly look at Krigere warriors that way. But it becomes easy to ignore them after my first bite of hot food. I moan as the crust of the bread gives way under my teeth and fills my mouth with its nutty, chewy sweetness.

"I sent a hundred attendants to provide your other warriors and andeners with a similar feast outside the walls," Nisse says loudly, though there is no need, as none of us are talking. We're all too busy stuffing our faces.

Thyra looks up from her food. "They'll need better shelter as the frost descends. In the north they had roofs over their heads."

"And they will have the same here. Tomorrow they can take their pick of the shelters in the city. The ones already taken by my own warriors and their families are marked with blood on the wooden posts outside each, but you may have any of the others."

Thyra frowns and glances at the Vasterutian attendants. The round-cheeked one stares steadily back. "Aren't their shelters already occupied?"

Nisse nods as he sinks his teeth into a chunk of hog loin. "By Vasterutians, though. Merely tell them to leave and they will."

"And go where?"

He shrugs. "They find shelter elsewhere within the city. It's not your concern."

Thyra stares down at the small pile of bread and meat and vegetables in front of her, and Nisse laughs. "Oh, come, Niece. You've always had a softer heart than the rest of us, but I of all people know you have a spine of iron when necessary. You won't put the comfort of the conquered over your own andeners'."

Thyra is still except for her eyes, which rise to glare at her uncle with open disdain. "Haven't you taken the conquered as your own? Are they not tribe?"

The only people who remain slaves are those who refuse to join our tribe, or at least, that is how it goes when we raid. Our warriors look at Nisse with the question in their eyes. How does it work when you squat on the conquered lands?

Nisse does not seem troubled by the question. "I'm still considering the wisdom of accepting responsibility for them."

The round-cheeked attendant's eyes flare, but when she sees me watching her, she quickly bows her head.

Thyra brings a sweet potato to her lips. "They were worthy of cooking your food, apparently. Or was this prepared by your andeners?"

Nisse's smile becomes tight. "Our andeners are focused on the young ones, as they should be."

I sit back at this pronouncement. The andeners do many things, including making weapons and armor. Raising young ones is only a piece of how they care for us. I want to say this, but I don't have status at this table, and I'm afraid of drawing more disdain from Thyra.

"Your own widowed andeners will need to choose new mates," says the dark-haired warrior known as Sten, who is sitting on Nisse's left. He elbows the warrior on his other side. "Many of them are still young. Not bad to look at, either."

Bertel clears his throat and lays his gnarled hands on the table. "This is how you speak of grieving widows?" he mutters.

Thyra looks out over the tables in the hall. "Are so many of your warriors unpaired?"

"No," says Nisse. "They all have mates. But given our predicament, I'm sure you'll agree that each warrior should have more than one andener capable of breeding."

"What?" The word slices from Thyra like a blade, cutting through any pretense at courtesy. "That bond is a sacred one. The andeners are not cattle."

Nisse gives her a patient smile. "I never said they were. They are valuable members of our tribe, and they will be provided for so long as they contribute young."

Thyra swallows a bite, though it looks like it's choking her. "And the males?"

Nisse waves his hand. "They'll be able to find themselves shelter within the city, as will the older females. But our focus will be on the women of breeding age."

I think of the male andeners, some of whom were paired with male warriors, some with female. Those pairings typically don't produce young, but they often take in orphans or children who were raid prizes. That was what happened to me—Jes was paired with Einar, Lars's war counselor, and the two men treated me like their own. I grieved Jes's loss from fever two winters ago, especially because it left Einar grim and gray, but suddenly I'm glad he's not here to suffer this indignity.

Thyra shoots to her feet. "This is unacceptable. My tribe is a body, each part as important as the next. Thanks to your son, the widows weren't even allowed a chance to grieve their lost mates, and now you expect them to choose new ones?"

Sten jumps to his feet as well. "Show proper respect when you speak to our chieftain," he shouts, even as Nisse places a hand on his arm. He slowly sinks back down, glowering at

Thyra. "Jaspar tolerated this kind of talk on the road, but in the presence of our chieftain, it won't stand. You're in Vasterut now."

"How well I know that," says Thyra. Her gaze flicks to Jaspar. "Though I was given to believe we were all free to speak our minds."

Jaspar inclines his head. "You had been through a terrible ordeal. Who was I to constrain your words and veiled accusations, however unfounded?"

"My veiled accusations? How dare—" Thyra begins.

"Peace," shouts Nisse, so that all the warriors at the lower tables hear, for all have stopped eating and are staring at Thyra. "We'll discuss this later, in private. Let's talk of the things that unite us instead of those that divide us, hmm?"

He sounds so amused and condescending that Thyra's cheeks are pink as she lowers herself down. "I propose we talk of Kupari," he says when she's back in her seat.

Jaspar leans forward, and he and Sander share a look. For some reason, it makes me want to drive my dagger right through the back of Sander's hand. I lean forward between the two of them and glare at him as Thyra says, "If you wish."

"The word of Lars's defeat came to us only hours after it happened, from a merchant we waylaid along the coastal road. We convinced him it would be in his best interest to return to the city and supply us with information about what takes place there."

Thyra arches an eyebrow. "You have a spy in Kupari?"

191

"He has no trouble getting through the Kupari city gates if he brings wares to sell or trade. And he brought us the most interesting news a few days after the catastrophe. It seems the witch queen did not survive the assault either."

I gape at him, as do Sander and Thyra. "But she looked strong," I say, before I can stop myself. My mouth has gone dry and my heart is pounding.

If her death didn't break the curse, what will?

Nisse's mouth lifts into a warm smile, making me regret speaking aloud. "Little Ansa. I remember you when you barely rose to my elbow, and now look at you. A warrior." He glances at Jaspar. "My son has already told me you and young Sander there were in the first wave. You saw the witch yourself, eh?"

"All three of us did," I reply. "We were in the lead ship." The memory of the witch's face and Lars's charred corpse makes my insides swirl with ice and fire and hate.

"Then you can celebrate her downfall. Whatever she brought down on you, it killed her too."

I should be happy, but all I feel is defeated. Her death did not free me. I didn't even know it had happened.

Thyra blinks. "Are they without a ruler?"

"Now there's where it gets interesting," he says. "We aren't sure." He inclines his head toward our Vasterutian servants. "The citizens here know a good deal about Kupari and its special brand of witchcraft. They were full of stories of the queen. They call her the Valtia."

"We know this already," Thyra says.

"But do you know of the Saadella and the line of inheritance?"

I bow my head over my food, saliva filling my mouth. I know that word. *Saadella*. Hulda mentioned it just before I—

"I can see that you don't," Nisse continues. "She is, essentially, the princess of Kupari. She inherits the Valtia's magic after she perishes. She lives in their temple—the fortress of the Kupari at the tip of the peninsula—and is raised by their priests, all of whom are also magic wielders. This is what they call their witches."

"The queen is not the only Kupari with witchcr—magic?" Preben asks. His iron-gray beard is trailing in his goblet of wine, but he doesn't seem to notice. "How many of them have magic? Are they *all* witches?"

"No, no, my friend. Only a few, and they all reside in their temple, protecting the Valtia and her heir. We'll have to find a way to crush them if we mean to take the kingdom. If we train and prepare, we could even make a run at them before winter closes in!"

At this, all his warriors raise their daggers. "Blood and victory!"

Thyra waits until they return to their food before speaking again. "You have barely a thousand warriors and are already occupying one kingdom, the citizens of whom have *not yet been brought into the tribe*. Wouldn't attacking another, especially so soon, stretch you rather thin? Not to mention that these magic wielders have powers we don't understand." For the first time, she looks at me, brows drawn together, and I know she is thinking of my curse. "Why should we rush to attack, if our next defeat could wipe us out completely? Why not focus on solidifying the tribe and looking after their health and well-being?"

Nisse's eyes flash with a cold kind of irritation, but it's Sten who leaps to his feet again. "Enough! You've come to our table with *nothing*, Chieftain. You're a beggar in our land. You bring hungry warriors, a herd of widowed andeners, a history of treachery, and a heaping pile of cowardice!"

There is a grumble of agreement. Thyra rises slowly this time, all intention, even as my own heart pounds with dread. "Did you just call me a coward?" she asks, her voice low and deadly.

Such an insult cannot be ignored.

"And a stinking schemer," snaps Sten, his black hair wild about his unshaven face. "I've had a chance to observe your hesitation and weakness on our journey here, along with your sneaky attempts to win allies. That is *not* the way of a warrior." He spits at his feet.

"This is an outr—" Bertel begins, but Thyra clamps her hand onto his shoulder and his mouth snaps shut.

"You tolerate this kind of insolence, Uncle?" she asks. "What is *your* reply to Sten's accusation of treachery and cowardice?" There is something blazing in her eyes that tells me this is between her and Nisse, that it is an invitation to an entirely different conversation. Every warrior at the table is completely still as we wait, the tension wrapping fingers white-knuckle-tight over hilts.

Except for Nisse. He strokes his beard and gazes up at Sten. "I offer my warriors the freedom to make their own decisions. I'm sure, as a chieftain yourself, you understand."

My chest is full of ice as Sten smiles, sizing up Thyra like prey. "I challenge you," he says in a low voice. "We need a united tribe, and you're a sickness that has to be cut out."

Every pair of eyes is on Thyra, no doubt waiting for her to respond with outrage or protest. Instead she stares at her uncle for a long, cold moment, and then spreads her arms and gives her challenger a mocking bow. "Then you are welcome to try, Sten." Her lips curve into an exquisite, lethal smile. "And I'll take good care of your widow when you fail."

CHAPTER FOURTEEN

Nisse wears a puzzling expression as he rises from his chair—the corner of his mouth is quirked up and his eyes are wide. I don't know how to read it, so I glance at Jaspar, who has gotten up too. He gives me a steady, confident look and goes to stand next to his father, who says something quietly in his ear. Jaspar is stone-faced as he nods in response.

"Given the gravity of this challenge, I think it best we adjourn to the fight circle immediately," Nisse shouts over the low, nervous rumble that has filled the hall. A few of our warriors have jumped from their benches and are standing in the aisles between the long tables, while others remain seated with Nisse's warriors, watching those of us on the platform nervously. The Vasterutian attendants are frozen where they were when the challenge was issued, but Nisse waves over the woman I noticed earlier, the one with the round cheeks and dark, springy hair. "Halina, escort Chieftain Thyra and her chosen armorers to the fight chamber to allow her to prepare."

The woman bobs her head and beckons to Thyra before striding toward a door at the back of the room. I stand up, preparing to follow Thyra. She is wearing a confident smirk, and it looks so wrong on her face. Like a mask she has donned to hide what lies underneath. And I wish I knew what that was.

Sten is selecting his own armorers, two senior warriors who wear marks down their right arms and partway down their left. I remember them from tournaments before Nisse was banished—Elo and Flemming, who surely would have been part of Lars's first wave if they hadn't chosen a traitor for a chieftain. Now they stand shoulder-to-shoulder with the dark-haired warrior who wants to take Thyra's life. I wonder if they believe the vague accusations of treachery that have been spreading like poison of late. What exactly has Nisse been telling everyone? He acted as if he was glad to see Thyra just a few hours ago—and now he's allowing her to face a challenge from his own warrior?

When I turn back to Thyra, she's walking away with Preben and Bertel on either side of her. I take a step after her, fear and rage crackling hot under my breastbone, but a hand clamps over my shoulder. I rip myself away and turn to find Sander, his palm outstretched to grab me again. "Don't do anything foolish, Ansa," he says, casting a wary glance at Nisse, Jaspar, and Sten.

My eyes sting as I watch Thyra disappear through a doorway. "After she fought Edvin, she told me she wanted me to be there for her."

"She's allowed to change her mind."

"Preben and Bertel don't know her as well as I do," I say in a choked whisper.

Sander presses himself in beside me as the others get up from their chairs to head to the clearing outside this horrid tower, where the fight circle lies. "*Did*, you mean." He lets out an exasperated sigh when he sees the look of rage on my face. "Ansa, think. Right now she must focus. Should she really have to worry about you, too?"

"Worry about me? What—" My eyes narrow as I remember what Jaspar said about Sander's accusations that I am a witch.

Sander doesn't look the slightest bit cowed. "She told me to look out for you this morning, and that's what I'm doing. And as for what *you* should be doing? If you truly care for Thyra, stay quiet and let her win this challenge."

I swallow the lump that has formed in my throat, but I'm pathetically relieved to know I entered Thyra's thoughts this morning, and I know Sander's right about this. I offer a quick, stiff nod, and together we follow the others down the platform, to a larger arched doorway at the front of the cavernous room, and out into the night. The clearing is lit with hundreds of torches, and more are being brought as hundreds of warriors crowd toward the fight circle. Like last time, I use my small size to my advantage, sliding my way between muscular arms and broad shoulders until I am just behind the people at the front, who surround the roped-off circle. There are two empty areas on either side of the raised benches where Nisse, Jaspar, and many of the men and women who sat at his table are now settled.

Halina, the Vasterutian attendant, is standing by a smaller wooden door set into the base of the tower, and at Nisse's nod, she opens it. Thyra and her chosen armorers stride out. She's wearing a long-sleeved tunic that covers her scant kill marks, and a new leather belt. She has a dagger sheathed at each hip. Preben and Bertel hulk at her sides, glaring at Nisse and his entourage. He could stop this farce at any time, but it looks like he's settling in to watch.

It suddenly occurs to me he might have wanted this all along.

"Blood and victory, Chieftain Thyra," I shout, and my cry is answered by shouts from some of our warriors, who are scattered throughout the crowd. It's too tight to move, to allow us to gather in this den of rivals and band together, and I wonder if that's also Nisse's strategy, to separate and conquer. For all his talk of harmony and unity, is this how he will crush us?

I frown as Sten enters the clearing. He has chosen a spear for the fight and also has a large knife at his hip. As he is of lower status than Thyra, his weapons are not as fine, but he wears a confident smile as he waves to a large group of Nisse's warriors, who let out a raucous cheer as he reaches the fight circle. Nisse and Jaspar don't cheer, but they do offer Sten slight nods as he approaches the raised benches. Sten swings his arms, his muscles flexing as he loosens himself in preparation. He's only a few years older than Thyra. In his prime. Not like Edvin, who was an experienced warrior but didn't have the speed he needed to take her down. A flutter of icy unease pulls my hand to my stomach.

Thyra draws her weapons and rolls her wrists, testing the daggers' weight and feel. She smiles at something Bertel says, and I cannot help a pang of jealousy. I should be there with her.

But she doesn't trust me anymore. She let one little lie erase her memory of years of devotion. I blow out a shaky breath as the truth seeps in. If that was all it took to destroy any feelings she had for me, they can't have been strong to begin with.

Or maybe I'm not the only one who's been lying.

That stinging thought doesn't stop me from wrapping my hands over the rope that fences off the ring. I hold on with pale knuckles as she and Sten step over the barrier and enter the circle. This is it—only one will walk out. And once she has defeated Sten, I hope she and Nisse will deal with each other as equals. Maybe this will truly bury the talk of treachery. Perhaps he only needs to see what she has become in order to understand that he should listen to her and consider her council as he makes his plans. Perhaps, too, she will listen to him, and consider that an invasion of Kupari might be the one thing that could make us whole again. Or . . . me, at least. I cannot help but hope that someone there, perhaps one of the so-called magic wielders in the temple, will know how to lift this curse from me.

Sander finally reaches my side. "Sten has always been overconfident, and that makes him impulsive," he says, watching the warrior scuff his boots against the hard-packed earth. "Also, his left side is weak."

There he goes again, showing off all he knows. But in this case, I don't tell him to shut up. It's actually reassuring. We are all taught to wield with both hands, but not everyone can do it well. Thyra can, though. She is staring at Sten with a predator's focus, one leg back to allow her to drive forward with force. Like always, her opponent is taller and heavier, but female warriors are so accustomed to that difference that we count on it and know how to turn it to our advantage.

Nisse stands and raises his arms. "Like all challenges to chieftain leadership, this duel will be to the death." He looks down at Sten and Thyra. "As long as you both fight with honor, you are assured of your place on the battlefield of heaven. No fear."

"No fear," roars Sten, his dark eyes glittering with the torch flames as he begins to circle Thyra.

"No fear!" Nisse's warriors echo, and then the cheering and chants begin, urging the dark-haired warrior on to victory.

Thyra remains silent. She gives her own warriors nothing to echo, because she has already disappeared into wherever she goes when she fights, a place where she reigns alone. She grips the hilts of her blades as Sten clutches his spear and makes a few feinting jabs, not even flinching as he begins to inch forward. And when he strikes, she easily blocks, using the thick base of her dagger to knock the advancing spearhead off track. Sten draws back and lunges again, and Thyra shoves the shaft to the left. He stumbles and rights himself, but as he does, she moves like lightning and slashes at his exposed right side.

He grunts as a thin line of blood stains his torn tunic and charges at her, his face twisted with anger. Thyra backtracks quickly, blocking jab after jab, spinning and slicing whenever she's presented with an opening. Sten doesn't give many, but there are enough that after a few minutes of this, he's bleeding from three different wounds. The cheers have subsided slightly as Nisse's warriors see she will not be easily defeated. When they fled our camp over the winter, Thyra was not yet a full-status warrior. She was still in training. And she has always been a reluctant fighter. But that is not the same thing as a *hesitant* fighter, and the difference is critical.

Thyra has only hesitated once. I was there to do her killing for her, and so it did not matter. She doesn't need me now, though. Her thrusts are smooth and controlled, and she looks utterly at peace, even as Sten plods heavily around the circle, glaring his hatred at her, his lips peeled back into an ugly snarl. I wonder if he realizes he is going to die soon.

I see the moment it dawns on him. He's just made yet another stab with his spear, and Thyra swings her dagger down so hard that his spearhead hits the ground. As it does, she jumps onto the shaft, and the wicked snapping sound echoes off the tower above. Sten stumbles forward as his weapon shatters, surprise and fear flashing in his eyes before he dives at his smaller opponent. She dodges his blundering charge and drives her dagger into his shoulder as he falls. It sinks deep, drawing a strangled shout from Sten and ripping it from her grip. He hits the dirt and rolls away from her, leaving a trail of blood behind.

She does not chase him. She merely waits, calmly transferring her remaining blade to her right hand. I glance at Nisse and Jaspar; both of them wear blank expressions, giving nothing away. But the warriors around them look frustrated and shout at Sten to rise. He does, with Thyra's dagger still protruding from just beneath his collarbone on the right side. The wound bleeds heavily—she's hit a large blood vessel by the look of it. Just as I'm thinking it would be wise to leave it, Sten reaches up with his left hand and, with a wrenching growl, yanks the blade from his flesh.

This is a mistake. Blood spurts from the wound, and he stares at the flood with stunned surprise. He clutches at the gash as he turns his hateful gaze on Thyra again. With another broken roar enhanced by the renewed cheers from his fellow warriors, he runs at her, the bloody dagger leading the way. Instead of dodging this time, Thyra charges too, but dives to the dirt as he nears, tumbling head over tail until she lands in a crouch between Sten's legs, her blade a blur of silver. It happens so quickly that the shouts from the crowd falter, not knowing if Sten struck or she did.

But when she jumps to her feet again and spins, the answer is clear. Sten falls to his knees. Blood flows down the inner thighs of his breeches and puddles in the dirt beneath him. He is facing Nisse and the others, who sit on their raised benches. Thyra approaches from behind as he braces himself on his palms. I watch her profile as she looks up at her uncle. I wonder if she's thinking he could have stopped this. If she is, she doesn't say. She merely grasps Sten's hair and draws her blade across his throat. No glory, no challenge or boast, no offer of mercy, just lethal action. She lets Sten fall forward onto his face, and then steps back.

Nisse looks down at Elo and Flemming, Sten's two armorers, and then at Thyra. He stands as the warriors crowded around me fall into hushed silence. Sander and I do not cheer. For some reason, it feels dangerous to do so. But I want to. She might have cast me aside, but she is so magnificent in this moment that I cannot help but love her with every shred of my body and soul.

"The chieftain has won her challenge and retains her chair," Nisse yells.

Thyra bows, a small, weary smile on her face as she walks toward the edge of the circle, her shoulders relaxing from their taut readiness. She's breathing hard, but she's completely unscathed. Sten couldn't even draw blood. I grin, so proud of her that I can barely breathe for the feeling. Jaspar catches my eye and gives me a little nod as Elo and Flemming trudge into the circle and carry Sten's dripping body to the other side, where they lay him gently on a length of rough cloth that has been brought over by Halina and another Vasterutian, a bearded man with a shaved head and bold black eyebrows. Both of them look disgusted as they watch Elo cover Sten's face.

Thyra reaches the edge of the circle and begins to step over the rope. Preben and Bertel offer their hands, wide smiles on their faces. Nisse holds up his arms again, a glint of strange amusement in his eyes. "And now—"

"I challenge her," shouts Elo, his kill marks shining silver in the smoky light. He holds his ax high from his position next to his fallen comrade.

Thyra's head jerks up, her eyes wide. "But—" Her words are drowned out as Preben, Bertel, and several of our warriors shout their protests as Nisse's cheer. I am so stunned that I can't find my voice. A *second* challenge?

"A challenge to a chieftain cannot be refused," Nisse shouts. He gives Thyra an apologetic look. "I am sorry, Thyra. I did not anticipate my warriors' feelings about your presence here."

Thyra slowly steps back from the rope, retreating deeper into the circle. Without taking her gaze from her uncle, she kneels and picks up the dagger Sten ripped from his shoulder. Two slashing swipes and his blood paints the thigh of her breeches with a thick red mark. "Come then, Elo," she says loudly, still staring at Nisse. "Just remember that once you enter this circle, there is only one way you will leave. Be certain."

Elo sneers as he stomps into the circle without hesitation. "I was fighting better warriors before you were even born," he says in a deep, rumbling voice. His beard is shot through with silver, and he looks to be nearly as old as Edvin, but he's lighter of frame and his arms are roped with muscle and vein. He is an experienced killer, and he hefts his ax, a double-bladed weapon with a short, thick handle, with comfort and ease. One solid blow would be all it took to destroy his opponent, and Thyra has already had one fight tonight.

"This is unjust," I hiss from between clenched teeth.

Sander is staring at the puddle of Sten's blood that is being absorbed by the dirt. "There is no rule that says one challenge cannot immediately follow another."

"But it isn't done. This isn't how warriors treat each other."

"We're on foreign ground, Ansa," he snaps. "Nisse doesn't have to rule the same way Lars did, and Lars didn't give him the choice to remain in our tribe."

"Where *is* our tribe?" I ask, looking around. A few waving fists mark the loyal, but there aren't enough of them to make any difference at all. Most of the warriors around us seem hungry for this fight.

I turn back to the circle to find Thyra watching us. Can she see that I am loyal? Does she know I would never abandon her? Her gaze softens for a moment when our eyes meet, but then her bottom lip trembles and she looks away quickly. Her grip on her dagger tightens, and her face loses any expression—she has gone again, and now she's alone in that circle. Her limbs move with a grace that makes my heart pound with want and wish. Her steps are sure as she crosses one foot over the other, circling as Elo begins to stalk her. He is vibrating with hatred, though she only did what any warrior would in responding decisively to Sten's challenge. I don't understand what drives him.

"You're a conniving little thing, aren't you?" he says to her. "Do you think we don't know what you did?"

"What's he talking about?" I murmur.

"No, Elo." Thyra tilts her head. "I *know* you don't know what I did."

I look up at Sander, but his face is a mirror of my own puzzlement. And we get no explanation, because in the next moment, Thyra strikes. Her dagger reflects the flames as it arcs forward, but the blade of Elo's ax knocks it away. And then they are a blur of metal and muscle, and Thyra has to backtrack rapidly under the strength of Elo's blows. Her speed is her best ally as she leaps to the side, her thighs brushing the rope of the fight circle as Elo's ax blade slashes only a few inches from the chests of the warriors standing just on the other side of the rope. They all shout and throw themselves back, but there is nowhere to go because the crowd is packed in so tightly between the tower and the stake-wall.

Thyra pants and quickly swipes sweat from her brow as Elo rounds on her again. He's more strategic than Sten was, and stronger. An icy splinter of fear begins to dig its way into my stomach as she parries another attack. Her arm buckles under its ferocity, and though she dodges, his next swing slices along her left shoulder.

Elo laughs as she staggers back. "If you hold still, I'll end this quickly."

She regains her balance and lowers her chin, glaring at him even as blood blooms along the sleeve of her tunic. "I didn't realize you needed a stationary target to be victorious." Her voice is jagged with contempt, her cool melted under the heat of her pain and this disrespectful, impulsive challenge.

Elo roars at the insult and swings his ax, a blow that would sever her head—if she had remained still. But she is fast as the wind as she lunges low and ducks inside his guard. Elo grunts and his ax flies from his outstretched hand, and the warriors on the benches dive out of the way as it whirls end over end, stopping only when the blade buries itself right where Jaspar had been sitting a moment before. Nisse is the only one who didn't move, and he merely looks down at the vibrating ax handle before raising his head to look at the warrior who challenged his niece.

Elo, like Sten before him, has fallen to his knees, and is embracing Thyra, his hands scrabbling along her back as she presses herself close. Relief nearly doubles me over as I realize what I'm seeing. Thyra's dagger is buried deep in his gut. She is kneeling in front of him, twisting it as he makes high, choking sounds until at last she yanks the dagger out again, spilling his blood across the dirt. Her breath rushing harsh and fast from her mouth, Thyra stands as he slumps at her feet. Her left arm hangs at her side, the weapon in that hand dangling from her fingers. "There you are," she says to Nisse in a weary, halting voice. "Surely I have proven myself now."

Nisse sets his booted foot along the edge of Elo's ax handle. "Impressive, Niece." He glances at Flemming.

"Oh, heaven. He had this planned," Sander mutters right as Flemming stabs his dagger at the sky and shouts, "I challenge her!"

"No!" I shout as fire melts the ice inside me, singeing my heart as it rises. Sander's hand clamps over my wrist, but he pulls back an instant later, gasping and shaking off the heat.

Preben and Bertel have drawn their knives and are approaching Flemming as he moves to step into the fight circle, but Thyra's voice cuts through the noise of the crowd, rising into the smoky night. "Stay back!" She glances over at me. "Stay back," she says again, more quietly.

"Flemming," Nisse says. He sounds so calm, as if this is merely a tournament instead of a fight to the death. "Are you sure?"

"She's not fit to lead," Flemming shouts. "She's a betrayer and a schemer! She's the one who should have been banished."

"Liar," I shout, but Thyra turns around and gives me a look so fierce my mouth snaps shut.

"I will not stoop to dignifying these pathetic insinuations," she says in a tight voice. "Especially when it's obvious that the truth carries no weight within these walls."

Jaspar looks right at me and Sander as he takes his seat again, next to Elo's ax, still buried in the wood of the bench. His blank expression only stokes the flames of my rage.

"Nisse's told everyone that he didn't try to poison Lars," I say to Sander. "Are they implying that they think Thyra did it?"

Sander shrugs. "I think the bigger question is—why isn't she denying it?"

"All of that is in the past," Nisse says blandly to Flemming. "We found our victory even in defeat, did we not?"

His warriors shout of blood and victory as Thyra wipes Elo's blood onto her breeches. Now there are two parallel stripes of crimson on her leg. But her hand shakes as she adopts her fighting stance again. The sight makes my throat constrict. "This has to be stopped," I whisper. "If their enmity is truly in the past, as he says, why isn't he stopping this?"

"What a dead clever plan," Sander says.

"What?"

"If he had executed Thyra, or assassinated her, he could not have won the loyalty of our tribe. So he's letting his warriors fight this battle in a way everyone must honor, because we all know and respect the basic rules of the fight circle. All he has to do is *nothing,* and his victory will be complete."

"There is no honor in this!"

"Thyra is a chieftain, Ansa. Warriors can refuse a fight like this, but chieftains must defend the chair or lose it."

I cry out as Flemming steps into the circle, his tan skin glistening with sweat. He is no taller than Thyra, but he is wiry and fierce, all sinew and strength. Like her, he has two daggers. Unlike her, he looks steady and smooth as he approaches.

And for the first time, she looks like prey. Her chest shudders and sweat drips from her chin. Her beautiful face is twisted with pain, and her left sleeve is soaked with blood. Flemming does not joke or preen, but the determined look on his face is just as bad. Heat blazes across my skin even as ice runs hard along my bones. I begin to tremble with the effort of holding them inside.

Flemming lunges, and Thyra staggers away from him. Their blades clash together, but Thyra isn't strong enough to hold him back, and he pushes inside her guard, the tip of his blade arcing toward her throat. She kicks him in the stomach, and he huffs, his eyes wide, but he's still able to block her next strike and shove her off balance. She stumbles over her own feet and falls onto her rear. As he advances, Thyra hurls her dagger, and it slices along his thigh as it flies past. She rolls away as he tries to stomp on her rib cage, so he stabs both of his blades down. One misses, but the other cuts along her flank, and she can't quite stifle her scream. She stabs up with her only remaining blade and sends Flemming arching back, then blocks one of his daggers as he sends it flying at her.

Thyra heaves herself to her feet, clutching at her side. Blood flows over her trembling fingers.

"No," I whisper.

Flemming walks toward her, unhurried, unconcerned. He doesn't look like he's exerting himself at all as he blocks and parries her next desperate strikes. Finally, he slams his blade against hers, and her dagger flies out of her grip. Before she can scramble for it, his fist crunches into her stomach, sending her to the ground.

She's on her knees, right in front of the wooden benches.

"This is it," whispers Sander, and even as Nisse's warriors scream their satisfaction, I hear him so clearly, each word penetrating my heart. I am paralyzed with disbelief. This cannot be happening.

Thyra raises her head. She must know Flemming is behind her. She must know what comes next. "Uncle," she says, and all go quiet. Will she ask for her life, even if it means banishment?

Ask for mercy, I silently beg. I'll leave with her. I'll follow anywhere she goes.

Nisse stands. "Yes?"

She lets out a pained breath and squares her shoulders. "Treat my warriors and andeners with respect after I am gone."

Flemming grabs a handful of Thyra's short hair and

wrenches her head back, his dagger rising to cut her throat.

I cannot let this happen. I will *not* let this happen. As the curse bleeds through my skin, begging release, I stop trying to hold it back.

Instead, I embrace it.

CHAPTER FIFTEEN

All the noise of the warriors falls silent, smothered by the rush of fire and ice in my mind, the swoop of it along my bones, its roar as it invades my very soul. I am barely aware of stepping into the ring, only that suddenly the rope isn't there anymore. Its ashes flutter in the air around me like moths.

I am the flame. It bursts from my palms as I stalk toward Flemming, who whirls around, perhaps when he feels the heat at his back. "You will not touch her," I say, and my voice is monstrous, teeth and claws and blades and hate made sound.

Flemming staggers away from Thyra, his arms reeling, his mouth gaping in a silent scream as I come after him, liquid fire in my veins. "Witch!" he screams.

It is the last word he ever utters. I hurl the flames, all my hurt and rage fueling an inferno that devours Flemming instantly. His cry is desperate and shrill and now it's gone and I don't care. I won't stop until he is cinders at my feet. This feels good and right and savage.

I raise my head at the flash and glimmer of a dagger blade, but the mere thought of wind brings forth an icy gale that sends it flying off course, its master thrown back into the churn of warriors with his eyes frozen wide and horrified. I turn in place, glaring fire at the tribe that was so eager to kill my chieftain. "Challenge *me*," I say.

Nothing has ever felt this magnificent. I laugh as a few warriors surge to the front and throw their spears. I swing my arms out, and the wind does my bidding once again— the long razor tips of the weapons fly past me on either side and into the crowd behind me. Let them all die. I don't care that they cry. I don't care about the terror on their faces. A moment ago they were salivating as they watched Thyra on her knees, a chieftain defeated by scheming. Not with honor. Not in a fair fight. I realize now it wouldn't have mattered if she'd defeated Flemming—another would have stepped up, and another, and another, until one landed a lucky blow, until Thyra fell from sheer exhaustion. I don't know what kind of chieftain nurtures a tribe that would do such a thing, but at the thought, I look up at the tiered benches where Nisse was sitting with Jaspar and the rest of his loyal entourage.

But Nisse is gone. So are his favorites. Only Jaspar

remains. He stands on his bench, his eyes round. "Did you know?" I shout, violent gusts lifting my red hair, ash and cinder swirling around me. The air is filled with the scent of burning flesh, sweet and bitter.

It's funny the small things one notices when the world is falling apart. Jaspar's throat bobs as he swallows, his skin shining with sweat and streaked with grime in the heat and light of my curse-fire. His fists clench. He shakes his head.

I could kill him. Perhaps I should, for spreading the rumors that broke people's faith and trust in Thyra. My heart squeezes at the thought of him burning in front of me, but I'm part of the fire now. I've accepted it as my own. It licks at my skin, striping it red and angry. Raising blisters. Pain surges into my awareness, along with an instinctive swell of ice to counter the heat. I wince as my blood runs so cold it feels like my bones will snap.

"No!" Jaspar roars, and I jerk my head up to see him leap off the bench and land at the edge of the fight circle, his hands up and waving as he runs past me and shouts at someone above us. I turn in that direction—battle archers are lined up behind a parapet that encircles the squat stone tower, halfway up its hulking height. "Do *not* fire!" he shouts, lunging forward to put himself between the arrows and me.

I turn my palms to the sky, shards of ice forming and swirling, lengthening into blades. At the sight, I smile. It *is* as easy as thinking cold thoughts. And now I am cold. So cold that the thought of these ice blades penetrating Krigere flesh can't melt me. They will freeze and fall and die, and it is what they deserve. What all of them deserve.

"Ansa?"

The broken, hitching sound of my name brings me whirling around. Relief turns my ice blades to mist as I stare at Thyra's red, heat-kissed face. Her blue eyes are filled with tears. She takes a slow step toward me, her injured left arm pressed to her body, her tunic streaked and stained with blood from her wounds. "Please stop this."

"I can't let them kill you." My voice cracks. Agony makes me sway, even as the fire and ice rages inside me, seeking a target.

"It's time to stop though. You have to stop."

My vision is tinted with an orange glow. I stare at her through the flames.

"You're my wolf," she says with a tremulous smile. A tear escapes and slips down her cheek. "I need you to listen to me now."

"Your wolf," I whisper. I clench my fists, trying to leash the massive storm inside me along with a rising agony that's trying to eat me alive. "I have never been anything else."

"Oh," she says, her voice high and shaking. "That's where I think you're wrong."

I blink at her in confusion. There's a roaring in my ears that won't fade. "What do you mean?"

She gives me a pained look and tilts her head, her right arm rising to embrace me. "You are a great deal more than that." She's alive and reaching for me, and I cannot deny her. I move closer. Her arm slides around my shoulders, and she pulls me against her, so that I can smell her, fire and sweat and a hint of sweetness. Her whole body is taut and trembling.

"Don't be afraid of me. I would never hurt you," I say.

She lets out a quiet sob. "I know, Ansa." Her hand slides up my back and into my hair. "I know." She kisses my cheek, and my eyes fall shut at the absolute perfection of her lips against my skin. But then her grip tightens and her body tenses. I open my mouth to ask her what's wrong, but before I can utter the question, my skull explodes in a thunder of pain and stars and black and I'm tumbling down, the deep darkness pulling me under.

She lies on the ground, blood soaking her dress, her eyes full of pain. Though the flames surround her, she doesn't pay them any mind. Her gaze is on me. *Never stop fighting.* Her mouth doesn't move, but I hear the words in my head, trilling and beautiful and true. *Never stop.*

I want to obey her, but I can't move. "Mama," I scream. I need her to stand up and come and get me, to scoop me from the ground and hold me in her arms, to laugh and stroke her fingers through my hair. I need to smell her scent, the one that means safety and love and home. But all I can smell now is the smoke.

I look down and realize I'm on fire.

"Be still," a voice hisses. "Don't touch those bandages!"

My eyelids are crusted shut, but I manage to open one,

enough to see a blurry brown face hovering above mine. "What?" It comes out as a rasping croak.

"If you rip those bandages off again, you can fix them yourself." The voice belongs to a woman, and she's speaking Krigere, but it sounds off somehow, like she's had too much ale, or too much honey. The sounds are drawn out and warm and round instead of the pointed fierceness I am used to.

A warm cloth is pressed to my eyes, knocking away the crust, and I blink my eyes open. "You're the one from the banquet," I say, wincing as the words abrade my dry throat.

The woman pats her spray of wild ebony hair with graceful fingers. She's younger than I first thought, not much older than I am, and her gaze is full of sharp wariness. "Halina."

"Vasterutian. I remember."

She lets out a cluck of incredulous laughter. "Do you? Wonder you can even form a thought."

My brow furrows. "What happened?" I glance down at myself. I'm clad in only breeches and a chest wrap, and my arms are bandaged from fingertips to shoulders. I can see every one of my ribs. Shock clenches cold and tight in my belly, and I try to sit up, but Halina holds me down. Her hand is encased in a thick leather mitt, like the kind some andeners wear when they handle iron in the fire. I collapse under the pressure, winded and weak.

"Thought you might not remember your own *name*, what with that knock to the head." She grunts, pure amusement. "The Krigere had no idea they had a wielder among them." She whistles. "Quite a show."

219

A shadow of memory hulks at the back of my mind, pushing its way forward. "Where's Chieftain Thyra?"

"Alive and safe. That's all I'm to tell you."

I try to get up again, but she keeps her hand pressed to my shoulder. "Why? Let me up!"

"Hush! You quiet down." Her skin is glistening with sweat, and her voice has risen in alarm. "Don't you turn that fire on me!"

My head sinks back onto the pillow, my lips tingling. "What did you say?"

The pressure on my shoulder lets up, but Halina is muttering to herself in a different language now, probably Vasterutian. It has the same drawling honey lilt she lent to the Krigere words. When she sees me staring, she gives me an exasperated look. "I don't want to be here. No one else would mind you, though. All afraid you would cook them or turn them into an ice statue."

How does she know? The dark shadow in my mind forces its way into the front of my consciousness. I remember. Fire bursting from my palms. Ice swirling in my hands. And my hate, and my rage, and Thyra's tear-streaked cheeks. I embraced the magic and it devoured me. "Oh, no," I whisper. "I thought that might have been a dream."

"A nightmare, more like." She flares her fingers and makes a *whooshing* sound. Then she looks me in the eye. "But you burn me and I'll haunt you. Drive you mad. I could do it."

My cheeks bloom with the heat of humiliation. "I don't want to burn you. I'm not—" I press my lips together.

Halina grunts and settles herself next to my bedside. I'm in a stone chamber, the air cool and heavy and wet, the walls dripping. A torch bracketed to the wall reveals a heavy wooden door but no windows. It feels like the whole thing will collapse and crush me.

"So many *brave* warriors, and they send me to tend you." She chuckles. "Not as brave as they like to claim."

I stare down at my arms, lifting them to examine my bandages in the firelight. "What's wrong with me?"

"Ha! Oh, so many things, it seems. But to begin with, your arms are blistered raw." She nods at my head. "And you got your skull cracked by a dagger hilt."

I squint, my head aching as I try to remember. But it's like trying to lift a heavy boulder to see what's underneath. I'm not strong enough. "Tell me."

"You went berserk, and the lady warrior stopped you. Crack!" She mimics slamming a dagger hilt into her own head and then rolls her eyes and lets her tongue loll.

"Thyra," I whisper. "She hit me."

"Mmm. A good thing, too. Would have burned down the world if she hadn't." She gestures at my arms. "Yourself included."

I try to clench my fists, but it feels like my flesh is tearing loose. I gasp, shaking with the pain. "Everyone knows about me now."

"Were you trying to hide?" She laughs. "If so, I must tell you that you're not very good at such things."

"I was cursed." I sigh. "The witch did this to me."

She clucks her tongue. "Don't know about that. But I do know you're a wielder. A Kupari."

My heart kicks against my breastbone. "I am *not*."

"Oh, you are. Only the Kupari have magic." Her round face twists into a look of contempt. "Who knows why? Certainly not because they deserve it." She mutters something in Vasterutian.

"I might have . . . magic. Or witchcraft. I don't know what it is. But it's not because I'm Kupari. I'm Krigere." Even as I say it, my mother's face flickers in memory. I shudder as my stomach clenches.

Halina arches an eyebrow as she points at my hair. "You were born to the Krigere? Because your hair tells me otherwise. The Kupari? So many with hair just like yours."

"I don't know where I was born."

"Then don't tell me who you are and who you aren't."

I stare up at her, stunned by the realization. I knew I was a raid prize, but always assumed I'd been taken from a tribe in the north or the west. I'd never considered . . . "Even if you're right, I'm no wielder. I wasn't born like this."

Her eyes narrow. "Not that you know of. But the magic can come out anytime."

"How do you know?"

"Oh. I know all about the Kupari." Her voice drips with contempt. "They sat quiet and smug as the monsters climbed our walls and killed King Dakila and his family. Refused to help even when we begged. They deserve whatever they get now that old Nisse's coming for them."

"I would think you would hate him. All of us, in fact."

Her dark eyes glitter. "Never said I didn't, little red warrior."

I see the fierceness in her gaze and suddenly remember what Nisse said about letting the Vasterutians join our tribe. I'm not sure they would even if he offered. "How long have I been here?"

"Long enough for me to kill you a few hundred times over," she says casually as she removes her leather mitt and begins to pick filth from beneath her fingernails with a small knife.

"Tell me how long."

"Days, little red."

"*Days?*"

She sets the knife down on a small table on her other side, one laden with a basin of water and a pot of greasy-looking tincture. "Weeks, really. Your head was right cracked. Thought you were going to die for a little while there. Kept burning the bandages right off your arms. Had to put you out a few times." She pretends to grab the water basin and dump it on me. "Had you tied down, but burned through the ropes. Decided it was best to leave you be, and that's when you stopped setting things on fire. Guess you don't like to be a prisoner." Her mouth curves into a sly smile. "Not that anyone does, eh?"

I'm having trouble meeting her eyes. Normally raid prizes are cowed and meek, but there's no real question that Halina has the upper hand for now. "You said Thyra's alive and safe. And she knows I'm here?"

223

Halina considers me for a moment. "I believe she does."

"But you're not sure? What happened to her?"

Halina wears that clever smile as if it were a shield. "Many things happening. *Many* things. Everybody here wears a mask." She traces a finger through the air, outlining my face. "Better choose *yours*."

My thoughts are so scattered. . . . I close my eyes and try to draw them together into a picture I can understand. Thyra was going to be killed in that fight circle, and I saved her. But she's the one who hit me. . . . "And Jaspar?"

"The prince is in the mix," she says. "Yes, he is. You Krigere." She laughs and shakes her head, but her lips are peeled back, tight and feral. "Come to squat in Vasterut. Think it's easy." She's not laughing anymore. Now she's just baring her teeth.

"Those are dangerous words, considering Nisse rules your city." I suppress a shiver, but it's not the ice inside me. Right now I can barely feel it. All I feel is weaker than I ever have, leaden limbs and shredded skin stretched over the knowledge that the moment I actually embraced the curse and set it free, it tried to kill me.

"Are such words dangerous, when I say them to *you*? Little Kupari wielder. You know what those Krigere call you?" She leans forward, so close that her sharp breath wafts across my cheeks as she says, "Witch."

"I'm not a witch. I'm a warrior."

"Like the ones who stole you away from your birthplace?"

I stare up at her, the breath knocked right out of me.

With a grimly satisfied look, she slaps her palms on her thighs and pushes herself to her feet, deftly pocketing the knife in her skirt. "You rest some more. Drink some." She gestures to a stone cup at my bedside. "I'm going to report to old Nisse. He wanted to know if you woke up. And if you were sensible. Wasn't sure you'd ever be sensible again after the crack in the head, but he'll be glad you are."

I push myself up to sitting, now that she's too far away to stop me. Dread has welled up in my throat, and I swallow it down. "Glad?"

Halina grins. "Oh, yes. I'm thinking he wants to know why you roasted or froze nine of his warriors, little red." She walks to the door, her hips swinging. "And I'm thinking you'd best think *very* carefully about your answer."

CHAPTER SIXTEEN

s I wait to hear of my fate, I stare at the ceiling and try to keep my thoughts in line. It is exhausting. Before, I was holding back the curse. Now I am holding back the memories. They used to only inhabit my dreams, hazy and horrifying. But now they hover at the edges of my waking moments, circling predators waiting for the right moment to pounce.

I was born Kupari. It must be true. It's why Hulda's language was so familiar, why the sound of her words scraped at the armor laid over the raw memories of my childhood home. The home I had before it was ripped away from me.

By the Krigere.

I clench my muscles and push that away yet again. I am a warrior, and I am a Krigere. I am part of a strong people.

I am part of a tribe. I fought and killed to become one of them, to have a home again.

You know what those Krigere call you? Witch.

Perhaps I am not part of a tribe after all. In saving Thyra, I doomed myself. And how did Thyra reward my service?

She pretended to love me and lured me close—she was the bait, and my heart was the snare.

And then she tried to kill me.

Halina comes back for me sometime later and tells me I've been summoned to the council room. My mouth is too dry to allow me to ask questions, and I'm not sure she could—or would—give me a straight answer if I did. But the way she watches me, her dark eyes glittering bright, her mouth curved but tight . . . it's like she's waiting for something.

I feel like a bundle of sticks stuffed inside a bag of skin as she helps me to sit up and unwraps my bandages. A lump rises in my throat as I see the swirls of scarring along my arms, red and silver and shiny and fragile. I have never given much thought to my appearance, save the number of kill marks on my arm, but suddenly I want to hide. I look like a monster.

Halina must see the shadow of shame cross my face, because she says, "Only your arms, little red. And it's not as bad as it looks—been moving them every day, not letting them get stiff—you still have full use of them! Rest of you is pretty all right too. Except for that spot on your leg."

I glance down at the red mark on my right calf, in the

shape of a burst of flame, and let out a choked laugh. "That's not a scar. It's a birthmark."

Halina leans back so that the light of the torch reaches my bare leg. "Is it now?" she asks quietly.

"I need boots," I blurt out, eager to cover the mark, even though I'm dreading what comes after.

Halina fetches me my boots, along with a new, overlarge tunic. It hangs from my scrawny frame and makes me look like a child, and Halina is obviously trying not to laugh as she steps back and lets me tie the collar with stiff, sore fingers. The long sleeves hang to my fingertips, but I don't mind that. For once, I want my arms covered.

I want a weapon, too, but it seems foolish to ask for one. As soon as I'm dressed, Halina yanks the door to the chamber open and leans out. "Got her ready," she says in a flat voice, so different from the warm, round tone of a few moments ago. She turns back to me with eyes so full that I can't sift through what's within. Curiosity? Regret? Fear? Hope? All at once?

"Step into the hallway," says a familiar voice.

"Sander?"

"Step into the hallway *now*, Ansa," he says from the corridor.

My stomach is a ball of ice as I obey him. Apart from Sander, three other warriors are waiting for me, including Carina, the one with the long, dark braid. All of them have unsheathed daggers, and they surround me as I leave the relative safety of the stone chamber. Halina has shrunk back into the room, but watches from behind the door with her keen gaze as Sander presses his knife against my neck.

"If you try to burn us or freeze us, we'll kill you."

I grit my teeth, trying to hold in the stinging tears that are filling my eyes. "I wouldn't."

Carina lets out a disdainful laugh. "We all saw what you did, witch. Don't pretend."

I look up at Sander, remembering what Jaspar said about how Sander is supposedly grateful to me, how he respects me. But now all I see in his eyes is a flint-hard wariness. "I won't hurt any of you," I say.

I'm not even sure if I could, given how weak I feel, but I'm scared to even think of the ice or the fire, for fear they would rise unbidden. They no longer feel like something foreign inside me. Instead, all of me is shaky and unstable, like a storm ready to burst to life on a muggy summer day. We are one now, the magic and me. I have become my own enemy.

"Forgive us if we don't take your word for it," Carina says. She's on my left, holding her dagger angled toward my belly, where a quick strike would send my guts spilling to the stone floor. The other two warriors are on my other side, knives poised.

Sander takes hold of my shoulder, but his grip is gentle. Perhaps Halina told him of the burn scars. He turns me around. "That way." He keeps his blade at my throat as they march me up the hall. I want to turn back and see if Halina is following, or still watching, but I am afraid to move without the other warriors' permission. There is no compassion in their eyes, nothing but suspicion and hatred.

They do not see me as one of them, and the knowledge nearly strangles me. My breath whistles from my throat, emerging in wisps of fear and sorrow. Although the memories of what happened are like shards of a shattered blade, fragmented and distorted, mixed with recollections of other fiery nights full of blood, I know I have done something terrible. Halina said I killed nine warriors. Nine. And all I recall is Thyra on her knees and my roaring desire for vengeance, strong enough to invite the curse to be my mate, to mesh itself with my bones and soul.

At the thought, I feel the heat caressing my spine, and I hold my breath until it passes. Sander's grip on my shoulder tightens, and his blade slides closer to my throat. "Careful, Ansa." The others press nearer, prepared to slice me neck to tail. The fear slides frigid and cruel along my spine.

"Please," I whisper. "Don't do that. Don't make it harder for me."

The tip of Carina's blade pokes my side. "Harder for you to roast us? That's rather the *point*." She pokes me again.

"Stop it," Sander snaps from behind me. "Back off, Carina."

Carina gives him a resentful look but does as he says. We march up a set of stone stairs, the air getting warmer as we ascend in a spiral. Torchlight is reflected off the wet rock walls. I don't know if it's night or day until we finally reach a door that opens into another corridor, where sunlight streams through a window above.

"Had our first snow a few weeks ago. Now it's thick on the ground," Sander says.

"What happened to the andeners and warriors outside the city?"

"They found quarters within the walls at Nisse's orders," says Carina.

Displacing all those Vasterutians right when they needed shelter most, something that clearly disturbed Thyra greatly. I want to ask about her, but I am afraid to. Halina said she was alive and safe, but where is she? Sander is here, but the other warriors are Nisse's. I don't know how Preben and Bertel fared, or if they stayed by Thyra's side. Halina said a lot had happened. I've awakened as an outsider in a strange land of unspoken rules and unknown allegiances.

Not for the first time. But this time, I'm not sure sheer ferocity will gain me a place among the Krigere once again.

I am guided up another, narrower set of stairs, to a narrow landing that ends in an open doorway. Sander pushes me forward. "In there."

He keeps a firm grip on my shoulder as we enter a room full of bright, cold sunlight. We are a tangle of malice with me at the center, and my breath puffs from my mouth as I fight the rising panic.

"Give her space!" Nisse's voice comes from my right. I'm scared to turn for fear of running into a knife blade, but at his loud command, my four guards all take a step away from me. Nisse approaches slowly, his long, graying blond hair arranged in a neat queue, his beard brushing the top of his fine leather vest. He has a dagger sheathed at his hip and another along his right calf, strapped to thick, fur-lined leather boots. He tilts his head and gives me a searching look. "Ansa. Are you going to use your fire to flay the skin from my bones?"

My heart is jolted by his words. "N-no."

The corner of his mouth slides up. "Are you going to freeze my blood in my veins?"

"No, sir," I whisper. Once, when I was a child, one of the warriors caged a wolf and brought it into our camp. It hunched, hackles up and teeth bared, while all us children gathered round, fear and curiosity drawing us close but jittery. The animal kept turning in circles, seeming to hate the idea of us creeping up on its back, but we surrounded it. This is how I feel now, wishing I could shrink into a corner. At least then I would know where the attack was coming from.

The other warriors look at me like I am that animal, but Nisse . . . There is something else in his eyes. Something bright and dangerous. "Leave us," he says.

Carina's mouth drops open. "That is not safe at all. You're giving her exactly the opportunity she wants!"

"I don't think so," says another voice. Jaspar's. He was standing so still in the shadows, behind the wall of sunlight flooding in from a large, high window, but now he strides into view. "She could have killed me that day, easily. And she chose not to."

"See, Carina?" Nisse says, waving his large, scarred hand at me. "Ansa means no harm." He chuckles. "At the moment, at least. Thyra is in no danger, so it's likely we aren't either. Right, Ansa?"

"Right," I breathe. I glance around the room, hoping she might be haunting the shadows like Jaspar was. I need to talk to her. I want her to look in my eyes and tell me the truth. Has she rewarded my sacrifice with hatred? The uncertainty squirms along my bones, impossible to settle.

But she's not here.

I wait until Sander, Carina, and the other two guards exit, and when Jaspar closes the door behind them, I can't hold it back any longer. "Where is she?"

"Ah," says Nisse, clapping his hands together. "We thought that might be the first thing you asked."

"She's fine, Ansa," Jaspar says. "But after what happened, we thought it best to keep her guarded and protected, away from the other warriors."

"So she's a prisoner."

Nisse holds up his hands. "Not at all. She dines with us every night, and she knows everything that's happened. She is treated with the highest respect. But we wanted to make sure she was safe while you recovered and alive when you awoke."

"So you got what you wanted," I say. "You've united the tribe at her expense."

Nisse's brow furrows. "You think *this* is what I wanted? Nine of my best, destroyed before my eyes, and two others slaughtered by my niece in the moments before. Several others injured. Burns. Frostbite that's taken fingers and toes and noses. And the survivors . . . ah. They crave vengeance as payment for their pain and grief. They want to stone the culprit in the fight circle—but they would be happy to stone the reason, too. And Thyra, my niece, my blood, is the reason."

Bile rises in my throat. "This isn't her fault. And I didn't mean to hurt so many. I've been cursed—"

"We know," Jaspar says, leaning back against a heavy wooden council table. The top has been painted with a map, a peninsula jutting into blue water. "I knew you were lying that day in the woods. But I had no idea you were *that* out of control." He gives me a rueful smile. "Even by your usual standards."

My cheeks blaze.

"The whole thing was unfortunate," says Nisse. "I confess that I should have reined in my warriors. But their mistrust of Thyra had been brewing for seasons, Ansa. You must understand that."

I glare at Jaspar. "I understand that both of you have a story to tell, and that the mistrust grew from seeds that *you* planted."

"Wrong." Nisse moves closer to me, looming, but not within strike range. It is almost as if he knows how near he can be without putting himself in danger. "You've been deceived, Ansa. All of Lars's warriors were shackled by these lies."

"Have you brought me here to tease me, or to tell me your truth?" I should not be so bold with this traitor, this false chieftain, especially since he is in control. But there is an earnest tension in his face that makes me believe he cares what I think.

"I will tell you the truth," Nisse says. "But you must understand that the reason it was hidden was the lives it saved."

I cast Jaspar a questioning look. "My father is being honest," he tells me. "The truth might have sparked a war."

"At the very least, it would have destroyed my brother," says Nisse, staring mournfully through the window to the white sky above. "And that is the one thing I could never do."

Confusion presses close around me, raising goose bumps. "But you're telling me now? I'm just a warrior."

Nisse pulls his gaze from the window. "Let's drop that pretense, shall we?"

I bow my head. "A warrior is all I ever wanted to be," I say in a choked voice.

"I remember," he says quietly. "I remember the day you were brought to me and Lars because you had bitten an andener and scratched her little boy. You could have been killed for that offense, but it was so clear you were meant to be Krigere. And instead of executing you, we made you tribe. We gave you to Einar and Jes, of all people. There was no better place for a warrior child."

"So why—"

"Because you are more, Ansa," he says, his fingers spreading, powerful and vibrating with energy. "You are more. And that is why I'm going to tell you what really happened."

I raise my head and meet his eyes. They are green like his son's, a primal, deep color. "I'm listening."

"I never would have hurt my brother," he says simply. "I would have served him unto death. And at his death, his daughter would have become chieftain, and I would have served her, too."

Jaspar folds his arms over his chest, but remains silent.

"But there was a problem," Nisse continues. "Many of the warriors could sense that Thyra was not with us. She would argue with attack plans. She would question every decision her father made. And over time, it made the others question *her*." He sighs. "Some of them began to whisper, wondering if perhaps I should be made chieftain when Lars passed into eternity."

"Lars told us Thyra would make a strong chieftain," I say. "He believed in her."

Nisse gives me a sad smile. "He loved his daughter. She was his only offspring to live past childhood *and* to become a warrior. He adored Hilma, of course, but he saw glimmers of himself in Thyra, and he worked so hard to fan those sparks into a full flame. And it nearly killed him. Because he had created something *else*, without even knowing it."

"What?"

"Maybe it was because she did not want to invade Kupari—Lars was making those plans even before I was banished! Or maybe it was that she was impatient to lead. Or maybe, just maybe, she was born with the spirit of a snake instead of that of a warrior. Perhaps she simply could not help herself."

Something unsteady has awakened in my chest. "Are you saying . . . Thyra was somehow involved in the assassination plot?"

"She was going to poison her father, Ansa. She wanted him dead before the support around me could spread beyond the inner circle. She wanted him dead before he could change his mind about the succession."

I shake my head. "Thyra would never scheme her way to power like a coward. That's not what happened."

"I was returning from hunting when I observed Thyra gathering the poison berries and leaves in the glen to the west of camp. You will recall Hilma was skilled in the art of crafting brews and poultices, and I knew she'd taught her sister a thing or two. Those berries—they have only one purpose," Jaspar says. "But I tried to tell myself otherwise." He frowns. "But then word came that very evening that Lars's celebration goblet was missing. I realized Thyra was planning to do something terrible, and I brought those fears to my father immediately."

Nisse grimaces. "It was agony deciding what to do. I knew of my brother's heart for his daughter. I love her too! But her treachery . . ." He shakes his head. "She is more skilled at it than I could ever have imagined. Knowing that would have killed Lars even if the poison hadn't—we all knew of his contempt for politics and scheming, and his own precious daughter had embraced it."

"But the poison—and Lars's celebration goblet—were found in *your* shelter."

Nisse nods. "And there is only one way they could have

gotten there. Thyra must have realized we knew of her scheming—and she decided to frame me."

"Who do you think sent that slave to find the damning evidence?" Jaspar asks, his tone bitter. "It was well hidden—we had no idea it was there! But that slave somehow accidentally stumbled upon it while fetching a forgotten cloak?" He scoffs. "She laid her trap well."

Nisse runs his hands over his face. "My own hesitation did me in. Perhaps I should have taken my information straight to Lars, but the consequences . . ."

"This is a lie." I fold my ruined arms over my stomach.

"If I had poisoned my brother, succession still would have passed to Thyra." Nisse's voice has hardened like the ground in winter. There is no give there now, no softness. "With most of the warriors supporting her as his daughter. It would have been foolishness for me to try to assassinate him, even if I had wanted to. And think what you will of me—but I'm not addled."

"If all you say is true, why didn't you tell Lars everything when the poison was found in your tent?"

"She ran to him," he says, clenching his teeth. "She took the slave, and the evidence, and she wove a web around him so tight that he couldn't see any other possibilities. He ate the lies from her palm."

"If the truth is so important to you, I would have thought you'd share it."

"I wanted to," says Jaspar, casting a frustrated look at his father. "I begged you to."

"And there you reveal your youth, which protects you from all the worries an old man must carry," Nisse says, suddenly weary. He trudges over to the table and settles his large body upon one of the benches. His palm strokes over the blue, flaking paint of the lake across the tabletop. "Lars's heart could not have allowed him to believe that Thyra craved his death. If I had made a counter-accusation, he would have been forced to choose between us, and it would have ignited a war. I had enough warriors behind me to put up a fight, and fight they would have. To the death. My own niece had made me look like a cowardly schemer, and I faced a terrible choice. What was I to do? Let my warriors die for me just to defend my honor? Let them kill hundreds of Lars's warriors in the process? That would have been a tragedy. Lars saw it as well. It's why he didn't have me executed, and why he let them leave with me."

Jaspar leans forward, the frustration still sparking in his gaze. "I wanted to tell you, Ansa. I hated leaving without you knowing the truth. But you're so loyal—and you honored Lars as your chieftain. I didn't want to make things difficult for you." He bites the inside of his cheek and turns away. "And I knew Thyra had her claws sunk deep in your heart. You wouldn't have believed me."

"And that was the way of it, with so many good warriors," Nisse says. "Because she reached him first, and because her lies tasted sweet as truth, Lars believed I had tried to kill him. He wanted to save lives. So he demanded that all of us who knew the truth conceal it and never speak it aloud, to avoid bloodshed—and to stifle more scheming. So given the choice between war and secrecy, we left in the night, the truth smothered beneath a veil of silence." He grunts. "Of course, the real story finds a way of pushing to the surface." He eyes me with a curious look. "Much like *magic* does."

A shiver passes through me at the word. "Your warriors call me a witch."

Nisse scratches at his beard. "They're afraid of you. As they should be."

"Your guards swept you away to safety. Afraid I would kill you." And I would have, if I'm honest.

"As chieftain, I had to allow them to protect me."

I look at Jaspar, who did stay. "They look at me as if I am a monster."

"It *was* monstrous," Jaspar murmurs. "But it was also transcendent."

"He's right, Ansa," Nisse says. "Such power. And a warrior must respect power wherever he finds it, in whatever form."

"I didn't want this." I rub my hands along my arms and wince as they pass over the scars. A wave of heat crashes over me, and it feels like my spine is melting, pulling me to the ground. I sway, and Jaspar rushes to my side, guiding me to the bench while barely touching me. "I never asked to be cursed," I say as I sink onto it. "I would do anything to rid myself of it." Although now I am afraid it is too late. I let it become part of me.

"Well . . . perhaps we can find a way." Nisse sweeps his

arm over the painted map. "Here is where it originated, after all."

Now I see—this is the Kupari peninsula. At its northern tip lies the city-state, and *temple* is scratched into a spot near the northeastern shore, black pigment rubbed into the letters. "Now that the snow has come, do you still plan to invade?"

"We still seek information as to who rules the Kupari. Some say the witch queen has perished, but I am told another is supposed to rise in her place. Yet this new ruler has not appeared in public. A day ago I sent an emissary."

"An emissary?"

Nisse grins. "Diplomacy! The south brims with it, and who am I to violate their traditions?" His smile disappears. "But I only want to know one thing—if the witch is on her throne. If she is, we must be very careful. If she is not, I see no reason why we shouldn't ride into her city and decimate it in payment for what she did to Lars and his warriors." He lays his hand on my shoulder, gentle but heavy. "And if we do that, I would want you with us, Ansa. I would want you to show those Kupari your wrath. Show them what it is to have such magic turned against them."

"You want me to *use* the curse?" A wave of sick sits bitter on the back of my tongue. "I don't know. . . . It's not under my control."

"Nonsense! You craved Flemming's death that day in the circle, and the flames wrapped around him like snakes, striking hard. It was thunderous and deadly and beautiful."

"I murdered your warriors," I whisper, the memories rising now, the opposite of beautiful.

Nisse leans close. "What if you could atone?" My eyes meet his, and he nods. "If you were to strike at the Kupari, at their queen, at their people, you would find forgiveness here. Deliver the warriors a victory, and you will be welcomed within this tribe."

My final memory becomes stark and bright in my mind. Thyra, tears running down her face as she begged me to stop. Even if her love was a lie, her fear of the magic—of what I had become—rang with truth. "Does Thyra know you're asking me to do this?"

"Given the nature of the truths I had to reveal, you can understand that she is not privy to all of it."

Because he has told me that she is the traitor. I don't know if I can believe it. I don't know *what* to believe, and the confusion is taking me apart. My entire body shakes with it. "I need to talk to her."

"Are you well, Ansa?" Nisse asks, his tone filling with concern. "You have become pale as the snow. Did that Vasterutian servant feed you adequately? Did she give you ointment for your wounds? Did she treat you with respect?"

"Halina did a good job," I say, knowing my answer might mean the difference between life and death for her. "I would not be standing before you if she hadn't." Except I'm not standing now. I'm slumped on the bench, my head throbbing, my body weighed down by the sickness of the last month and all I have heard in the last several minutes.

"I thought I might never see your eyes open again," Jaspar says. "Thyra hit you so hard we thought you might not ever wake up."

Nisse looks at his son, and they share a moment. "Perhaps that was her intention."

Jaspar gives him a curt nod. "It had occurred to me. I was trying to call off our archers and calm things down when Thyra hit Ansa."

"Thyra wouldn't . . ." The protest dies on my tongue as they echo my suspicions. "I saved her," I say lamely.

Jaspar kneels in front of me, his blond hair glinting gold as he leans into a shaft of light. "And once again I must ask: How has she rewarded your loyalty?"

I close my eyes. "I need to rest. Please."

They do not press me further. Nisse calls the guards but tells them to keep their weapons sheathed as they take me back to my chamber. Jaspar gives me a long, hard look before I go, wrapping his hand around my upper arm and stroking his thumb over the kill mark he gave me, as if he is drawn to it. "We'll talk again soon, I promise," he says.

I cannot meet his gaze. I let Sander and the others lead me back down into the earth, the stone behemoth swallowing me down until I find its stomach, the little windowless tomb where I am to be kept. Halina is waiting when we reach it. She bows her head meekly and nods as Sander tells her to get me dinner and make sure I am comfortable.

As soon as I sink onto my bed, though, she is pulling me up again. "Come with me, little red. Dinner is this way."

Her tone isn't amused and joking as it was earlier, but nor is it meek and scared like it was in the hallway. Instead, it is urgent. Determined.

"Where? I can't be around the other warriors right now. They all hate and fear me." If I am to win my way back into the tribe, it will require me to loose fire and ice on Kupari. I glance at my arms, where the scars lie red and silver beneath my sleeves. The curse would have eaten me alive that day. If I unleash it again, will it kill me?

Halina has the door open and is peeking into the corridor. Evidently satisfied with what she sees, she comes back inside and pulls me by the wrist. "Stop your spinning mind and follow me," she says. "You may find something that will nourish you."

Fatigue gnaws on my bones, but the desire to see the sky again brings me to my feet, along with the need to be in the open, out from under all this rock. I have no idea where she's taking me, but the question temporarily silences the blizzard of knowledge and questions raging in my head. Grateful for the relief of curiosity and purpose, I trail Halina out the door and into the corridor.

CHAPTER SEVENTEEN

My wish for sunlight is crushed as Halina leads me through a recessed wooden door to a staircase that descends further into the earth. But when I balk, she tugs at me, relentless. "Come *now*," she whispers. "Time is never our friend."

"How do you know our language?" I ask as I begin to follow her again, needing something to get my mind off the press of stone and dank air as we enter a tunnel so low that even though I'm not that tall, I must hunch to keep from conking my head.

"I am good with language," says Halina. "I know Kupari as well. And Korkean. Ylpesian, too. My father was a trader and he took me on his travels when I was little. As for Krigere . . . I learned fast out of a sincere desire to survive."

She tosses me a smile pulled taut by the ghosts in her eyes.

I clear my throat. "Ylpesian? Korkean?"

"The city-states of Korkea and Ylpeys lie west of here, through the Loputon Forest." She looks back, and her gaze is cautious. "Allies."

"Does Nisse know of these city-states?"

Her eyes linger on mine. "Well, now. I don't know, little red. What did his big map say?"

If she means his map on the table in the tower, the answer is no. The area to the south and west of Kupari was blank. Unpainted. "He'll find out."

"Because you tell him?"

I run my tongue along my teeth, uncertainty filling me again as all the revealed secrets of the afternoon stack on one another, high as the tower itself. "I don't know."

Her eyes narrow. "Maybe I'll help you figure it out. Best believe old Nisse is cautious, though. He doesn't allow riders to leave the city, not since we sent an envoy to the Kupari to beg for help after the initial attack. No one in or out, save Krigere. That's the way of it now. Vasterutians are prisoners in our own city."

But considering how easily we just departed my little prison chamber, perhaps things are not as locked down as Nisse hoped. "Where are we going?"

"Not far now." She skitters along the passage, raw earth held up with wooden posts, some still green. As if it has been newly dug and braced, though such an endeavor would take months. Months . . . perhaps since the early spring.

I stare at her back with new suspicion. "Where do your loyalties lie?"

"What a question."

"What an answer."

She lets out a grunt of laughter. "Loyalty is precious, little red. Hard won, hard lost. Easily given, easily betrayed." She pushes through a door, and suddenly we are outside the tower, outside the stake-wall that surrounds it . . . and below the hill on which it sits. I'm in a narrow lane between two tall shelter buildings, ankle deep in snow that melts away from my boots as if afraid of me.

Halina stares down at the retreating ice and whispers something in her own language. Or, who knows, perhaps Korkean or Ylpesian. She is full of surprises. "Ooh. Be careful there. Your tracks will be easy to spot."

I am outside the tower without permission, without Nisse's knowledge. I smile down at the snow, a friendly, welcoming look, I hope. The frost stops fleeing from my ankles and nestles close, reforming as ice. Halina frowns. "And now they're frozen. Great," she says in a rueful voice. "I'm not going to regret this at all." She jabs her finger at me. "Best remember that you have as much to fear from the Krigere as any Vasterutian."

"Just tell me where we're going!"

Her mouth twists. "My brother's house. Because I often make risky decisions. Hopefully I won't regret this one." She grabs my hand and pulls me along the snowy lane. The air is crisp and bitter, but the walls are close and radiate warmth.

Somewhere inside one of these shelters, a baby is crying. Someone is singing. Others arguing. All in a language I do not understand, though I recognize the round honey sound as Vasterutian.

Halina treks through a maze of these shelters until finally she stops in front of a rickety set of wooden steps leading up to the second level of a building. Light pours from within. "Up there," she whispers before starting her climb.

The stairs creak and rattle as we ascend, and a head pokes out of the doorway at the top, a wild spray of black curls framing a heart-shaped face. "Mama," says the little boy, who is perhaps three or four and begins babbling in Vasterutian. Halina answers, her voice firm, and he disappears within once more. She purses her lips when she sees my surprised expression.

"My husband was one of the king's guards. Old Nisse's raiders cut his throat from ear to ear. The day the Krigere came to Vasterut was the day I became a widow. I do whatever I have to do to stay alive—for *that* little boy in there." She doesn't look away from my gaze as she lets her words sink in, and then she enters the shelter with me on her heels.

The chilly room is tiny and cluttered with wooden toys and cooking implements. A low table and a stool are the only furniture. Three figures hunch by the fire, covered in patched cloaks with hoods drawn up. The boy has withdrawn to a corner, his feet wrapped in thick cloth, wearing an ill-fitting, filthy wool tunic. He's crouching next to a basket containing a baby, rosy cheeked and sleeping. Both children have round faces and earth-brown skin.

Halina gestures toward the fire and says something in Vasterutian, and two of the cloaked figures, a woman and a man, toss back their hoods. One of them is the man with the shaved head and black beard who was serving with Halina in the great hall. The other woman doesn't look familiar, but she, too, has a round face and curly black hair, though hers is tamed and pinned against her head.

"This is my brother, Efren," Halina says. The bearded man nods. "And his partner, Ligaya." The woman gives me a wary jerk of her head.

I glance toward the third hooded figure and arch an eyebrow. "And . . . ?"

The third figure pushes back her hood with pale fingers. My breath catches in my throat and I stagger back as Thyra turns to me, looking worried and thin and anxious. "We won't hurt you, Ansa," she says quickly. "You must stay calm. These people mean no harm."

"What are you doing?" I whisper.

Her blue eyes are deep and sorrowful. "Whatever I have to, like I always do."

Her words send a pang straight through me. Today Nisse told me of a Thyra different from the one I thought I knew, one who framed him as an assassin after he caught her plotting to poison her own father. A clever, ruthless Thyra.

Exactly the kind of person who could use someone's love and trust against them. "I've heard a bit about what you *have had* to do."

Her lip curls. "I know who's been whispering lies in your ears." She looks up at Halina and says a few words in halting Vasterutian before adding, "For bringing us here."

"You're welcome." Halina pulls an offered cloak over her own shoulders. "But I didn't do it for your benefit alone. Now I want to talk about how we help each other."

Thyra gives me a sidelong glance. "Give us a moment?"

Halina's nostrils flare, but she says something in Vasterutian to Efren and Ligaya, who step away from us. The three of them turn to the corner where the children are, talking in low, round tones. When I look back at Thyra, she is nearer to the fire, staring into the flames. "You're too skinny," she says quietly.

"Weeks lying flat on one's back with a cracked skull does cause a person to shrivel."

She bows her head. "I had to do it, Ansa. You know that, don't you?"

"Do what?" I ask lightly, even as the curse-fire awakens in my chest, cinders glowing and stinging. "Try to kill me?"

She presses her forehead to her clasped hands. "If our positions were reversed, I'd hope you would do the same."

I look at her in shock. "I would never hurt you." I leave the rest unsaid, but it hangs ugly between us—she hurt me. So badly I can barely breathe now that she is so near. I was in her arms. I thought she loved me. And her heart was cold as stone as she slammed her hilt into my skull.

The fire in the hearth swells with my resentment, snaking tentative tendrils over the stones as if waiting for my command. Thyra scoots back. "Our warriors are in danger," she says. "A great number of them fled the tower the night I was challenged. They were joined by the warriors outside the walls and have barricaded themselves in a group of shelters at the eastern edge of the city."

"Displacing a good number of our people in the process," Efren growls from the corner.

Thyra gives him a troubled look. "I am working to correct all that has gone wrong."

Ligaya tosses her hair and makes a skeptical clucking noise with her tongue, but then the Vasterutians return to muttering among themselves.

I frown as I consider the plight of our tribe. Nisse did not mention any of this when we met this afternoon. "Nisse values warrior lives."

"He values his army." Thyra scoffs. "If he valued their hearts and souls, he would let me speak to them. Instead he keeps me locked away for my own *protection*."

"And yet, here you are. Free within the city."

Thyra smiles and glances toward the three Vasterutians in the corner. "There is help within the tower, offered at great risk."

"For those who defy Nisse," I guess. "What are you *doing*? If he finds out—"

She jabs a finger toward Halina's back. "If he finds out, *they* will be gutted in the square, and their children left to starve, assuming they aren't killed as well," she whispers harshly. "Is that what you want?"

251

"I don't want more *warriors* killed. I want our tribe to be strong again." But I can't help glancing toward the little boy in the corner. I can't help thinking I was about his age when my family was destroyed.

Thyra's fingers tighten over her knees. "You sound like Sander. Does it matter what the price is, Ansa? Will you follow anyone?"

My throat constricts. "I followed *you* until I realized what you were capable of. You cast me aside and almost ended my life, and still you demand my loyalty?"

Thyra gives the fire a nervous glance. Its tendrils are growing like a vine straight out of the hearth, fingers of flame seeking someone to embrace. "I didn't want to hurt you, Ansa. I had to stop you, though. Can't you understand that? Do you remember anything about that night?"

"I remember Jaspar trying to stop the archers and you . . ." *Pretending to care about me so you could sneak inside my guard.*

"You saved me," she says, reaching to touch my cheek.

I lean back out of her reach, unwilling to be snared yet again.

Her hand falls back to her side. "I was trying to do the same for you."

"Jaspar definitely was," I say. "He stood between me and the danger."

"You were the danger." Her expression turns hard. "Has it occurred to you that he was trying to save *them*? You were about to kill those archers."

"You didn't have to hit me!"

252

"I had no idea how to stop you. There were flames in your eyes, and your arms were on *fire*, your tunic burning black and falling right off your body, even as you juggled knives of ice. You didn't even seem aware that the magic was devouring you." She shudders. "I don't regret what I did."

She still sees the monster when she looks at me, I can tell. "Why did Halina bring me here, then? You seem to wish I'd never risen from the ground where you left me."

Her eyes flare with surprise and pain, and she presses her lips together. She turns back to the fire, as if to confront it directly as it tries to caress her. She says nothing to defend herself, nothing to stave off the flames. She merely stares at them, as if daring them to touch her. And the sight reminds me of that night in the fight circle, the way she faced Nisse, and instead of begging for her life, she told him to respect her warriors. Not the act of sacrifice I would expect from a traitor.

The flames pull back, as confused as I am.

She glances at me from the corner of her eye. "I need you to get a message to our warriors. They will not emerge from their enclave if they do not hear from a member of our tribe—if they do not trust the words come from me. They are rapidly running out of supplies, and Nisse has assigned a heavy guard to block all access to them. But I can trust y—"

"*Now* you suddenly trust me again?"

She flinches at the sharp snap of my words. "I'm sorry, Ansa. I regret some of the things I said to you."

"Is that only because you need me right now?"

"No. It's because I've had plenty of time to think about

it while held prisoner by a man who is only keeping me alive until he figures out how best to use me."

"So you've hit upon the best way to use *me*—as your messenger. I'm seeing a family resemblance."

Her mouth is tight, as if she is trying to hold her words captive. Finally she says, "My uncle needs our numbers if he's going to invade Kupari. We comprise nearly a quarter of the warriors within this city. But if Nisse invades Kupari while the snow is thick on the ground, our warriors will emerge from their exile only to die. Imagine what the witch could do with all that ice and cold."

"She might be dead. They may have no ruler."

"Yes. Nisse has sent someone to find out."

Now I know he spoke the truth when he said he had kept her informed. "If the witch has fallen, we could take them over."

She waves her hand toward the Vasterutians. "Like he took them over? You see what he has done here? He's sowing the seeds of our destruction and he doesn't even recognize it because he believes so strongly in our superiority. He is blinded by arrogance."

"I *see* that our warriors sleep safe in a warm city instead of freezing by the northern shore."

"Are we safe?" She waves her arm toward the door. "We are enclosed in a wall of stone, along with an unknown number of people who crave freedom more than their own safety, and another many thousand only awaiting a sign that freedom is possible."

Halina raises her head. Her young son is curled on her

lap, his head against her shoulder, and her arms are tight around him. "Old Nisse might have cowed us for a time, but that does not mean our spirits are crushed. We're going to take our city back." She gives Thyra a frustrated look. "And you said little red would help."

My mouth drops open as I turn back to Thyra. "You did *what?*"

"I said you would be an ally," Thyra says slowly. "You saved me that night in the fight circle, Ansa. It made both of us dangerous outcasts among Nisse's tribe."

But Nisse promised me redemption, if only I do as he asks. I swallow those words. I have a feeling I know what she would say to that, and I'm not in the mood for her questions—they always tear the lid off things I thought were locked down. "So you thought I would join you in helping the Vasterutians defeat the Krigere?" I ask, my voice shaking. "Now who is the traitor?"

Thyra winces and gives Halina an apologetic look. "The Vasterutians want the same things we do, Ansa. We are not so different."

"We *are* different! We're warriors and they aren't."

"There's the arrogance that blinds our tribe," she says. "Don't we all bleed red?"

"It's not arrogance—it's pride in who we are! And our chieftain should have it in abundance."

"I am proud of who we are." Her brow furrows. "I cannot always be proud of what we do. I love our people—and that is why another invasion must be stopped. It is lunacy."

All my doubt and frustration over her refusal to avenge

our tribe rises to the surface once more. "At least Nisse is taking action! He means to give our warriors their vengeance, and their pride."

"So you've chosen your side, little red?" asks Halina.

"I haven't done anything except wake up from a stupor and find myself hopelessly tangled in intrigue and lies!" I glare at Thyra. "But perhaps I was before as well, and I simply didn't realize it."

Efren reaches beneath his cloak, possibly for a weapon.

"If any of you make a move against me, you will instantly regret it," I snarl. "I don't need fire or ice to make people bleed." I don't care if I'm half starved and scarred; I know how to turn people's weapons against them.

"Ansa won't hurt anyone," Thyra says to Efren, then turns her authoritative gaze on me. "She's smarter than that."

"You still haven't told me exactly what you're planning. And don't give me that 'whatever I have to' dung. I don't want to hear it. Are you stirring some sort of rebellion?"

"We don't need either of you for that," says Halina. "But you could help save lives. Krigere and Vasterutian both."

Thyra sighs. "Haven't you ever questioned our way of life, Ansa?"

I squint at her. "Why would I?"

"We live by taking from others."

"Because we are warriors. What else are we to do?"

"Here in the south, they trade with one another."

"So? Why trade when you can simply ride in and snatch what you want?"

"We don't treat our andeners that way." Her jaw tightens. "Or, we shouldn't."

"Our andeners are tribe."

"Ask Nisse how he's treating them next time you see him."

I groan. "What are you getting at?"

"Ansa, do you ever wonder what happened to your parents? Your real parents. The ones who birthed you and loved you?"

I edge backward. "No. And I don't want to."

"Why?"

Because it's too painful. "Because they were victims!" I jump to my feet, my breath rushing from my throat in a cloud of frost as the image of my mother invades my mind. She reaches for me with eyes full of love as she bleeds and burns and dies. "Because they were weak," I say, my voice cracking. *Too weak to protect me from the monsters.*

I push the thought away yet again before confusion can swamp me.

When I open my eyes, Thyra has risen to face me. "Look at her," she says, pointing to Halina, who is hunched protectively over her child. Efren and Ligaya are in front of her, putting themselves between the children and me—the enemy. "Is she weak, Ansa? Is she a victim?" Thyra leans forward. "She's still fighting. Just not with daggers or axes."

I look into Thyra's blue eyes. "Is she like you, then? Does she fight with poison instead?"

Her gaze flickers with suspicion. "What exactly did my uncle tell you?"

"That he never tried to assassinate Lars. But that you

257

did." I watch her, waiting for her to bluster with the outrageous accusation.

She goes still. "And you believed him?"

"I never would have. Never." I swallow the lump in my throat. "But now, after that night in the fight circle . . ."

"I had no choice!"

"You sound so righteous, Thyra. I think you could convince yourself of anything." And me too, sadly. But not this time. "Is that why you framed Nisse for the crime? Because you had no choice?"

Her face is like polished granite, so perfect, so unyielding. "I saw the chance and took it. And if I see another chance, Ansa, I'm going to do the same. Halina told me you met with Nisse this afternoon. The fact that you're still breathing only confirms what I suspected—he wants to use you. And that means you might be the only person who can carry a message to our trapped warriors."

"What about Sander?"

"I haven't talked to him or seen him since that night in the fight circle. Please, Ansa. Do this for our warriors. Tell them that we can liberate ourselves from this city and make our way north again. Nisse might have sealed the exits to this city, but with the help of the Vasterutians, we could get out. In return, we'll help them get their city back."

I stare at her in disbelief, then suck in a deep breath, pushing the ice and fire down, down, down. "I am such a fool," I whisper, my teeth chattering. "I actually felt bad for lying to you about Hulda and Aksel. Your anger was so sharp that it pierced my heart. And here you are, telling me how you've been lying to me all along, and you're not even sorry." I look over at Halina. "*She's* the one responsible for what happened here! If she hadn't schemed to get Nisse banished, he never would have come here!"

"You don't think Nisse was urging my father to sack this place as well?" Thyra asks. "The Torden itself couldn't quench his thirst for power and domination. He wants to turn the entire south into his domain."

"And you unleashed him, and your silence kept everyone from knowing the truth of your part in it."

"My father forbade us to speak of it at all! It seems I'm the only one who honored his wish, though. And as for you . . . I was scared, Ansa. I didn't know how to help you, and we were nearly to the gates of the city when you killed Aksel. I knew what awaited me here, and I was afraid that if you were close to me, it would expose you to more scrutiny and suspicion, right when you seemed most vulnerable to being discovered. I had to keep you at a distance."

"You're a liar. You were only trying to *protect yourself*," I say in a mockery of her voice, her words. "Now be honest, because I see how you look at me. You're only talking to me because *you* want to use me. But you're still disgusted and horrified at what I've done."

She puts her hands up, as if trying to calm me down. "Ansa, that's not true."

"You think I'm a monster. Say it. You hate what I am."

"I don't know what you are anymore," she shouts. "But I could never hate you."

My hands shake as I push them through my hair, knocking off the frost clinging to my brow. It falls in a glittery powder as I glare at her. "You make a very good show of it. But then, you made a good show of loving me, so I shouldn't be surprised."

"Ansa, please. I never wanted it to be this way between us." Her hand crosses the distance.

"*Don't* touch me," I snap, jerking back. My shoulder hits the door frame. "I don't want to hurt you." But I will. I swear, if she puts her hands on me, something terrible will happen.

"I've made mistakes and so have you," she says. "But I need you just as I always have. Our tribe is depending on us. Don't abandon me."

"You abandoned me first!" I yell, and the Vasterutians wince at the sound of my voice.

"You'll be heard," says Halina. "Krigere warriors and andeners have commandeered some of these living spaces, and squads of warriors roam the streets to keep people scared and crush any hint of rebellion. Please. Don't do this here."

I glare at her. "You never should have brought me, then."

"We thought you might help, for her sake." She inclines her head toward Thyra. "Because of what you did for her in that fight circle."

"I will do *nothing* for her sake. Not anymore." I turn

my icy gaze to Thyra. "First you want me to deliver a message, but then what? Use my power to burn Nisse in his bed? Freeze Jaspar solid? It would be convenient for you, wouldn't it? How many more Krigere would you like me to kill on your behalf, *Chieftain?*"

"None! I don't want you to use magic at all!"

Heat sears its way along my bones. "Right. 'Hold it in, Ansa. Control yourself, Ansa. For *once*.'"

"I'm trying to save us! I want to find a way for our whole tribe to live and thrive."

"By asking them to fight against their own?" I ask.

"If I can avoid that, I will." She looks over at the Vasterutians. "But freedom has a cost."

"You'd rather sacrifice your entire tribe than allow them to fight at Nisse's side in Kupari. You'd rather them die for you than live for anyone else."

Thyra steps back as if I've punched her. "It seems I've truly lost you."

The pain in her voice, the betrayal there, causes sparks of confusion and rage to flare and catch inside me. My arms burn and itch and tingle, and there is something wet and sticky running down to my wrists—new blisters burst under the heat. Or the cold. I don't even know which, only that I am full of it, so full that it leaks from me, eating me alive. Halina rises to her feet and pushes her son behind her. "She's losing control, Thyra."

A distant shout from the maze of shelters outside the door makes Thyra pull her hood up over her face. "That's only one of our concerns—Nisse's guard is coming. They must have heard us."

"What are you going to do?" Efren asks her. "We have to get you back to your chamber before your guards wake up."

"Did you poison them, too?" I ask.

Thyra doesn't answer. She heads for the door, her movements smooth but urgent. "I'll buy you time. If they catch you and Ansa here . . ."

Halina presses her son's head to her thigh, her eyes shining with tears of terror that strike a painful note inside me, but Thyra waves her hands. "I'm not going to let it happen, Halina. I made you a promise."

"But if you're caught—" Efren begins.

"This is why I stored the herbs in my own chamber and put them in the guards' goblets myself. No one will take the blame but me." Thyra opens the door just far enough to slide out, and then I hear her footsteps descending to the alley.

I turn to the Vasterutians. "What's she doing?"

Halina rushes toward the door. "We have to get you back to your chamber." She beckons me out into the night with only a brief, loving glance at her family. "If you're caught out, it will be bad for everyone."

I follow her, my cloak billowing around my throbbing arms, my thoughts a maelstrom. Thyra wants to align with the Vasterutians against Nisse. It seems there's no limit to how far she's willing to go to remain in control of our tribe. But . . . all the reasons I loved her still beat within me, refusing to melt or evaporate no matter how hot my fury burns. Blindly, lost in the churn and shatter of devotion and deception, I trail Halina until her arm shoots out and bars my path.

"Shhh." She peeks out, then shrinks back. "Oh . . . this is bad."

"What is it?" But already I hear the sounds of a struggle. I push past Halina to peer from the shadows.

Thyra is on the ground in the middle of a wide lane, surrounded by Krigere warriors. My fingers curl into the stone wall of a shelter as one of them kicks her in the ribs. Her breath explodes from her mouth and she draws her knees to her chest, curling in on herself. From the way her limbs shake with pain and weakness, I know that's not the first time she's been struck.

Stay down, I think.

She rolls to her stomach and clumsily gropes for a dagger sheathed along one of the guards' calves. He knees her in the chest and she falls backward. "I know we're not to bruise her face, but if she doesn't stay down—"

"She will," says a stout female warrior as she quickly kneels behind Thyra and wraps her arm around her throat. Thyra makes a wheezing, choked sound as her face turns crimson. She claws weakly at the warrior's sleeve. The air around us starts to steam as my unspoken guilt and panic simmer inside.

"She's pulled their attention away from finding us," Halina whispers as Thyra goes limp. "Don't betray yourself now—she sacrificed herself for your safety."

Nisse's warriors yank Thyra up by the arms. She is limp, barely conscious. Her feet drag against the frozen ground as they lug her back to the tower.

Halina tugs on my cloak. "Come on," she whispers. "I know another way to get back to the tunnel. Come with me now if you don't want to share her fate."

I have always wanted to share Thyra's fate. Always.

Until today, when I realized I didn't understand her at all. And now she belongs to her enemy once again.

Without another word, I whirl around and follow Halina back to safety.

CHAPTER EIGHTEEN

Halina is silent and jumpy as she leads me back through the dirt tunnel to the tower. She keeps tossing wide-eyed looks over her shoulder as if wondering when I'm going to shout for Nisse's guards and tell them all I've just heard.

I do not relieve her fears. She's lucky I don't strangle her, though in my present state there's a good question of which of us would come out on top. She's put me in a hideous position. She's conspiring with other Vasterutians, and with Thyra. And she's trying to drag me into it.

Halina presses me back into the tunnel as we reach the corridor that leads to my windowless chamber, but when she sees the hall is clear, she pulls me by the wrist. I hiss with the pain of new burns, and she lets me go, biting her lip as she looks down at my sleeve, dotted with ooze. "I'll take care of that," she says.

"Why would you?"

Her eyes are black in the almost-darkness of the hall. "First, because that is what I've been told to do, and if I don't do it, Nisse will have me killed." She rolls her eyes. "And second, because this isn't your fault, and I know it hurts."

I blink at her. "But after all I just said—"

"No matter, little red. Doesn't change who I am." She flashes me a rueful half smile and pulls the key to the chamber from her pocket. She's just bundled me into the tiny room when there's a banging on the door.

When she opens it, Sander is standing outside. "I came to make sure Ansa is . . ." His gaze shifts to me. "Thyra's just been captured out in the city."

I do my best to look surprised. "What? How? Nisse told me she was in protective custody."

His eyes are like keys, probing at every lock I have. "She was. And now she is again. I thought you might have—"

"Been helping her?" I ask.

Halina lets out a jittery chuckle. "Little red's been here the whole time, sir. I'd never let her out—wouldn't want to risk displeasing the chieftain."

Sander turns his prying eyes to her, but she stands steady beneath the scrutiny. "You'll be questioned," he tells her. "All the Vasterutian attendants will be. Thyra managed to get friendly with the guards outside her chamber, and slipped some kind of herb into their mead that left them in a stupor. Nisse will want to know how she got hold of it."

"I saw her gathering herbs on our journey here," I say quickly. And even though it's a lie, I realize bitterly that this latest act against her guards fits what Jaspar said about her. What if I'm only telling half a lie, one that actually captures the truth? "She may have had them when she entered the city. You know she wanted to be ready for anything." And if Sander believes me, it will protect Halina. I'm not completely sure why I want to, except that I can't quite rid myself of the vision of her hunched in the corner, her arms around her little boy.

The taut line of Halina's shoulders curves toward ground. "We'd never want to anger old Nisse," she says, her voice meek, cowed like she's supposed to be.

"Good." Sander is quiet for a moment, long enough to make me squirm. And then he clears his throat and says, "I'm wondering if you want to stretch your legs, Ansa. Will you walk with me?"

"With a blade pressed against my neck the whole time? No, thanks." In truth, I'm dying to lie down on my pallet and let Halina tend to my arms.

"No blade. I just want to talk."

I eye him. "About what?"

He sighs impatiently. "Things that can only be discussed among Krigere."

I glance at Halina, and she pushes my chamber door open and smiles. "I'll just wait, little red. Take care of you when you come back." Her voice is unsteady, dripping with fear. She wonders if I'm about to betray her to Sander.

"Fine. I'll be back soon," I say, and right now it's all I can give her as a reassurance.

"Little red?" Sander asks as we slowly walk up the length of the corridor. He sounds amused.

"I guess it's fair," I say, touching my hair. "She could call me dunghead if she wanted, as long as she keeps treating my burns as she has."

He glances back at my chamber. "You trust her?"

She's too complicated to trust—or to betray right now. "Why wouldn't I?"

"She's Vasterutian."

"Would any of our warriors have spent the last month helping me piss in a pot?"

He snorts. "Fair enough."

We pass the stairs that lead up to the rest of the tower. "Speaking of trust . . . You didn't bring Carina and the other guards."

He looks up the steps. "I don't know who to trust, Ansa. I always knew where I stood with you, though."

"Jaspar said the same to me once."

"Because it's true. And it's a relief. Heaven, the past month." He bows his head, and I can see the weariness bracketing his mouth, lining his brow. "We're fractured, Ansa. I don't know if we'll ever be whole. And now that Thyra's tried to escape . . ."

"Do they know where she was going?"

"No, but they suspect. Preben, Bertel, and over a hundred fifty of our warriors have holed themselves up at the eastern quarter of the city, along with their andeners, and they refuse to cooperate until Thyra tells them what to do. They're surrounded by a squad of Nisse's warriors to prevent the rebellion from spreading to the populace, but the squad has been ordered not to attack. Word is that Thyra may have been trying to get to them. I don't think Nisse will be surprised to hear it, either."

"Why has he let her live, I wonder?"

"That many warriors willing to fight to the death, loyal to the end . . . They'll meet their end before they swear loyalty to a new chieftain, and Nisse knows that."

"They'll starve, if they're isolated like that."

"Nisse's supplying them with food and wood for their fires."

Thyra told me they were running out of supplies. Another lie to manipulate me? "Why is he making it possible to stay where they are?"

"He wants their loyalty, Ansa, not their blood. He's hoping some of them will give in. He doesn't care if he wins in a trickle or a flood."

"He might, if he wants them to invade Kupari. We are a large enough force to make a difference."

"We are. If only I could puzzle out who *we* is these days." He rubs the back of his head. His hair has grown in the past month, and it stands on end as his hand returns to his side. "But that's why Thyra is still important. Nisse is trying to win her over too."

I open my mouth to say that perhaps his warriors didn't get that message—I just saw them beating the stuffing out of her. Then I remember that I was supposed to be in my room the whole time. "Has he won *you* over, Sander?"

He stops and leans against the wall, tapping his skull softly against stone. "Everything is sideways, Ansa. I don't know where I belong. I'm not built for intrigue."

"Me neither." And part of me hates Thyra for forcing it on me. But another part of me hates myself for not saving her tonight.

He smiles. "I know."

"I thought you hated me."

"I hate what you can do. And I have to fit in with Nisse's guard. Understand? I won't keep my freedom otherwise."

"You want to have liberty to jump in either direction." Which is probably why he's not with Preben and Bertel right now.

He shrugs. "And you?"

I sag against the wall next to him, winded from all the walking I've done today after a month of not setting my feet on stone. My ankles are blistered, but not with fire—with the simple rub of leather and wool stockings. My brain feels blistered too. "I don't know. It was so simple, before." But now I can't stop thinking about who I was, who I am, and there's nothing simple about it. And that's before I even begin to think about Thyra and who *she* truly is.

"I think there was more going on beneath the surface than we ever suspected."

"You're more right than you know." I wish I didn't know the half of it.

"What do we do, Ansa?"

"You're really asking me?"

He touches the jagged pink ridge at the bottom of his mangled ear. "It matters. And you've always been Thyra's wolf. Are you, still?"

The image rises like a water spout—Thyra lying, bleeding, in the snow as warriors beat her near to death. "I don't know, Sander," I whisper. "Take me back to my chamber, please?"

He's frowning as he guides me back, clasping my elbow gently. "I understand. Believe me, I do. But the messenger will return from Kupari any day now. That's when Nisse will make his decision whether or not to invade." When we reach the half-open door of the chamber, he glances inside at Halina. "And at that point, we're out of time. We're both going to have to decide which way to jump." He looks down at my feet. "But until then, if you value your life and that of this Vasterutian here, I advise you to clean the mud off your boots."

He strides away as my blood runs icy with fear.

The summons comes two days later, two days spent with Halina's silence and wary watchfulness. I ask her for news—of Thyra, of what's happening in the city, of how our warriors are faring—but she offers me nothing. She comes back from hours gone, her skin clammy and her hair frazzled, and

I know she's been questioned by Nisse or his warriors, but even then she keeps silent. But she changes my bandages, so gentle that it barely hurts. She patiently walks me up and down the hall to help me regain my strength—Sander, who has apparently decided not to tell anyone about the telltale mud on my boots, got permission from Nisse for such things, as long as a warrior guards the stairs. I suppose they don't yet know about the hidden doorway that leads out of the tower, and I don't mention it.

If I even hint that Halina has helped smuggle Thyra out of the tower, or that she is stirring some sort of resistance, she will be executed, made an example.

I should. I know I should. But every time I consider it, I think about the little boy and the baby, their round cheeks and big eyes, their faith that their family can keep them safe. I cannot bear to shatter that faith, to fill their world with more grief and blood. And Halina . . . she looks nothing like the mother who haunts my dreams, the red-haired woman on fire, her blood staining the dirt, who reaches for me with only love in her eyes . . . and yet, sometimes my Vasterutian attendant takes her place, and I see devotion that carries a person past fear of pain and darkness and monsters that come up from the water to take your entire world away. . . .

I wonder what carries a person past the fear that she *is* a monster. That she *delighted* in the violence. The magic did not make me this way. I embraced it ages ago.

I embraced it because I could not bear to be the prey, and my only choice was to become a predator.

I cannot force these thoughts away—they're too powerful. I used to take such pride in killing. I dreamed of kill marks to my fingertips. And now . . . I have shed so much blood that it warrants marks down to my forearm, and I don't want a single one of them. Hulda, Aksel, Flemming, all the others I destroyed . . . Another drop spilled and I might drown in it.

I may not have a choice, though. Now I will have to jump. Because Nisse has summoned me, and it can only mean one thing—word has come from Kupari. Halina helps me with my boots and clothes. Her hands shake as she fastens the ties. I reach down and touch her fingers. "I won't betray you."

She looks up at me, brown eyes wide. "Will you help us?"

I straighten. "I didn't say that."

"Same as betraying, then," she mutters.

"Not by half," I snap. "You should be grateful."

"I should be grateful for your silence, when it allows the injustice to continue?" She curtsies. "*Thank you* for not trying to stop my people being turned out of their homes and left to starve in the cold. *Thank you* for doing nothing while the best food and fuel is given to the invaders, while the people who built this city grow skinny and weak and despairing. *Thank you* for being part of the monster that crushes us. You think because you don't wield the knife, you have no part in the slaughter?"

"You are bold. Too bold."

"Oh, forgive, little red. I should be quiet and sweet all

the time, then? Would that make it easier for you?" She throws up her hands. "I've tried that. You value bravery, but only in the Krigere, I suppose. And you despise meekness, but you demand it of me if it makes you more comfortable!"

My heart thumps hard with confusion and frustration. "But I'm not telling Nisse of whatever you're doing. I won't cause your death."

"If Nisse decides to invade, who do you think will carry your supplies and make your fires? Who will he drag into the winter cold to keep his warriors fed and watered?"

I step back from her, my mouth open to tell her about the andeners, but then I realize—the andeners always stayed in camp when we raided, waiting for us to return. But this, another invasion . . . "Vasterutians?"

She nods. "Able-bodied men and women whose backs can bear the load, whose legs can carry them far away, into the land of magic and treachery. Me included, and who cares about what happens to my baby boy? He's just a Vasterutian, after all." She lunges forward, so quickly that I fall back onto my bed with her standing over me. "Think I'm going to let that happen? Think I won't fight?" She grimaces and steps back. "Think I won't die?" she adds softly. "Think you won't have killed me, just because you didn't speak out against me? *Thank you*, then."

I edge to the end of the bed and stand up. "Stop it. We don't . . . we don't even know what's going to happen yet."

She stares at me for a long moment, then laughs and shakes her head. "Right. Well, then." She gestures to the hallway as the sound of footsteps reaches us. "I am eager to find out."

Still reeling with her sudden brashness, I step into the hallway, relieved at the familiar sight of warriors, even ones who look at me with suspicion. Sander gives me a tight, barely perceptible nod as he steps behind me. Carina, on the other hand, keeps her fingers wrapped tightly around her sheathed dagger as she walks beside me. It's a tense journey up to the top of the tower. I'm dying to ask Sander if there's word of Thyra, or Preben and Bertel and the warriors who hold the eastern part of the city, but I know it's not safe here.

When we reach Nisse's council chamber, the guard steps back and lets me walk in alone. Nisse and Jaspar look up from the painted table as I enter. Nisse smiles. "Our rider returned from Kupari this morning. Their city looks worse than ours, apparently. Not the wealthy stronghold we expected."

"Does that mean there is no witch queen in the temple?"

Jaspar shrugs. "Apparently there is, but they delayed her coronation."

"Why?"

"Their politics are a mystery," Nisse says, a smile pulling at his mouth. "But perhaps we can still uncover the truth. They have invited us to witness her ascension to the throne."

I cross my arms over my chest. "So will you invade or not?" I hate the thoughts I'm having, of Halina and the other Vasterutians being taken away from their children, just to supply our force.

"I haven't decided," says Nisse. "But I think, in this case, I will follow the path my dear niece is always urging. We'll be cautious."

My eyebrows rise. "So you won't invade?"

"Not immediately." His green eyes are full of eagerness. "So—what do you say?"

"To what?"

"Will you come with us?" Nisse asks. "You could be our hidden weapon."

"But you said you weren't invading."

"Not yet, but if you were to come with us, perhaps you could . . ." He waves his hand toward me. "We'll be very close to the queen. She won't expect magic to come from one of our own. If she is just being crowned, it is likely she is new and young and inexperienced."

"You want me to assassinate her. With magic."

He smiles. "It would clear the way for our warriors and save many lives. It would make them all indebted to you. No one would remember what happened in the fight circle."

"And it would be your chance for vengeance," says Jaspar. "Perhaps not on the queen who cursed you, but certainly on her heir."

I turn toward the fire, thinking of my fantasies ever since that horrible day on the lake, of striding into the witch's throne room and ramming fire down her white throat. Heat courses down my arms, a powerful rush of cursed magic. But the pain follows hard on its heels, raising new blisters that burst and weep. I cry out, tears starting in my eyes. "Something has gone wrong with me," I say between gasping breaths. "The curse has turned against me. It's killing me."

"What?" Nisse asks in a hard voice. "I saw you in the fight circle. You had complete control of it."

I shake my head. "I think it controlled me."

"I don't believe that," says Jaspar. "Ansa, you knew what you were doing. The elements obeyed every wave of your fingers."

"My head, then. It's . . ."

Nisse's fists clench. "Thyra hit her so hard that it damaged her ability to wield the magic."

"I'm not blaming her," I say, not even sure why I'm defending her, only that I cannot help fearing for her when I hear the blade of his voice. "I'm sorry. I know I'm disappointing you. If I had a little more time to recover . . ." I don't want him to punish her for this. But also—if I don't figure out how to control this magic inside me, I'll never have a place within the tribe again.

Nisse lets out a long breath. "Of course. You must stay here and continue your recovery. We must get you strong so that you can be the fearsome force of vengeance we saw only a month ago!"

"I'm sorry," I say again. "I know this was a good chance to go and assess their capabilities."

"Oh, we'll still go. This is too important, for many reasons other than the opportunity you presented." He calls for the guards. "Bring her in!"

I turn toward the door as Thyra is led in. She looks pale and walks stiffly, though she is not shackled. I stare, wondering what has been done to her in the last two days. Though I despise her for lying to me, for not being who I always thought she was, I take no pleasure in the pained look on her face. "Thyra?"

Her gaze lingers on mine for a long moment before shifting to her uncle. "How nice to see you again, Uncle. Your warriors have faithfully—and frequently—offered me your greetings these past few days."

Nisse smiles. "I'm so glad we were able to bring you back into our circle of protection, Thyra. You're lucky we found you before you stumbled into a dangerous part of town." He approaches her, and she tenses but refuses to backtrack as he nears. "And you'll be seeing a great deal of me over the next few days, it seems." He lets that sink in before adding, "We're riding to Kupari. We leave immediately."

Her eyes go wide as he instructs her guards to take her back to her chamber and help her pack for the journey. Nisse's hand settles on my back. "See? Despite her betrayal and ongoing treachery, I respect your chieftain." There is a question in his eyes, though, as if he is wondering whether she still has my allegiance.

"Is she your hostage?" I ask.

He chuckles. "What an unpleasant way of putting things. I am merely keeping my niece close, because I recognize her importance. Though I also recognize that she may present . . . a temptation."

I swallow hard. "To me?"

He smiles. "To many." He pats my back. "Now. You go rest. We'll be back in a few days, and I want to see your progress." The mirth in his eyes disappears, replaced by determination. "You could be our salvation, Ansa. The treasure of the Krigere. I hope you recognize how much you mean to us. Do not question your worth. And don't let anyone else do it, either."

He calls Sander and the others to escort me to my chamber, and once again I trudge away from his council room, my head packed so full of information and questions that I can't think straight. *Do not question your worth*, he said. But right now—with Thyra being taken to Kupari, with Halina glaring at me as if I'm failing some important test, with the entire future of the Krigere depending on my ability to control and wield a cursed magic that I don't understand and that might well kill me, against a people I once belonged to—I am questioning everything.

CHAPTER NINETEEN

I am moved to a chamber on one of the top floors of the castle, in time to have a view of Nisse, Thyra, and a squad of his warriors leaving the protection of the tower and the stake-wall to ride through the city, on the road to Kupari. Thyra has been given a helmet and new cloak, as well as a sword that is probably too heavy for her to wield competently.

But Nisse wants to put on a show, I suspect, and so he gives her the weapons they fear, because they don't understand us. I hope it works. He is taking a tiny force into enemy territory.

I am left behind with all my questions, fearing the march of the sun through the sky. Halina is back to being quiet and cautious, gentle but remote. I tell her that Thyra has been taken, and she doesn't seem surprised.

She says nothing more to me about helping her, and I am glad. In knowing her, I've come to wish no harm on the Vasterutians, but they cannot be my people.

Truthfully, I don't know who my people are anymore.

I fit with the Krigere so neatly, or so I always told myself. I took so much pleasure every time a true Krigere told me I was one of them. I took pride in being a victor, and security in being part of a tribe so strong that no one could tear us apart and take me away.

Like they had torn me away from my Kupari family.

I don't know where I belong now. The loss eats at me, loneliness with teeth.

Jaspar comes to see me only a few hours after his father leaves the city. I look at him with surprise as he enters my chamber. "I thought you would go with them."

His smile contains a hint of bitterness. "Someone had to be in charge while the chieftain was away."

"But you wanted to go." I watch him as he walks to the window and peers out. "Do you miss sleeping under the stars and raiding in the morning?"

"Ah. You know me too well." He leans on the stone sill. "Shall we walk? I think we both need the air."

I glance nervously at the door. "I'm not eager to face more hateful stares."

"Come." His smile is warm as sunlight. "You'll breathe free when we're up high." When I don't move, he goes to the door and opens it. "You'll feel like a bird, I promise."

"Why—are you going to push me off the parapet?"

"Only if you leap on my back and bite my ear off." He winks and heads into the hallway. I follow, my shoulders drawn up when I hear the laughter of warriors coming from a chamber down the corridor. But Jaspar ducks into the staircase that spirals up, and we walk until we reach a door directly over our heads. "Wait until you see," he says, pushing the door open.

What I see is sky, and it calls to me like a lover. I smile as he boosts me into the cold winter air and scoot to the side as he pulls himself up to join me. It's a relatively large space, enough for a ring of twenty archers to kneel comfortably. I crawl over to the low wall and gasp as I see the Torden, vast and white-gray under scattered, wispy winter clouds. The cold nips my nose and fingers but is pushed back immediately by the fire inside me. I shake my head in confusion as Jaspar joins me.

"What's wrong?" he asks.

"Sometimes this curse protects me, and sometimes it causes me agony. I can't tell what it wants or how to please it." I bite my lip. "Or how to rule it." I know that's what Nisse wants.

Jaspar looks down at my hand, where scarring swirls across my knuckles. "I am sorry you have suffered so much. Do you ever regret surviving the storm that day?"

I stare at the waves, only ripples compared to the churn of water in my memory. "That is a complicated question."

He traces a fingertip along a swirl of silver across the back of my hand. "I hope someday it will be simple. And that the answer will be no."

"Me too," I whisper.

"There is no one fiercer or stronger to bear this burden, though," he continues. "I have no doubt about that."

I laugh. "I do."

"I know. But only because you've been pushed there."

"What do you mean?"

"What if you had a chieftain who loved what you are, instead of fearing or despising it?"

I groan. "Are you here to convince me to join Nisse?" I am so tired of being the animal hide in this game of tug of war.

"I don't want to convince you of anything. You'll make the decision on your own. I'm just asking you the same kinds of questions I've been asking since the moment I saw you again, standing so strong at my cousin's side—without knowing what she'd done, or who she really was."

"She didn't—" I clamp my lips shut. I was about to tell him she hadn't denied the accusation when I asked her, but that would reveal that I've spoken to her. "I don't know why she didn't just tell me the truth in the first place."

"I do. She knew you would have struggled with the truth, because you are an arrow, Ansa. You fly straight. You find your target. You do not twist and bend."

"I certainly feel like I've been tied in knots now."

"Who could blame you? It should be simpler. For you especially. Whether you can't wield your magic because of the blow to the head she gave you—or the shame she's piled upon you for simply being who you are—"

"I lied to her, Jaspar. I killed that slave, a woman who

hadn't threatened me. It was an accident, but I did it to keep her silent. I'm not innocent. I killed Aksel, too."

"Out of necessity, I have no doubt." Jaspar looks down at me, looking entirely undisturbed. "Thyra has never accepted you just as you were. Even before you were cursed." He lets loose a grunt of laughter. "She doesn't accept anything. Always sowing doubt. But when she had to swallow that bitter brew herself, as she did on our journey from the north, she bristled with the taste. And yet, still, she seems intent on destroying us."

My brow furrows. "That's not . . . I don't think that's what she wants. It wouldn't make any sense. She could have ordered us to fight to the death when you came to the camp—she had every reason to fear coming here. But instead, for the sake of the andeners and her warriors, she came quietly. And when she had the chance to beg for her life in the fight circle, she only asked for the safety and health of her warriors."

"I'm sorry, Ansa. It's hard for me to see past the damage she's done. And when I look at you, I can see her marks on you. I see you struggling to hide who you are, and to hold everything inside to meet her approval. . . ." His hand covers his chest, his fingers fisting over his tunic. "It enrages me. Why do you love someone who doesn't love who you are?"

Tears sting my eyes and I turn away from him. "Stop," I say hoarsely. "No more."

"My father and I—we see who you are. We value that."

I close my eyes. "Thank you."

His hand covers mine, careful and warm. "I hope it helps. Doubting yourself and what you can do—and whether you should wield the power you have—that cannot be healthy for you. And I wonder if that is why it's hurting you."

I sniffle. "I hadn't considered that."

"I know." He smiles and squeezes my hand. "And that is why I needed to make sure I said it. And now, I want to ask you something." He nudges my shoulder with his own. "Will you spar with me?"

"What? Are you addled?"

He purses his lips. "Maybe? But I have missed it so."

"You might be taking your life in your hands."

"Stepping into a fight circle with you is *always* that way." He rises and holds his hand out. "Let's give it a try. Just grappling. Please?"

I let him pull me away from the wall. "Here?"

"Why not?"

My heart is skipping with an eager, happy rhythm. "Are you sure you're not just planning to throw me over the side?"

He widens his stance, beckoning me forward. "I guess you'll have to trust me."

My laughter is high and happy and real. "Fair enough." And then I charge.

I lie on the cool wooden floor of my new chamber, staring up at the timber braces above. I ache all over, but not with new blisters. Instead, it is a pure pain, one I welcome—I've been sparring with Jaspar every afternoon for the past three days. I can feel my strength returning, the simple, uncomplicated joy of fighting with only my wits and my speed. I am nowhere near as good as I was, nowhere near able to subdue Jaspar, but I can get away from him nearly every time, which is almost as good—he can't keep me down. And his grin every time I rise from the ground makes me feel like a conqueror. It has helped keep my mind off the mission to Kupari, what might happen when Nisse and Thyra return—and the fact that I am running out of time.

Halina has just taken my noonmeal scraps away, and I know she will be gone for a good long while, cleaning up and chatting with the other attendants in the kitchen, where no warriors bother to go. I've noticed this. I have no idea what the Vasterutians are discussing as they mull about down there, whether they have rebellion or pot scrubbing on their minds, and I push thoughts of it away. It doesn't matter right now.

All that matters is the curse, and whether I can control it. Regardless of what happens, wielding this power will help me. I close my eyes, seeking the fire and ice inside me. It rushes forward eagerly, like a child who wants a sweet, or perhaps just to be noticed. I breathe slowly as it floods my chest. It feels huge, as if I'm poised on the crest of a giant wave, deadly potential and unstoppable momentum. I remember this force as it rushed to my aid that day in the fight circle, as it rolled deadly and vicious from my hands and thoughts. The memory is both terrifying and seductive. Are we friends, or enemies?

I spread my palms and turn them toward the ceiling. So many times over the last many days, I have pressed the magic down, knowing that allowing it into my consciousness would bring more pain, more burns. Before that night in the fight circle when I let it loose, before I gave in to it so completely, it did not hurt me, but once I wielded it with intention, somehow it burrowed deep inside me, setting roots inside my marrow. Now my arms are raw meat, and there are spots of agony along my torso and my legs. The disease has spread, and when Halina saw the damage, her shocked expression told me exactly how hideous it was. But if I can wrestle the curse into submission, I will find my way back to my people. I will be able to walk among them without fearing the jab of a knife or a stare just as sharp and lethal.

I could be Krigere again. I could forget everything else. I crave the safe simplicity of it.

Carefully, I think of ice. Not a blizzard, not a gale, but only frost on leaves and grass, a kiss of cold in the still air. And I feel it caress my brow, so gentle. The quiet creep and crackle of it draws my gaze, and when I turn my head I see the maze of crystals growing around my body, slithering slowly along the floor as my breath fogs the air. It feels so good. This cannot possibly be wrong.

I sigh and settle into it, summoning the heat now, letting it scamper up from where it was hiding and burst into the open. It is hungrier than the ice, but more play-ful too. Wisps of flame appear above me, spiraling around my body, making me dizzy. The fire glows, melting the ice, though the frost re-forms only moments later as if challenging the heat.

Surely I can control this. Surely this magic won't hurt me. It seems to love me. It kisses my skin so sweet, like relief, like joy. And I need it, after so much fear and pain. I sit up slowly, hope taking root. Here is the ease I craved, that I feared would never be mine. This curse, given with malice, has a life of its own, but now it belongs to me, not the witch. It doesn't do her bidding. It is mine.

I rise, my palms upturned. On one hand sits a ball of fire, and on the other, a swirl of frost and untainted cold. I tickle them with my fingers, and they dance for me. Jaspar was right—I should not question what I am anymore, even if I question where I belong. I should not listen when Thyra urges me to doubt, when she tells me to control myself.

Why do you love someone who doesn't love who you are?

A swell of resentment surges within me. It's not my fault I was cursed and invaded, burned and frozen by the violation of fire and ice.

Suddenly the ball of fire on my palm is as large as a shield. I gasp and clench my fist, but it becomes a maelstrom, rising toward the ceiling.

The *wooden* ceiling.

"Stop," I whisper. "Obey me." But my heart is beating so hard, full of fear and anger, and *that* is what it seems to be listening to. I grasp at the flames and hiss as they cling to my fingers, biting too hard. I summon the cold to fight it, and blades of ice form and spin on my other hand. They begin to stab at the fire as a bitter chill descends on the room, so sudden and frigid that my face is numb in an instant. I cry out, and the fire rises higher and spreads wide, blackening the ceiling and reaching for my bed.

"No!" I shriek as my blanket catches fire, and then the straw tick pad beneath it. My breath comes out in a spray of frost as the fire doubles back on me.

My tunic catches fire, and I scream.

A shout from the hall is followed by a crunching crash, and Sander and Jaspar barrel into the room. I flail, my sleeves aflame, as Jaspar grabs the pitcher on a side table and flings its contents at me. My back hits the floor and shouting fills my ears. More water splashes onto me, followed by soaked, heavy cloth and an unyielding body that presses me down. "Calm yourself," Sander huffs. "Please. Don't kill me, too. Ansa. Please. Be still."

I collapse under the weight of failure and despair and horror, the pain so intense that it makes me writhe and shiver. Voices bark various orders above me, for more water, for bandages, for Halina, for medicine, for a fire in the grate, for no fire at all. Confusion reigns as I wish for darkness and quiet. But there is no such mercy for me. I am completely aware as I am peeled from the floor and doused with water yet again. Sander shouts at someone to bring him heavy leather gloves, and I realize I must be burning him. But when I wish for the cold, he yelps and lets me go, stung by the ice. Someone, probably Carina, offers to kill me, but Jaspar roars at her to leave the room. "My father wants her alive!" he shouts at her retreating form.

Nisse wants me alive.

I am his broken sword.

Tears run down my face as I begin to laugh. My skin is ruined and weeping and steaming, all over now, not just my arms. The fire and ice are rabid and mad, and I'm not strong enough to wield them. They slide silent and venomous back inside me as I am laid on a fresh blanket on the floor. Sander leans over me. "Your attendant is coming," he says. "She will do what she can for you."

But I hear the crack in his voice, the rasp of helplessness. I remember it from that day on the Torden. "Am I going to die?"

His eyes meet mine. "I don't know."

There is a shout from the corridor. "Are you sure?" Jaspar calls from his spot just behind Sander, where he holds a full water pitcher, just in case. When he hears the answer to his question, he nods. "Tell them to get up here immediately, then! We'll take whatever help we can get!"

"What's happening?" I whisper.

"The party from Kupari has returned," Sander says, sounding bemused. He looks down at me again, and I see my own ruined face reflected in his dark eyes. "And apparently they've brought someone who can help you."

I am shaking with agony as dark-cloaked figures rush into the room. "Better hurry," Jaspar says. "I think she's dying."

Thyra reaches me first, her eyes wide with horror. "Oh, Ansa," she whispers, "I'm so sorry. But this will all be better soon. I promise."

I blink up at her through swollen eyelids. "H-how—"

Nisse leans into my line of sight. "She's right, Ansa. Try to stay calm." He raises his arm, welcoming a third person to my side.

This one has the thick stubble of black hair around his jaw and over his head, as if he had shaved it all off but now it's growing back. His lips seem swollen, two fat slugs sitting on his face. But his eyes are alight with curiosity. He says something in the trilling, looping language I recognize as Kupari. Halina is shoved to her knees next to him. "He says you must have a great deal of fire, to have done this to yourself," she says in a flat voice, wrenching her arm away from Sander.

"Ice, too," Jaspar says, and Halina translates for the dark stranger, who nods. He smiles down at me and speaks again. His voice is gentle. Comforting.

"He says he's going to heal you," Halina says.

"Please," I murmur. "It hurts."

The stranger looks up at Thyra and Nisse and gestures for them to give us space. He asks a question. Halina turns to Nisse. "He wants to know if his apprentice has been provided for."

"He's been put into a bed chamber to rest," says Nisse.

Once Halina conveys this to the stranger, he smiles and nods, then pokes his fingers at my body while babbling in his ridiculous language. "He wants to know what pains you most," Halina translates.

My heart. But that doesn't make sense. He can't help me with that. "My face."

"Then close your eyes," Halina says as the stranger speaks. "He says it won't hurt."

I obey, and almost immediately thereafter I feel the strangest sensation across my cheeks—wisps of fire and ice, sinking into my skin, making it tingle. It feels like a million tiny needles poking me at once, and yet somehow it numbs me instead of causing more pain.

"Amazing," Nisse murmurs.

"Oh, thank heaven," Thyra says, her voice thick with tears.

I remain still, grasping any straw of hope, relieved that the horror has left their voices. I sink into the sensation as it moves across my scalp, and then into my throat, across my chest, down my torso, along each of my legs and then my arms. . . . I am turned over, and the tingling begins anew across my back.

The stranger asks Halina something. "Yes, the scars on her arms are over a month old." She waits and listens to his reply, then says, "He says he can't fix those. Only new wounds."

"Then we're grateful we got here when we did," says Nisse. "She looks so much better."

I open my eyes as I'm turned onto my back again. The pain is gone. I glance down at my body, my scarred arms, the rest untouched . . . and covered in soaked, blackened rags. I shiver, and Jaspar calls out, "A blanket, please!"

Sander strides over with a fresh wool blanket a moment later, and Thyra spreads it over me. I blink up at the people around me. One would think that after what has happened, I would have more on my mind than embarrassment, but it rises just the same. I don't like that all of them are looking down at me with their eyes full of questions. I glance at Nisse. "I was trying to use the magic," I say, my voice a ruin from all the screaming.

Nisse looks at the stranger. "So here, obviously, is the warrior I was telling you about."

Once Halina translates, the stranger chuckles as if that were obvious.

"Who is he?" I ask. "What's happening?"

"Oh, forgive us, Ansa. We are only just catching our breaths." Nisse gestures at the stranger. "This is Kauko. He was an elder in the temple of Kupari."

"He has quite a story to tell," says Thyra, suspicion in her voice.

"And we'll hear him out once Ansa has had a chance to rest," Nisse says firmly, glaring at her.

"How did he heal me?" I ask as I look up at Kauko, who is wearing the same kind of black robe the witch queen's minions wore.

Kauko smiles down at me and answers slowly, so Halina can translate. "He says he wields the same magic you do, little red." Kauko leans forward as he continues to talk, setting his large hands on his thighs. Halina's eyes go wide as she listens, then takes a breath before translating. "And he says if you let him, he can teach you how to use it too."

CHAPTER TWENTY

I don't know how long I sleep, but when I awake, my hair is a soft fuzz over the top of my head, already starting to grow back after being burned away by the hateful magic. Halina sits next to my bed, her face drawn, dark circles under her eyes. She's probably been acting as translator in addition to being my attendant, and looks like she hasn't slept for days.

I suddenly wonder if she's seen her little boy. If he wonders where his mother has gone. If he cries for her at night.

"Evening, little red. Welcome back."

I look up at the ceiling. I'm in the tiny stone chamber where I spent most of the last month. "Am I a prisoner again?"

She shakes her head. "But this room does not have a

wooden floor or ceiling. It seemed safer. Come. Now I take you to old Nisse. He got himself a Kupari priest somehow." She shudders. "And a ghost of an apprentice."

"What?"

"You'll see." She gives me a tight smile. "I'm glad you didn't die."

"Really?"

Her eyes narrow. "Mostly."

She helps me get dressed and joins me in the hallway as the guards gather around us. Sander smiles when he sees me and runs his hand over my fuzzy head. I blink at him—he doesn't usually touch me unless we're sparring. He leans in and whispers, "I didn't like watching you burn to death, all right?"

I smile. "Thank heaven for that." Because if he and Jaspar hadn't burst in and tried to help me, I might have been a pile of ash before the stubbly priest even reached me.

We march up to Nisse's council room, and this time, Thyra is present, as is Jaspar. The elder sits at the painted table. Another man, this one young and pale, with black-brown eyes and a short fuzz of hair the color of winter sunlight, haunts the corner. Kauko sees me looking at him and smiles, speaking once again in the trilling Kupari language. "That's his apprentice," Halina says. "His name is Sig. Apparently he's been through a terrible ordeal and you should forgive him."

"For what?"

Halina rolls her eyes. "Chances are you're about to

find out." She mutters something under her breath in Vasterutian but clamps her mouth shut when Nisse gives her a cold glare.

Sig is staring at me with a blank, blunt sort of look. His face looks as if it has been carved from stone, sharp cheekbones and jaw, straight nose. He would be frankly handsome, except there is a swirl of burn scars across his brow and along his cheeks. He's clad in a tunic and breeches that don't quite fit—on his lean frame they hang loose, clearly not his own. Sweat beads on his brow even though this room is barely warm, with only torches and the fire in the hearth to chase away the dead winter chill.

"Hello," I say.

He tilts his head and speaks in Kupari, his voice shaky. Halina sighs. "He wants to know if it hurt, when you caught fire."

My gaze traces the line of scarring down his throat. "Looks like he would know."

"Please sit down, Ansa," says Nisse, drawing my attention back to the players at the table. Thyra is on one side, opposite Jaspar, who sits next to Kauko. Nisse sits at the head.

I sit at the opposite end of the table, not wanting to take a place next to Thyra. Jaspar's words ring too readily in my head for that. He gives me a reassuring nod as I settle myself in the chair, and Thyra clears her throat and looks away. Halina remains standing at Nisse's side, quietly translating what is said into Kupari for Kauko's benefit.

"We have had quite an adventure," Nisse says, scratching his face. I peer at the blackened stubble on the right side of his jaw, and he chuckles. "My beard was almost a casualty."

"You're lucky any part of you survived," Thyra says. "We both were." She gives me a hollow-eyed look. "Two of the warriors who went with us did not live through the experience."

"What happened?" I ask.

"We rode into the city to see the coronation of the new queen—the Valtia. Or, at least, that's what we *thought* we were seeing."

Kauko sighs and shifts uncomfortably, as if the bench is too hard for his soft bottom. Thyra turns to me. "They had us on the steps leading up to a platform. First they brought in the little princess. The Sabkella—"

"Saadella," says Kauko.

"Right. She's the heir to the Valtia's magic," says Thyra. "She was a tiny thing. Only four or five at the most." She looks like she finds the whole idea disgusting. "She sat on a little throne and wore a little crown—"

Kauko begins to babble. "He says it's an important symbol," Halina interprets.

"Our only symbols of power are our broadswords," says Jaspar.

Kauko smiles when she translates, nodding at Jaspar as if he's made a joke.

"Anyway," Thyra continues. "Then they trotted out their queen, lifted high on a throne they carried through the streets.

She had on a gown that seemed to be made entirely of copper, a copper cuff—"

"With red marks on it," I murmur.

"What?" asks Nisse.

"I saw it," I say, feeling hollow. "When she called down the storm on us."

Thyra's expression has softened. "I saw it too. And she had a blood-red mouth, and a face painted white like the snow."

I wince at the sudden, stabbing memory of the witch queen's cracked face. "It was paint?" I suppose that makes sense, but it was thick as a mask.

Kauko nods and speaks to Halina, who grunts. "He says the Kupari people expect such things. It comforts them."

"Then they are comforted by the oddest things," I blurt out. Was I really one of them, at one time?

"Kauko speaks of them as if they were children," Thyra says. "And they looked so desperate in that square."

Nisse chuckles. "And perhaps they are, Niece. Sheep in need of shepherds. And now that we've established that, let's continue to tell Ansa what happened, maybe?"

Thyra's cheeks flush. "So they brought this queen out and set her on the platform, and a bunch of black-robed priests"—she waves her hand at Kauko's round belly—"put a big crown on her head."

Nisse lets out a huff of amusement. "And that's when the show began. The fire in the torches around the square rose and twisted and entwined until they caged us in."

I glance at the torch bracketed to the wall. "It can do that?"

Thyra arches an eyebrow. "You've done something very similar, Ansa. Just not as . . . big."

From the corner of my eye, I see Sig tilt his head as Halina translates, and I turn to see that a cold curiosity has stripped the blankness from his stare. He whispers something, his voice just a hiss. Halina swallows. "He says he'd like to see that."

The flames of the torch nearest to him flare.

"Sig," barks Kauko.

Sig's mouth snaps shut and the flames bank, but I'm left staring at them, my heart pounding. "How did you escape, if the flames trapped you? Is that how you were burned?" I ask Nisse.

"No. For a short while the Valtia seemed to be controlling it," says Thyra. "She raised her arms and the flames went higher. But then . . ." She stares down at her hands and shakes her head.

"The fire turned on her, Ansa," Nisse says. "It arched over the platform and slammed down upon her, devouring her. We ran for our lives." He touches his singed beard. "It nearly ate us, too."

Sig chuckles softly from his corner. Nearly everyone at the table looks at him with wary dislike as he laughs at the thought of their peril, but Kauko merely gives him a chiding glance before launching into a speech. "Kauko says he has been in the service of the magic of the Valtia for longer than he can remember," Halina translates. "And—"

Sig begins to giggle, his whole body shaking with mirth. A tear runs down the side of his scarred face. He mutters a question, a strange light flickering in his brown eyes. "He wants Kauko to tell us exactly how long it's been," Halina says with a frown.

Kauko rises slowly from his chair, addressing Nisse while Halina renders his words understandable. "And now he's saying, 'I am afraid my apprentice has been undone by what happened.' He wonders if you could summon your guards to bring him to his room. Preferably one made only of stone. Apparently he's a danger to himself."

Kauko walks over to Sig as the torches in the room flare and takes the young man by the arms. Through gritted teeth, he mutters to his apprentice, round trilling words that sound wrong when uttered in such a low, menacing tone.

Halina's eyebrows shoot up, but she doesn't translate as Kauko releases his apprentice and gives him a little shove toward the door. Sig skulks away, stopping only to give me one final, curious glance over his shoulder before disappearing into the corridor, surrounded by warriors with drawn blades.

Thyra looks worried as she stares at the place he had been standing. "He seems troubled. And dangerous to more than just himself."

"Kauko here reassures me he'll be kept under control," Nisse says.

Jaspar arches an eyebrow. "I guess they don't have the same rule we do about banishing unstable warriors."

"You give them too much credit," Nisse says. "But let's allow the priest to tell us his story." He smiles and speaks loudly. "Please. Tell us what happened after the fire destroyed your Valtia."

"He can hear just fine," Halina says quietly, before translating Nisse's words. Kauko nods and begins to speak, and Halina reveals the story:

"Our true queen perished in the storm she created to defeat your navy. And after her death, her heir, the Saadella, was supposed to inherit her magic. But the Saadella could not wield the magic at all, and she ran from the castle before we could help extract it from her."

Thyra shudders. "Do I even want to know how they were going to do that?"

"Quiet," Nisse says. He looks rapt as Halina translates the elder's words:

"We searched the whole of our kingdom for the new Valtia, but the girl had gone into hiding—with a band of criminals, some of whom were outlaws who wield magic to hurt and terrorize innocent citizens. Without a queen to provide for them, the Kupari people were in a bad state. Starving. Freezing. They needed their queen. And when the elders received the message from the Krigere inquiring about the Valtia, we felt we had no choice but to assemble a ruse to protect the kingdom. We dressed a servant girl as the Valtia and used our own magic to create the illusion of her power. But someone . . ." Halina trails off as rage distorts the elder's voice. He takes a deep breath and loosens his clenched fists. "*Someone* sabotaged it and caused the tragedy that nearly killed you honorable warriors. The next day, the criminals stormed the temple and took it over, chasing away or brutally killing all the loyal elders, priests, apprentices, and acolytes, some of whom were mere children. The survivors have scattered into the Loputon Forest. My apprentice was gravely injured in the attack, and I only barely escaped with him, on a boat."

Nisse looks delighted. "And we found them on the shore at the edge of the Kupari kingdom. The apprentice was as badly burned as you were, Ansa. We couldn't understand what they were saying, but we could see they had magic. The apprentice was dying from his burns, and Kauko begged us to allow him to heal the boy."

"So we let him do it, and then began our journey back," Thyra says. "It seemed like they might be able to help you." She narrows her eyes. "Or kill us all."

Nisse laughs. "Always focused on the bad things, Niece. I feel so sad for you."

Jaspar gives me a meaningful look. "Obviously he helped Ansa," he says. "Looks like she fared better than that apprentice, at least."

I think back to the silver swirls of scarring on Sig's cheeks and the fire in his eyes, and can't help but be curious. "I'm glad you brought them," I say, smiling at Kauko. "I owe you my life."

He grins when Halina translates my words, and then gestures at my hair and face. "He says you have lovely copper hair and ice-blue eyes," Halina says.

"Er . . . thanks," I say as Thyra stares at the round-bellied elder with distaste.

"So!" Nisse raises his hands. "I think the big question is—where is the true queen? Halina, ask him where she might be. Could she be dead?"

"That would be good," says Jaspar. "Nothing stopping us from taking the kingdom, then."

Halina asks Kauko the question, and he smiles, his eyes glinting with intrigue as he stares at my newly sprouted hair. I was burned and bald the first time he met me, but now he seems particularly fascinated by it. Halina frowns as she translates for him. "He says the Valtia has worn many different faces throughout the years, but some things are always the same, and those are the features they look for when they find the Saadella among the little girls of the kingdom." She points at my head. "She always has copper-colored hair and pale blue eyes."

Nisse's eyebrows rise as he looks at me, and my heart pounds. *You could be Saadella*, Hulda said. "But surely those things aren't that uncommon," I say. "Hulda the Kupari slave had hair this same color." I point at Thyra. "Thyra has eyes of the color he describes."

Kauko listens to Halina translate and nods before replying, all the while eyeing me as if I were a succulent roast pig.

"He says there is one more feature that helps identify the Saadella, who becomes the Valtia when the current queen dies—when the magic leaves the dying queen and enters the body of the new one," Halina says. "She has a—" She presses her lips together, her nostrils flaring.

"Speak, Halina," Nisse says, his voice a warning.

She gives me a bright, scared look. "He—he says she always has a mark. A red mark. Sh-shaped like a flame."

Nisse looks puzzled, but Thyra gasps. Like Halina, she has seen my bare legs on more than one occasion. "Ansa," Nisse says, glancing at the two women with dawning realization. "You have such a mark?"

My entire body is shaking. "This cannot be true. It doesn't make sense." My skin has turned icy and my teeth chatter.

"Show it to us," Nisse commands, rising from his chair as I shrink into mine.

There is no hiding this. There is no escaping it. All of them are staring. Jaspar's green eyes are so wide and shocked that I have to look away from them. With shaking fingers, I push the edge of my boot down my calf. Kauko blinks and shuffles over, his mouth dropping open. For a long moment, he stares at it, and in that space I plead with the heavens— *Let this be wrong. Let this be wrong.*

He falls to his knees before me, trilling words exploding from his fat lips. His hands clamp over my knees and he looks up at me with tears in his eyes. "Valtia," he whispers. "Valtia."

"Oh, heaven," whispers Thyra as her eyes meet mine. And in them, I see the truth.

I was not cursed by the witch queen that day on the Torden.

I *became* the witch queen.

CHAPTER TWENTY-ONE

I stand up so suddenly that my chair overturns, and then I stumble over its legs and end up on the ground, frost spreading across the wooden floor. The torches in the room flare as the flames begin to grow.

"I'm . . . I'm not . . . ," I stammer, backing away as Kauko comes toward me. I seek Nisse's muted green eyes, because I can't even look at Thyra now. "Please. I'm not . . ." *I'm not the enemy.*

Jaspar pulls his father away to the far side of the room, his jaw rigid as he watches the frost crawl across the planks toward them. "Ansa, stay calm. No one's going to hurt you."

Kauko is talking to me in that stupid, weak, trilling language that wrenches up memories faster than I can push them down. "Shut him up!" I shriek, covering my ears, but my hands are dripping fire, and I scream again as the flames lick my scalp. Tears turn to steam as they escape my eyes, then become flakes of frost that fall through the air around me.

"He's trying to help you," Halina says loudly from across the room, her voice high and terrified. "Please, little red. Let him help before you hurt yourself."

Kauko is the only person here who does not seem terrified. He kneels next to me, his brow furrowed with gentle concern. He looks over his shoulder and asks Halina a question. "Breathe," she replies.

He looks down at me again. *Breathe,*" he says. "Breathe." He presses his lips together and his nostrils flare as he draws in an exaggerated breath, then blows it out through his mouth, then gestures for me to do the same as he asks Halina for more Krigere words.

"Not afraid," he says as I let out a shaky, frosty breath. "Not afraid."

"Very afraid," I whisper, laying my head on the floor as the storm inside me rages. This is no curse. This is who I am now, who I'll be until I die. The knowledge is too painful to accept.

Kauko spreads his fingers, and the frost around my body melts. When it tries to reform, it turns to water again, then steam. He points to the torches, and their flames shrink, becoming docile once again. I stare with envy and awe as he controls the things that so easily control me. "Teach you," he says, nodding in thanks at Halina for giving him words. "Teach you. Not be afraid."

Halina speaks in low tones with Nisse, who is nodding. Thyra has her back against the wall and her arms folded over her chest, her mouth set with tension. She doesn't look happy that I'm not burning to death in front of her, and it resurrects my resentment. Nisse blocks my view of her a moment later, though. "Ansa, Elder Kauko has taught many Valtias how to use the magic."

"I'm not the Valtia," I plead. "I'm Krigere. I'm a warrior."

"Of course you are," he says. "You are part of my tribe, no matter where you came from. But you must learn to control this gift you've been given, so you can use it on behalf of your people. Will you obey me in this? Will you let this priest instruct you?"

I glance at the others, at Jaspar, who looks resolute and hopeful, at Halina, who wears her stark wariness like a veil, and at Thyra, who is biting her lip and staring at the ground. She doesn't speak up, doesn't insist I am hers, not Nisse's. This must have been the final crack in the ice for her. Not only am I not her love, not her wolf, I am not even her people. Defiance rises in me, brittle but bracing. "Yes," I say to Nisse. "I'll do my best to learn quickly."

Jaspar and Nisse smile, and they look very much alike in this moment. "Perfect, Ansa," Nisse says. "I know you will make us proud."

I lose count of how many times Kauko has to heal me in the following days. Fortunately, he's very good at it, and since he does it as soon as the ice or fire sinks its fangs into me, my skin is restored quickly and completely.

It doesn't save me from the pain. But warriors can endure pain.

Halina stays with us to translate, but Kauko learns the basics of our language quickly and does his best to speak to me directly. He brings Sig into the chamber in which we practice, but it seems he does it mostly to keep an eye on him. The deranged apprentice usually sits in a corner, his collar untied and hanging wide, revealing the scarring down his pale, sweaty chest. His eyes burn as he watches me. Sometimes he seems amused, laughing at jokes that only he hears, but sometimes his gaze is so full of hatred that I swear I see flames in his eyes. Kauko ignores him, mostly, but Halina speaks to him as Kauko works with me, her voice gentle and motherly.

First, Kauko teaches me to breathe, because apparently I haven't been, at least not when the magic is rising inside. Instead, I've been holding my breath and letting it out in gusts, unsteady and sudden. So I breathe and breathe and breathe as I bring the fire and ice up, little by little. It helps, but I still lose control often, requiring Kauko to intervene. Sig sits in his corner and sweats—I think he enjoys when my ice fills the room. He tilts his head back and sighs.

"The boy has fire inside him," Halina says to me one morning. "It tortures him. Day and night."

"He told you that?"

She shakes her head. "Isn't it obvious, though?"

When next I see him, I think cold thoughts and let them blow his way, and he blinks at me, like kindness surprises him.

Next, Kauko teaches me to focus. "If you don't, it spreads everywhere," Halina translates as the elder sets up a row of stone water basins along a table. "You have to have a goal."

He instructs me to freeze the water in specific basins while leaving the others untouched. I try, but when I glare at the water, it turns to steam as often as it does to ice, and usually all the basins are affected instead of just one. We spend days on this, and I show little improvement. Nisse comes to watch one afternoon.

"We're halfway through the winter," he says to me. "When do you think you might be able to wield as you did before?"

Before was *one moment*, an invitation that couldn't be rescinded, when I hurled fire and ice like spears—until they turned on me. "I don't know."

He smiles and nods, but there's an impatient snap to his stride as he summons Halina and crosses the room to talk to Kauko.

"Please, sir," Halina says, bowing her head as she stands before Nisse. "I've had an idea."

Nisse raises his eyebrows, his lips twitching with amusement. "You have?"

She gestures at Kauko. "He has said that many of his priests and apprentices fled to the Loputon wood."

Nisse nods. "A miracle if any of them survived. I lost

311

two warriors there—they went to hunt and never returned! It bears the stink of a cursed place."

"I know a few trappers who can move through it as easily as our city streets." She glances at me, and the cunning in her eyes sends a tremor through me. "With little red still struggling, perhaps you could pursue other options." She holds her hands out, palms facing each other. "Two parallel paths. Either will lead to where you want to go."

But only one will bring me the acceptance of my tribe again. I stare at her, betrayal choking me.

Nisse must read the clammy panic on my face. His smile is kindly as he pats Halina on the shoulder. "I happen to have a great deal of faith in—what did you call her? Little red?" He laughs. "You Vasterutians and your pet names. It's charming."

Halina bows her head again and meekly translates as Nisse begins to speak with Kauko about what might be the best material to acquire for my new tunic and cloak, so that I will look fearsome when we invade—the Krigere version of a Valtia.

Relief and gratitude nearly buckles my knees. He's not giving up on me . . . yet.

Sig lets out a quiet chuckle, and I turn to see him watching me. With a smirk, he points to the nearest torch, and a tendril of flame sprouts from its center, spiraling into the room like a ribbon. I gape at it as it snakes prettily toward me. Sig swirls his finger, and the flame obeys, following its motion with loving attention. He stares at it with such devotion, a melancholy wistfulness that makes my chest ache as I watch.

"I wish I could control it like that," I say. And I'd better learn quickly.

Sig opens his palm, and the fire jumps into it, forming a ball that grows until it's nearly the size of a shield. I take a step back as sweat streams down his cheeks and chest, wishing for cold to temper the flame. The fireball shrinks a bit, but my cold wind fills the entire room and draws the others' attention.

"Sig!" Kauko shouts. He jabs his hand forward, and Sig makes a choking sound as his back slams against the stone wall, his face cherry red with heat. Despite his apparent love for fire, he's very sensitive to it.

"Did he hurt you, Ansa?" Nisse asks, running toward me.

"No, not at all," I say, wincing as blisters cover Sig's handsome face. "I think he was just showing me."

"He's unpredictable," says Nisse. "Kauko controls him, but you shouldn't get too close."

"What's wrong with him?" I ask. "He's treated less like an apprentice than a prisoner." Or a caged animal.

"When the temple was overtaken, many atrocities were committed," Nisse says. "And apparently Sig was nearly burned alive when his magic was turned back on him. Kauko saved him, but he couldn't heal him for hours, so Sig has been left with his scars. Kauko says it has affected his mind and memory, and that Sig does not know friend from enemy right now. The elder seems devoted to the boy, though." He bows his head and speaks very quietly. "And apparently he has fire magic in abundance, and he is a good ally to have when we invade. Between the elder, this fire wielder, and you, there is no chance the criminal wielders who hold the temple now will triumph over us. They've put an impostor queen on the throne, but she has no power of her own. However, the wielders around her are very powerful, and they are the ones we will face on the battlefield."

"We have a month of winter left."

"But we don't want to give them time to prepare for our attack. There are rumors they are raising an army, and that means warrior lives will be lost if our victory is not decisive."

I bite the inside of my cheek as I look out the window at the gray sky. "I . . . I heard a rumor that there are many warriors who have sealed themselves up in a different part of the city."

Nisse's green gaze turns decidedly cold. "I wonder who you've been talking to." But then he sighs, and the ice melts. "Truthfully, I fear for them. They've been holed up for weeks, and though I've supplied them with food, it's not all they need. With so many people packed into such a small space, with inadequate drainage, I'm afraid disease will come to visit them."

A chill shimmies down my back. "No," I whisper, thinking of all those andeners and children, all those warriors. "They still refuse to come out?"

"They demand to hear from Thyra. They will act on her will, and her will alone."

"Have you let her speak to them?"

Nisse scratches at his beard, which he's cut short as the singed bits grow back. "I would, but I am afraid that what she has to say will doom them as surely as her silence."

"You think she would tell them to fight you."

"I don't think she's going to encourage them to join me, do you?"

I shake my head. She was utterly determined to stop him, and he seems to know that, but still he has allowed her to live. "You've been generous with her," I murmur.

His mouth curves into a small smile laced with surprise. "I've tried, though she resists any attempt to win her over. She won't even come out of her chamber—or eat the meals we provide. Hasn't for days. She's starving herself to death." He pauses, looking down at his feet. "I don't suppose you would consider speaking with her? You know and love those warriors as much as she and I do. Maybe you could persuade her to tell them what they need to hear?" His chuckle is dry as a summer drought. "Including that I'm not the one starving her? She tries to make me into the villain at every turn, and it turns out she's extremely good at it. But if we can convince all the warriors that uniting our fractured tribe is best for all, we'll be stronger than ever. And then, when you're in control of your power, we'll be prepared to make our march on Kupari as one united force."

"I'm trying," I say, watching as Kauko kneels next to Sig,

who is crumpled on the floor, his eyes swollen shut and his blisters weeping. Most of my days end with me looking just like Sig does now, or stiff with frostbite. But I don't tell Nisse this. He has accepted me into his tribe when he could have stoned me as the enemy. Just as he could have executed Thyra. But instead he gives her chance after chance. "And I will speak to Thyra. Though I'm not sure she'll listen to me."

Nisse puts his hand on my shoulder. "Thank you, Ansa. You are a true Krigere."

I am smiling as he leaves the room, and I continue my lesson, with Sig hunched in the corner, healed and handsome once again, but the fire gone from his eyes. He seems dull now. Numb.

Despite my hopeful conversation with Nisse, though, and my new determination to speed my preparation for war, my control is no better. I struggle through the afternoon and end up sweating ice pellets of frustration. Even Kauko seems flummoxed. Halina hands me a cloth to wipe my brow as she translates for him. "He says you have no balance between the ice and the fire. Without balance, neither can be controlled. The Valtia is supposed to have perfect balance in her magic."

"Maybe I'm not the Valtia," I say.

"Oh, he's sure you are." She frowns as she watches him yank Sig up by the arm and usher him toward the door. "He keeps saying something about how *she* took your balance."

"She? The witch queen?"

She shakes her head. "No, it's someone else. The impostor. I'm not completely sure who he means."

"Ask him."

Halina calls Kauko over and questions him. "He says they . . . read the stars wrong. He says you lack something all other Valtias have had, and . . ." She grimaces.

"What is it?" I glance at Sig, who has come back into the room as Kauko speaks, and is staring at his master with that strange light flickering in his dark eyes.

"Kauko says the only other way to achieve balance is for him to bleed you," Halina says.

"Bleed me?"

She nods. "He would make a cut in the vein and drain a quantity of your blood, to siphon off the extra magic."

"How would that help me achieve balance? Wouldn't that just leave me weak?"

Kauko has produced a small blade from the pocket of his robes, and he demonstrates making a quick cut in the crook of his elbow while Halina watches with her mouth tight and downturned, as if she's trying not to be sick. "He says it always works, especially when done regularly. Every Valtia has been bled to stay balanced at some point."

I think back to the impatient flick of Nisse's stride, the edge in his voice as he talked of the timeline for invasion, the possibility that those rebel Kupari wielders and their impostor queen are preparing for our attack. "I'll do it."

The torches in the room flare as Halina gives Kauko my answer. He grins and ushers me over to a chair, then grabs a basin and tosses the water out the window. He gestures for me to raise my arm and slides the basin beneath it. Sig approaches the table with wide eyes. He's shaking, staring at the knife as if it were a sword. Kauko doesn't seem to notice—he's very focused on my arm.

I grit my teeth as the blade cuts deep, the pain lancing along my bones. My blood flows bright and sure, forming a small puddle in the basin after several long moments. "How much am I supposed to shed?" I ask.

Halina translates my question, but Kauko doesn't seem to hear. He's utterly absorbed by what he sees in the basin. His hands shake as he finally presses a cloth to my arm. "I guess that's enough?" I ask.

Kauko licks his lips as he lifts the basin from the table, but then he shouts in surprise and drops it as its contents start to steam, and the basin falls to the floor and cracks. My blood doesn't spill, though. It's dried to flakes in a matter of seconds. Kauko stomps his foot and turns to Sig, who starts to giggle again. He grabs Sig's arm and shoves him toward the door, barking at him nonstop in Kupari. Both of them head into the corridor, and Halina and I stare after them.

Finally, she turns to me. "That boy . . ."

"What just happened?" I look down at the cracked basin, my dried blood.

"Sig did that."

"Cooked my blood to dust? Why?"

Her brows are drawn together. "Is that the right question, though, little red?"

"What do you mean?"

She picks up a cracked half of the basin, and my blood becomes a brown haze that clouds the air. "Maybe the better question is—why was old Kauko so upset about it?"

CHAPTER TWENTY-TWO

Kauko did not return after he bundled Sig out of our training room, so my arm throbs with its new, unhealed wound as I walk with Sander toward Thyra's chamber. It's on the other side of the tower, just below the main level. "What have you heard about our warriors?" I ask. "How are they faring? Nisse is concerned that disease will find them."

Sander gives me a nervous glance. "He'll know I told you."

"He didn't seem upset. He wanted me to talk to Thyra about it."

"And what will you say, Ansa?" He tilts his head. "Have you jumped?"

I suck in a breath. "Don't ask me that right now." For

some reason, it makes my cheeks burn, though I have no reason to be ashamed.

He looks down at me for a long moment. "Have you given it much thought? All of us who are raid prizes, we grow up knowing we come from someplace else. We all have to make peace with it."

I lower my gaze to the floor. I'm not sure I ever did.

"None of us have ever discovered we were meant to rule in that other place, though," he adds.

"It doesn't matter. I am Krigere."

"I won't argue with that. All I'm saying is—that's not all you are. And I would think it would complicate things, especially as you consider helping your chieftain . . . whichever one you end up choosing . . . to destroy the people over whom you could have been queen, had you not been stolen as a child."

"Not now, Sander," I growl. The thoughts swirling inside my head are already too much, and they threaten my control.

"All right," he says softly. "I suppose your choice will become obvious soon enough."

I chew my lip. "Did you know she's starving herself?"

"I've seen the guards handing off her dishes, piled with untouched food, to the kitchen staff." He rubs the back of his head, quick and frustrated. "This can't go on forever. Something—or someone—will break. I suppose I have a choice to make too." He gives me a rueful smile. "Though I think yours might matter a good deal more than mine."

That truth sits sour in my stomach. I grab his arm as

we enter the corridor where her chamber lies. "I just want to belong to a tribe, Sander. I need to be part of something strong. You of all people understand that."

He looks down at my hand, curled into his sleeve. "I do, Ansa, though my opinion isn't one that holds weight."

"It does with me," I say. "We've had our differences, but we are alike in many ways."

He nods, though his smile is drenched in sadness. "Then I suppose . . ." He sighs, looking up the hall to the six guards sitting outside Thyra's door. "I suppose whatever strong thing you choose should depend on how you define strength. I've been thinking on that a lot lately."

It feels like something massive is pushing against the walls of my skull, demanding attention I can't offer right now. "Speaking of strength . . ." Eager to move away from the subject, I wave toward the guards, one of whom is using a stone to sharpen his dagger. "Is she so fearsome that she requires half a squad to guard her?"

"After Thyra escaped her chamber, Nisse tripled the guard and threatened all of them with death should they fall asleep during their watch. He won't let anyone but his own hand-picked warriors near her." He arches an eyebrow. "So I guess that means he trusts you now."

Part of me feels pride and relief at that, but a small part of me, a tiny, tenacious kernel of loyalty to Thyra, itches and aches. "I'm only speaking to her for the sake of our warriors. They shouldn't suffer for this loyalty."

"Sometimes that's what loyalty demands," Sander says,

coming to a halt halfway down the corridor. "And I will leave you now. I'm not allowed to get any closer."

The guards have risen to their feet and are eyeing him. He waves, and they nod as he turns and walks away. "Nisse told us you would be coming," says one, a young warrior with sandy hair and a scar cutting through his eyebrow. "Good luck in there. If she offers you anything to drink, I advise you not to accept."

All of them laugh as he pushes the door open, and I enter with my heart galloping. Thyra sits on a straw pallet on the floor, her knees drawn to her chest. Her hair has grown these past many weeks, and it curls at the nape of her neck and at her temples. Her cheeks are hollow and her eyes are bloodshot. "I know who sent you," she says, her voice raspy with disuse and weakness.

"He is worried about our warriors."

"*Our* warriors? Whose do you mean?"

I sigh. "Is this the argument you want to have?"

She leans her head against the wall. "Should we bother talking at all? The last time we spoke, you seemed very determined not to hear half of what I said." She looks toward the cold hearth. "And to deliberately misunderstand the rest."

"Deliberately misunderstand?" My jaw clenches. "You are guilty of that, Thyra, not me."

"Tell me, then, Ansa. Share your wisdom."

I scoff. "You've always been the smart one between us, haven't you?"

She smiles and shakes her head as her eyes grow shiny.

"No. Just the one who couldn't see the world in black and white, blood and victory." She glances at me as she swipes her grimy sleeve across her face. "I tried, though. Everything would have been easier if I'd succeeded. Or perhaps I would have died a lot sooner. I'm not sure."

"You're talking in riddles." And so softly I can barely hear. I can't tell if she's broken or quietly defiant.

"I considered becoming an andener. Did you know that?"

My eyebrows rise. "You've always been a warrior. And a good one."

She nods. "But not the kind of warrior my father hoped for. Neither role really fit, but I couldn't be both."

I sink to the floor, remembering how Lars shouted at her to come back with a raid kill, or not at all. "Your father just wanted you to be strong."

"Is that strength? The ability to pierce soft flesh with a sharp blade?"

"You make it sound petty when you describe it like that. But there is no greater power than the power to take a life." I learned that the night my parents were killed.

"What about the power to preserve life?" she asks. "What about the power to sustain and nurture a people?"

"But that is *how* a chieftain nurtures us! He gives us a mission, and we reap the riches if we succeed. We come away from each raid and battle with the understanding that we are strong, and that *no one* can defeat us." Something is so wrong inside me, making every word I utter exhausting. It's like swinging a blade that's too heavy, one that used to be easy to wield. And yet I press on, because stopping would force me to figure out what has changed. "If you don't believe that, why did you ever want to be chieftain?"

She winces. "I was stupid enough to believe I had something to offer. I was so determined to change things. Think about it—as the tribes gathered from the north, as we began to build our ships and shelters—we had so many mouths to feed that raiding for our food would never have been sustainable."

"And that is why we were sailing south," I remind her. "To plunder here, where the riches are abundant!"

"So we are a pestilence," she says. "Like locusts. We eat through one field, then find another."

I groan. "How is it you can make anything sound pathetic and distasteful?"

She lets out a hoarse laugh. "That's my gift, I suppose." She runs her hands over her wavy hair. "Nisse was pushing so hard to invade Kupari the season before I became a warrior. He had my father convinced of the riches in the south, of the ease of the coming victory."

"And you opposed it from the start."

"I did, Ansa. I couldn't see an end in it, and I didn't think it was what our people needed. I also knew so many innocents would die as soon as we hit their shores." Her eyes meet mine. "I kill without mercy or regret when I have no choice. But the idea of killing someone who could not or would not threaten my life or my people?" She shakes her head. "I can't. I've always wondered how you could, actually.

I know your parents were killed in a raid. You used to cry out for your mother in your sleep."

Saliva fills my mouth. "Don't."

"You of all people should question why we live this way, and whether we should."

"I of all people *can't*," I shout, fire trying to push its way up from my core. "And you can't possibly understand."

"Make me, then."

I shake my head. "It must have been meant to happen. I was meant to be Krigere."

"You were forced to be Krigere, Ansa. You were never given a choice."

"Enough." My voice is pure warning. My hands are shaking.

"As you wish. But I have trouble living with the knowledge that we tear children from families, that we kill when we don't have to, that we see it as a point of *pride*. That we mark our own skin as a boast to the heavens!" She makes a disgusted face. "It sickens me."

I think back to that night in the woods, when we stood over the old man from the village we'd just raided. He'd run, carrying a bundle of food and nothing else. He had no weapons, though he tried to throw a few pebbles at us as we approached. It was pathetic. When Thyra refused to kill him, I saw weakness. I reminded her of what her father had said. *Maybe I can make him understand*, she'd whispered.

I thought she'd wanted him to understand her hesitation. But now . . . "The night I killed for you, the night you hoped you could make your father understand. You weren't talking about one man. You wanted to change Lars's mind about our entire way of life."

"That was the night I realized I couldn't change anything—until I was chieftain."

My heart skips. "And is that why you tried to poison your father?"

She does not look away from my eyes. "Now you are just Nisse's horn, playing his tune for whomever will listen."

My mouth twists with contempt. "Come, Thyra—you admitted it that night in Halina's shelter."

"No, I did not." She sits up, leaning forward. "I admitted to sending that slave to find the poison, and to telling my father Nisse was trying to assassinate him. I am guilty of deceiving my father, and of the scheming that he hated so much. But I never set out to assassinate him." Her fingers clutch the blanket that covers her straw tick mattress as she sways, looking dizzy and unsteady. "I never set out to assassinate anyone."

"You succeeded in getting Nisse banished—along with several thousand warriors. Isn't that what you wanted?"

"Yes!" she shouts. "That's exactly what I wanted. But would you like to know why, Ansa? Would you believe me if I told you, or has he won you over so completely that you are packed full of his distorted version of truth?"

"That's a very good question, since he's the only one who's been willing to *tell* me the truth," I yell.

"No," she says in a shaky voice, rising to her knees.

"He's willing to tell you whatever story brings you his way, whatever story keeps you quiet and useful."

I jump to my feet. "Is that better than using silence for the same purpose?"

Her head falls back and she takes a deep breath. "I have made many mistakes. I never claimed to be perfect. But I loved my father and would have followed him into eternity. You saw me, Ansa, on the deck of that longship. After we heard of Nisse's invasion of Vasterut, my father was dead determined to invade Kupari, and I was right there at his side. Reluctantly, yes. But I was loyal."

"You split our tribe by framing Nisse!"

"I split our tribe because Nisse tried to kill me!" she shrieks. "I found the poison in my own cup, Ansa. The only reason I didn't drink it was pure luck—a mouse got to it first and died right before my eyes. But I knew there was only one person who wanted me dead—the man who would take my place as heir, who would offer no counterbalance in his demand for war and death. And I had a choice—publicly accuse him and light the fuse on a civil war within our tribe, or create a situation where he had no alternative but to leave quietly. I stole my father's celebration cup and planted it in Nisse's tent, along with the poison he had intended for me. But I did not strike first. Believe that."

I gape at her. "I don't know what to believe."

"Then we are strangers," she says, sagging on her pallet. "It's my word against his. You are free to choose." Her voice is weary but cold.

"Why should I choose you when you didn't choose me?" I blurt out.

She raises her head. "What?"

All my sorrow and rage forces its way up, propelling my words from my throat. "As long as I can remember, Thyra, I wanted to be next to you. I'd never seen anyone fight like you, so beautiful and deadly." My voice cracks, broken by memory. "I never understood you. I know that. But there was always something . . ." I sniffle. "Something I couldn't stop craving. You were a mystery, and I wanted to be the only one who could puzzle you out. All I ever wanted was for you to look at me, and to tell me I was yours. I knew I couldn't be your mate, but my only desire was to be your wolf."

"You've always been a force all on your own," she says. "I loved watching you fight too. You possess a ferocity I lack."

I let out a pained laugh. "And you have a grace that is foreign to me." The lump in my throat makes it hard to speak. "But if you admired me so much, why did you push me away? Because you did keep me at arm's length, even before I was cursed."

Her blue eyes are steady on me, though the rest of her trembles. "I let you as close as I could, Ansa. Can't you see that? Is there anyone closer? Has there ever been? But when one is born a stranger in her own tribe, when she must wear a mask every day to be accepted, can you blame her for being terrified to show who she really is?" She inclines her head toward me. "Especially to one who fits so perfectly.

Regardless of how you came to us, you have always been more Krigere than I." She laughs. "Even now, when you're revealed to be the queen of a foreign tribe."

"Do you have any idea how much I loved you?" I whisper.

She nods. "I also saw the fear and disappointment in your eyes when I refused to kill."

"It seems neither of us could accept the other." I swallow. "And I can't control this magic if I don't feel accepted, Thyra. You've made me feel as if I was evil. You *said* I was evil."

"I said what you had done was evil." A tear slips down her pale, sunken cheek. "But I never thought of you as anything but my Ansa." She wipes the drop away. "That hasn't changed. But how will you use this magic, now that it is a permanent part of you?"

"To bring us victory." Assuming it ever learns to obey me.

"So you are to be Nisse's sword on the battlefield," she murmurs. "He will wield you as it suits him."

I take a step back toward the door. "He wants me to be a good warrior. He is giving me a chance, Thyra—I can be accepted by the tribe again."

"We always accepted you."

"Because I fought! That's the only reason I'm alive. I *earned* it."

She sighs. "Do you ever wish you hadn't had to? Do you ever let yourself feel the anger you must bear deep inside you, knowing it was the Krigere who stole you from your native land, who killed the people who—"

"That is deep in the past." How I wish it felt that way. "And the present holds more than enough to occupy us."

"We agree on that, at least." Her eyes are bright with hope. "You are still part of our tribe, Ansa. You were never banished. Don't act like you were."

"Where *is* our tribe, Thyra?" I ask, waving toward the window. "They're dying in some maze of mud and human waste, all for their loyalty to you!"

Thyra's lips are a gray line as she nods slowly. "And what would Nisse have me say to them? What would *you* have me say to them, since you wouldn't deliver my message?"

"Tell them to join us," I snap. "Tell them to live and die like warriors, not mice!"

"And help Nisse destroy another people, another land? *Your* people, no less!"

"They are not *my* people!" My voice cracks over the denial.

She gives me a wary look, perhaps seeing the fire in my eyes. "As you wish. But tell me—why is Nisse so afraid of what I would say to our warriors that he's cut me off from any communication with them at all? If he was so worried about them, so unwilling to let them die, why wouldn't he allow Preben or Bertel to come to the tower and see me?"

"It's not my place to know," I say, backing toward the door as she sands away the last layer of my control.

"Oh, so it's only your place to do his bidding now, without thought or question? You're not his wolf, then—you're his dog."

"Shut up." I close my eyes as fire and pain streaks along my limbs.

"Do you trust that elder he has training you? Do you believe the story he tells? How do you know he's not leading everyone into a trap?"

"Nisse trusts him," I say, because I can't quite claim that I do.

"Nisse only cares about what you can do for him. He doesn't care that the magic burns you. He doesn't care about how it hurts you—and I can see that it does. Right now, even."

"At least he lets me have a place at his side!" I roar, the fire dripping from my fingers onto the stone floor. "At least he lets me be who I am!"

"Is *this* who you are? Just fire and ice magic, controlled by rage and fear and a wild desperation to belong to a tribe, even a twisted, corrupted one? Because that's when this power becomes vicious and unstoppable. Have you noticed? You have a perfectly good mind, Ansa—you'd be more powerful if you let *that* rule you, instead of fury and terror!"

I breathe and breathe and breathe, but the heat rises unbidden.

"I love you, Ansa," Thyra says breathlessly, her skin turning pink as the air becomes searing. "I love *you*. And this magic is part of you now. You can kill . . . or show mercy. You will decide to be in control . . . or not." Sweat streams down her face and she grimaces with the pain. "You can only . . . blame yourself. . . ."

She slumps against the wall as I slam the side of my fist into the door.

"Let me out, for heaven's sake," I shout, calling to the ice as Thyra faints.

The door swings open and Carina pokes her head in. "We heard the shouting. Did you kill her? You weren't supposed to kill her!" She waves her hand as I rush out of the room, wincing as the heat reaches her.

"Get Kauko up here to heal Thyra," I bark, fear jittering along my spine. Thyra's starving and weak already. What have I done? "Summon him now!" I stalk down the hall with no idea where I'm heading as Carina runs past me, on her way to find the elder. My entire body is burning with the magic—and with Thyra's words. She's reached inside me and poured out all my thoughts, scattering them to the wind, leaving me jumbled and spinning. I walk blind and stumbling, my vision blurred with hot and cold tears. I shiver and sweat. So badly, I want to hurl fire. I want to rage. I want to call to the magic and let it loose. But if I do, it could kill me. Bleeding or not, I've never felt less balanced than I do now.

A hand closes around my wrist as I reach the very bottom of the spiraling steps, and I'm yanked into an alcove. I slam my hand against a hard, sweat-slick chest—and my assailant lets out a hiss of pain as his back hits the wall, followed by a shaky laugh.

"Sig," I say as he leans into the torchlight. "What are you doing?"

"No. More. Bleed," he whispers, pressing his thumb to the wound in the crook of my elbow.

I stare up at him as the torch flares, and I'm not sure if he's causing it—or if I am. "Why?"

He shakes his head. "No more," he says again. He puts an imaginary cup to his lips and pretends to drink.

"Have you had too much mead?"

"Bleed? No," he says. "No more."

This is hopeless without Halina. "What are you doing outside your chamber?" I point down the corridor, where I know he's being kept. Through the gloom, I can just make out two prone figures lying next to an open door.

When I try to step back from him, he holds my arm tight. "No," he says. His mouth twists with frustration as he mutters something in Kupari. He points at my hand. "Teach you."

"Yes. Kauko is teaching me. Not that it's working."

He seems to understand the frustration in my tone, if not the words. His grin is a bright, deadly thing. "*I* teach you."

I peer at him through narrowed eyes. "Um . . ." I glance up the hall toward the guards, sincerely hoping he hasn't killed them. At the same time, I can't bring myself to call for help, or to fight him, because no matter what he's done, and no matter how gentle Kauko has been with me, I have come to hate the way the elder treats his apprentice. I wish I could ask Sig what really happened, but without translation, we must remain strangers. But I am running out of time to learn how to control the magic, and at some point Nisse will give up on me. "All right. Tomorrow."

His brow furrows. "Teach? Yes?"

I nod. "Yes." I put a finger to my lips.

Sig lays his own finger over his smug grin. And then he releases me and heads up the hall. As he walks by a torch, I gasp at the horizontal stripes of blood that have bled through his shirt. He's been whipped.

Sig enters his chamber and pulls the door shut without giving the felled warriors so much as a glance. To my relief, they start to stir. Whatever he did to them—perhaps making them faint in the heat just like I accidentally did to Thyra just now—the effect was temporary. But it only makes his power clear; he kept that heat in place while he crept down the hall and talked to me. I don't understand how someone with that much control and power could allow anyone to whip them.

I lean against the wall, trying to sort things out. I don't know who to trust. Nisse or Thyra, Kauko or Sig. Each of them has an agenda. I'm not naive enough to believe otherwise. But two kingdoms and a thousand warriors might depend on which way I jump. Only a few hours ago, I thought I had made my decision.

Now I realize I'm frozen midair, and I have no idea where I'm going to land.

CHAPTER TWENTY-THREE

As soon as my back collides with stone, I have my legs up. I jab my foot into Jaspar's middle and roll before he can wrap his hands around my ankle. My head throbs with the jarring aftermath of the fall as I jump to my feet, but my blood sings.

Jaspar rubs his stomach and chuckles. "You're even faster than you were."

"Or you're slower." I swipe my hand over my sweaty face, glad that for once the heat is only caused by exertion—not magic. It's nestled in the pit of my stomach, quiet for now as I focus on the slam of body against body, on dodging blows and landing strikes. Or perhaps it burned itself out by torturing me last night. A flash of the dream jolts me— Thyra, her pale skin clammy and reddened with heat, her hand outstretched—*you can only blame yourself.* . . .

"And clearly your words hit just as hard." Jaspar draws his shoulders up as a gust of wind makes him sway. We're up at the top of the tower again, and the Torden blows us frigid and forceful kisses.

"Or your skin has thinned." I say it quickly, clinging to the animal simplicity of this time with him, eager to chase away the haunting tremors in my bones, even as they swell into my consciousness once again. *Please, control yourself,* she whispered as her hair caught fire, as her skin wept and split. *I can't,* I screamed as she died right in front of me, just as Aksel did.

"Are you all right, Ansa?" Jaspar asks, and I snap back to the moment, blinking in the daylight.

"Fine," I say. "Though I didn't sleep well."

He sighs. "I thought it might be hard for you, after you'd spoken with Thyra."

"Why?"

"She twists what should be straight," he says. "Including you."

"Do I seem so easy to manipulate?"

"Of course not." He turns away, leaning on the low stone wall and gazing out over the squalid city. "But I knew that seeing her again would move you." He gives me a sidelong glance. "I just didn't know the direction."

I can't admit to him that I don't know, either. I'm still angry at her—for what she's doing to herself, for what she's done to us, for how she said she loved me and for how badly

I want to believe her. "Neither of us budged," I say lightly.

"But not because your feelings for her have changed."

No, because we are opposites, and we crash and crash and always end up in the same place. She peels away my armor and pokes what's underneath. Part of me hates it. And the rest of me doesn't want it to stop. "Do my feelings matter, Jaspar? She has her strange and lofty ideas to keep her warm." I let out a bitter laugh. "And I have fire magic."

He touches the back of my hand with his fingertip. "Is it getting any easier to control? You've been spending hours each day with Kauko. Every time I come looking for you, it seems you're with the Kupari wielders."

My fist clenches. "I'm doing my best. And I think I'm getting a little better at it." How I wish that were true.

"Good. Because we need to leave here, Ansa. We've been within these walls too long."

From here, it is possible to see the gate through which we walked six weeks ago, and the road and forest beyond. But between us and all that open space is nothing but mud and ice and thousands of suffering people. "You were here for three seasons before we arrived. If it was so terrible, why stay? And why bring us into it, crowding everyone even more?"

"We arrived here at the end of winter—nearly a year ago. We were so glad of warmth and shelter that our desperation made us fiercer, I think. We were a terrifying sight, I have no doubt. And in the spring and summer and fall, we rode out to hunt and spar in the fields, slowly regaining health and strength. So we could at least leave the city. But now, with the snow drifting high, we've all been stuck in this stinking warren for nearly two months. I never imagined how it would feel. I doubt any of us did."

"Then I suppose no one is content within these walls. And the Vasterutians will be glad to have their kingdom back when we're done with it, I'm sure." I wonder if that is why Halina made that suggestion to Nisse, to venture out to find the refugee wielders—perhaps she is eager to see us defeat Kupari and to be more quickly rid of us, especially since her hope that our rebel warriors would join a Vasterutian resistance force to take back the city has been dashed.

"Oh, we're not giving Vasterut back," Jaspar says. "My father will leave ten squads behind to hold the city, and the andeners will remain here. Many of them are with child, anyway. They shouldn't be marching."

The news sits like a stone inside me. Thyra had told me to ask about how the widowed andeners were being treated, and I recall that Nisse was going to bind them to his warriors, even though the men already had mates. "Have you heard word of Gry?"

"Cyrill's andener? She was claimed by Kresten. I believe I heard she's to be blessed with a child."

My stomach turns. "She wasn't even given a month to grieve her mate. She can't have entered that bond willingly."

Jaspar shrugs. "She was willing enough as the winter descended."

Meaning she made the choice to save her children from the cold, and now she is to have another. "So a new generation of Krigere will grow up within a city wall?"

"They'll grow up as rulers," Jaspar says. "They will know their place on this earth."

"Because the Vasterutians will be the mud beneath their feet," I mutter, thinking of Halina's sharp wariness, of the way Efren and Ligaya watched me that night out in the city. "Do you really think these people will stand for that?"

"They'll have no choice. We'll have many of their young men and women with us in Kupari, so hopefully they will realize that any rebellion would be met with the slaughter of their best and strongest."

"So they're not just to be attendants for the warriors. They are to be hostages."

"It will save many lives."

I can't get Halina's curly-haired little boy out of my head, or her words—*Think I won't fight? Think I won't die?* "Krigere ones, at least."

He turns to me, his brow furrowed. "Thyra *did* twist you up. What did she tell you? Did she make you ashamed to be Krigere?"

"No." But she and Sander made it impossible to convince myself that is all I am.

"I told my father it was a mistake to ask you to speak to her. If he'd talked to me first, I would have—"

"Why, Jaspar, do you think I'm weak?" A trickle of ice makes its way up my back, a warning.

He takes me by the shoulders, unaware or unheeding of the danger. "I could never think you were weak. But I do think she shames you. She makes you question who and what you are."

"Should I never question who and what I am—or the things I do?" I ask.

"My heaven, you sound just like her! No wonder you can't control your magic—your strength is sapped by all this doubt."

I wrench myself out of his grasp. "I wish people would stop telling me how to fix myself," I shout, my words accompanied by a thunderous burst of icy wind that knocks Jaspar back against the low wall. His arms reel as he tries to keep his balance. Horror lances through me, and I grab his hand as he nearly falls. We collapse to the ground.

"I'm sorry," he says, panting, his hands fisted in the sides of my tunic. "I'm so sorry. I don't know how to help. And I want to help." His hand wraps around the back of my neck, his fingers sliding into my hair. "My father reconsidered your attendant's suggestion about sending out Vasterutian scouts to search for the Kupari priests and apprentices that fled into the Loputon."

I go very still, tightening every muscle to keep my fear from forcing frost through every pore. "What?" I whisper. "He changed his mind?"

When I pull away, Jaspar looks worried, like he's sorry he mentioned it. "No, I'm sure he hasn't, not about you, anyway. He thinks you're very important. It's just . . . we're running out of time. We got word late last night that the impostor queen of Kupari is definitely raising an army—including rebel wielders from their outer territories. We don't know how powerful they are, but Father wants every advantage. And if we were to march into Kupari with hundreds of warriors *and* dozens of trained wielders in our force? The battle will be over before it even begins, especially if we act quickly. The elder thought it was a good plan."

The elder. Thyra's words about him slink into my head unbidden—what if he's leading us into a trap? "Do you . . . do you ever wonder *why* he's helping us?"

"He wants to oust the rebels from his temple, I imagine," Jaspar says, pulling back to look down at me. "He seems eager to reclaim his seat of power. And we can help him with that."

"But once we do, then what happens? Is the elder likely to want to share that power with us?"

Jaspar grins. "Wait—you think my father actually trusts that old man?"

"He certainly makes a good show of it."

"Oh, Ansa." He laughs. "Kauko is a means to an end. We need him right now, but that won't always be true. And as soon as it's not . . ."

I stare at him, my fragile hope shifting and cracking like ice over the marsh. "As soon as he's not useful, Nisse will find a way to end him," I say.

Jaspar pulls me to my feet. "Don't tell me you feel pity for that elder."

"No," I say. "I don't feel pity for him." I smile, though it's flickering, a candle flame in a cruel wind. "But I'm late for my lesson with him, so I'd better go."

I practically dive for the hatch that opens to the stairs. "Thanks for sparring with me."

I don't hear if he replies—the door slams above me and I jump halfway down the stairs, turning my ankle as I land. I want to beat my head against the wall to rid myself of the look on Jaspar's face just now, how much he resembled his father, and his complete lack of awareness of the truth he'd just revealed.

Kauko is a tool for Nisse, to be used and discarded.

What makes me think I'm any different?

After the evening meal, I tell Halina I'm tired and need to sleep. I don't tell her I know Nisse has followed her advice and sent scouts into the Loputon Forest to find more magical allies for our invasion, because I'm afraid it would stir up my anger and desperation. Especially after the look Kauko gave me after I failed yet again to control the magic inside me this afternoon—like a child mourning a broken toy. The ice and fire simmer beneath my surface tonight, begging release. I feel like I did last night, when Thyra collapsed under the heat of my jagged, rage-driven fire and needed Kauko to revive her, and I spent a night roiling with nightmares that brought it back over and over, sharper and hotter and more devastating each time.

Her eyes, staring. Refusing to let me hide. Her words.

Refusing to let me blame my crimes on a curse that never was. *You can only blame yourself.* . . .

The guilt makes me sick, and I don't need the weight of Halina to make it worse.

I also don't trust her, though. It was childish to ever have trusted her at all.

"Maybe you could go check with the tailor and find out when my new cloak and tunic will be ready," I suggest.

I expect her to argue, but perhaps she senses my mood, if not my plan, because she immediately heads for the door. "Of course," she says. "I know you'll probably be glad to have some clothes that fit."

I grin. "You have no idea." I don't either, really. I don't actually care. I wave her out the door with a yawn, telling her I plan to sleep like a bear in the winter. But as soon as the noise of her footsteps fades, I'm peeking into the corridor and praying Sig hasn't given up on me like Nisse and Kauko have.

My heart beats unsteadily as I jog up the corridor, through the maze of dim, dank stone, until I reach the hallway where Sig sleeps—both of us are kept here, away from sunlight and wood. Before I make it two steps toward his door, he loops his arm around my waist and hauls me into an empty chamber. I buck against him instinctively, and he clenches his teeth over a groan of pain. As I turn to him, he's lifting the fabric of his shirt off his back—where only a day ago I saw oozing wounds from a whip. "Did Kauko do that to you?" I ask, gesturing at his back.

Sig's eyes go half closed. He nods.

"You have power," I say. "Fire." His chin lifts when he hears the familiar word. He glances at an unlit torch in a bracket on the wall, and it bursts into flame. I step away as the flames flutter toward the ceiling. "So why would you allow him to whip you?"

I'm not sure he understands all my words, but he seems to hear the question, and guesses the meaning as I stare at the fire he brought to life with a mere thought. "Only fire, no ice," he says quietly, looking away. "Kauko . . . both. Both ice and fire. Like you. Very strong. But . . . you are strongest."

I snort. "If I am, it doesn't matter. I can't control it."

"The Valtia is *strong*. The Valtia *is* magic." His Kupari accent mangles the words, but he speaks slowly so I can understand. There's something almost pleading in his voice, and it's tinged with frustration. I can tell by the way he's looking at me that there is so much more he wants to say. Does he want me to help him get away from Kauko?

"I'll be stronger if you teach me. You said you could."

"Teach." He arches an eyebrow and points to the torch. "Make dark. With ice."

"Are you insane?" He's seen me fail at tasks like this before. "I'll fill this entire room with a blizzard and make your blood turn to frost." And even then, the torch will probably remain lit.

He laughs, and flames dance in his eyes. "Try, *Valtia*."

I shove him. "Call me that again, and I'll cut your tongue out."

He's still laughing, and he taps his fingers to his thumb, as if telling me he's not impressed by my talk. Or maybe that he doesn't understand it. And then he crooks his finger at the torch flame, and a tendril of fire slides from its center, snaking toward my face. "Make dark with ice," he repeats.

Already regretting taking this risk just to fail yet again, I glare at the flame, wishing for a cold so pure that there is no escaping it. The ice grows along my bones, frosting my skin and making me shudder, and as the fire twinkles merrily, even Sig gets goose bumps along the pale skin of his throat. But then he winks, and the room grows hotter again. "More," he whispers as the flame creeps closer, making me wince.

He's using his fire to counterbalance my cold. Battling a swoop of frustration, I redouble my plea to the ice. "Come on," I mutter. "Ouch!"

The flame shrinks back after licking my cheek, and Sig sighs. He says a word in Kupari as if he expects me to understand it. *Terah*, it sounds like. He says it over and over, and finally I step back from him, from the heat he's radiating and the undulating torch flame. Both are making me sweat despite my ice. "I have no idea what you're saying, you idiot!"

Sig makes an irritated noise in his throat, then bends over and swipes the dagger from my leg, the dull training blade I used in my sparring session with Jaspar this morning. I forgot to take it off in my desperation to get away from him. Sig waves it in the air and points to the blade. I don't strip it from him because he's clearly not threatening me with it—he's tapping his fingers along the edge and saying that same word again.

"Blade?" I ask, touching the edge of the dagger. "Is that what you're saying?"

He closes his fingers around the metal. "Blade?" he asks.

I nod, and so does he. "Blade *magic*," he says. Before I can move, he presses the dagger into my hand, then steps behind me. He places one hand on my waist and closes the other around mine, lifting the weapon and pointing it at the torch.

I gaze down the length of my arm, down the edge of the blade, which is now aimed right at the center of the fire. If it was my enemy, all I'd have to do is lunge, and I'd stab it right in the heart. "Oh, heaven," I whisper. This, I understand. This, I know how to do.

"Ice," he murmurs, shaking my hand a little and making the tip of the blade tremble. "Blade."

I concentrate on the ice inside me, drawing it up from the bottomless well where it hides. And this time, instead of begging, I command it. I imagine it sliding along my arm and into the blade, and I gasp as I feel the hilt turn frigid in my grasp. Sig's hand is hot and clammy over mine, but he smiles as my own skin turns cold, as a lattice of frost begins to grow along the blade, heading for the tip, which is still pointing at the flame. The dull glint of the blood groove that runs the length of the blade focuses my gaze, giving me a path to the heart of my target. Joy bubbles up inside me at the sight of the metal turning white and my ice magic moving toward the fire. This is it. He put a dagger in my hand and it was all I needed. I push the magic forward with all my might, intent on darkness and bitter cold, and delight in watching it eat up the length of the blade.

The weapon shatters with a sharp crack, followed by the spatter of metal splinters pinging off the walls and floor. Sig cries out and stumbles back with his hands over his face, and when I pull them away, his cheek is pocked with two dark shards, blood welling around them. I grimace and pull each of them out as he clenches his jaw and fists, obviously trying not to scream. They plink coldly when I drop them into an empty, shallow stone basin. Failure makes my eyes sting as Sig does the same for me, tugging a needle of metal from my shoulder.

He presses the sleeve of his tunic to the wounds on his face and sighs. "Tomorrow."

"What? Did you see what just happened?" I gesture at the bloody splinter of metal he pulled from my skin. "It got so cold it shattered like pottery! I could have killed you."

His brows draw together. "Tomorrow," he says, even louder. "Like this, tomorrow." He offers me the splinter. "Magic. Like this." When he sees the confusion on my face, he rolls his eyes and points to one of the shards in the basin. His nostrils flare as he aims his fingertip at it, and I watch in awe as it turns red hot before melting—while the one only a few inches away from it remains gray and unaltered. He holds up the blood-covered needle of metal again and stabs it at the basin. "Like this."

Magic so focused that its target can be the size of the point of a needle. "I can't hit a target the size of that entire basin, let alone something smaller!" The only time I even came close, when knives of ice danced on my palms, when I hurled fire, was in that fight circle—only moments before the magic turned on me like a mad wolf. "I can't control it!"

"Control?" He shakes his head, sweating in his frustration. "Don't control magic! *Be* magic!"

I rub my eyes and laugh. "Be magic," I say, mimicking his accent. "Thanks. That helps a lot."

He tosses the metal splinter into the basin. *"Soturi,"* he whispers. His lip curls, and he spits on the floor at my feet.

The Kupari word for warrior. Except . . . I think he's telling me I'm a coward. I square my shoulders. "Fine, if you want me to scar the rest of you, that's your choice." And if I want to have even a chance of regaining Nisse's confidence, I don't have a choice at all. "Tomorrow."

Sig's smile is so blood tinged, so brutal, that it suddenly occurs to me he would make an excellent Krigere warrior, unstable or not. "Tomorrow," he says in that shaky, eager voice of his.

He gives me a mocking little bow and disappears into the hallway, his footsteps silent on the stone.

CHAPTER TWENTY-FOUR

As I hurry back to my own cell, my mind tosses like a ship in a storm. I am fighting so desperately to wield this power, the magic of the Valtia, but if I succeed, am I more of a Krigere . . . or more of a Kupari? If I use this magic to conquer the Kupari, am I loyal, or am I a traitor?

I know what I have always wanted. But now, I am questioning why I wanted it. *You were forced to be Krigere*, Thyra said. Do I love the Krigere because I truly had no choice, or is there some spark in them that has always called to me, that fits with who I really am? If I had remained a Kupari, would I have been as out of place among them as Thyra is among the Krigere, even though she was born to rule?

Apparently I was born to rule too, but not over warriors. Is it better to lead a soft, timid people or serve a fierce, strong tribe?

These questions burn inside me. I don't know where I belong. Trying to figure it out is exhausting me.

I have just made it back to my chamber and dived onto my mattress when I hear footsteps in the hallway. Frantically, I extinguish every candle in the room and lie in the dark, feigning sleep as another cadence of footsteps, this one more rapid than the first, approaches. I let my mouth drop halfway open and breathe deep and slow as a slant of light from the hallway penetrates my eyelids. It's only there for a moment, though— whoever looked in on me seems satisfied that I'm asleep.

"Did you deliver the message?" a man asks as soon as the door closes most of the way, leaving only a crack of torchlight. I recognize the accent and the deep timbre of the voice—it's Efren.

"I did," Halina whispers. "The tunnel is narrow, though, hardly big enough for me to get through. It will need widening if we expect all of them to do it. Have you seen the size of some of them?"

"But it worked."

"Yes, it worked. It opens into one of the shelters, and I spoke to the iron-bearded one myself."

Iron-bearded one. My blood drains from my face. She must be talking about Preben. Her resistance force hasn't given up—they've dug a tunnel to get to the warriors who have stayed loyal to Thyra, and they're planning to get them out!

"What did he say?" asks Efren.

"He was grateful for Thyra's message, and they will be ready when the signal is given."

Thyra didn't give up, then. She just gave up on me. But now she has found another way to reach her warriors in exile. I clutch at the mattress beneath me.

"Good," Efren says. "They'll flank the guards and head for the tower. Nisse's warriors will be completely caught by surprise. But it has to happen before the group of priests and apprentices reaches the gates. We don't want them interfering."

"That's why it has to be precisely midday. I thought there would be only a few, but it seems nearly a hundred are coming! If they side with Nisse, the battle would be over too quickly."

"So if they don't make it into the city before the signal, do you think the girl chieftain actually stands a chance?" Efren asks.

Halina grunts. "Of course not. She's half starved, and so are all her warriors. Old Nisse's been giving them only subsistence rations, trying to convince them to come out and join him."

"But they're loyal to her. They'll fight."

"Oh, yes. All we have to worry about is the signal tomorrow. After that, we'll let the Krigere destroy each other."

And there it is. The plan laid out, so clear.

Did she *want* me to hear it? Or are these Vasterutians stupid enough to speak outside my door with no thought for who's listening? They were speaking Krigere—was that deviousness or because they have been punished for speaking Vasterutian within the fortress walls?

I'm not sure it matters. One way or another, they are guilty of treachery.

Any trust or affection I ever had for Halina is gone. If what she said is true, she's crafted a brilliant plan, using Thyra's stubbornness and our warriors' loyalty as a weapon against Nisse, never mind that it will result in hundreds of warrior deaths. My anger is a fire, and I wince as I feel my skin grow feverish. If I don't control this rage, it will devour me before I can save even one life. So for once, I'll follow Thyra's path and not let my fury guide me.

Halina comes through the door a moment later. She has fresh bandages folded over one arm and carries a pitcher of water. She lights a candle with the one she brought from the corridor, and I make a show of sitting up and yawning. "Did you find out about my cloak?" I ask, hoping she pays more attention to my light tone than the searing heat of my breath.

"Cloak—oh! Oh, yes. Yes, it will be ready by tomorrow afternoon," she says, smiling broadly, all innocence.

I wonder if she hopes for all of us to be dead by then. "Are you all right?" I ask, noticing the flush on her round cheeks and the wild spray of her hair, even more wild than usual. I glance down at the hem of her dress. It's edged with mud, just as I would expect. "You've been out in the city."

"Just needed to see my boy," she says, but the quaver in her voice betrays her.

"And did you see anyone else?" I meant to stay calm, but my voice has grown sharp.

She sets down the bandages and pitcher and blinks at me in surprise. "No. Who on earth would I see, little red?"

I lean back against my mattress, seething yet smiling. "No idea, Halina. No idea. I hope you enjoyed the visit, though."

Her hands still for a moment, but then she jumps back into motion immediately, peeling back my sleeves to look for new blistered patches. Oddly, though, there is nothing, despite my little meeting with Sig. "It was nice to be out in the city," she says quietly as she tugs my sleeves back down to my wrists. "I've spent so much time in this tower that I feel like my skin has faded to the color of the stones."

"Then maybe the journey to Kupari won't be so bad after all," I say, watching her face. "You'll be out in the open air."

She pauses to look at me, and in her eyes I see a million questions. "As you say, little red," she says softly.

Does she suspect I overheard? If she does, she could arrange for the signal time to be changed, which would render my knowledge useless. "Thank you for taking such good care of me," I tell her. "I want you to know—when we're in Kupari, I'll protect you."

She tilts her head, then gives me a warm smile. "Much appreciated, little red. I'd do the same for you if our positions were reversed. I mean it. We might be from different tribes, as you call them, but I see you struggling to make it to the light. I think you will, one day."

I feel the hurt of her betrayal in my chest, though I know it's not really fair to expect her to tell me the truth and be on my side. I just . . . wish she were, that's all. I like her. I admire her. She would make an excellent Krigere.

Or perhaps she is simply an excellent Vasterutian.

"I'm trying," I whisper. "Good night." I turn over and close my eyes as she pulls a blanket up over my shoulders, making my throat constrict with the truth of what I must do.

When tomorrow dawns, we will be enemies.

I lie awake all night, trying to figure out what to do. If Halina and Efren meant me to hear, should I keep what they said to myself, for fear of playing a part in their deception? But if they didn't want me to hear, then I must tell, or the Vasterutians' plan will cause the deaths of everyone I care about. The Vasterutians are trying to get us to turn on each other. Instead of raising a resistance, they simply want us to kill our own and take care of the problem for them.

I hate how clever it is.

Thyra has no idea. She wanted to be their allies, but instead they're setting her up—she has no way of getting information from the city or the warriors, except through them. They could have told her anything, promised an alliance that will dissolve as soon as Nisse's warriors close in to seal our tribe's doom. Why can't she see it? Or is she fully aware that this is a disaster in the making? After all that talk of protecting our warriors from yet another rout, why would she ask this of them?

If I had helped her instead of turning my back, if I had been the one to make contact with our warriors, would all of this have happened differently? Could I have saved the tribe?

Can I save them now?

By the time Halina arrives with my breakfast, I am bleary-eyed and jumpy, my head pounding and my stomach sour.

"I'm not hungry," I tell her as she sets the bowl of porridge in front of me.

"Sweetened it with honey. I know you like that," she says, backing away.

"Did you hear me?"

"Little red," she says, slowly, like she's considering each word. "I think you best eat up. You'll need your strength. Priests will arrive today from the Loputon. Our scouts found them in the woods and are bringing them here. Should arrive after noonmeal."

"And I have you to thank for that," I say in a flat voice.

"Nothing but good. More magic, less pressure on you to deliver a victory."

I close my eyes and rub my hands over my face, trying to summon some energy. I don't know how to explain to her how badly I needed to be the one, how the wish has grown huge inside me these past weeks, as isolation sank its teeth into my marrow. "I wanted to deliver victory," I whisper. I wanted to be accepted within my tribe again, to know who I am without question. I wish Thyra hadn't made me think about the cost.

"Maybe you will," she says, pushing the wooden tray closer to me. "Still a chance."

My hands fall away from my face and I look up at her. Her brown eyes make me ache, and the words I wish I could say make my tongue feel hard and twitchy. What will I do as our warriors face off against each other in this betrayal she's arranged? Which side will I take?

If I don't try to stop the coming catastrophe, then I don't deserve either tribe. "I need to see Nisse."

Her eyebrows shoot up. "Why?"

"Is it any of your business at all? I need to see him. Make it happen."

She scoots away from the edge in my voice and turns for the door. "Of course."

She goes and comes as quick as a hare, and by the time I've swallowed the last bite of my porridge—she was right, I can't go into today starving and weak—she's back with a few guards from Nisse's personal entourage. She pulls open the door with her head down, the meek Halina she presents to all Krigere except me, it seems. The warriors lead me up the stairs to Nisse's war chamber. My heart beats out a fierce rhythm as I try to puzzle out the best words, the way to stop this clash between those loyal to Thyra and those who belong to Nisse.

I step into Nisse's chamber, sweating and shivering as my trapped magic squirms just beneath my skin, awakened by my desperation. The memory of my temporary triumph and control last night is just that. I've run out of time. I would beg for more if I thought it would matter, but now there is something so much more important to think about.

"Ansa!" Nisse calls from over by the massive fireplace. I turn to see him set a goblet on the mantel. "I heard you wanted to speak with me, but I would have summoned you this morning anyway. How's the magic?"

"Better," I say. "Perhaps in another few weeks—"

"Ah," he replies, clasping his hands in front of him. "That is time we don't have. They may not have had an army a few months ago, but with every day that passes, the impostor queen is gathering more power and preparing her people for our attack."

I look down at my hands. How I wish I could be in the same room with that fraud, if only for a few minutes. Yes, it might destroy me, but I think killing the impostor queen might be worth it. After all—that is a throne that is rightfully mine.

I blink as the thought hits my consciousness and look up to find Nisse with his head tilted, regarding me closely. I am thankful he can't read my mind. "You have decided to march soon, then?"

He nods. "In two days' time, once we're armed, packed, and ready. I received excellent news this morning. The refugee priests who escaped from the ambush at the temple were found by Vasterutian scouts two days ago. I sent two warriors to meet them, along with a host of horses so they could reach us quickly. They will arrive this afternoon."

Just as Halina said. "I am ready to go with you," I tell him.

He smiles. "I will welcome you at my side, Ansa."

His gaze is so warm on me that it catches me by surprise—I had expected him to be cold, to discard me as he plans to discard Kauko, assuming he still can. "Thank you." Now I must tell him what I came here for. Now I have to save warrior lives without wielding magic. "But I did not come here to talk to you about Kupari."

He sits down on the bench at the painted table. "Then tell me your purpose."

I draw in an unsteady breath. Surely I am doing the right thing. "How do our warriors barricaded in the eastern part of the city fare?"

"They're all alive as far as I know. Like I told you, I've made sure they have rations."

But only enough to keep them alive. "Have they given any indication of when or if they might emerge?"

"Last I heard, they are refusing unless they hear from Thyra."

And they have heard, apparently. "Has she shown any indication of changing her stance?"

He chuckles, but it's heavy and low. "Not yet," he says softly. "I fear for her warriors, and because of that concern I am afraid I have made a very difficult decision. In fact, that is why I was going to summon you this morning, had you not come to me first."

My stomach clenches. "Yes?"

"I'm afraid I'm going to have to use a bit more force when trying to persuade Thyra. We need those warriors to join us, and she's only leading them to their deaths."

Now I feel like vomiting on his boots. "More force?"

"I have to make her see reason, Ansa. Surely you can understand that. But every attempt at persuasion thus far has only hardened her resolve." He sighs. "Every body has limits, though."

"I overheard something," I blurt out, as hot and cold splinters poke at my soft spots. Maybe I can protect Thyra from herself. "And that is why I came here."

He casually examines his grimy fingernails. "From Halina?"

I shake my head quickly. "No. Of course not." Despite her betrayal, I cannot give her up just like that, not after all she has done, not when I know she has that little boy at home, waiting for his mother. Loyalty is hard won, hard lost, she once said, and she is so very right. "From . . . another servant. I heard . . . that the warriors barricaded in the eastern part of the city have grown restless."

He arches an eyebrow. "Restless? We're all restless after a winter spent caged within these walls."

I clear my throat. "Yes, but . . . what if they emerged all at once?"

"To challenge us?"

I fidget where I stand. "And if they did?"

His eyes darken like a thundercloud has passed overhead. "It very much depends. If you know something, you should tell me. I know you love many in those ranks, and this is your chance to save their lives."

"I know," I whisper. But at what cost?

"And otherwise you wouldn't be here. What's happening?"

"I think they have an escape route," I say. "They're going to emerge and attack."

"And with over a hundred and fifty warriors, they'd be formidable," Nisse mutters. "Very well. There's only one solution. When they emerge from their burrow, we must be waiting, with so much force that they cannot consider fighting. They've had their andeners and children with them this whole time, and surely they won't endanger them."

"It would take a large force to intimidate them."

Nisse nods. "They're counting on us not being ready, and on most of our warriors being elsewhere in the city when they emerge. But if we're waiting and can steal the element of surprise, they'll be so shocked that perhaps they'll reconsider." He shoots to his feet and approaches me quickly, taking me by the upper arms. His gaze is so intense, his muted green eyes burning. "Do you know when they're planning to make this escape attempt?"

"Noon, I think," I say. "I believe there's going to be some sort of signal."

He squeezes my arms. "You have saved them all, then. Carina!" His voice is still echoing when the warrior enters. She must have been waiting outside. "Gather every warrior you can find and take them to the eastern part of the city where Thyra's tribe fled. Have them surround the place. I want every point of egress covered."

"And if they come out fighting?" she asks.

"Overwhelm. Disarm. Intimidate. But do what you can to avoid killing or maiming."

I nearly sag with relief. "Thank you."

He turns to me and puts his hand on my shoulder. "Every warrior life is precious. Well. Most of them. The loyal ones—as you turned out to be." He smiles, and a chill runs through me as his voice turns cold. "As for the disloyal ones . . . Bring in the traitors."

Halina walks stiffly through the door, her eyes wide and her hair a frazzled mess. Sander stands behind her, his hand on her shoulder, the point of his dagger between her shoulder blades. But when he turns, his eyes find mine, dark and unreadable. *You jumped*, I almost say. . . . But then I realize I've done exactly the same thing. Now I must live in the wreckage.

"I said it wasn't Halina who told me," I say, my voice breaking.

"I know," says Nisse. "But tell me this, Ansa—if you overheard something and understood it, the messenger must have been speaking Krigere, not Vasterutian. And how many of the servants in this castle can do that? But no matter. I already had several pieces of the puzzle. I just needed the rest."

My blood seems to be draining from me, pouring into my feet. "Oh." I look over to Halina, who is staring out the window. They meant me to hear. "What will you do now?"

"Make an example of her. But not only her." He gestures toward the door as Thyra walks in. She looks pale and thin, but her eyes are full of defiance as she sees me standing next to Nisse. Jaspar is holding her upper arm and his dagger is unsheathed.

"Oh, no," I breathe.

She can't possibly hear me, but perhaps she reads the horror on my face. "This is not your fault, Ansa."

But it is. I know it is.

"It's time, Carina. Take all the warriors and go," Nisse says, his voice echoing off the stone walls. "When you have the rebel warriors subdued and disarmed, bring them to the courtyard."

Nisse crosses the room to stand in front of Thyra and Halina. "It turns out this diplomacy of the south is useless. Now we do things as Krigere should. Now we will show every soul in this city what it means to cross me." He looks Thyra up and down. "We found the messages you sent to your warriors, Niece. Carved into your dinner plates. You were starving yourself to keep them covered so your Vasterutian friends could shuttle your instructions to your tribe."

Thyra glares at him, but her lips curve up at the corners, a ghost of a smile. I stare at her hollow cheeks, her sharp shoulders, her skinny wrists. All this time, she had a plan, and was willing to destroy her own body to see it through. She will never beg for mercy. She will never even bend. "Your warriors thought cleaning my dishes was beneath them," she says. "They'd grown accustomed to having Vasterutian servants do it for them."

"And we will hunt each and every one of those servants

down. We'll let them live just long enough to regret helping you," Nisse says as he waves at the door. "Take these two up to the parapet and wait for me there. I'll come when we have gathered all our warriors and the Vasterutians who will travel to Kupari with us. They'll be witnesses to the unification of our tribes."

My entire body trembles, and I know this feeling—I've had it before. My hold on the magic is cracking like thin ice beneath a heavy boot, the weight of my love and fear. "What are you going to do?"

Nisse's hand closes over the hilt of his dagger as he turns to me. "I'm going execute Thyra and Halina for their treachery while their fellow rebels watch."

CHAPTER TWENTY-FIVE

N o!" Fire bursts from my palms as a bitter cold wind roars through the room. I draw back my arm, thinking only of saving Thyra and Halina, preparing to hurl flames at Nisse and his guards.

But the air swirls warm around me, and the fire disappears as quickly as it formed. I blink down at my hands, and the flames sprout instantly, only to disappear again. Hands close around my arms, hot and cold. I cry out as Sig and Kauko pull me away from Nisse, who is immediately surrounded by his personal guard. "Let me go," I shriek, jerking back and forth as I try to loosen their holds.

"Be calm," says Kauko as his fingers dig into my flesh. Every time my skin flashes hot, his palms turn ice cold. Every time my skin frosts over, his hands flush warm as a summer day. Sig holds just as tight, providing heat as my magic tries to freeze him, but he curses each time my skin turns hot, just until Kauko can cool me down again. They're countering my magic, and I don't have the focus or control to fight them.

I'm powerless.

"They will keep you from hurting yourself," Jaspar says loudly. "I had them at the ready. I suspected this news would upset you."

"This isn't about me," I shout. "Our warriors will never stand for it! You're condemning them to death too!"

"They'll be disarmed," Nisse says as Thyra eyes him with fury. "And we will reveal the full extent of Thyra's betrayal."

"Her betrayal? What about yours? This is exactly what you wanted, isn't it? First you try to kill her with poison!"

Nisse's face contorts with rage. "How *dare* you accuse me of such a thing!"

"You tried to kill her again through challenges in the fight circle," I yell. "Don't pretend you're righteous now."

Spittle flies from his mouth as he rages. "She tried to kill *me* by framing me for murder," he roars, drawing his dagger and pointing it at her. "She cost me my tribe and my family!" His nostrils flare as he sucks in a deep breath and sheathes his weapon once more. "I have been the soul of mercy and patience. All I ask for is your loyalty. Your obedience." His eyes meet mine. "Stand by me and be the treasure of my tribe, Ansa. Betray me, and you will be caged like an animal for the rest of your days."

I lunge for him, struggling against my captors. "The only way I would stand by you is if I were about to cut off your head!"

Jaspar waves toward the door. "Kauko, she's all yours."

His cold words strike right at my heart. "How can you do this?"

He glances at his father, who has turned away to stare at the map on the table. "Because you didn't choose us, Ansa," Jaspar says simply.

I give Sander a pleading look as Kauko and Sig drag me to the door. "Don't let them do this!"

"I jumped, Ansa," Sander shouts just before the wooden door shuts in my face. The last thing I see is Thyra's eyes, clear and blue and hard and cold.

It's going to be the last time I see her. This can't be happening.

I scream with the agony of it, arching and fighting, kicking and clawing, but held tight between two magic wielders who are raising blisters and the white crust of frostbite on my arms right through the fabric of my long-sleeved tunic, I can't get purchase. My feet barely touch the ground as they wrestle me down the stairs. Kauko speaks in a trilling, round tone that he must think is soothing, but every syllable cranks my rage higher. Sig is silent and grim on my other side, the ridge of his jaw sharp enough to cut stone. He will not meet my furious gaze.

I am bruised and blistered and torn by the time they force me into a tiny, windowless stone chamber that I recognize as the room where Sig has been sleeping. There's no bed here, though. No torches or candles, either—the only source of light comes from the torches in the hallway. The room contains only a few things—a filthy-looking blanket, a stone bowl, a knife . . . and a set of copper manacles bolted to the rock walls. The cuffs are crusted with blood. I glance down at Sig's wrists, where his swirled scars lie, and then at Kauko.

"You chain and bleed him every night, and then you heal him every morning, don't you?" I put as much venom into my words as I can, but the elder only smiles.

"I must," he says. "To keep the balance."

He and Sig each wrestle one of my wrists into the manacles, still using their magic to subdue mine. Between the two of them, there's too much for me to fight, and the pain from my injuries is so intense that I can barely think past it. They chain my ankles, too, tight to the wall, making it impossible to kick. "No fighting," says Kauko, stroking my arm as I fight in vain to pull away. "I will help you."

Sig looks away, and it's the last betrayal I can take. "I thought *you* were helping me," I say in a choked voice. "I thought you were on my side."

Kauko chuckles. "Sig is a naughty boy. He needs very much discipline."

Sig lets out a shaky breath that warps the air with its heat.

"Sig," Kauko says as he rolls my sleeves to my upper arms, revealing what I already knew was there—skin so damaged and broken that it's a wonder it's still holding together. Then he says the Kupari word that I know means "blade."

Sig kneels over the stone bowl and the knife, his back to us. He's moving slowly enough that Kauko gets impatient. He gives Sig a little kick in the rear and snaps at him in Kupari. In response, Sig turns toward us with the knife and the stone bowl, the latter of which he hands to the elder. Kauko takes it and then pokes at the crook of my elbow, still chattering at his apprentice, whose blond hair is so pale it almost glows in the dark as he moves closer. He clutches the knife tightly.

Kauko is telling him to cut me. I try to twist my arm away, but Sig's clammy palm presses the limb to the cold stone. "Shhh," he murmurs. His thumb strokes gently over the tender skin on the inside of my forearm.

"You told me not to let him bleed me," I whisper, standing on my tiptoes to hiss in his ear. "You said not to let him."

Kauko chuckles. "So naughty, Sig. Make it deep."

Sig nods. His brown eyes meet mine, just briefly. But in them I see flames. I grit my teeth as the blade cuts into my flesh and fight the urge to be sick as I listen to the *pat-pat-pat* of my blood flowing into the bowl, which Kauko holds just beneath my elbow to catch every drop. Sig stays close, holding me to the wall as I bleed. I glare up at him, and he stares down at me, letting me see the fire. The flames are entrancing, the way they undulate within the bottomless black-brown pools of his eyes. Why, I want to sob. Why are you doing this?

Why am I surprised, though? Thyra pushed me away. Halina turned on me. Sander has joined Nisse. And Sig is serving his master, perhaps to avoid more whipping or whatever torture the elder has forced him to endure.

And why am I angry? The realization descends on me like a massive wave on the Torden. I've given none of them any good reason to stand by me. I've been a crumbling wall, a stalk of wheat, a puddle of cloudy water. I've stood for nothing. I never jumped, not really.

I was so hungry for acceptance that I played every side. I served Thyra. Nisse. Kauko. Jaspar. Halina. Sig. Anyone who would give me kindness, I swayed in their direction. While each of them stood firm, held to their positions by principle or greed or hunger for power, I swirled like a flame in the breeze. I deserve every betrayal—after all, I betrayed all of them first.

I close my eyes and bump my head against the stone. These thoughts are shredding my mind, pulling me even farther from the one thing that could save me—a focus on what I'm willing to give, and on what I truly want. If I don't figure that out, I deserve to die.

Kauko presses a cloth to my wound just as my lips begin to tingle. I glance down to see the bowl full to the brim with my blood, black in the dimly lit, dank chamber. He takes a step back, eyes only for the contents of the bowl. It's as if I've ceased to exist—or he only cared about my blood in the first place.

The image rises in my mind as Kauko licks his thick

lips. Sig, the night he told me not to let Kauko bleed me, pretending to drink from a cup. I'd thought he was saying something about drinking too much mead, but as Kauko lifts the bowl, understanding dawns.

And as Kauko begins to drink, revulsion makes my stomach clench, and I have to fight to keep that porridge I ate for breakfast from spewing from my mouth. I glance at Sig, expecting to find him just as disgusted, but instead he is watching Kauko with his head tilted, his expression blank.

Kauko lifts his head and shudders, his lips covered in my blood. He looks at me and smiles. "So much power," he says in a low, shaky voice before lowering his head to drink again. The wet slurping sounds make bile rise in my throat. He drinks like a man dying of thirst.

"The magic—is it in my blood?" I ask.

Sig looks at me from the corner of his eye and nods. "Blood *is* magic." He rolls up his own tunic sleeve and reveals a scar in the same spot as my wound, confirming my suspicions. Now I understand his pallor, the circles under his eyes, the way his scarred flesh stretches over his skull like thin fabric over a frame of twigs. I wonder how powerful he would be if he hadn't lost this much blood—powerful enough to escape?

Horror flows like ice through my heart, turning it cold. Kauko has magic of his own, but he's used it to dominate Sig and now me, just so he could have more. "Did you do this to the Valtia, too?"

The question springs from me without thought, as does

the memory of the witch queen's face. I've barely allowed myself to think of her since the day it was revealed I was her true heir, that her magic had entered me upon her death instead of entering the girl the elders chose as the Saadella—the girl who now sits on the throne of Kupari, trying to make people believe she's the real queen.

Kauko slowly swallows a full mouthful of blood. "Every Valtia," he says.

"*Every* Valtia," Sig echoes, his fiery gaze on Kauko again.

"You were supposed to protect her," I say, my voice breaking. I don't even know where this anger is coming from, but it's welling up from the same spot inside me where I felt the witch queen reach and touch that day on the Torden—my heart. She wouldn't let her priests hurt me that day. She was protecting me.

From people like Kauko.

"You were her enemy," I say. "Is all of this your plan to snatch power for yourself?"

Kauko's thick, bloodstained lips curve upward. "Krigere will help me."

I would bet every drop of blood in my body that he has the same strategy Nisse does—use your allies to get what you want, and then dispose of them when you want to sit on the throne alone. Nisse and Kauko use people like weapons, like tools. They don't care about tribe or family or loyalty. They only care about themselves.

"I'm going to kill you," I murmur.

Kauko chuckles as he upends the bowl and lets the last

thick drops fall fat and crimson on his tongue. "No," he says. "You are going to feed me."

I struggle against my chains as his plan wraps around my throat, choking off any intelligible words, clouding my thoughts. The air in the room snaps with bitter cold, but Kauko dismisses the ice with a flick of his wrist. "Today the traitors die," he says. "And then we march." He grins like a drunk, revealing blood-tinged teeth and a slightly unfo- cused gaze. "To kill the impostor and take back my temple. I will . . . rule the . . . Kupari."

As the manacles cut into my wrists, Kauko blinks a few times, like he's trying to clear his head. He leans on the stones as he bends to set the bowl on the ground. He walks his hands up the wall to bring himself upright again, and he has the strangest look on his face as he turns to Sig. "You . . ." he says weakly.

Sig smiles, his eyes glowing now, pure sunlight. "Me."

Without another word, Kauko sinks to the ground and slumps forward, his eyes falling shut and his limbs going slack.

CHAPTER TWENTY-SIX

As soon as Kauko's head *thunks* to the floor, Sig is on his knees and digging through the pockets of the elder's robe. He comes up holding a little copper key, which he uses to unlock my manacles.

"You poisoned the cup," I say, staring down at the now-snoring old man.

Sig pulls a small cloth sack from his breeches and waggles it at me. I catch a whiff of something that smells like a strange combination of death and springtime. "From Halina," he says.

I press the cloth to the wound in the crook of my elbow, and Sig reaches over and ties it tight for me. As I roll my sleeve down my arm, I nudge Kauko with my toe. "Are you going to kill him?"

Sig stares down at the man, and now I can see the utter loathing he's been concealing for so many days. "Yes," he hisses. "But not today."

"Why?"

He steps back from Kauko, his entire body trembling. "I want him to . . ." He mutters something in Kupari, then uses two fingers to point at his fiery eyes.

"You want him to look you in the eye," I guess. "You won't kill him when he's asleep because you want him to know what's happening." He wants him conscious, so he will feel every second of pain and know Sig is the source. The heat of his hatred fills the whole room and makes both of us sweat.

A slow, malevolent smile decorates the ruins of Sig's once-handsome face. He wrenches Kauko's limp body up to sitting and chains the elder's chubby wrists, leaving him slouched against the wall, his arms in the air, spread as if in celebration or pleading.

"Now we go," Sig says as he admires his handiwork.

"I have to get to the parapet," I tell him. "That's where Nisse is keeping Thyra and Halina."

I'm going to save them, or die trying. For both their sakes, but also for Preben, Bertel, all the warriors who set their faith in Thyra, and for that little boy who should not be torn from his mother. And not just for them—for Nisse's tribe, who have been steered in this deadly direction by a man who sees people as resources to be used up for his benefit, who sees andeners as nothing more than wombs with legs, who sees Kupari as yet another land to ruin while their people simmer with hate that will kill us all. Just like the hatred of the Vasterutians has festered, driving Halina and her friends to lethal lengths in their silent war to regain their freedom.

Thyra was right, I realize. She was right all along. And my need to be a warrior, my need to belong, my need for *her* to belong, blinded me.

Sig leads me into the corridor, but he turns before we reach the steps that lead up to the parapet. "Stop," I whisper, tugging at his wrist, which he yanks out of my grasp like it pains him. I pull my hand back, but point toward the stairs. "We have to go up."

Sig shakes his head. "Astia," he says. "You need it."

"What's an Astia?"

He curves his fingers around one of his forearms. "Astia. For balance." He turns and jogs down the passage without bothering to check if I'm following. I do, telling myself that if this takes too long, I'll just peel off and find a weapon. I'm running out of time—once the signal is given and the warriors emerge from their barricaded stronghold, stunned and disarmed, Nisse is going to kill Thyra and Halina to break the spirits of their supporters and force everyone's allegiance. But Sig's promise of balance is too tempting—would this Astia thing allow me to do magic without hurting myself?

We reach a chamber, this one also windowless, but sumptuously furnished with a soft bed topped with thick pillows and blankets, a table upon which sits a pitcher of wine and a copper goblet, and a half-unfurled scroll revealing a partial map of Kupari. An open trunk sits next to the table, revealing a few black robes like the one Kauko wears every day.

"Is this Kauko's chamber?"

Sig nods and grabs the mattress, yanking up the top and hurling it over the end of the bed frame. A small cloth pouch lies in a carved out hollow in the wood, and Sig scoops it up. He turns to me and pulls out a copper cuff covered in some kind of runic writing, which glints red in the torchlight.

My breath *whooshes* out of me. I remember. "The Valtia was wearing that when she called down the storm." It glinted red and copper in her patch of sunlight, shining as she pointed her finger at the sky.

Sig flicks a clasp and the cuff falls open. He holds it out to me. "For balance."

"That's what Kauko said about bleeding me."

Sig's nostrils flare. "Astia is for balance," he says, his voice hard. He takes a quick step forward, and before I can protest, he tugs my sleeve up and fastens the thing to my wrist.

A warm tingle flows through my body, and I look up to see Sig watching me with a satisfied look on his face. The cuff is cool and comforting against my scarred flesh, but the sensation is one of unsteadiness, more power than I can control. "Balance will keep the magic from hurting me," I say. "But will it help me control it?"

"Don't *control* magic," he says, frustrated with me yet again.

"Be?" I guess.

He winks. "Be."

From somewhere above our heads, a single note is blown on a horn. The faint noise hits me like a bolt of lightning. "That must be the signal," I yelp, lunging for the door. This time I'm in the lead, and I'm honestly not sure Sig is following. I have to get to the parapet before our rebel tribe is brought to the courtyard.

I hit the stairs and begin to sprint, my breath rushing alternately hot and cold. The cuff at my wrist is soothing and centering, not a distraction so much as a reassurance—as are Sig's footsteps behind me. I'm not sure what I did to deserve this strange, scarred boy's allegiance—I have to wonder what he wants from me—but right now it runs warm through my veins.

Normally, these stairs are crowded with the warriors who reside here in the castle or who have been chosen to work within the walls. But today, Carina has gathered them all and taken them to the eastern part of the city, to lie in wait for Thyra's rebels, to overwhelm them and end the uprising before it begins. It will save their lives but crush their spirits, and Thyra's execution for treachery will make all that struggle meaningless.

I look up the broad spiral of sunlit steps, knowing the parapet is located three levels above the ground. Just as it is occurring to me that I should develop a strategy—I am one small warrior who will be facing Nisse, Jaspar, and their personal guard, which apparently includes Sander now—Sig yanks me to a stop. "Shhh."

Just around the curve of the steps, I hear the buzz of voices. We won't be able to pass unnoticed. But then Sig presses something soft into my hands.

It's a pillow. And a robe. "Be Kauko," he says as I realize he's thrown another robe around his own body. Without so much as a question, he pulls at the rope that holds my breeches up, and as I grab for them, he stuffs the pillow under my tunic, reties the rope, and pulls the robe over the whole thing, tugging the hood up over my head.

I glance down at my puffed out belly. "You certainly are a clever madman."

He pulls his hood over his own head. "Go now."

I start up the steps, and as we turn the curve I see that the way is blocked—dozens of Vasterutians are coming down from the upper levels and being herded onto the main level by a few helmed and armored warriors who crowd them toward the exit to the courtyard. If we try to barrel past them, the alarm will be sounded and Nisse will know I'm coming for him.

He could kill Thyra in a heartbeat. One slice is all it takes. I know exactly how easy it is.

I glance behind me, at Sig, and put my head down as I trudge out of the staircase, following the Vasterutians. I stroke my paunch. One of the warriors says, "We thought you were downstairs with the witch."

Sig bursts into a trilling cascade of Kupari, chuckling as he mimes chaining someone to the wall. I glance at the tree-trunk legs of our warriors, firmly planted but not in a wide fight stance, and silently pray that I look like an old, fat priest.

The warrior guard laughs. "Can't understand a single stupid word you're saying," he says to Sig. "Go on, then. You must have her secure if you're up here to watch the show."

He shields me from sight a moment later and stays close as we walk with the Vasterutians toward the courtyard. Even through the thick robes, I feel the heat he gives off. By his own admission, he has no ice to balance it with. It simply flows from him like a current on the lake, constant and powerful. I wonder how strong he really is, if he has this much fire after being bled for so long. Either his magic is a very deep well or his spirit is unbreakable.

Then I consider the look in his eye as he promised Kauko's death. Unbreakable, maybe, but definitely cracked.

We flow with the crowd of Vasterutians—there must be at least a hundred of them, all young and strong, all muttering among themselves in low, tense tones. These are the ones who will be taken as hostages to Kupari, to ensure that Vasterut remains under Krigere control.

When the sunlight reaches me, warming the black fabric of my robe, I chance a look around. Sig looms dark and hooded to my left, and we stand out among the Vasterutians, many of whom are wearing grayish-brown tunics and breeches, their feet covered in cloth boots that barely keep out the cold and damp. None of them are armed, but their dark eyes carry that sharp, wary look I have grown so familiar with. Do they know what Halina and Efren have done? I don't see the black-bearded Vasterutian here, and I wonder if Nisse has already caught him, if he is somewhere in the bowels of the tower, chained and bleeding.

High above us is the parapet, and I hold the hood over most of my face as I look up. Sander and Halina stand on one side of the wooden-fenced walkway that surrounds that level of the tower, and Jaspar and Thyra stand on the other. Nisse stands in the center, wearing his broadsword and helmet, his graying blond hair loose over his shoulders. He looks dominant and deadly, and I know that is his intention. He raises his arms and smiles as a loud, eerie horn sounds off somewhere out in the city. The noise is repeated by a warrior just inside the courtyard, who blows a curved horn of a mountain sheep. Nisse grins. "My friends," he shouts. "Do you know that sound? It's our arriving allies, the priests of Kupari." He leans forward and gestures at Halina to translate.

He's about to execute her, and he's demanding that she translate his words for her captive people. It only drives my understanding of him deeper into my darkening heart.

Sander pushes Halina forward, and she grips the railing of the parapet and gives him a resentful glare before turning back to the crowd. She shouts her words in Vasterutian, and they no longer sound round and honeyed—now they ring with a ferocity that makes me wince.

"I have to stop this," I whisper to Sig. "I can't stand here and watch him kill them."

Sig's fingers clamp over my shoulder. "Not close enough," he whispers back. "Wait."

Nisse raises his arms. "Open the city gates," he roars.

Halina wears a strange, grim smile as she shouts her words in Vasterutian. As the warrior blows his horn three times to signal Nisse's command to the few guards stationed near the gate, a strange ripple of energy seems to run through the crowd.

The horn out in the city blows a single, high-pitched note that cuts off suddenly.

Nisse's victorious smile fades as he peers down the long, wide road that leads straight downhill from the tower to the city gate. We all turn to see what he's looking at; nearly a mile up the muddy road, a long procession of black-robed riders emerges over a rise. They ride with their heads low to their mounts, galloping at full clip, not the way I would expect soft priests to approach. I squint as the noonday sun glints off metal, a shimmer that's nearly blinding within the black horde.

All of the riders are heavily armed.

"Oh, heaven," I whisper as the truth crashes down. "Those aren't priests." And I don't know who they are, but I'm guessing I am staring at an advancing force of Korkeans and Ylpesians.

Halina said they were allies. She told me the Vasterutians hadn't been able to get riders out of the city since they'd sent a plea for aid to Kupari. She's the one who volunteered Vasterutian scouts to go fetch the refugee priests, right when Nisse was most thirsty for magical allies.

She wasn't betraying me—she was betraying *him*.

Something tells me those scouts rode without stopping to the other southern city-states. And then Halina spread the story that the rebel warriors were planning to escape, ensuring that nearly all of Nisse's force was occupied with the rebels—and very few of them remain here at the tower to guard Nisse. She made sure I "overheard" the story; it only bolstered the knowledge Nisse already had.

"We have to get to Thyra," I cry, pushing back my hood to get a clear view of the parapet.

It's already in chaos. As I lunge forward, trying frantically to push through the churning, shouting mob of Vasterutians, some of whom have already charged the few warriors in the courtyard, Sander shoves Halina toward a window farther along the parapet and whirls around with his dagger in his hand.

Nisse sees Sander's attack just in time and gets his dagger up to block the strike. I stare, wide-eyed. Sander did jump, then. Just not in the direction I believed. Love for him beats in my breast as I watch him take on the older warrior, fighting with a strength and frenzy that I know well.

A cry of pain draws my eyes to the right. Thyra has taken advantage of the moment. She has one of Jaspar's daggers in her hand. Jaspar draws one from his boot, a wooden smile on his face.

"Close the gates," Nisse howls as the Vasterutians around us let out a fierce, ragged war cry. He kicks Sander in the stomach and backs up a few steps. "Close the gates!"

But instead of three quick notes, the horn sounds off in one long, eerie tone, cutting over the noise of the riot in the yard. I glance over to see the warrior who previously had the horn lying on the ground, clutching his head while a stout Vasterutian woman fills her cheeks and blows the horn yet again.

There is utter mayhem all around me. The southern warriors will be here in minutes. Sander, Nisse, Jaspar, and Thyra are still grappling on the parapet. One Vasterutian tackles Sig, who crashes into me but then whirls around with balls of fire bursting from his palms. This ignites a very different type of chaos, with Vasterutians scrambling to get away from us. It draws the attention of the fighters in the parapet. Thyra's blue gaze meets mine. *Ansa*, she mouths. Her smile is exquisite relief.

But the distraction costs her dearly. Jaspar backhands her, so hard that her head hits the stone wall of the tower. At the same time, Sander slices Nisse across the arm, sending the older warrior staggering back. He falls, and Sander descends on him, raw determination shining on his face.

He chose Thyra. My fellow raid prize chose mercy and loyalty and faith. He chose to break from our brutal past and trust in a fragile future. *I suppose whatever strong thing you choose should depend on how you define strength*, he said to me. And now I know what his answer was.

His blade shines as he brings it down.

His force and momentum are so powerful that he has no chance to reverse course.

Sander's eyes go wide as Jaspar's dagger pierces his gut. Jaspar's face is monstrous and animal as he twists the blade, then wraps his arm around Sander's torso and jerks him forward, sending him tumbling over the edge of the parapet.

CHAPTER TWENTY-SEVEN

Sander falls as if held up by a cloud, slow and agonizing. I see every second, and I know the screaming I hear is my own. I shove and push, calling to the wind to bear him up, and a gale swirls around us, battering the crowd. His body slows in its plunge from on high, but not enough. He hits the ground at the base of the tower, and I finally break free to reach him. I skid to my knees and wrap my arms around him. "Ansa?" he says weakly, blood flowing unchecked from his mouth, his eyes black and unfocused.

"I have you," I say, glancing up at Sig, who has his back to me, fire still sitting on his palms—he's making sure the mob doesn't attack us in their frenzy. He looks over his shoulder, and I can tell by his expression that he has no hope for Sander. It squeezes in my chest, only confirming what I already knew.

"I failed," Sander says, his voice as broken as his body. Unbelievably, his fingers are still wrapped firmly around the hilt of his dagger, as if not all of him has admitted defeat.

"You didn't fail. You fought until the very end." I press my lips to his bloody forehead. "And Hilma will welcome you when you get to heaven."

He closes his eyes, and a tear slides down his cheek, the only one I've ever seen him shed. But when he speaks, it isn't of his lost mate. "Get Thyra," he says in a halting voice. "The foreign fighters . . . won't attack us if she's chieftain. That was the bargain . . . we made with the Vasterutians."

I don't want to leave him. These are the final minutes of his life, and I don't want him to be alone. But . . . I close my hand over his—the one that holds the dagger. "Give this to me now. I will carry on your fight," I say, my voice cracking beneath my grief. "My victory will be yours."

He smiles. "I would choose no other warrior for the task. Blood and victory, sister."

"Blood and victory, brother. I will return your weapon when the battle is over," I murmur, gently laying his broken body down. His great shuddering sigh is his last breath. When I rise from the ground, the cuff around my wrist makes my whole arm tingle, power craving a target. But if I were to unleash my grief-driven magic now, it would destroy every soul in this courtyard. I look down at Sander's weapon and pray it is enough. "We have to get to Thyra," I say to

Sig, and he nods and begins to walk forward, his hands outstretched, the deadly fire dancing at his command.

There's a thunderous noise down the hill—the foreign fighters approaching our undefended tower, and possibly the entire able-bodied population of Vasterut hard on their heels. Empowered by new allies, I have a feeling they'll attack us with hammers and scythes, whatever they can wield. This is a people ignited after a year of being held down. If they are not willing to honor the deal they apparently made—to spare our tribe if Thyra is made chieftain—then we will all be slaughtered. No matter that our warriors will kill hundreds before they go down. With no leader and the city engulfed in confusion, chaos will reign.

"Hurry," I say, pushing Sig's sweaty back. I don't know if Nisse understands what's at stake—the lives of his warriors may hinge on whether he keeps Thyra alive. The entrance to the castle is blocked by Vasterutians, pushing to get back inside. At first I think they're trying to find shelter and protection from the oncoming horde of foreign fighters, but then I hear Nisse's name, shouted over and over. They are calling for his blood.

"Can you clear that entrance?" I ask Sig. I don't trust myself—there must be fifty Vasterutians between us and the arched doorway, and half of them are beating one of our warriors to death. Their fists are clenched, their eyes wide. They will not be denied their vengeance—or their freedom. "Try to do it without killing anyone. It would only enflame them."

Sig chuckles, a shaky, unstable mirth. "Enflame?" He wiggles his fingers, and the tiny infernos in his palms grow tendrils, spiraling up like vines made only of sunlight.

I touch his back. "No killing." Part of me can't believe I'm saying that—two months ago I dreamed of kill marks every night. But now that wish seems petty in the face of all that is at stake—and the possibility that I could preserve life.

Sig nods as his fire grows, moving almost playfully as it slithers over the heads of the Vasterutians. His control is terrifying to me, but so is the extremity of his power— his body is drenched in sweat. It flows down his neck and soaks his robe. His skin is pink from the heat. My ice magic seems to protect me from it, but he has none of that. I close my eyes and think of a cool breeze, then lean forward and blow a frosty breath against his back and neck. He shudders and looks over his shoulder, a tiny smile playing on his silver-scarred face.

Then he turns around and pushes the fire forward. It arcs over the crowd and doubles back, sliding down the wall of the tower. The people at the front scream as the flames creep down the walls over the archway. For all the world it looks like the tower is on fire. They throw themselves back from it, and when the ones behind them catch a glimpse, the entire writhing mass of them switches directions, fleeing through the courtyard. I don't know if they're heading back out into the city or merely seeking another entrance, but we don't have time to find out. As soon as a path opens up, Sig and I are running for it, stopping only to drag an unconscious Krigere warrior to the safety of a little alcove near the steps that lead up to the castle entrance. With any luck, invading foreign warriors will think him dead and pass him over. "I'll be back for you," I whisper as I rise from his side and leap back onto the steps.

Sig moves aside and lets me pass him at the entrance, then summons a fire to burn in the archway to discourage anyone else from following us. The courtyard is still a churning storm of humanity, and the riders are approaching the base of the hill that holds our tower. We only have a few minutes to—

There's a crash and a *thunk*, and I whirl around to see Sig hit the ground in a boneless sprawl. His fire dies, and I blink in the sudden gray wash of daylight. Jaspar stands just inside the arch with a chunk of splintered wood in his hands. Sig's blood decorates the edge of it. "Kauko wanted him alive," he says to me as he kneels next to Sig and feels for the pulse at his throat.

I back up, brandishing Sander's dagger as Jaspar rises to his feet. He wears a smirk that hardens his face and makes him look more like his father. "Lovely disguise. The paunch is a particularly nice touch."

I grit my teeth and keep my eyes on him as I shed the overlarge black robe and yank the pillow from my middle.

Jaspar chuckles as he watches me tighten the rope around my waist. "I suppose it would be difficult to tussle with one's pants around one's ankles," he says, then purses his lips.

"Depending on what type of tussling we're talking about."

"The kind that leaves you bleeding at my feet."

"Are you going to kill me, Ansa?"

"Like you killed Sander?" My grief is a clenched fist in my chest.

"Can you blame me? Sander turned on us!"

"He was your best friend," I shout. "And he was serving his chieftain."

"It didn't matter," he says. "Like you, he didn't choose us."

My brow furrows at his flat, cold tone. "Where's Thyra?"

He arches an eyebrow. "Are you imagining you'll rescue her?" he asks, tossing his wood club to the side and drawing his dagger, still stained with Sander's blood.

"I'm not imagining," I say, dropping into my fight stance.

He grins. "Ah, Ansa. This is what I love about you. It's always so simple. Fight. Kill. I envy you that."

Simple—fight, kill. Right now nothing could be further from the truth. "I suppose I've changed. You don't know me at all."

His amusement falls away. "I wanted to, though. That was real. It always has been."

"Liar. You wanted to control me. You wanted to steer me in whatever direction suited you and your father. You soothed me and comforted me—you tried to *stop* me from thinking! I'm not your dog, Jaspar. I'm nobody's dog."

"That's not how it was. Think about what we shared," he says, circling slowly—putting himself between me and the spiraling stone staircase.

"I *am* thinking now." Finally. Finally, I can see it clearly. That moment I heard Thyra's footsteps in the wood, the instant I pushed Jaspar away from me—the look of triumph on his face as he saw her there. "What I think is that you were always trying to hurt her. You used me to do it."

His lip curls. "An added benefit. The kissing was quite nice as well, however."

"Did you know that your father was going to poison her? Were you in on it all along, even from the beginning?"

He stops his circling, because now he's between me and the stairs. "Was I in on it?" He closes his eyes and breathes in, then exhales his deadly truth. "Ansa, I did it all. *I'm* the one who poisoned her cup."

A chill runs across my skin. "And Nisse?"

"Doesn't know. And doesn't ever need to."

And in the moment it takes me to swallow my new reality, he attacks. I barely parry his strike. His fist collides with my stomach, sending me staggering back, but I get my feet up in time to kick him away. When I roll to my feet, sucking hard to get enough air into my lungs, my magic pulsing inside me loud as my heart, Jaspar is waiting.

"If I had my way, and if Thyra hadn't ruined everything," he says, "all this would have been over a year ago. My father would have been Lars's heir, and the succession would have shifted to our line."

"And you saw yourself as the someday-chieftain," I say, the words bitter as bile. "For all your questions, this was never about loyalty for you. It was about your thirst for power."

"Power is the only thing worth having! I am a true Krigere. So is my father. So are *you*, Ansa."

"I don't yet know what I am," I admit. "But now I know why I fight." I slice at his dagger hand, quick as lightning, fire magic tingling so hard inside me that sparks fly off the edge of my weapon.

Jaspar's eyes go wide as he sees the flame dripping from my blade, and then he laughs. "Careful, Ansa. Wouldn't want you to burn yourself again."

Me neither. Though the cuff of Astia is warm and comforting and heavy on my arm, I don't know how to use it—no one ever taught me. And the fear of all the times I've lost control still looms. Even as Sig's exasperated command to *be* echoes in my head, I push down the magic as best I can. I know how dangerous it is, and I haven't had time to practice.

Jaspar charges me again, not intimidated in the slightest—he's seen the magic turn on me over and over. We collide, and this is no friendly tussle—his jaw is hard and his blows are merciless, and soon I'm fighting just to soften his strikes and keep them from my most vulnerable spots. The fire and ice crackles in my chest, as if offering to take over, and my breath gushes icy from my mouth when he lands a solid hit to my side.

I dive for the ground and roll, desperate to catch my breath, and then I hear Sander's voice in my head, almost as if he's next to me. The way he always used to analyze an opponent's strengths and weaknesses, because he knew

I never bothered to notice—I just fought with instinct. I always thought he was showing off, but now I realize . . . he was trying to help. He was being my true brother. My true friend. *Jaspar is weaker in the forearms and wrists,* he whispers. *Stretch him out so he can't use his chest and upper arms to power in those blows and strikes.*

I jump to my feet and backtrack just as Jaspar comes forward again, and as he pursues me, I dance just out of his reach, dodging and slashing at his hands, his fingers. His mocking smile becomes a grimace of frustration. "You're running out of time," he says between heavy breaths. "Those riders are going to charge in here at any minute and kill us both. That was probably Thyra's plan all along." He spits on the floor.

"You, of all people, accuse her of being conniving?"

"Isn't she? You claim I used you—but you don't think she's done the same thing?"

Somewhere in the near distance, a horn sounds off. The distant rumble of horse hooves reaches us, vibrating through the stones beneath our feet. "Maybe she has," I admit. "She is a chieftain, and that's her prerogative. But I think she just wanted me to be my best self." Now I see her for what she is—human, striving, aspiring, reaching past power to cling to the light, and hoping others will do the same.

"So I guess that leaves it up to me to choose." I feint, and he lunges forward to block it. Leaping to the side, I slice downward, opening a gash in his sword arm. He cries out and hits the ground, and I jump away as he grabs for my legs.

I back up—the stairs are now just behind me. "You were right. I choose her," I say. "I'm nobody's dog. But I guess I'll always be her wolf."

I have another choice now, as Jaspar gasps and cradles his arm to his chest. I could continue this fight until I finish him. Or I can go after Thyra. And it's not just her I'm trying to save. I glance over at Sig, who is stirring against the wall just inside the tower entrance. If anyone comes barreling in, he'll be safe from being trampled. I look out into the daylight of the courtyard, where a din of war cries battles with the thunder of horses for supremacy. And then my eyes meet Jaspar's, and they shine green and pleading.

But I feel nothing for him. No love. No regret. No rage. "We are not tribe," I say. "And if I ever see you again, you will not survive it."

I leave the would-be prince of Vasterut to face the oncoming horde and sprint up the steps.

CHAPTER TWENTY-EIGHT

I barrel upward with Sander's dagger clenched tightly at my side. Every single breath hurts. I wince and wrap my arm around my ribs, and my hand comes away slick with blood. Vaguely, I realize Jaspar must have sliced me, and perhaps I am just propelled by magic and will. If so, I'll collapse when I'm done. But not until then. I am strong enough for this.

My love for Thyra and my faith in her vision beats relentlessly inside me, as strong as any fire or ice. I don't know exactly what she wants for our tribe, but I know what she believes in. I know she loves her warriors. And I know she loves me, enough to let me figure out my path.

I am nearly to the level that holds Nisse's chamber when

a pair of hands shoots out from the floor below and yanks me off the stairs. I stagger and start to bring my dagger up, but wide brown eyes and a wild spray of black hair stops me cold. "You're alive," I say stupidly.

"Thanks to Sander," Halina says sadly. Then her brows draw together. "You're bleeding bad, little red." She comes forward, pulling her apron up to press it to my side.

I gasp at the pressure and agony of it. "Where's Thyra?"

"Old Nisse has her up at the very top," she says. "Don't know what he's going to do."

"Is she hurt?" I saw her go down, hard.

"Don't really know," she says. "After Sander shoved me inside, I hid behind a tapestry until Nisse and the guard were gone. But they're waiting at the top of the stairs. You can't go that way."

"I have to try. Sander told me the foreign fighters and the resistance will spare the warriors if Thyra is established as chieftain."

She gives a quick, curt nod. "Efren was waiting for the riders on the other side of the stake-wall. He escaped through a tunnel as Nisse's guard tried to arrest him. But our people can't be easily appeased, little red. So many hungry for blood."

"Does Thyra know all of this?"

"She negotiated the agreement. Got a promise of cooperation from her warriors, that they wouldn't get in our fighters' way."

"The whole story about them emerging through a tunnel—

that was a lie, wasn't it? You made sure I overheard it, hoping I would take the information to Nisse."

Her mouth twists in apology and she takes a few steps away from me, as if she's afraid I'll strike at her. "Had to make him believe it, little red. And if it came from you as well as—"

"I know. It's all right. You knew I would try to protect my tribe."

"That I did." She smiles. "Always clawing your way to the light. All any of us can do." She rubs at her round cheeks, and I see the tearstains there. "But it went all wrong on the parapet. Sander and Thyra thought they could best Nisse and Jaspar, but those two . . ."

I swallow back the cost of their victory. "Now Nisse holds captive the one person we need to survive the day."

Tentatively, she squeezes my arm. "I'll help you get to Thyra. You're the only one who might be able to do it." She touches the cuff around my wrist. "That crazy boy said he would get this for you."

"He's downstairs."

"Dead?"

I shake my head. "Hurt, though."

She frowns. "So many will die today."

My cheeks burn—she is not saying as much as she could. All these weeks, she's held back, maybe out of kindness, perhaps out of hope that I would come to it on my own.

This is the price of their freedom, won back from those who took it from them—*my* people.

"I'll do whatever I can, Halina."

"Then so will I."

My brain shifts through my memories of the top levels of the tower. "How high can we get?"

"There are windows maybe two lengths of a man below the top. And the guards are just beneath that trapdoor."

"How many?"

"Six. And they have nothing to lose."

But maybe I could save them, too. Not by confronting them, though. "Can you distract them?"

She bites her lip. "I can try."

"That's all any of us can do. Come on." I re-enter the staircase with her behind me, my dagger drawn. Below us, I imagine I can hear the shouts of warriors, but it may just be the roaring in my ears or the rush of magic in my veins. I need it now. I can't go without it anymore. But that means I have to trust the foreign thing inside me. I have to accept it as mine. I have to accept it as *me*. And suddenly, Sig's instruction makes sense. My heart races as I consider what I'm about to do, and I barely breathe as we creep our way to the level just beneath the guard. Halina is utterly silent behind me, a ghost tracing my steps. She grips my wrist as we huddle in the corridor outside the staircase.

"What are you going to do?"

I sheathe Sander's dagger and look down at my hands. "Claw my way toward the light, I suppose." And hope she's still alive when I reach her. I walk toward a window set into the curved outer wall of this narrower level near the top.

We are two levels above the parapet, and I can see much of the city from here—the streets are filled with people, too far away to discern if they're fleeing or fighting or rioting or cheering. I look to the east, but the view is obscured by a cluster of tall shelters. I can only hope Preben and Bertel have kept our warriors in safety as the world collapses around them.

Cautiously, I lean out and look up. Three of my body lengths above me, I see the round, flat wall that rings the roof of the tower, the place where Jaspar and I sparred, the place where he tried to poison me, not with powder or toxic berries, but with carefully crafted words. And now Nisse is up there with my chieftain while doom closes in.

"Give me a few minutes," I whisper. "If my body doesn't plummet past this window, do your best to keep the attention of those guards."

"And you?" She points at the cuff. "Are you Kupari or Krigere right now?"

I lift the cuff to the light, examining the blood-red runes along its surface. "I'm both," I say, knowing only as I hear myself speaking that this is the only way I can be, and that it will never be simple again. "From now on I will always be both."

Refusing to let terror close its fingers around my heart and mind, I jump onto the stone sill and dig my fingers into the rough spaces between jagged rocks. I will have eyes only for the sky. *Please*, I whisper to the magic, *do not let me fall. We are together in this.*

A hard breeze gusts at my back, pushing me against the outer wall of the tower. I think that's all the reassurance I'm going to get. With my whole body clenched tight, I begin to climb, slowly inching toward the top. It's not terribly far, but from my position clinging to the side of the tower, it feels like miles. Sweat beads and trickles from my brow, but is dried by the steady wind at my back. I don't know if it's a gift from the Torden or the push of my magic, and I don't care. All my focus is on not falling to my death. I kick and wiggle my toes into crags and crevices, pushing my bleeding fingers into any place that will give me a good hold. I ignore the throbbing pain in my side, the slick smear of blood as my belly slides upward.

Finally, when I am just beneath the edge of the roof, I hear the low rumble of Nisse's voice. "By now Jaspar will be on his way to our warriors," he is saying. "You've made a nice effort, but like before, you will fail to defeat us."

"I hope your arrogance comforts you as you die at the hands of black-robed invaders," Thyra says, then seems to stifle a whimper of pain.

I press my forehead to the stones and hold in a sob made of fear and relief. She's alive, and she's at his mercy. And if I go up there now, Nisse's personal guard will flood through the trapdoor and—

A huge crash echoes up from somewhere below me, followed by a scream. "Witch," Halina shrieks. "Witch!" She lets out another bloodcurdling wail that cuts off suddenly.

She is possibly the cleverest person I've ever known.

"Ansa is coming," Thyra says weakly. "It seems your pet magic wielder couldn't keep her caged."

Nisse curses. "Hold her back," he shouts, presumably to his guards. "She can't control that magic—if you can keep her at bay, it will turn on her! Go!"

I'm about to find out if he's right. With one last burst of effort, I heave myself up and over the side, rolling onto the floor of the roof and rising unsteadily to a crouch. Nisse is standing over the door, and Thyra is sitting at his feet. His thick fingers are curled into her hair, and she's bleeding from a gash somewhere in her hair. She's ghastly pale, but her gaze is clear as she focuses on me, just a moment before Nisse notices my presence.

He curses and drags her up, holding her back pressed to his chest, a shield. "So you were in on the scheme too?" he asks. "Jaspar said you couldn't lie to save your life. Another mistake." His face is drawn tight with fear as he slides a dagger from its sheath and holds it pressed to Thyra's throat.

Thyra's eyes meet mine. "Ansa wasn't part of the plot. She found her way here on her own." Her mouth is curved into a pained smile.

"She used you, Ansa," Nisse says. "She's always used you. She had your Vasterutian attendant plant the story and—"

"I know all that already." I take a step forward, my fingers tingling. "I know everything, and I still made my choice."

"You'll die up here with us, then."

"Maybe. Or you could let her go and allow her to save

us all. Your son is the true schemer, Nisse. He tried to poison Thyra—she merely discovered the trap and struck back. Jaspar's greed and deception was the birth of all your suffering—and your thirst for power allowed you to nurture it."

Thyra's eyes flicker with a sudden uncertainty, as do Nisse's. "You're better at telling lies than I ever imagined," he says.

"No, I'm not. Let her go. You didn't try to poison her. You can undo the damage Jaspar has done—to her and to you, and to everyone else."

"Uncle?" Thyra asks in a strained voice.

He takes a quick step back, bringing him within a few paces of the low wall. "Or I could wait until Jaspar marshals all the warriors who went to the eastern part of the city. Once they surround this place, the fighters of the south will be forced to bargain."

I clench my fists. I'm the one who allowed Jaspar to live. "The riders and the Vasterutian resistance have flooded the streets. He'll be lucky to reach them."

"Jaspar will find a way." His eyes shine with the simple faith and pride of a father in his son.

"Jaspar has destroyed you," Thyra says. "He pitted us against each other, playing us both for fools. But now we can—"

"At what point will you stop scheming?" Nisse pricks Thyra's throat, making her bleed. "My son is loyal, and he will not fail me. You, on the other hand, have more than earned your execution. I wait only until Jaspar sends the signal that he's on his way back for me."

A signal that could come at any minute if Jaspar is half as determined as I know him to be. I only injured his arm, not his legs, and given the time that has passed, if he was able to escape the courtyard, that signal could come at any moment. The foreign fighters will take the tower because there were no Krigere to stop them, but with all of them here, it won't be hard to place it under siege as long as Jaspar's warriors can intimidate the Vasterutian people into staying back.

My mind spins with all the possible outcomes, but then Nisse takes another step back from me, and I am caught by a painful flash of memory—Jaspar throwing Sander over the edge of the parapet. "Don't take another step."

Nisse smiles. "Why, Ansa? Are you going to stop me?" He presses the blade tighter to Thyra's throat.

I draw Sander's dagger, and when I lift it, the cuff of Astia shines in the bright sunlight directly over our head. Nisse squints at it. "What is that?"

"Balance," I say. "A gift from elder Kauko."

Nisse's face twists with rage. "That priest betrayed me?"

"Weren't you going to betray him?"

"All he wanted was you, and we delivered you to him!"

I smile with the realization—no matter what I chose, Nisse would have betrayed me. He is no innocent victim— he only fathered a snake because he is one himself. I couldn't be wielded as a weapon because I couldn't control the magic, and so he gave me up. "Because I was worth something to Kauko. Or, my blood was."

Nisse looks me over, appearing to notice my wounds for the first time. "And it seems you're shedding quite a lot of it. I'm surprised you're still standing."

I aim the dagger at him, focusing on the beating pulse in his neck. "Let her go, or you're the one who will be on the ground."

He laughs. "You seem to forget that I've watched you for weeks. If you aim your magic at me, you'll kill Thyra as well. You're a storm, Ansa. You'll take everyone down with you."

A drop of fear slips icy down my back as my chieftain's blue eyes meet mine. Suddenly I'm in the fight circle on a new spring day, and I'm bleeding and hurting and defeated as Sander walks away from me, and hers is the one voice I hear shouting for me to get up. Like I could that day, I can read the simple faith written across the planes of her cheekbones, etched into the curve of her mouth.

A distant horn blows once, and then again, pulling Nisse's lips into a lethal grin. "And now we're out of time," he says, pressing a hard kiss against Thyra's bleeding temple.

He draws back his blade, preparing to cut her throat.

"I love you, Thyra," I whisper, and then I let the magic loose, fueled by devotion and determination and all the adoration that's in me, powered by hope in the future and acceptance, finally, of who I have become. The ice winds along the blade of Sander's dagger, but this time, instead of focusing on its progress, I focus on my target. It's the size of my fingertip.

Nisse's jugular.

As his weapon descends, I thrust my blade forward, even though I know the iron will never touch his flesh.

Nisse makes a strangled grunt and his dagger swings away from Thyra. One hand claws at his frozen throat as he staggers back, the weapon falling from his hand as it grasps desperately for something to stop his collision with the edge.

His fingers find the back of Thyra's tunic. Her mouth drops open as she reaches for me, and I lunge forward as both of them tumble and fall.

CHAPTER TWENTY-NINE

My hands close around her ankles. A rending yank from below pulls me forward, and for a moment I know I am heading over the edge as well, but I refuse to let go of her. She is mine, and I am hers. Her wolf, her blanket, her fire, her dagger. And then I am jerked to a halt, and I glance over my shoulder to see ice fastened like manacles around my ankles, spread over the floor of the tower, rooting me in place.

My fingers dig into the leather of her boots as she screams. In the courtyard, so far below us, Nisse's body hits hard, falling only feet from where Sander lies, still and broken. All around them are black-robed fighters, swords drawn, staring up at us. Maybe waiting for us to fall too.

"I've got you," I say from between gritted teeth.

She lets out a laugh. A *laugh*. "I know." Her flesh slips beneath the thick shield of her boots, and she screams again. My fingers grasp at her with white knuckles, and ice grows from my fingertips, snaking around her ankles.

I gaze at it with wonder. "I'm pulling you up."

With my feet fastened and Thyra's ankles encased in ice, it's now up to me to bring my chieftain to safety. My body is so torn, a faulty, fragile vessel for the magic that has brought us both to this point. But it has been my ally for far longer than the fire and ice that have now made me their temporary home. I draw in a breath and pull, ignoring the agony of my legs, my back, my arms, my chest. I tug until my rear sits on my ice-encased heels, until Thyra's knees rest on the edge.

"Up to you now, Chieftain. Can you sit up?"

She grunts, and I can feel her effort as her trunk rises off the wall of the tower, as she brings herself up and up, and as she reaches for me. Like it understands what I need, the ice around my right hand, the arm that bears the cuff, melts instantly, and I grasp her hand, our fingers entwining. I pull her back, and the ice around my ankles melts and turns to steam as I land on my back with her on top of me.

It is the best feeling in the world, and it makes all my pain disappear. She strokes my hair back. "I thought you would be furious when you discovered that Halina deceived you."

"I deserved to be deceived. I refused to help you reach our warriors. You did what you had to do."

She kisses my forehead, and the feel of her lips is heaven

itself. "I had no idea Kauko was going to take your blood. I would have found a way to warn you."

"Sig tried."

"Thank heaven for him."

I hope heaven is not where he is right now. "Will our warriors be safe?"

She lays her forehead on mine. "I hope so. I told them to stay where they were and hold the barricades. With any luck we'll find them alive. And hungry, probably."

"Will they be able to help us when Jaspar and the other warriors lay siege to this tower?"

"They'll do all they can, I have no doubt. They have proven their loyalty time and time again. My father's memory is clearly a powerful thing."

"It's not just his memory," I say, stroking her cheek. "You gave them something to believe in, however foreign and strange it might be."

She smiles. "I had no idea how dangerous peace truly was, but I'll fight for it anyway."

That is why I love her. It's why I don't care that we aren't really meant to be mated. It's why I crave this moment like water and air. It's why I draw her down and press my mouth to hers. And when she moans and parts her lips, a taste of heaven is my reward. My magic simmers and shivers inside me, drawn tight and chaotic by the churn of want surging along my bones, but with the cuff of Astia around my wrist, the storm is quelled, and our kiss is just that. Because we are reconciled, because the magic is part of me now, maybe it recognizes her as someone I could never hurt, someone I would die to save.

The wounds that mar my body are nothing, not with her hands on me, not with her mouth on mine. Our enemy could be storming the gate right now, and I still smile and nip at Thyra's bottom lip. I still grin when her fingers twist in my hair. I still gasp as she yanks up my tunic and lays her cool palm on my bare skin.

The trapdoor slams open and makes both of us jump. I crane my neck and see Halina's upside-down face, her bright eyes, her grin. "Everyone settled down there," she says.

"Nisse's guard?" Thyra asks.

"Surrendered to about three dozen foreign fighters. The tower is under our control."

Thyra gives me one last, brief kiss before sliding off me. She winces as she raises her head and sways in place. "Jaspar and his warriors? He must have reached them. We heard the signal that he was coming to lay siege to the tower."

I push myself up to sitting on shaking arms, and Halina gives both me and Thyra a concerned look. "Do you have tunnels that could help us get a message to Preben and Bertel?"

"No need, little red. Jaspar isn't coming. He had different plans than old Nisse. Guess he wasn't so loyal after all."

"What's happened?" Thyra asks, her voice going flat and sharp.

"He ran," Halina says. "Everyone was clustered up here in the north of the city, so once he reached his seven hundred fighters, you think he came here to face hundreds of

Vasterutians, Korkeans, and Ylpesians who wanted a taste of Krigere blood? No. He gave up. He took them south and they escaped the city. Stole any horse they could find on the way. Bunch of their families running too."

"Is anyone trying to stop them?" Thyra asks.

Halina shakes her head. "We want them gone, Chieftain," she says softly, her gaze somber.

Thyra looks over at me, and I read the worry in her eyes. The Vasterutians want us gone too. We are merely guests here now. "I understand," Thyra says slowly. "I hope you will give us time to recover from this battle."

Halina nods. "Of course. We honor you as an ally now. You will be able to stay until you know where you will find your new home, whether it be Kupari or elsewhere."

Thyra gives me a speculative look. "Let me consult with my war counselor here," she says, reaching for my hand. Our fingers clench tight, holding each other up. "And then we'll let you know."

CHAPTER THIRTY

I heal faster than Thyra does. Faster than Sig, too. He tells me it is because of the magic, and if I work at it, maybe I can even heal others. "Like Kauko?" I ask.

Sig's mouth crimps with distaste. "I know another who heals," he replies. "In Kupari."

"Is he among the group who attacked you and chased all the priests from the temple?"

Halina translates for him. Somehow, she and Sig have formed a bond, and she seems to understand him better than anyone. She knows he has a story to tell but won't tell it for him.

Sig sighs and looks away, muttering something in Kupari. Halina touches his arm. "He says this man was his friend before. He says maybe . . . but that is all he says."

"I have to know this story, Sig. We need to reach out to the impostor queen. We need her to understand who I am and what it means."

Thyra shifts next to me and glances at Preben and Bertel, who look gaunt but otherwise healthy after their ordeal barricaded in the east. We are all sitting around the table in what is now her chamber. She refuses to call it a war chamber, but we all stare down at the map of Kupari painted on the table's surface. "If she can be made to understand that we want peace . . ."

"And a home," I say as Halina murmurs the translation to Sig. Because this is where Thyra and I landed—apparently Kupari is a vast land, with the city at one end of the peninsula, and the rest of it occupied by a stretch of largely uninhabited marshland and mines. There's enough room for us there. We could make a home and figure out who we are now, and who we want to become.

Because I am the rightful queen of Kupari. All that remains is convincing the impostor to step down.

"Elli," Sig says, continuing on in Kupari.

"He says the impostor's name is Elli," Halina translates. "He says that she is the one who scarred him as he tried to kill Kauko."

My fists clench. "I can repay her for you."

Thyra's hand closes over mine, and I relax slightly. "Our aim is not revenge."

Sig mumbles something, and Halina frowns. "He says she is not a mere impostor."

Sig leans over and touches the cuff, which has not left my body since that day in the tower a few weeks ago, when it helped me save my chieftain. "Sig says she is . . . this." Halina points at the cuff too.

"What? She has one of those?" Preben asks. "I thought you said she had no magic? What good would it do her?"

"No," says Halina. "She *is* one of these. And she has an ice wielder at her side . . . and he is as strong in that ice as Sig is in fire."

"Like two halves," Thyra murmurs, looking between me and Sig.

Bertel leans forward, and his white beard brushes the tabletop. "So perhaps we have a chance. She's not powerless, but neither are we."

Preben nods. "If we can come together, surely we can negotiate a lasting compromise that will result in a permanent home for our people."

"As long as Jaspar and Kauko don't interfere," I say. This is the galling truth—when our warriors went down to retrieve Kauko, to secure him before he awoke, they found him gone—chains sliced through with what was probably a broadsword.

Our best guess is that Jaspar rescued him and took the crafty old wielder with him as he escaped the city. And now he's out there, possibly trying to find the refugee priests and apprentices, along with hundreds of warriors. The Vasterutians tracked them to the Loputon, but were thwarted by a fire that drove them back, with winds coming

414

from the west. Either it was very bad luck—or there was a very powerful wielder pushing the flames in their direction to cover his tracks.

"I don't know what Jaspar wants now," says Thyra. "Apart from my death."

"He'll never have his satisfaction, then," I reply, moving a little closer to her.

She looks over at me, and then at the others. "Give us the room, please," she says quietly.

Sig, Halina, Preben, and Bertel rise and do as she asks. Thyra walks over to the window on the far side of the chamber, which looks out over the city. I follow, and I lay my hand on her back, needing the contact. I can feel each of her ribs, but she stands straight, steady once again. "I don't know what's going to happen," she says.

"None of us do. That's the annoying thing about the future."

She chuckles. "Very annoying." She touches my cheek. "How will this go, Ansa? For now, I'm your chieftain, but if our future unfurls as we hope, you'll be queen of your own land."

My hand slides down the bumps of her spine to settle at her waist. "We can rule together," I tell her. "It's not like I know anything about being in charge, anyway."

"Neither of us knows anything about the customs of these people. They'll be terrified to find out their Valtia is actually a Soturi."

"A Soturi is still a person," I say. "A Valtia is a person."

"Not just a person," she whispers, leaning her head down until it touches mine.

I close my eyes, savoring this moment, knowing that what is coming will test us. "I don't feel like a queen, Thyra," I admit, my throat going tight.

"Shh." She brushes a kiss across my lips. "You'll do what you think is right, always. All you have to do is remember the people you serve. Remember that what you do is for them." She raises her head, and a shadow flickers behind her eyes. "Not just for me, all right?"

My cheeks burn as she traces the outline of my devotion, as she tries to pry it from my hands and place it on a shelf. "But I'm your wolf," I mumble.

She tips my chin up with her fingers. "Promise me. Promise me that if it comes down to protecting your people, our people, or protecting me, you'll choose them." When my lips press tight, she gives me a disapproving tilt of her head and squeezes my cheeks.

"Fine," I say. "As you wish." But I silently swear that it will never come to that. Thyra *is* my people, and I will be her castle, her sword and shield.

She smiles. "All right." She kisses my cheek. "We're agreed."

"We are," I murmur, staring beyond the walls of the city to the distant line of green beyond. The trees are budding. Spring is on us. And with the warmer weather comes the future, all the blank swirl of mystery, all the possibility, all the danger, and all the hope. We have nearly two hundred warriors and a few thousand andeners to care for. We are not a powerful invading army. We are only two girls who bear the responsibility of our people on our backs. But with my arms around Thyra, the weight is lighter, because we share it.

We stare at the world beyond these walls, a world we are about to explore, the next step on our journey. Kupari and Krigere, enemies whose future is entwined. Together, Thyra and I will save them all.

ACKNOWLEDGMENTS

Thank you to the team at McElderry for all their work and advocacy, including Justin Chanda and Natascha Morris, and particularly my editor Ruta Rimas, whose thoughtful questioning about arc and character somehow pushes me miles down the road every single time. A huge thank you also goes to Zlatina Zareva who captured all of Ansa, both warrior and Valtia, with one powerful image and design, and to Leo Hartas for designing the map of the wider world of the Krigere, Kupari, and Vasterutians, and to Debra Sfetsios-Conover for the beautiful overall book design.

To my agent, Kathleen Ortiz, what to say? This is book number fifteen and we're still going strong. Thank you for everything. And my gratitude also goes to the team at New Leaf Literary for all manner of assistance, organization, and support. In addition, thank you to Gaby Salpeter for marshaling the online charge—I am so happy you tolerate me.

I'm grateful for my friends—Lydia, Brigid, Amber, Sue, Claudine, Jackie, Paul, and Jim—in different ways, each of you lifts me up and guides me closer to being my best self. Without you I'd be lost. To my parents and my sisters, thank you for your unconditional love. To my children . . . Asher, thank you for your enthusiasm and critique as I read this book aloud to you. Alma, you are my inspiration, warrior girl.

And to my readers, thank you for caring about my characters and worlds. Thank you for telling others about my books. Thank you for reaching out. Thank you for existing in the world.